THE
SOUND OF **Rain**

THE SOUND OF Rain

Part One of the Jayson Wolfe Story

a novel

Anita Stansfield

Covenant Communications, Inc.

Cover image: *Rock Man World Tour* © 2008 Artur Achtelik / istock

Cover design copyrighted 2008 by Covenant Communications, Inc.

Published by Covenant Communications, Inc.
American Fork, Utah

Printed in Canada
First Printing: August 2008

14 13 12 11 10 09 08   10 9 8 7 6 5 4 3 2 1

ISBN 13: 978-1-59811-688-5
ISBN 10:1-59811-688-6

This story is dedicated to all of the great musicians,
who have deeply inspired me,
and who have struggled much to honor their creative gifts.

And especially to my sons, for all the music and the memories of making it.

Prologue

The Oregon Coast

Jayson Wolfe looked out over the rushing waves to where the sea met with an overcast sky. The subtly shaded gray horizon was almost invisible. The scenery felt eerily familiar. As it should, he thought. He couldn't count the times he'd come to this beach, even though he'd only lived in this area for fewer than two years. And how many years had it been since he'd stood in this very place and surveyed this view for the first time? It took him a minute to figure it out, and then he actually gasped. *Twenty years.* Had it really been that long? It seemed like a lifetime ago, but then he'd only been sixteen at the time. He *had* lived a lifetime since then. He couldn't deny that much of his life had been good. But there had been hardships he never would have imagined, never could have foreseen.

Jayson took off his shoes and walked the familiar length of beach, even though the day was cool; he kept his coat on, pulling it more tightly around his lean frame. The sand had a comforting effect on his feet. It was much finer and softer than the California sand he'd become accustomed to. He squatted down to scoop up a handful, and he watched it sift through his fingers. Its fine, white quality enhanced his memories. He still wasn't certain what had compelled him to make the lengthy drive up the coast from his southern California home just to be able to stand in this spot. Perhaps he simply felt a need to find some grounding in his life, to see and feel a point of constancy in a world that continued to change so quickly that he just couldn't keep up. Perhaps it was the fact that certain key events in his life had unfolded in this very place. In spite of the passing years, he still had trouble understanding some of those events—or rather, one in particular. To this day he found it difficult to accept that Elizabeth had not wanted to share her life with him. It had felt wrong then; it felt wrong now. But perhaps it wouldn't bother him so deeply if he weren't completely alone. He was grateful at least to know that Elizabeth had remained his dearest and truest friend. Through all these years she had been there for him through every joy and crisis in his life. And he had done the same for her. In many ways they were more like a brother and sister. Their friendship was a one-in-a-million, and he knew it. But she was happily married and raising a family in some little town in Utah, while he aimlessly wandered the world, questioning his purpose—and why he would be tortured with such strong feelings for a woman he couldn't have.

Feeling as if a familiar dark cloud might overtake him completely, Jayson uttered a silent prayer. He'd never put much faith in organized religion. His memories of going to church in his youth were of a pulpit-pounding preacher who bellowed the fear of God to his congregation. Jayson's mother had softened such teachings with her belief that God was loving and benevolent. And instinctively Jayson believed that was true. He'd stopped going to church once he'd left home after high school, but he'd never stopped praying. It was likely the only thing that had kept him remotely sane through all he'd endured. And now in what felt like his darkest hour, he prayed fervently that he could be given some kind of light, some meaning or purpose, anything to give him a reason to keep getting up in the morning, to keep putting one foot in front of the other.

Jayson was startled by the ringing of his cell phone. It didn't ring very often, because there were very few people who had the number. His heart quickened as it always did when the phone rang, but a glance at the caller ID let him know it was not the call he'd been aching to receive for many months. Instead, it was his agent.

"Hello, Wendy," he said into the phone, pushing a hand absently through his brown hair that was cut short on top and hung in a ponytail down his back.

"You're psychic," she said, and he just grunted. "Hey, you still want some work?"

"Sure, why not?" he said, his tone bored. Then, as an afterthought he added, "Well, maybe I should ask *what* before I'm so agreeable. I'm not singing TV commercials."

She laughed in her typically obnoxious way. "Would I do that to you?"

"Yes, you would," he said with no trace of humor. "What is it?"

"Phil Gordon asked me to call you," she said, and Jayson made a noise of interest. He knew Phil was a decent guy; they shared a deep mutual respect, even though their tastes differed greatly.

"I'm listening," he prodded, knowing she would purposely drag this out if only to tease him. And he wasn't in the mood.

"His band is starting its European tour next week; dates scheduled, tickets sold. Sold out in many cases."

"Okay," he drawled impatiently.

"And the lead guitarist just broke his arm. Phil thinks you're the only man in the world who could fill in and make it work. So, what do you say?"

Jayson didn't even have to think about it. While he felt bad for the guitarist, he couldn't deny this was an answer to his prayers. It *would* give him some purpose—for at least as long as the tour lasted. "Sure, why not?" he said. "Tell him I'll do it."

"Great," she said. "That means you need to be ready to roll the day after tomorrow so you can learn the stuff. And then you're going to be working some long hours until you do."

"Fine," he said. "Email me the details. I'll be home tomorrow night."

"Where are you, anyway?"

"Oregon," he said and hurried to end the call.

Jayson sighed and took a good, long look at his surroundings before he walked back down the beach to where he'd left his car. Before he got there, it started to rain. He stopped for a moment and turned his face skyward, allowing the water to bathe his skin while he breathed in the memories, not certain whether they soothed his ache or deepened it. Either way, he had no choice but to keep on living.

Chapter One

Twenty Years Earlier

Jayson looked out over the rushing waves to where the sea met with an overcast sky. The subtly shaded gray horizon was almost invisible. Still, the openness of the sea was a refreshing change following days on the road, staying at cheap motels along the way only when absolutely necessary. He glanced over his shoulder at the U-Haul truck he'd been driving, with the small family car being towed behind. He and his brother Drew had been taking turns driving and sleeping. Their mother had refused to drive the truck, certain she'd bring them all to inevitable destruction with her lack of experience. She'd expressed great confidence, however, in Jayson being able to handle the truck, even though he'd not actually gotten his driver's license until after his mother had made the decision that they would be moving, leaving their Montana home for a job opportunity in Oregon. Not that the job was all that great; waiting tables at a family diner was hardly a justifiable corporate move. And the apartment a friend had found for them had been described as *adequate until they could find something better*. Considering their budget, Jayson wasn't sure if finding something better would ever happen. They'd had to sell practically everything except their beds in order to make the move. And until he and Drew could find work, there would be no money for anything beyond survival.

Jayson felt no real regret for anything they'd had to leave behind—except the piano. And thoughts of the piano made him almost physically ill. It was only a month ago that the old piano had truly become his best friend. He'd taken lessons for years, and he could play by sight almost as well as he could play by ear, but he'd not truly conquered the piano until his mother's birthday last month.

* * * * *

Back then, Jayson had stewed for days over what he could get his mother for her birthday. She was the most amazing woman he'd ever known. He knew that most guys his age did not feel that way about their mothers, but then most guys his age had not been through what he'd been through—and they had not seen their mothers rise above abuse and harassment and conquer it with peace and dignity. Leslie Wolfe was a woman among women, and everything she did, she did for her two sons. Now Leslie's birthday was less than a month away, and Jayson knew if he didn't start coming up with a plan he'd never be able to do something memorable for her birthday—something worthy of her. Then, right after lunch, it came to him. During his afternoon classes he planned it out carefully in his mind. He knew it would be a lot of work, but he could do it. He knew he could do it.

Once school was out, he felt pumped with nervous excitement just wanting to share the idea with his brother. It just wouldn't be the same if Drew wasn't willing to do this with him. Oblivious to an early autumn chill, he paced next to the little red Chevy his brother had recently purchased from wages he earned at a local movie theater. Since he'd turned eighteen, Drew had actually been promoted to assistant manager, and the money helped their family situation immensely— especially since Jayson hadn't been able to find a job at all. Of course he was only sixteen, and there weren't many jobs available for guys his age that were close enough to get to without a car of his own. But for the first time in weeks, he was actually grateful not to be working. He was going to need every possible minute just to make this come together, and his mother's birthday wasn't far off.

Jayson's heart quickened when he saw his brother approaching. Drew was a senior at the same high school where Jayson was a junior. While Drew was nearly two years older than Jayson, they were only one year apart in school. In spite of being Jayson's elder brother, Drew was nearly a head shorter and slightly nerdy looking with fluffy blond hair. He wore wire-rimmed glasses and was constantly reading a science-fiction novel. He generally went through two or three a week. In addition to their difference in height, they barely looked like brothers. Jayson had brown hair and brown eyes, but he also had a slightly rugged look that had nothing to do with the way he dressed—which he did with the studied purpose of being different from anyone else in the school. He had a tendency to mix clothing pieces that no one else would ever think of. He wore Sunday shoes with jeans, or slacks with a T-shirt, or a suit jacket with his oldest jeans and shoes. Most of all he loved vests. He collected vests and wore one with almost everything, although he never buttoned them. He was different, and he knew it. And that was the way he liked it. Drew, on the other hand, wore jeans and a T-shirt every day, and he'd about passed out with embarrassment when Jayson had pierced his left ear and started wearing a little silver ring there. And while Drew kept his hair neatly trimmed every three weeks without fail, Jayson clipped the top off his occasionally to keep it reasonably respectable—although he usually did it himself. The result was a haphazard look that he often gelled to give it a neatly mussed look. The back hadn't been cut in several weeks, and it was almost long enough to pull it into a ponytail—another source of embarrassment for Drew. Still, Drew loved and accepted Jayson without question—and the feelings were mutual. They had common bonds that far outweighed any possible differences. They had the same amazing mother, the same deplorable father—and the same love of music. And that was what Jayson needed to talk to him about today.

"Drew," he said before his brother even reached the car, "I figured it out. I know what to do for Mom for her birthday."

Drew chuckled dubiously, and they both got into the car. "In case you haven't noticed, little brother," he said, turning the key in the ignition, "we have no money. Since I got the car fixed and helped Mom with that doctor bill, I'm broke. And *you* don't have a job."

"That's just it," Jayson said. "This is something that doesn't cost money."

Drew looked intrigued as he pulled out onto the highway from the school parking lot. "I'm listening," he said.

"Okay, well . . . you tell me what Mom loves more than anything."

"Ice cream."

Jayson laughed. "Even more than ice cream."

"Oh, that would be music," Drew said, then he laughed as if he'd been suddenly enlightened. "Music!"

"That's right," Jayson said. "But what is her very most favorite song of all time? We both know she loves all kinds of music and she has a lot of favorites, but what does she listen to when she's depressed? The song that she said got her through the divorce."

"Oh, oh." Drew snapped his fingers. "I know what you mean. It's that . . . that . . ."

Jayson gave him a hint. "She always says that even though most of the lyrics have never applied to her—and never will—there's something about the song that speaks to her spirit. Isn't that what she says?"

"Yes, it's . . . it's . . . give me another hint."

"It's got all of that really great piano in it and—"

"Wait a minute. You can't play *that* song on the piano."

"You don't even know *what* song we're talking about."

"I can't remember the name, but I know the song. And the piano is incredible. We're talking about Elton John, little brother." Drew loved to call Jayson that, given that the younger brother was taller. "You're great with the guitars, and you're not bad with the piano . . . but it's Elton John."

"Yes, it's Elton John, and it's amazing. Mom has the music in a book. I know where it is. I tried to play it a few years ago, and it was too complicated, but I've learned a lot since then. I really think I can do it. You do the drums; I do the piano. Mom's working lots of evening shifts the next few weeks; she told me so yesterday. We'll let the neighbors in on the secret, and they'll gladly put up with the extra noise if they know what it's for."

"Okay, I'm with you," Drew said. "But—"

"You *can* do the drums, can't you?"

"Yes, I can," he said with no hesitance. "But there're just two of us, Jayse. That song has some hefty guitar and a lot of synth."

"So, I'll improvise. I can make adjustments on the piano to make up for the guitar and synth enough to make it work. We'll just . . . figure out a piano and drums version, and she will *love* it."

Drew laughed as if the idea were fully sinking in. "I like it. I really like it. She is gonna freak out."

"Yes, she is." Jayson laughed with him.

"You really think you can do it? We're talking about . . ."

"'Funeral for a Friend,'" Jayson finally stated the title.

"That's it."

"And 'Love Lies Bleeding.' It's actually two songs blended into one, you know."

"I know. And you really think you can do it?"

"I really do. I can hear it in my head, Drew. I know I can do it."

Drew was more serious as he said, "Yes, I'm sure you can."

Jayson sighed and absorbed the music going through his head, even now. And Drew was one of the only two people in the world who really understood him in that respect. The other was his mother. And he could almost bet that God had put this song into his head as an answer to his prayers. He'd prayed to know what to do for his mother's birthday. She was a wonderful woman, and she deserved the best. And this was the very best that he could give her.

For as long as Jayson could remember, Leslie Wolfe had seemed to sense the need for music in her sons' lives. He had needed to sit on two phone books to reach the piano keys when he'd first shown an interest in it, but he had soon wanted his very own guitar—an electric one with an amplifier. And this was about the same time Drew had decided he wanted his own drum set. Leslie had sat them down and told them if they could each learn the piano well enough to play a particular song for her, she would help them buy the instruments. They had stuck with the piano lessons long enough to meet their end of the bargain—and she had met hers. With great zeal and pleasure, Leslie had scrimped and saved her tips and took on extra shifts in order to give her sons what they wanted most. And when the instruments were paid for, she scrimped and saved to give them lessons. But it soon became evident that they each had a talent that went far beyond anything they could be taught. Still, Leslie insisted that talent had to be honed, and it was important for them to learn the rules. And they had.

Nothing could make Leslie's countenance more bright than hearing evidence of some new level of progression with the music

Jayson and Drew played—especially when they played together. She often said that God giving her sons such musical gifts had compensated for every rotten thing she'd ever dealt with in life. As Jayson had grown older, he'd come to learn that was a lot of compensation. She'd been victim to a variety of abuses in her childhood, and to top it off, she'd married a violent alcoholic—and eventually divorced him. She often told them that the only good thing Jay Wolfe had ever done for her was give her the two greatest sons in the world. Jayson had trouble accepting this horrible man as his father, and he didn't even want to think about having any part of that man in him, but he did his best to focus on all that his mother gave him to compensate. She'd taught him that if you look closely at life, you can always find that God is compensating you somehow—you can always find something to be grateful for. And Jayson knew she was right. They didn't have much, but they had each other, and they had music. And now he was more excited than he'd ever been in his life to perfect his mother's favorite song and give it to her as a small way of giving her back the music she had given to him by always believing in him.

Drew dropped Jayson off at home before he went to work. Jayson first went to the four homes where he knew Drew's drums could be heard when he practiced. He explained the situation, and the neighbors were all pleased. Of course, they'd had a long-standing agreement that the boys would never practice loud music before ten in the morning or after nine in the evening. And if it were ever a problem for any of those living nearby, they should feel free to call. There never had been a problem, for which Jayson was extremely grateful. He'd learned long ago that being nice to the neighbors and communicating with them gave him the opportunity to do what some people would never tolerate. He imagined one day sending them all autographed copies of his platinum-selling records. As always, when he had such thoughts, he chuckled to himself—just because the idea was so thoroughly pleasant and felt so completely right.

With the neighbors taken care of, Jayson went home and straight to the front room. Leslie often joked about their having the strangest decor in town. Their front room furnishings consisted of a sofa, a lamp, a drum set, a guitar amp, a couple of guitars leaning on stands, and the old piano. The piano had belonged to Leslie's mother; it was the only thing she'd inherited when her mother died, and she proudly declared that it was all she had wanted. It was an upright, and it *was* old. But Leslie had put a high priority on keeping it tuned and in good repair. She frequently polished the wood surface, and it was a striking contrast to the rest of their meager furnishings. Near the piano sat the drums; they were set up on a sheet that covered the carpet since they had learned the hard way that drum pedals leave ugly, black stains on the floor.

Jayson quickly found the music book that went with the album. Elton John's *Good-bye Yellow Brick Road.* Leslie owned two copies of the double-record set, and she had copied many of the songs to cassette tapes a number of times, since she always managed to wear them out. She had often said that, just as with many albums she owned, there were usually a few tracks that she didn't like, and there were some with questionable lyrics. And that's why she liked to copy them to tapes, so she could listen only to the ones she liked. She'd often used music as a metaphor for teaching her sons about sifting good from evil in the world. She taught that good music could come from bad people and bad music could come from good people, and it was important to pay attention to the way a song made you feel. She knew a little something about every musician she listened to. From Elton John to Mozart and dozens in between, she was well aware of their human imperfections but declared that their musical gifts were not to be questioned. She frequently expressed great faith in her sons to make a positive contribution to the music of the world. And Jayson was determined not to disappoint her.

Jayson couldn't count the times that his mother had taken on a dreamy look and started talking about the vision she could see of her children on stage with their music. It wasn't fame she sought for her sons; it was the possible impact that their gifts could have on a world starving for *good* music. *Good* was a term she defined as being completely different from *quality;* she expected both from Jayson and Drew. She frequently looked each of them in the eye and told them straightly that they had to follow their hearts and bring their gifts to fruition. It seemed to Jayson like part of a routine. Teach your kids to say their prayers, brush their teeth, and to make their dreams come true. And the teaching went a step further. In guiding her children through the good, she taught them how to handle the bad. Don't play with matches or sharp objects, look both ways before crossing the street, and don't fall into the traps of the music industry and ruin your life. Leslie Wolfe was neither gullible nor naive. And the news was full of famous people with horrible lives. She taught her sons very plainly that their music could bring them—and others—great joy. But if they indulged in promiscuity, street drugs, or drinking, they might as well just throw their musical gifts out the window right now. The drinking was something she emphasized to the point of nearly driving them crazy. She felt that drugs and sex were easier to steer clear of, because the lines between right and wrong were more easily defined. But the drinking was more shady and gray. For many, social drinking was acceptable, but getting drunk was not. She'd been married to an alcoholic, and she would not allow liquor of any kind into her home. She cautioned her sons to never drink at all, no matter how tempting the offer of just a little drink might be. She told them that the tendency to alcoholism could be genetic, and it wasn't worth the risk. For Jayson, the thought of genetically inheriting something so atrocious from his father made him sick to his stomach. He'd seen firsthand what alcohol had done to his father's life—and theirs. He didn't have a problem with following his mother's advice on that or anything else.

For the next several days, Jayson used every minute when his mother wasn't at home to work on the song. He listened to the recorded version over and over, sometimes with headphones so that he could play along. He practiced it with the sheet music, trying to embellish and improvise where other instruments were more prominent than the piano. He knew that once he mastered the song, Drew would be able to put the drums in without too much trouble. He was a genius with those drumsticks, always leaving Jayson in awe. Jayson had actually toyed with the drums a little, and he could pick out some basic rhythms. He only used what little knowledge he had to give Drew an idea of what he could hear in his head, and then Drew could take over and fly with it. Beyond learning music that their mother loved, most of the music they played together was directly from the source in Jayson's head. He was often scribbling lyrics and notes and futilely attempting to keep up with the music in his mind. He only enjoyed playing someone else's music when it was for the purpose of entertaining his mother.

Even though Jayson *could* hear this song in his head, the undertaking proved to be much more difficult than he'd imagined. When Drew finally insisted on hearing what he had, he said quite honestly, "It's . . . getting there. We've still got two weeks," Jayson insisted. "I can do this. I know I can. Run through it with me a couple of times, and I'll keep working on it."

"Okay, let's do it," Drew said.

"Have you been listening to the tape?"

"Every chance I get. I know it the way Elton plays it, but you've got a different twist, so just . . . tell me what you want. It's an eleven-minute song, you know."

"Yes, I know. But we're cutting off the first minute and a half which is purely synthesizer. We're starting where the piano comes in with a quiet cymbal beat. Okay, from there. Give me a one-two-three."

They worked together until Leslie came home from work, and they pretended to be working on a song that she'd already heard a hundred times. For the next week and a half, Drew had something going every night, and he was working long hours on the weekend. Jayson worked so hard on the piece that his fingers developed new calluses, and his hands and arms ached. He hoped his mother would forgive the poor grades he was getting in school when she heard the results of his practice.

Five days before Leslie's birthday, Jayson hooked up the microphone he'd gotten from Drew for his sixteenth birthday. He started singing the lyrics that came into the second half of the song, trying not to think of how the neighbors could probably hear him when he kept messing it up. He reminded himself that the voice had to be done with the amp if it was ever to be heard above the piano and the drums, and he had to get used to the sound and feel of the microphone. So he kept singing it— over and over. Playing the song masterfully was one thing; singing at the same time was quite another. He'd always felt confident with his voice, but he was trying to sing it like Elton John.

Four days before Leslie's birthday, Drew finally had an evening off. He sat down behind the drum set and hit the sticks together for the one-two-three. And they were off. Nine and a half minutes later, Drew comically tossed the sticks into the air and laughed. "That was *incredible!* Holy asterisk, how many hours have you been working on this?"

"Every one I could get away with."

"I can't believe it," Drew said.

Jayson laughed. "Is that an insult or a compliment?"

Drew shook his head. "You are amazing, little brother." He held up his hand, and Jayson gave him a high-five. "California, here we come," he added, and they both laughed.

"Eventually," Jayson said. "We promised Mom we'd get high-school diplomas before we go to LA to get famous."

"So we did, and if you don't start doing something *besides* playing that piano, that's not going to happen."

"Well, if you'd do something besides read those stupid *Star Trek* novels, *you* might get something above a D in any given class."

"At least a D isn't failing."

Jayson laughed. "Okay, let's do it again. You've got to stay with me on that first transition, and I think you should do a little embellishment when the tempo picks up."

"You got it," Drew said and hit the sticks together.

The song came together perfectly during the last couple of opportunities they had to work together. The neighbors were invited over for a dress rehearsal the evening before Leslie's birthday while she was at work. They cheered and applauded and promised to keep quiet about the surprise. Jayson felt blessed to have good neighbors; he wished the kids at school could have even a degree of the acceptance toward him that these people had. Of course, nobody at school had actually heard his music. But in truth, he preferred it that way. They already thought he was odd. He didn't want to give anyone there an opportunity to make light of his deepest treasure.

On Leslie's birthday, Jayson and Drew were both disappointed to learn that she wasn't scheduled to get off work until ten. Even with patient neighbors, they couldn't get away with playing loud music at ten-thirty at night. At eight she called to see if they were all right and admitted that it was slow and she was standing around, but that she couldn't leave. Jayson wished her a happy birthday and promised her they would celebrate when she got home. Twenty minutes later, Drew called the diner where their mother worked and asked for his mother in a panicked voice. When the manager said she was in the ladies' room, Drew told the manager that they had an emergency and she needed to get home right away.

Ten minutes later Leslie came running breathlessly through the front door to demand what the problem was. "Happy Birthday!" they both cheered, and she laughed and hugged them—once she'd recovered from her heart-pounding panic and had given them a good scolding for scaring her like that.

"And what am I supposed to tell my boss the emergency was?" she demanded with a little laugh while she absently fluffed her curly brown hair that hung to her shoulders. She was about the same height as Drew, with a figure that implied she was twenty years younger than she really was. Only her eyes and the subtle lines in her face hinted at her age and the horrors she'd lived through.

"I don't know," Drew said, "but you'll think of something."

When she realized that her sons had been cooking and the table was set for the three of them, she squealed with excitement. She moved toward the table, but Jayson said, "Oh, you can't eat yet. First you have to open your birthday present."

"Oh, you guys," she said with chagrin. "I told you not to spend money on me; we don't have the money to—"

"Don't go jumping to conclusions," Drew said.

He guided her to the couch and told her to close her eyes.

"Okay, you can open them now," Jayson said. She did so, only to see them seated at the piano and drums. She let out a delighted squeal as the implication sank in. "We had to improvise a bit," he added, then cleared his throat and said dramatically, "Leslie Wolfe, this song is for you."

The music began, and only four notes into the song, Leslie squealed again as she recognized it. And then she started to cry. She was well-known for what she called "a high water table" that made her cry easily. Jayson tossed her a quick smile, then focused on what he was doing, wanting it to be perfect. When the first song merged into the second, she made another excited noise, and when Jayson started to sing she actually stood and started jumping up and down. As the lyrics sailed out of his mouth, Jayson couldn't help recalling how his mother had said there were certain phrases that had spoken to her spirit, that had—in some abstract way—given her the strength to keep moving through an ugly divorce with the hope of making a better life for herself.

When the song was finally done, Jayson and Drew turned to find their mother sobbing into her hands. "Mom?" they both said and moved to either side of her on the couch.

"Oh, my gosh," she said, wiping at her tears. "That was the most fabulous thing I have ever seen . . . heard . . . in my life." She hugged Jayson tightly, then Drew. "You've made me the happiest woman on the planet. Do you have any idea . . . what it means to me . . . to have you do . . . *that song* for me? *Me?* What did I do to deserve such incredible sons with such unbelievable talent?"

"Maybe it was the fact that you're the most amazing mother on the planet," Jayson said.

"Amen," Drew added, and she hugged them both again, still crying.

While they shared the birthday dinner that Jayson and Drew had managed to cook, they told her all about their plans and how they'd been working on the song for weeks. She made them promise to practice the song enough so that they could always remember it and play it for her whenever she got depressed. She insisted that from now on, Elton's version would never be as good.

Lying in bed that night, Jayson felt so filled with light and warmth that he could hardly sleep. He wondered how it would feel to play high-impact music on stages around the world for the sole purpose of lifting people's spirits and making them feel like they could keep going through whatever their struggles might be. It was a dream he intended to make a reality.

Jayson finally slept and woke to a strange sound. Heart pounding, he listened in the darkness, wondering what might have jolted him from a deep sleep. Childhood memories made his palms sweat and his mouth go dry before he heard a distinct sound and knew that his memories were merging into the moment. *It was his mother crying.* But it wasn't with happiness as she'd done earlier; no, he knew this cry well. It was pain and fear. And apparently they had all been foolish enough to think that they had seen the last of such events a few years earlier—the last time Jay Wolfe had paid a late-night visit.

"Oh, not again," Jayson snarled under his breath and pulled on his jeans. He rushed into the kitchen where he wasn't surprised to see his father, staggering drunk, just raising his hand to hit Leslie again. She was crouched in the corner, her face already bleeding.

As a familiar anger surged through Jayson, he was struck with a realization that gave him a perverse pleasure. Something significant had changed since the last time this had happened. He was big enough to do something about it.

"You filthy scum," Jayson snarled just loudly enough to get Jay's attention. He turned just in time for Jayson to throw a fist into his face. Jay cursed and lumbered backward. He leaned against the wall and touched his bloodied lip before his eyes focused on Jayson.

"Well, look who grew up," he said with a familiar slur that made Jayson sick to his stomach.

"You bet I did," Jayson growled. "And I will *never* let you hurt her again."

"Don't be so sure," Jay said with a sneer and lunged toward Jayson.

"No!" Leslie screamed as Jay knocked his son to the floor, hitting Jayson twice in the face before Jayson was able to get the advantage. He hit his father over and over until he realized his mother was begging him to stop. He hesitated long enough to hear her say, "You're better than he is, Jayson. Don't lower yourself to this. Drew called the police. It's over now."

Jayson looked at his father, bleeding and cowering on the floor. He looked at the blood on his hands and backed away, horrified at the reality. Before he could fully react to what he'd done, he heard the sirens and knew his father was too incapacitated to run or do any more damage. He shifted his attention to the blood on his mother's face and grabbed a dishtowel, which he pressed over the cut on her cheekbone.

"Oh, I'm fine," she insisted.

"Of course you are," he said with sarcasm. "It's right between the other two scars he gave you and—"

"Hush," she said and took the towel, pressing it to *his* face. "It looks like you've got one yourself. I think we're both going to need a couple of stitches."

"Well," he chuckled without humor, "at least you've got a good *emergency* story for your boss. He doesn't have to know the encounter occurred a few hours later."

Drew guided the police into the kitchen, and it was an hour later before the three of them were finally left alone. The EMTs had attended to the cuts and bruises, and Jay Wolfe had been taken away in handcuffs, after which all the paperwork had to be done. They'd done it all before, and they all knew that Jay would spend a cursory amount of time in jail, and then they could all begin to wonder when he would come around again. Would it be years? Or weeks? The broken window made it evident that changing the locks wouldn't keep him out.

Drew taped up the window while Jayson cleaned up the glass and Leslie put the kitchen in order, attempting to clear away any evidence of the drama. Before they all went back to bed, she looked hard at each of her sons and stated firmly, "I'm not going to live like this any longer. We're moving. And we're doing it soon. With any luck, we can be gone before he gets out of jail. He'd never have the gumption—or the money—to track us down. This way, we can finally be free of him."

Jayson didn't go back to sleep. He fought to push away the anger he felt toward his father, and he thought long and hard about the changes before him. He really didn't have any close friends. He had buddies he hung out with here and there, but no one he'd really miss. Overall, he was considered a joke at school, and he certainly wouldn't miss that. Drew had a way of blending in more easily, but Jayson had a nonconformist streak that made him stand out. He was doing lousy with his grades and figured a fresh start in that respect couldn't hurt, even though he felt some hesitancy at the idea of going into the foreign territory of a different high school with no familiar face beyond his brother's. Still, he figured he could handle that. In fact, he felt relatively fine about moving. Being away from his father gave him great incentive to face the changes.

The following day at school, Jayson answered inquiries about the damage on his face by simply saying, "My face got in the way of some drunk idiot."

That afternoon when Drew gave him a ride home from school, he was surprised to hear his brother say, "You were incredible last night, little brother."

"I feel good about how it turned out. Mom certainly loved the song and—"

"I'm not talking about the song," Drew said, and Jayson looked at him sharply. "I mean . . . it *was* incredible. You really conquered the piano on that one, kid. But I'm talking about the way you handled Dad. I never could have done it. I was scared out of my mind."

"So was I," Jayson admitted.

"But you stood up to him the way I always wanted to. I just want you to know you're my hero."

"Oh, give me a break," Jayson said with mild disgust.

"I mean it," Drew said. "I may be your older brother, but you'll always be my hero."

"It's the other way around," Jayson said. "I'd be lost without you. And considering that we're moving soon, we're all we've got."

"I'm okay with that."

"Yeah, me too," Jayson said.

The following day Leslie got paid, and she took Jayson to get his driver's license. He'd been sixteen for five months, but they hadn't had the money to actually get the license. On the way home, with him at the wheel, she said, "Now you can help drive the moving truck."

Jayson figured he could handle that. In fact, he figured he could handle just about everything related to this move until the following day when Leslie sat her sons down to make a plan.

"Okay," she said, "I've talked to my friend Janice in Oregon. She's been trying to get me to move out there for years. She's got me a guaranteed job at the diner where she works, and there's a vacant apartment that she's putting deposits on for us. She says I can pay her back a little at a time after we get settled. I've figured how much it will cost us to move with renting the truck and paying for gas, meals, and motels along the way, plus what it will cost for us to get settled there. If we have a big yard sale and sell all the furniture, except the beds, and everything else we have that we don't really need, I think we can make it work, if . . ." She hesitated, and Jayson held his breath. In his mind he prayed. *Not the piano. Please don't tell me we have to sell the piano.* Her eyes went to Drew. "We're going to have to sell your car, honey. Of the two cars, mine is in better condition and is more practical. We can tow one car to Oregon; not two. Are you okay with that?"

Drew shrugged his shoulders. "Sure," he said, but Jayson knew this was hard for him. He'd worked hard and saved long for that car. "I can get a job and buy another one when we get out there."

Leslie sighed loudly and forced a smile. "You're such a good sport. I don't think there are two finer teenagers on the planet."

Her eyes shifted to Jayson, and he held his breath. His heart started to pound. "Jayson," she said, and he could feel it coming, "we're going to have to sell the piano." He felt like he'd been kicked in the stomach even before she went on to say, "Besides Drew's car, it's the only thing we have that has any *real* value. And we just . . . can't haul a piano to Oregon." She started to cry. "I can't even tell you how it breaks my heart to sell it. And not because it was my mother's, but because . . . it's yours and . . ."

Jayson rushed out the back door. Not because he was angry—even though he was. But he wasn't angry with his mother; not even slightly. No, he was angry with his father. So angry he wanted to hunt him down and finish what he'd started a few days earlier. Knowing that such anger would accomplish nothing, he relented to the sorrow. That was the real reason he'd fled the room. He'd inherited his mother's high water table, and he didn't want his own tears adding to her grief. He couldn't recall ever feeling such sorrow in his entire life. He'd never experienced the loss of a loved one or friend, and his parents' divorce had been more a source of relief than grief. But all he could feel now was a deep, tangible ache—as if a literal part of him had just been amputated. That piano was his best friend, and the time they'd spent together the last few weeks had given him a fulfillment and joy he'd never imagined possible. How could he ever say good-bye to that piano? And with their financial situation, it could be years before they would be able to afford another one. By then, he'd be on his own. And what kind of money would he ever make with nothing but lousy grades to recommend him?

He was startled to hear his mother say close behind him, "Jayson." He frantically wiped at his tears and turned more fully away from her. She set her hands on his back and said gently, "Oh, Jayson, I'm so sorry. There's nothing I can say that will ever make this easy or right. But there *is* something I have to say."

"I'm listening," he said when she didn't go on.

"I need you to look at me," she said.

He sniffled loudly and again wiped tears away before he turned reluctantly to face her. She hugged him tightly, making it plainly evident that he was a head taller than she was. Then she took his shoulders into her hands and looked him in the eye. "Great people rise out of the dust of adversity, Jayson. You have a gift and the drive inside of you to bring that gift to its fruition. Don't you ever forget that. Don't you ever let go of it. God sent you to this earth to make magic with the instruments you play. Your guitars will go with you. They will keep you connected to that gift. And I promise you . . . *I promise you* . . . that God knows the sacrifice you're making to help keep this family safe, and He will bring a piano into your life. I don't know when or how, but He will. You just have to believe in Him, and in yourself, and it will happen."

Looking into her tear-filled eyes, Jayson actually believed her.

Chapter Two

The drive to Oregon was long and hard. But Leslie manned the tape player and radio, making certain they had a wide variety of music to listen to. They listened mostly to Elton John, while the three of them sang along at the top of their lungs, if only to keep the driver awake through long, tedious stretches. They stopped at a motel only twice, where they all slept long and deep and then forged on, with everything they owned tucked into a truck that wasn't terribly big.

When they finally arrived in Oregon, Leslie insisted that they were going out of the way to go to the beach first before they backtracked a little less than an hour to the small city where they would be living. Her sons had never seen the ocean, and she wanted them to experience it before they faced the challenges of a new life. Jayson had to admit that he felt a certain fascination with the rhythm of the waves and the unique aroma in the breeze. The overall effect was soothing somehow, almost hypnotizing, and he wanted to stand there forever and never face moving into a dumpy apartment. Leslie insisted they would make it their home no matter what it was like. And he knew they would. But it would still be a home without a piano.

Leslie finally insisted that they had to get moving or they'd be searching for the apartment in the dark. They found it without too much trouble, according to Janice's directions. Leslie's friend was there to greet them, since they'd called her from a phone booth and let her know they were nearly there. Jayson and Drew had only met Janice once, and that had been years earlier. Leslie was obviously comfortable with her, and that was good. Jayson figured his mother could use a friend. Jayson and Drew had each other, but she could likely use a peer.

The apartment wasn't as bad as Jayson had expected it to be. He and Drew would be sharing a room, but that didn't bother either of them. The boys dug in and started unloading the truck so they could return it and not pay for another day. By late evening they had the place fairly livable, which wasn't terribly difficult when they had brought so little with them. Since they had no living room furniture and the bedrooms were small, Leslie insisted that the drums and Jayson's guitars be set up there. She meticulously set out the two stands and carefully leaned Jayson's guitars into them as if they were priceless porcelain. And when Drew had his drums put together, she admired them much the same way.

"We'll never be able to play, you know," Drew said while they sat on the floor eating a pizza that wasn't very good. "In an apartment complex like this, we'd never get away with the noise."

"I'm sure you're right," Jayson said, trying not to sound as sad as he felt.

"At least you can play the acoustic guitar without waking the baby next door," Drew said.

"And you can beat your sticks on the carpet or the practice pad," Jayson countered, "just like you used to before you actually had drums."

"You'll find a way," Leslie said with a bright voice that Jayson knew was taking great effort. "Somehow, you'll find a way to be able to play again. I just know you will."

"Of course we will," Drew said, forcing a smile toward his mother. Jayson wanted to believe her, but at the moment it all just felt too far out of reach.

* * * * *

Throughout the next several days, Jayson and Drew agreed privately that they would do their best to have a good attitude and not create any more difficulty for their mother. They knew her heart was breaking on behalf of their music, but she was doing her best to be positive. Drew got a job after only a few days. His experience with movie theaters fit perfectly with a job opening. Jayson kept applying, and kept trying to smile—at least when he was around his mother. But two weeks after their arrival, Jayson wondered if he'd ever hated life so much as he did walking the halls of a high school that felt like some kind of prison in a foreign country. He couldn't be angry with his mother for making the move, and he couldn't be angry with the students around him who didn't know him and likely wouldn't care to, so he chose to be angry with his father. Still, that was relatively pointless. Reminding himself for the hundredth time in a month that anger wouldn't do him—or anybody else—any good, he put his focus on his music. It was in his head; always in his head. He felt completely distracted from what he knew he should be learning in these classes, but coming into them in the middle of a term already made him feel too far behind to know what was going on. And he didn't feel the motivation to do anything about it. The only thing that stuck in his head at all was the buzz in the air about the school play that was opening that night. He'd always enjoyed going to such things in Montana, but he had no desire to go alone. Drew wouldn't go; it wasn't his thing. And his mother was working practically every evening. Jayson was on the way out of his last class, feeling terribly sorry for himself, when a girl named Patty asked if he would like to go to the play with her. "Not really a date," she said, "but I have tickets."

Jayson eagerly accepted her offer and was glad to get out of the house, even though he felt mostly awkward with Patty, who was a little too funky for his taste. At the school auditorium, she introduced him to some other people as they went by, looking for seats. They were friendly, but Jayson still felt lost. He was relieved when the lights went down and the play began. For a couple of hours he could become completely lost in another world, filled with drama and music. He'd seen *West Side Story* before, but he was extremely impressed with the way it was being done. The acting was good, and the presentation of the musical numbers was excellent. He was most impressed by the performance of the character Anita. The actress had a voice that chilled him. Her ability to belt out loud, clear notes was incredible. And she was beautiful, as well. During the intermission he looked at the program he'd been holding during the play and learned the name of the actress he'd been admiring. *Elizabeth Greer*. He'd have to remember that name. By the time the play ended, he wasn't worried about forgetting her name. He was more concerned that he would *never* forget *her*. Long after midnight he laid awake in his bed, contemplating this dark-haired enchantress oozing with talent and a simple beauty that left him thinking over and over, *I'm in love*. He knew it was ludicrous. Such feelings were equivalent to getting a crush on Jane Seymour. He knew absolutely nothing about her personally, and if he did he would probably hate her. Still, the impression was deep.

The following morning Jayson was glad to sleep in. Saturday felt like a miracle at the moment. He woke up to the smell of French toast and felt a soothing comfort to realize that his mother evidently had the morning off. He got up to find her sipping a cup of coffee and reading a magazine. She smiled when she saw him and said, "I thought the aroma would bring you around. Sit down. I'll heat it up."

"Thanks, Mom," he said and yawned. "Where's Drew?"

"Working. I guess the Saturday matinees start pretty early. He had to be selling tickets by ten, I think."

"Wow," Jayson said. "Who thinks about seeing a movie this early?"

"That's what I was wondering," Leslie said. "So, how was the play?"

"It was great," he said while his mind wandered to Elizabeth Greer.

"What's up?" Leslie asked as she slid two pieces of French toast onto his plate.

"What do you mean?" he asked absently.

"You have a silly grin on your face," she said lightly. Jayson pretended to be astonished until she added, "I'm guessing it's a girl."

He heard himself chuckle and was forced to admit sheepishly, "Yeah, it is." Then he heard himself admit something he'd never even contemplated before last night, "I think I'm in love."

"Ooh," she said, "that's pretty extraordinary from a guy who has never been in love with anything but music. Sometimes I've wondered if you'd ever have time for a girl."

"Oh, I think I could make time for this one," he said lightly.

"I want to hear all about it," she said, sitting across from him. "Is it the girl you went to the play with last night? What was her name? Patty?"

"No, Patty was nice enough, but I'm relatively certain this was our first and last date. Actually, this girl was *in* the play. She played the part of Anita."

"Wow," Leslie said, "it takes talent to play that part and do it well."

"And she did it well."

"Tell me about her."

"There's nothing to tell. Beyond seeing her on stage I know absolutely nothing about her, so why do I feel so . . ."

"So? So what?" she pressed.

"It's almost like . . . I knew her in another life; like my soul is supposed to be linked with hers."

Leslie stopped what she was doing and stared at her son in amazement. Jayson could almost imagine her thoughts. She was wondering if this was simply his artistic mind attempting to describe a typical first crush. Or was there some merit to what he was feeling?

"Do you think I'm crazy?" he asked, wishing he knew the answer to those questions.

"No, of course not," she said. "Why would I?"

"Well, it feels crazy. I know absolutely nothing about her."

"Then you need some time and an opportunity to get to know her better. There could be something to what you're feeling, or it could simply be a . . . crush. Either way, you're sixteen. You're entitled to such feelings, and you should enjoy them. But remember, you've always been more mature than your age in many ways. You think . . . and feel . . . deeper. You even talk older than you are. You always have. That's not a bad thing, but don't get ahead of yourself. You're still very young. In the long run, you need more information in order to know if your feelings are worth pursuing. All the attraction and passion in the world will never compensate for a bad match."

Jayson read between the lines and asked, "Is that what happened with you and Dad?"

Leslie sighed. "Yes, that about covers it. I was so infatuated with him that I didn't bother to look at the warning signs. We were ill-matched, and he had some serious problems, but I naively believed that marriage would solve everything. In truth, it only brought out the worst in him." She looked at Jayson directly. "Which is why I want you to choose carefully. That intense attraction you feel is important to a relationship. But it's only a small part of what makes a good relationship work. So, look for opportunities to get to know this girl, and time will let you know what's right. She would certainly need the same kind of maturity you have, for starters. When your heart and your head can agree, then you'll know you're on the right path. And just enjoy the journey. You've got years before you need to worry about getting serious with *any* girl."

"I'm sure it's nothing," Jayson said. "I'll probably forget about her in a week."

Nothing more was said throughout the remainder of the weekend, but on Monday Jayson actually felt some appeal in the prospect of going to school. It wasn't a small school, but it wasn't terribly large, either. Surely he would eventually cross paths with Elizabeth Greer. He scanned faces in the hall, looking for her dark hair, but he didn't see her. While he'd previously been fairly oblivious to his surroundings, now he carefully observed the other students in his classes, searching for that familiar face. He settled into his third-period English class with a sigh when he realized there were no girls with long, dark hair in the room. He felt somewhat embarrassed to realize that an oral book report was due, and when his name was called he had to admit that he wasn't prepared. He digressed into his usual oblivious state of mind while other students went to the front of the room, one at a time, to tell the class about their favorite book of all time and why it was their favorite.

"Miss Greer," the teacher said, and Jayson's head shot up. "I assume you're prepared."

"I am," a voice said from directly behind him; and yes, it sounded familiar. Was that the voice he'd heard reciting lines on stage? He stole a quick glance as she stood and walked past him, but he couldn't see her face—only curly blond hair hanging down her back. He was telling himself it was a different Miss Greer until she got to the front of the room and turned to face the class. It took great self-discipline for him to keep from gasping aloud. *It was her!* He'd been looking for dark hair, but . . . of course, the part she'd played had been Hispanic. She'd put temporary color on her hair for the play. Jayson felt like a fool from the inside out as he realized how his heart was pumping and his palms sweating. He listened intently as she said, "My favorite book is *Pride and Prejudice* by Jane Austen. When I first read this book in junior high, I thought it was great because the main character's name is Elizabeth, and as you all know, that's *my* name. Anyway, as I read the book, I discovered that I really liked it, and I've read it several times since." She went on to analyze the plot and characters, while Jayson was mesmerized—not with her book report, but with her. And she'd been sitting right behind him in this class all along. Of course, he'd only been going to this school a couple of weeks, but still . . .

His heart quickened again as she passed by him and sat down. Through two more book reports, he fought to think of something he could say to her that wouldn't sound idiotic. When the bell rang, he turned quickly as he stood. "Elizabeth?" he said.

She looked up from gathering her things, apparently surprised. "Hi," she said and smiled, but he could almost imagine her impression of him. While he'd considered Patty a little too funky for his taste, Elizabeth would surely consider *him* a little too funky for *hers*.

In response to her expectant expression, he quickly added, "Your performance last Friday was incredible. It left a deep impression on me."

Her smiled widened. "Thank you. That's very sweet. What kind of impression? A good one, I hope."

"Oh, yes," he chuckled. "Let's just say that sitting in that auditorium was the first time I actually felt glad that we'd moved here."

She laughed softly and picked up her books. "Well, I'm glad you enjoyed it," she added. "Jayson, isn't it?"

"That's right," he said.

She moved toward the door. "I'll see you later, then."

Throughout the day Jayson realized he had two more classes with her: algebra and science. Their brief conversation had left him elated, until he realized over the next week and a half that she was polite and friendly to everyone, and she often greeted people by name. He couldn't be sure if she was genuinely kind or just gifted at being diplomatic. Maybe she intended to run for a student office eventually and was hooking votes in advance. Then he realized that she already had a student office. Why wasn't he surprised? He went to see *West Side Story* once more, then convinced himself while he watched it that he needed to get a life. He was hopelessly pining for a girl that he felt certain would never have any interest in a guy like him. The more he learned about her, the more he realized they were from different sides of the tracks—figuratively speaking. By putting the pieces together he knew that she came from an affluent family. She was active in debate as well as drama. She sang in the school choir and played in the school orchestra. She played the flute and the violin. She was amazing and beautiful, and he was out of his mind to think that this could ever come to anything in this lifetime or the next.

"How was the play?" his mother asked when he came through the front door to find her reading, leaning against the wall with a couple of pillows. "As good as the first time you saw it?"

"Better," he admitted.

"You okay?" she asked.

"Not really, but I'm not sure I want to admit to anything."

She gave him a scolding glare and patted the floor next to where she was sitting. "Talk to your mother," she insisted. He sat beside her while she asked questions of genuine concern about school, job hunting, and friends. He answered her honestly. He hated school; he couldn't focus or concentrate, and he was getting lousy grades. He hadn't found a job, in spite of applying at several places and being willing to do just about anything. And he had no friends.

"What about that Patty girl you went out with?" she asked. "Is she friendly?"

"She asks me how I'm doing. She's one of the few people who is friendly with me. But she's got her little group of friends, and they're not my type. I'm not brokenhearted over Patty."

As if Leslie had read between the lines, she leaned forward and looked at him closely, asking with a severe voice, "Who *are* you brokenhearted over?"

Jayson looked away quickly, embarrassed at having her guess the problem so easily. "Jayson?" she said in a mock-scolding tone; a tone that made him chuckle. She touched his chin and forced him to face her. "Is it the girl you told me about?"

"Yeah."

"That *is* why you went to the play again, isn't it?"

"Yes," he admitted, knowing it was pointless trying to avoid being honest with his mother. But in truth, he was relieved. He needed to talk to somebody, and she'd always been a source of perfect under-standing. "She's incredible, Mother. I've never felt this way about a girl before. But I don't even know her, and I'm not sure she's my type."

"What *is* your type?"

"I don't know, but . . . she's like . . . a straight-A student, and everybody likes her. She looks like the kind of girl that every teacher would point to and say, 'This is how the rest of you ought to be.' She's clearly not my type."

"And why not?"

"I don't know, I just . . ."

"Would you change the way you appear to others just to impress someone like her?"

"No!" he answered abruptly.

Leslie Wolfe touched the little silver ring in Jayson's left ear and smiled. "You have just a tiny bit of rebel in you." She pressed her hand down his ponytail and smiled, as if she were genuinely fond of it. "But that's one of the things I like about you. I don't think you're trying to defy anything or anyone; you're just unique, and you want the world to know that. Underneath, you're probably not so different from this girl. If she's too judgmental to not see past the surface, then she's not good enough for you. Do you think she has any idea how talented and sensitive and awesome you are?"

Jayson chuckled. "No, and she probably never will—unless you tell her."

"Maybe I will one day. If your feelings for her are as strong as you say, then perhaps something will change eventually. Right now, your heart is speaking very loudly. You're both very young. You need to give the matter some time. And perhaps you can actually *meet* her."

"I already have, actually."

"And you didn't tell me?" she scolded lightly.

"Well, it was a bit of a shock." He told her about the encounter in his English class and why he'd not figured out that it was her.

Leslie listened, then asked, "What's the name of this Princess Charming?"

"Elizabeth Greer," he said, loving the way it felt to say it.

"Elizabeth is a nice name."

"Yes, it's the name of the heroine in *Pride and Prejudice*," he said. "That's her favorite book."

"Maybe you should read it," Leslie suggested. "You *do* know how to read."

"Yes, I do," he said, pretending to sound insulted. "I just . . . don't like to."

She pushed her fingers lovingly through the hair that was cut shorter on the top of his head. "How can you possibly concentrate with all that music in your head?"

Jayson couldn't answer that. He simply said, "Elizabeth Greer probably doesn't even like rock music or care anything about it. If she listens to anything at all, it's probably Mozart."

"Mozart's not so bad," Leslie said.

"No, Mozart's not so bad," he admitted. "But I wonder if she likes Elton John."

"I bet she'd like *your* rendition of Elton John."

"Maybe," he said, "but I doubt it."

"I wish you could play it for me now."

Jayson forced away the heartache he felt over *that* wish. He hurried to say, "Even *if* we had a piano, I don't think the neighbors would appreciate it, especially this late in the evening."

"Probably not," she said. "But I look forward to the day when you can play it for me again."

"I look forward to that, myself," he said and kissed her good-night.

The next day Jayson was offered a job at a quick-lube place after school and on Saturdays. Changing oil in cars wasn't his idea of a good time, but it was a job, and he needed the money. His mother had none to give him, and with some steady income, he could meet his own needs and help her out some.

Within a few days, he became accustomed to the job, grateful that his older brother had taught him the basics of maintaining a car a long time ago. Weeks passed while he became accustomed to his life, but it felt gray and devoid of color—devoid of music. He picked at his acoustic guitar enough to not go insane, but it just didn't feel right without being able to jam with Drew on the drums. It just didn't feel right without the piano.

The holidays came and went while the Oregon sky remained as gray as his mood. Christmas was nice in a safe, secure kind of way. They didn't have much to give each other, and they had no extended family or close friends to celebrate with. But they had each other, and they had strong Christian beliefs that gave the holiday a deeper meaning. And they didn't have to worry about Jay Wolfe coming around. Still, Jayson was struggling. He felt as if something inside of him was shriveling up and dying.

As the second semester began in January, Jayson used the opportunity for a fresh start to do better on his schoolwork, but he struggled anyway. Still, he kept trying, wishing that by staying busy he could keep Elizabeth Greer out of his head. She was polite and always smiled and said hi to him, but he knew he was just another face to her.

As Jayson got to know the guys he worked with, he became more comfortable there. He particularly liked a guy named Derek, who was barely younger than Jayson and also a junior at the same school. Derek was thin and nearly as tall as Jayson, with swarthy blond hair that always looked like he'd just gotten out of bed. He had a sense of humor unlike anything Jayson had ever encountered, and once Derek warmed up to him a bit, he would do and say things at the oddest moments that provoked Jayson into laughter. And laughter felt good for a change.

Jayson also discovered that they enjoyed listening to the same kind of music in the rare moments when the manager wasn't there with the radio tuned to a country and western station. He and Derek could usually find something to talk about when the work allowed bits and pieces of conversation. But Jayson felt a heart-quickening affinity with Derek when he heard him say, in reference to a song playing on the radio, "Oh, can you believe the awesome bass line in this?" He said it with passion, then he stopped what he was doing just long enough to tap the rhythm out with his hands on the toolbox at his side. Jayson stopped what he was doing as well, realizing that what Derek had just done had a unique flare to it. The movement of his hands had given Jayson a neon message. Derek was a musician.

"Derek," Jayson said, sliding out from beneath the car he was working on. "Tell me about the bass line." He looked puzzled, and Jayson said, "Just . . . tell me why it's so awesome."

Derek went into a detailed explanation that confirmed Jayson's suspicions, while something inside of him wanted to throw his arms around Derek and hug him. How long had they been working together, oblivious to this amazing connection? He knew he'd found a soul-mate, even before he asked, "Do you play?"

Derek answered matter-of-factly, "I've messed around with guitars more than a little; every chance I get, actually. I'm much better with the bass, but I can manage to pull some tunes on a six-string."

Jayson laughed out loud, then asked, "When do you get off?"

"Same time you do; at six when we close."

"I'd love to hear what you can do," Jayson said, and Derek grinned.

"Really?" He sounded as if he'd just been awarded a dream vacation, which made Jayson wonder if Derek had anybody in *his* life that he connected with musically. Jayson had Drew, but because of the noise factor, they'd hardly been able to touch their instruments since they'd left Montana. He felt as if he was shriveling up inside when he thought about it, so he'd tried not to think about it.

During the remainder of the workday, Jayson glanced at the clock every ten minutes. He called his mother to let her know that she didn't need to come and get him. Derek overheard and said, "I can take you home later."

Jayson repeated this to his mother and promised to be home by ten at the latest. When they finally got off work, they both got into Derek's car, and for the first time Jayson noticed that it was actually quite nice, but he could tell from the stereo and certain embellishments that it was obviously not his parents' car. The reason that a guy his age could afford to drive such a car became evident when he pulled it into a three-car garage attached to one of the largest, most beautiful homes Jayson had ever seen—much less been inside of. He followed Derek in through a door that led from the garage to the kitchen. It was obvious that no one else was home. They went straight through the kitchen and down some carpeted stairs, then through a huge room with a big-screen TV, lush couches, and a pool table. Derek opened a door and flipped the light switch, and Jayson actually had trouble breathing. The room was huge, but in it was only a small desk, a few chairs oddly placed—and three guitars, leaning on stands, a few amplifiers, a microphone on a stand, and some mixing equipment. And there was an electronic keyboard. He felt as if he'd just stepped into heaven. He let out a delighted laugh as Derek closed the door and commented, "The room is basically soundproof. It was built as a home theater by the people we bought the house from, but nobody ever watches TV enough to care, so I took it over."

"By . . . soundproof . . . you mean . . ."

"I can play it pretty loud without bothering anybody. If they're actually trying to sleep or something, then you can hear the beat through the floor, but then . . . the bedrooms are on the top floor. So for the most part, nobody notices."

Jayson laughed again and silently thanked God for giving him a job changing oil. For the next two hours, Jayson and Derek took turns showing each other what they knew, both in awe of the other's talent and the fact that they had found such a strong common bond. For Jayson, having his fingers on the guitar and keyboard soothed something inside of him that had been aching for many weeks now. He'd picked at his own guitar in his room a bit, but this was different. Oh, so different!

He was startled when the door came open and a man appeared. He nearly expected Derek to be scolded, but the man smiled and said, "So, you *are* here. I thought I detected a subtle ambience from the basement."

"Hi, Dad," Derek said. "This is Jayson. He works with me. He's amazing with this stuff."

"That's great," Derek's father said, stepping toward Jayson with his hand outstretched. Jayson stood and returned the handshake. "It's a pleasure to meet you, Jayson. Call me Will."

"Thank you," Jayson said.

Will took special notice of Derek's obvious pleasure, and then he chuckled. He turned to Jayson and said, "I'm assuming you are the reason my son is so happy. Where have you been all his life?"

"Montana," Jayson said, suddenly grateful for having made the move. Never before had he found anyone besides his brother to connect with musically.

"Well, I'm glad you're here," Will said, chuckling again. "I'm throwing together some pasta if the two of you are hungry. It'll be ready in about twenty minutes."

"Thanks, Dad," Derek said. "We'll be up."

Will left the room, and Derek said, "My dad loves to cook." Jayson felt a moment of envy for having any kind of a decent father at all, but he quickly turned his focus to the instrument in his hands.

Jayson looked around himself and asked, "What do you think we could do if we had a drum set down here?"

"Oh, that would be way awesome," Derek said and did a little dance that made Jayson laugh. "If we knew somebody who could play it, that is," he added with exaggerated resignation.

Jayson chuckled and looked at Derek. "My brother Drew not only owns a set, but he's one of the best drummers on the planet—in my humble opinion."

"Are you *serious?*" Derek said with such amazement that Jayson laughed again.

"Quite serious. So, what do you think? Should I have him bring them in? Do you think we could come up with something . . . extraordinary?"

"I'd bet my life on it," Derek said, and they laughed together.

When Derek and Jayson went upstairs to have pasta with Derek's father, Jayson noticed it was nearly nine. Derek bragged profusely about Jayson's talent, then with great excitement, he told Will about Jayson's brother. Jayson almost expected Will to protest having drums brought into the house, but he seemed pleased, even eager. More than once he said, "I can't wait to see what you boys might come up with."

"So, what do you listen to?" Jayson asked Will.

"Oh, lots of stuff," he said.

"But . . . who is your favorite musician of all time?"

"Oh, that's easy," Will said. "Steve Winwood, especially the classic stuff."

Jayson grinned, then softly sang some classic lyrics, which Will immediately recognized.

"Yes," Will said and laughed. "That was very good. Do you play any of his stuff?"

"Not really, but my mom listens to it, and his work has had a great influence on me."

"So, what do you listen to?" Derek asked Jayson.

"A little bit of everything, but . . . I have my own stuff in my head too much, I guess. The radio is too distracting."

"You write your own stuff?" Will asked.

"I do," Jayson said, wondering why he seemed so impressed. Embarrassed for some reason, he asked Will, "Are you familiar with Elton John's older stuff?"

"Some of it," Will said, practically beaming.

"My mother loves Elton John. For her birthday my brother and I gave her one of his songs."

"I don't understand," Will said, but he said it with a delighted chuckle. Derek just ate ravenously, apparently thrilled by the conversation.

"My brother and I put together a somewhat renovated version of one of her favorite songs. We had to refurbish it, since it was only piano and drums. But she loved it."

"I'd like to hear that," Will said eagerly.

"That might be possible eventually," Jayson said, aching for his piano.

Once they'd finished eating, he told Derek he needed to get home. He thanked Will profusely for the pasta, and Will told him he was welcome in their home any time. They were on their way to the garage door when Will said, "Oh, there's a video on the bench in the front room. Would you drop it off on your way home?"

"Sure," Derek said, and Jayson followed him in the other direction as he added, "Come on; we'll go out the front door."

When Derek flipped a light switch in order to get the video, Jayson's breathing once again became difficult. In fact, he actually saw stars as the blood rushed from his head. There, before him—the focal point of the front room—was a full-sized, black grand piano.

"You okay?" Derek asked.

"A little dizzy, actually," Jayson said. He was relieved when he managed to force back the threat of tears and turned to meet the eyes of his new friend, certain Derek would understand when he added, "This is the most beautiful piano I've ever seen up close." Derek laughed as if it gave him great pleasure to see Jayson so awestruck. "Do you play?"

"Not really. My sister does."

"May I?" Jayson asked.

"Go ahead," Will said from behind them, apparently there to investigate their conversation. "No one else is even home."

Jayson sat down and reverently brushed his fingers over the tops of the keys, as if to offer a greeting. He laughed as he went through a typical warm-up run, then he said, "Okay, I just have to play one song, if that's okay, before I go."

"I was hoping you would," Will said, and Derek sat down, looking as if he were about to witness a miracle.

"All right." Jayson gave a nervous chuckle. "This is that Elton John number I learned for my mother; seriously renovated. But I haven't practiced for weeks."

"Just go for it," Derek said eagerly.

Jayson actually heard himself laugh as he started to play. He'd played it in his mind a hundred times, and he was amazed at how fluidly the notes went through his fingers. He stopped about halfway through, certain he'd outstayed his welcome with these people by now. He heard them applauding and felt embarrassed by their overt praise. On his way to the door, Derek's father said, "You are welcome to use the piano any time you want, son."

"Thank you," Jayson said and again had to fight tears as he followed Derek to the car.

During the brief drive to Jayson's apartment, Derek said five times, "This is unbelievable." Apparently he was as happy as Jayson about this arrangement. And that was pretty happy.

As Jayson got out of the car, he told Derek that he'd talk to his brother and that he'd see Derek tomorrow at work. He practically ran to the apartment door. His mother wasn't going to believe this. Or maybe she would. She'd all but prophesied this turn of events. She was a woman who believed in miracles.

Chapter Three

Jayson stepped through the front door. "Mom?" he said, and she poked her head out of the bathroom.

"What is it, honey?" she asked with a toothbrush in her mouth.

He laughed and picked her up, turning her around once before he set her down. She laughed and spit into the sink before she said, "You got a date with Elizabeth."

"Even better," he said and laughed again. "I just played 'Funeral for a Friend' on a black grand piano."

"Really?" she asked and laughed with perfect delight. "Tell me," she added with tears in her eyes. Nothing good or bad happened to any degree without her shedding tears.

He repeated the events of the evening, finding great joy in the way she gasped as he told her about the soundproof room, the high-quality instruments there, and the hospitality of Derek and his father.

"It's a miracle," she concluded with a sparkle of fresh tears in her eyes.

"Yes, it is."

"Didn't I tell you God would find a way for you?"

"Yes, you did," he said and kissed her loudly on the cheek. "You're something else, Mom."

"No, *you're* something else," she said, and he felt like he could do anything, as long as she kept believing in him the way she did.

Drew was as pleased with the news as Leslie had been, but he had to work long hours the next couple of days and wouldn't be able to transport his drums until he got a day off. While Jayson felt anxious to see what he and Drew could do with Derek's obvious talent and the opportunity before them, he didn't necessarily feel impatient. It seemed they had all the time in the world to just become friends, and become great.

* * * * *

Elizabeth Greer slipped into her English class, not certain why she was in such a foul mood. Perhaps it had something to do with the echoes of her parents' late-night argument pounding through her head. Perhaps it was the ongoing exhaustion she felt from being involved in so many extracurricular activities that she could hardly keep them straight. If she complained to her father, he would tell her she needed to lighten her load, that she needed to enjoy life at a time when it could bring her so much joy. If she complained to her mother, she would tell her to buck up and stop acting like a baby; real life wouldn't be as pleasant as high school. Elizabeth generally tended to lean more toward her father, mostly because her mother was never there to lean on at all. But perhaps that was the very reason Elizabeth had found herself in the whirlpool of being an overachiever. Somewhere deep inside she clung to the belief that if she followed her mother's example, working every waking hour for gain and recognition, she might just get her mother's approval—or at least her attention.

Elizabeth was distracted from her dismal thoughts when Jayson Wolfe walked into the room, flashing her a warm smile before he sat down. During the weeks that he'd been sitting just in front of her in this class, and directly in her view in two other classes, she'd found herself examining him rather closely. She'd actually been relieved when the semester had changed to find that the situation in English hadn't changed, and they still had a math class together. Why she had any interest at all, she couldn't possibly understand. His very existence just seemed to get on her nerves, and she had no idea why she even cared. He'd never done or said anything to her to cause such disdain. In fact, he'd been perfectly polite, even friendly. Still, she often found herself just wanting to yell at him and tell him to go back to wherever he came from and stop smiling at her.

Elizabeth could analyze her dating experiences in two words: pathetic and hopeless. The guys she'd gone out with could be put into neat, predictable categories. There were those she'd met through her drama or music classes, who were so absorbed in their own talent that they had little else to talk about. Then there were those she'd met elsewhere who were so oblivious to drama and music that they might as well have emerged from some Neanderthal existence where culture had not yet been invented. This category could easily be divided into the jocks and the nerds. The jocks tended to be more enthused about life in general—as long as it revolved around their sporting events. The nerds were so preoccupied with numbers or science or computer technology that they had no room for girls in their lives at all. Elizabeth had associated with, and even dated, guys from every slice of the high school spectrum, and she had found no one who held her interest for more than one or two dates.

Every slice of the spectrum but one, actually. There were the rebels. And Elizabeth had no interest in rebels. There were many degrees of rebels, from those who were mildly snotty about life, to those who drank and smoked and did hard drugs. But they all had a certain nonconformist look about them, and they all had one thing in common. They were so preoccupied with kicking against the system that they couldn't be bothered with schoolwork or being responsible. They were underachievers and would live out lives of failure, eventually becoming a burden to society. And Jayson Wolfe was clearly a rebel. She knew he was barely surviving in his classes—if that. He was so unfocused on his schoolwork that he couldn't even answer a question in class without fumbling. He dressed in a way that clearly stated he would not conform, and the way he wore his hair plainly said, "I'm a rebel." The earring clinched it. But what bothered Elizabeth most was her very lack of indifference. There were all kinds of people attending this school, and she was accustomed to being kind to everyone—even the rebels. But there was something about Jayson Wolfe that made him cling to her mind—against her will. And it made her angry. What business did a guy like him have in holding her interest when he was so clearly not her type? As busy and exhausted as she was, the fact that she would waste her time and energy on such thoughts made her even more irritated.

Once school was over for the day, Elizabeth endured an extra chorus practice, a play audition, and a student-body officers meeting. And then she went home, hoping there would be something worth eating before she changed and hurried back to the school for the chorus concert dress rehearsal. Her only relief was in knowing that her mother wouldn't be home from work for hours yet. At least what little time she spent at home would be peaceful.

* * * * *

Jayson got through the day with an eager anticipation of being able to spend some time at Derek's house after work. They arrived to find Derek's father in the kitchen working on something at the stove that created a pleasant aroma. Will greeted Jayson with a warmth that soothed him deeply. Perhaps it was the absence of a decent father in his own life that made him feel so drawn to Derek's father. His kindness and perfect acceptance of Jayson were a nice reprieve from being the new kid at school.

"Oh, Derek," Will said, "before you start playing, you need to take the garbage out and get the cans on the street."

"Can I help?" Jayson asked.

"No, that's okay," Derek said, looking a little embarrassed. "Just . . . play the piano or something."

"Make yourself at home," Will said as if to add his approval.

Jayson's heart quickened as he went to the front room and turned on the light. He sat at the grand piano and reverently touched the keys before he began a simple melody that reminded him of his childhood lessons. He closed his eyes and allowed the music and the memories to fill him. He could get through almost anything as long as he could get his hands on a piano every day.

* * * * *

Elizabeth parked her car in the huge garage, noting from the other vehicles that her father and brother were home. She walked into the house and smelled something cooking. That was a good sign. But something felt unusual. Then she realized she was hearing piano music. She wondered for a moment if it was a recording her father was listening to on the stereo in the kitchen, but it was too sporadic. Someone was playing the piano. And nobody in the family beyond her had touched the thing in years.

She moved quietly toward the front room and peered around the corner. She heard herself gasp, grateful that the music was loud enough to buffer the noise. *She couldn't believe it!* His back was turned to her, but she knew the back of that head very well from sitting behind him in English. *She couldn't believe it!* Not only was Jayson Wolfe in her home, he was playing the piano. It was a simple song and not necessarily indicative of any notable talent. But he was playing the piano. She never would have guessed that a rebel would have any degree of interest—or training—in such things. She gave herself a quick, silent scolding in regard to being judgmental at the same moment that her heart quickened unexpectedly. She was attempting to analyze the reasons when she was startled by hearing her father call, "It's nearly ready."

Jayson stopped playing and slid off the bench as he turned and stood. Their eyes met, and there was no way for her to pretend that she hadn't been listening to him play. The way she was leaning in the doorframe made it evident she'd been there longer than a moment.

"That was pretty impressive," she hurried to say.

Jayson didn't know whether to laugh or cry. His heart beat audibly, and his palms turned sweaty. Elizabeth Greer was standing in the same room. Without thinking he blurted, "What are you doing here?"

"I live here," she said. "And I know what *you're* doing here. You must be the new friend my brother was bragging about. He didn't know your last name, or I might have made the connection."

"Well, I didn't know his last name either, or I might have done the same," he said, relieved to see that she was at least polite. But there was something condescending about her air with him. And he hated it. He realized he was staring at her just as she looked abruptly away from staring at him.

He was wondering what to say to fill the silence when Will came into the room, wiping his hands on a dishtowel. "I see the two of you have met," he said, leaning over to kiss Elizabeth on the top of her head.

"Oh, we've met," she said. "Jayson is in a couple of my classes."

"How nice," Will said, while Jayson felt some relief to know that she'd at least remembered his name.

Derek came in, and Will insisted they come to the table and eat while it was hot. Jayson felt both disappointed and relieved when

Elizabeth insisted that she had to hurry and change and get back to the school for a dress rehearsal.

"What are you rehearsing this time?" Derek asked her, sounding slightly facetious.

"Your sister's in a choral concert tomorrow evening," Will said with pride in his voice. Toward Elizabeth he said, "I wouldn't miss it. I've got it on the calendar. Why don't you hurry and get ready and you can eat a little before you go."

She nodded and hurried away.

"I didn't realize she was your sister," Jayson said. "She's in some of my classes."

"I'm sorry," Derek said, then chuckled.

"You're both in the same grade," Jayson pointed out as if Derek didn't know. "You're not twins, are you?"

Will chuckled. "No, but close. Elizabeth is actually eleven months older, but they ended up in the same grade at school because of the deadline placement."

"I see," Jayson said, thinking that was the same reason he and Drew had ended up only one year apart in school, even though they were nearly two years apart in age. Once he and Derek had eaten, they went to the basement after Jayson thanked Will more than once for supper. He enjoyed his time with Derek and soon forgot about Elizabeth while they toyed with the guitars and he messed around a little with the electronic keyboard. They talked and laughed, and Jayson felt as if he'd known this guy forever.

Derek took Jayson home at ten, and Jayson found himself alone. He picked at his acoustic guitar, looking forward to moving his electric guitar and amp to Derek's house in the next couple of days, where he could play his own instrument with some volume. Without Derek there to distract him, his mind strayed to thoughts of Elizabeth Greer. Derek's sister. He couldn't believe it. He didn't know whether he should be happy or angry about the connection. At the moment he felt more angry.

When Leslie came through the door, she took one look at him and said, "What's wrong?" She tossed her keys and purse on the table and sat down next to him on the floor, where he had his guitar on his lap.

"You'd never believe who I saw at Derek's house this evening."

"Who?" she said. He gave her a hard stare, and she added with astonishment, "Elizabeth Greer?"

"That's right," he said sourly.

"She's dating Derek!" Leslie guessed. "Oh, my gosh. That is so—"

"No, Mom," he interrupted. "She's Derek's sister."

"Really?" Leslie seemed delighted. "Wow."

"Wow what?" he asked, unable to appreciate her enthusiasm.

"Well, that's a pretty amazing coincidence, don't you think? I don't believe in coincidences. This girl that you have described as . . . what did you say? You felt as if you'd known her in another life? And now you find out she's a sister to a guy you described as your musical soul mate. That's too weird, Jayse."

"Yeah, it's a little too weird for me."

"I would think you'd be happy; you're obviously not."

"Why should I be?"

"Well, this is a perfect opportunity for you to get to know her better."

Jayson sighed. "Maybe, but . . . this is not how I imagined having that opportunity."

"Well," she laughed softly, "opportunities rarely come the way we expect them to. But I sense some destiny at work here. Whether Elizabeth ends up being a part of your future or not, you must remember that we can gain experience from the contacts we make with other people in this world that help shape who and what we are. Even if Derek and Elizabeth are only a temporary part of your life, you may still have great things to learn from them—or maybe to teach them."

Jayson felt sure she was right; she usually was. But he wondered why he felt like anything less than forever with Elizabeth Greer would be a crime.

The following day Jayson dreaded his English class. He slid into his seat, grateful that Elizabeth wasn't there yet and he didn't have to make eye contact with her. With any luck she would say nothing to him about last night's encounter. He didn't stop to analyze why he was feeling so uncomfortable over the connection; he only knew that he was.

From the corner of his eye he saw her come into the room, and he pretended to be reading. He was startled when she said brightly, "Hi, Jayson."

"Hello," he said, looking up. She smiled before she took her seat, but again he couldn't help feeling that her attention to him had an edge of condescension.

From behind he heard her say, "I must admit I was a little surprised to find you at my house last night."

"I was a little surprised to find you at your house, as well," he said without turning around.

Not knowing what to say, Elizabeth attempted a little teasing that might open a conversation. "Derek told me his new friend was into music, but I was thinking you were more the screaming guitar type."

Jayson felt angry over the comment; he knew beyond any doubt that it was laced with prejudice. He wanted to yell at her and tell her she knew absolutely nothing about him. Instead he turned and said with exaggerated boasting, "Oh, I am." With sarcasm he added, "I don't really make music, I just make noise."

Elizabeth almost looked hurt before her eyes hardened and she said, "No wonder you and Derek get along so well. He's very proficient at making noise."

Elizabeth noticed then that he had a little scar on his cheekbone. It had a pinkish hue, as if it weren't very old. It was exactly the spot that would split open in a typical fist fight. He'd probably been in some gang wherever he'd lived before coming here. He was probably a bully and full of anger—the kind of anger that would make a person throw sarcastic retorts into a conversation.

She was relieved when class started and he turned his back to her. She sensed that he was angry with *her* and she wondered why. Had her teasing been misunderstood? Then she wondered why she cared. She was attempting to distract herself with the class discussion when the teacher announced that they would be dividing into small groups. Each group was assigned to come up with a famous person and write a brief biographical outline that would be read orally in twenty minutes. They were supposed to come up with as much information on that person without having any research resources available. Part two of the assignment would be to do some research and report the actual facts in two days, when they would compare the two.

Elizabeth was intrigued with the assignment until she was put into the same group with Jayson Wolfe. She tried not to look at him as four other students circled their chairs around and he turned in his seat. The other students made a few suggestions on who they could do their report on, but it quickly became evident that no one really knew anything about these people that would hold up.

Elizabeth was stunned to hear Jayson say, "How about Mozart?"

No one else said anything so Elizabeth asked, "What about Mozart?"

"He was a pretty amazing guy," Jayson said.

"Do you know anything about him?" another student asked.

"A little," Jayson said. "He was born in Salzburg, Austria, in January of 1756. His full name is Wolfgang Amadeus Mozart. He is considered one of the greatest musical composers of all time. He wrote nineteen operas, a hundred and three minuets, fifty-five symphonies, and thirty-nine concertos. He changed the way musicians were perceived by society. He died tragically at the age of thirty-five and was buried in an unmarked grave."

The others in the group scrambled to write down all the facts on Mozart while Elizabeth stared at Jayson Wolfe, wondering how her previous assessments of him could possibly include a profound knowledge of Mozart. Then she realized that he was staring back at her. She looked away abruptly and cleared her throat, and she spent the rest of the day trying to push thoughts of Jayson Wolfe out of her head.

* * * * *

At work that afternoon, Jayson took the opportunity to ask Derek some questions about his family. He learned that Will was an accountant and that Derek obviously admired his father a great deal. Derek's mother was an attorney who was almost never home, and it was evident that Derek was not close to his mother at all. Jayson found their home situation ironic, with the father home more and doing most of the cooking. He really liked Will Greer and wondered again how it would be to have a decent father. Of course, Jayson had an incredible mother, something it seemed Derek didn't have.

Jayson was cleaning his hands, nearly ready to leave work, when Derek asked, "You coming to my house, bud?"

"I'd like to, but . . . I'm going to that concert at the school tonight."

"Oh, man," Derek said. "I forgot about that. My sister's in that. I guess I should go too."

"Yeah," Jayson said lightly, "you probably should."

"Okay, so maybe I'll see you there, and . . . if it doesn't go too late, maybe we could jam for a while after."

"Sounds good," Jayson said.

In the school auditorium, Jayson had barely walked in the door when Derek flagged him down and invited him to sit with him and his father. "How are you, Jayson?" Will asked.

"I'm good. How are you?" he asked, shaking Will's hand.

"Doing well, thank you."

While they were waiting for the concert to begin, Will asked Jayson questions about where he had lived and the reason for the move. Jayson tried to be as vague as possible, sticking to the point that his mother had just needed a change for several reasons. He doubted that Will Greer would be impressed with his upbringing if he knew. For many reasons, he figured it was better left unsaid. In the same vein, he could only imagine how Elizabeth Greer might respond to knowing that his father was an alcoholic derelict and his mother a struggling waitress.

Just as the lights were going down, Derek asked Jayson, "So, who do you know that's in the concert?"

Jayson hesitated a moment to respond, then said coolly, "I just like concerts." And that was true. But deep inside he knew that his fascination with Elizabeth Greer had motivated his coming to this one. When he saw her come onto the stage, his reaction was so intense that it almost scared him. He cursed himself for feeling this way about a girl who was so obviously beyond his reach. And he still felt angry with her for her attitude toward him in English earlier that day. Forcing negative thoughts out of his mind, he relaxed and enjoyed the music. Oh, how he loved music! And he had to admit it was a good choir, and they did some impressive numbers. When he wasn't focused on Elizabeth, his eyes were drawn to the piano in the center of the stage. Different members of the choir took turns at the piano to accompany the numbers. He actually wondered if *he* should join the choir next year. He knew there were auditions for such things, and he knew he could do it. But he'd never been fond of the forced structure of music classes and the restrictions of working with such a large group. His mind was wandering when he realized that Elizabeth was moving onto the piano bench. His heart quickened, and he straightened in his seat. Derek had said that his sister played, but he'd not consciously made the connection. And boy, could she play! She accompanied the song with confidence and ease. Watching her play he felt something strangely calm filter through him. He'd become infatuated with Elizabeth Greer knowing absolutely nothing about her. Now he knew that she shared something wonderful with him—even if *she* didn't know it yet. Of course, she probably wouldn't care even if she knew, he reasoned. But in that moment he felt incredibly patient and completely at peace. It was as if some inner voice whispered to him that Elizabeth Greer would be a significant part of his life, and he simply had to allow time to work his destiny into hers.

When the song was finished, the applause was full and deep. He watched her stand by the piano and take her bow, and he felt richly blessed just to be in the presence of her talent. He could have basked in it forever. When the applause died down, he leaned over to Derek and said, "I didn't know she could play like that."

"Oh, she's at least that good with the violin. And she messes around with the flute too."

"Of course," Jayson said, only slightly caustic. Her talent was apparent. But her tastes obviously differed a great deal from his own. She would probably never even listen to rock music, let alone play it. He felt sure she could never appreciate his talents the way he did hers. Already he questioned the calm feeling he'd had only minutes ago. Surely such expectations were unrealistic and ridiculous.

After the concert, Jayson was grateful for Will's offer to give him a ride home, since Drew had dropped him off on his way to work and he'd been intending to walk home. In the car Derek asked if Jayson would have time to come over for a while. Jayson glanced at his watch. "Sure," he said. "I just don't want to wear out my welcome."

Will said with pleasure, "Son, you are always welcome in our home. The way you've lit up Derek's face these last few days, I'm deeply indebted to you."

Derek gave a sheepish chuckle. Jayson just smirked at Derek and said, "I think it's the other way around."

"Why is that?" Will asked.

Jayson hesitated, then felt compelled to admit, "We had to sell our piano when we moved. It was pretty hard on me. And the apartment we're in now is too close to everybody else to be able to play much of anything on the guitar. Being able to play means more to me than I could ever say."

"Wow," Derek said. "I didn't know that. Glad I could help, brother." He playfully slugged Jayson in the shoulder.

Jayson chuckled and added, "Besides, Derek understands me. There aren't many people who do."

Will gave a good-natured laugh. "Well, believe it or not, I think I understand both of you."

"Why is that?" Jayson asked.

Will said, "I can't play a note of anything. But I love music; always have. It's been evident from early on that my children were gifted, and it's something that gives me a great deal of pleasure."

Jayson said, "That would give you a great deal in common with my mother. I don't think she enjoys anything as much as seeing her kids play music."

Will asked some questions about his family. Jayson answered them, and Will said he would look forward to meeting Drew and to hearing what the three of them could do when they were able to spend some real time together. He also said that Jayson's mother was welcome to come over any time and listen. Jayson just thanked him, praying this wasn't a short-lived dream. It just seemed too good to be true.

At the house, Jayson was secretly hoping that Elizabeth would show up before he left, but she didn't. Either that or she'd slithered up to her bedroom unnoticed.

The following day he and Drew moved every piece of musical equipment they owned into the Greers' basement. Drew and Derek hit it off well, and the three of them were quickly able to pull some things together that gave Jayson a deep sense of fulfillment he'd never experienced before. He'd always toyed with writing music, and Drew could put a beat to anything. But Derek just had a way of adding the right ingredients to make it work—and the result was magic. Still, he wanted what they were doing to be just right before he let anyone hear it.

As weeks passed, Jayson was at the Greer home nearly every day, but he rarely saw Elizabeth there. And he had yet to meet Mrs. Greer. He knew Elizabeth was involved in another upcoming play, and the school orchestra she was in had been practicing for a concert. At school she was polite but said little to him, and he figured that was just as well. He felt relatively certain that admiring her from a distance would be far better than outright rejection. Jayson attended her concerts, and he went three times to the play she was in, all the while inwardly praying that one day these feelings would come to something beyond being her biggest fan.

Jayson felt some gratification in seeing evidence that his mother seemed more relaxed about life than she had been in years. Not having to fear an intrusion from her ex-husband probably had a lot to do with it. With Drew and Jayson both working, they were able to get some things they'd been needing, and someone that Leslie worked with had given her some used furniture that was actually pretty decent. Having a table and chairs and couch made life much easier.

At the end of the third term, Jayson was pleased to have pulled passing grades. They weren't great, but he hadn't failed any classes, which meant he didn't have to take any of them over. Leslie wasn't terribly pleased with his report card, but she just gently encouraged him to try and do better and left it at that. She was one of the few people who understood how distracting the music could be.

Spring settled in fully while Jayson developed a friendship with Derek that was unlike anything he'd ever known. In regard to music, they could practically read each other's minds. And they had great fun together no matter what they were doing. Between their jobs and their schoolwork, they weren't able to spend nearly as many hours together at the music as they would have liked. And it was even more rare that Drew could find the time to play with them. But eventually, they were able to smooth out a couple of songs that had come from Jayson's head. With much practice they finally decided they were ready to unveil them. Jayson asked Will if it would be okay to bring his mother over so she could hear what they'd been doing. Since she would be off the following evening, it would be the perfect opportunity.

"I would love to meet her," Will said. "And if you'll let me hear what you're doing, I'll even feed you."

"You always feed us anyway," Jayson said.

Will chuckled. "It's a delight to have someone appreciate my cooking. Why don't you invite your mother over for supper tomorrow, and we'll make an evening of it."

"She'll be thrilled. Thank you," Jayson said.

"However," Will said, "I do have my selfish motives for feeding you."

"You do?" Jayson asked, wondering if there was something Will expected of him that he might not like.

"Yes," Will said severely, "I keep hoping that at least once a week you'll play 'Funeral for a Friend.' I absolutely love the way you do it."

"You do?" Jayson asked again, his tone brighter.

"It's incredible, young man. In fact, I think you should do it now and I can listen while I finish up this salad, and then we'll eat."

"You talked me into it," Jayson said and went to the piano.

Later that evening when Jayson told his mother their plans, she was so excited she could hardly stop talking about it. "You're like a real band now, aren't you," she said.

"Well, we're getting there. But you have to be able to do more than two or three songs to get anywhere."

"One step at a time," she said with a proud smile. "And this is a glorious step."

The following evening, Leslie was in awe when Jayson pulled the car up in front of the Greer home. Drew was in the backseat reading science fiction. "Don't worry, Mom," he said as they got out. "They'll love you."

Jayson rang the bell, and Will came to the door. "There're my boys," he said brightly, then he extended a hand to Leslie. "And this must be the woman responsible for raising such fine and talented young men."

"This is our mom," Jayson said as the two parents shook hands, "Leslie Wolfe. Mom, this is William Greer. We call him Will."

"Come in, come in," Will said.

"It's such a pleasure to meet you," Leslie said. "The boys have told me how kind and gracious you've been. I can't tell you what it means to me to know they have a place where they can rehearse."

"The pleasure has been mine," Will said. "With that big empty basement—and a soundproof room—it's hardly an inconvenience.

And your boys have been wonderful friends to Derek. He was pretty much a loner until Jayson came along."

"Stop talking about me, Dad," Derek hollered from the kitchen with exaggerated offense.

Leslie laughed softly. "Derek's a fine young man. Although I haven't had much of a chance to get to know him. They're always here. I hope they haven't been a problem or—"

"Not at all," Will said. He looked at Jayson and added, "Well, I think it's show time, son. The lasagna won't be done for another half an hour."

Jayson actually felt nervous. He cleared his throat and wiped his sweating palms on his jeans. "Okay, well . . . let's do it."

Derek let out a little laugh and led the way down the stairs. More than once Leslie commented on what a lovely home it was. Jayson felt certain she was as overwhelmed as he'd felt the first time he'd come here. She'd likely never been in such a fine home in all her life. Jayson wanted to make so much money selling records that he could buy his mother a home like this. She deserved it.

Chapter Four

Leslie gasped when they came into what had been dubbed "the music room." Drew closed the door and sat at the drums. Jayson motioned Will and his mother to the chairs that were strategically placed in the audience position as Derek flipped all the switches to turn on the amps. Jayson's nerves increased. He didn't want to disappoint his mother, and he didn't want Will to think that all his efforts and encouragement on their behalf were misguided. They both knew the boys had spent endless hours in this room. He didn't want them to start thinking it was a waste of time.

"Okay," he said, putting the guitar strap over his head, "here goes." He cleared his throat. "It's gonna be loud. We have to match the volume of the drums."

"I like it loud," Leslie said with enthusiasm.

"We're waiting," Will said with a little smirk that made it evident he'd picked up on their nervousness.

Jayson turned to Derek as he asked, "What are we doing first?"

"The best, of course," Jayson said and tapped the floor switch with his toe. He forced his nerves down by going into humorous mode; he purposely lowered his voice as he said into the microphone, "Ladies and gentlemen. Put your hands together and welcome the newest, hottest band to hit the planet: A Pack of Wolves." Leslie let out a delighted laugh at the name. He added facetiously, "And their number-one hit, 'Predator.'"

Jayson started on the guitar, the drums came in, then Derek on the bass. He was amazed at how the moment he started playing, his nervousness ceased completely. He put his mouth to the microphone and sang with strength and clarity, *"Time will stalk you like a predator, yeah, never giving you a chance. Just when you think that you've got it beat, time will knock you off your feet, feet, feet."* And then the chorus, beginning with a strong drum sequence and Derek echoing each line. *"And I'm feeling like something's in the wind. Something's coming for my soul. And I'm feeling like something's in the wind. Something that I can't control."* Through the interim, Jayson glanced at his audience and found their faces pleasantly interested. A good sign.

Jayson started the second verse. *"Time's no friend; she is my enemy. The destroyer of my dreams. Just give time the time and then you'll see just exactly what I mean, mean, mean."* They did the chorus again, then a catchy little riff that Jayson was especially proud of, ending with the lyrics, *"You can't run, you can't hide from what you can't see."* They did the chorus once more and ended on a strong beat and a long, clean note.

The room became eerily silent. Jayson focused on the faces looking back at him. His mother had tears streaking her face and a hand pressed over her mouth. Will look stunned, expressionless. Jayson's heart quickened, but he wasn't certain if it was dread or elation he should be feeling. He finally said, "It was that bad, eh?" Will just shook his head. Leslie waved her hands frantically in front of her face as if that could get her emotions under control. Jayson pointed out the obvious. "You're crying, Mom." He looked at Will. "Say something."

Will shook his head again. "I don't know what to say. I am . . . speechless." He chuckled. "That was . . . incredible." Jayson blew out a long breath and Will went on. "Honestly, guys, I . . . expected to hear something that remotely sounded like music. I was prepared to tell you it's got potential and you keep working at it. But this is . . ." He chuckled again. "Forgive my previous pessimism, but this is . . . incredible."

"Wow," Derek said. "Really?"

"Really," Will said.

Leslie was still crying. She just stood and rushed toward Jayson, hugging him tightly once he'd swung the guitar to his back. She then hugged Drew and blew her nose on a tissue before she said, "I knew you could do it. I knew it was just a matter of time and the right combination and . . . you've done it. You're . . . oh, my gosh."

"Mom, it's just one song," Jayson said.

"A very good song," Will said. "Where did you get this song, anyway? I've never heard it before."

Jayson exchanged a glance with Derek. He'd assumed that Derek had told his father. He was leaving it up to Derek to tell him now. "Uh, Dad. Jayson wrote that song."

Will looked at Derek to see if he was serious, then at Jayson as if he'd just sprouted wings. "Well," he said, "it would seem I'm going to need to keep you boys well fed. I feel a record deal coming on."

Leslie made an emotional noise as if she agreed, but she'd started crying again. To break a sudden tension in the air, Jayson said, "Did you want to hear another one?"

"Do I?" Will said, motioning with his arms.

Leslie sat back down and sniffled loudly before she said, "Oh, yes, I want to hear more."

Jayson and Derek made some adjustments on the amps and guitars. Jayson nodded at Drew, and they started together. This song had a softer sound and an entirely different mood from the last one. This was a love song, even though the tempo was quick and steady. Jayson crooned into the microphone, *"I see you walking down the hall. What I'd give to give you a call. You are the most beautiful thing . . . that these eyes have ever seen."* And the chorus, *"Why can't I . . . say hello? When I try . . . my lips don't go. I get tongue-tied."*

Jayson caught his mother's eye and saw her smile. He felt certain she knew the source of these lyrics, especially when he sang the second verse. *"Now you're with your group of friends. And I wish I was one of them. Love is such sweet pain to me, 'Cause I can't touch but I can see."*

Will seemed to be enjoying the song, but Jayson figured it was good he didn't know it had been inspired by his daughter.

"Incredible," Will said when the song was finished. "That was every bit as good as the first one. Just so . . . different. Diversity; that's good."

"Thank you," Jayson said and removed the guitar, setting it gently into its resting place. "I was hoping you wouldn't think all of your cooking and letting us use your electricity was just a waste."

"Heavens, no," Will said. "Even if it was bad music, I'd consider your time well spent. You're having fun, aren't you?"

"I know I am," Derek said eagerly.

"Works for me," Drew said and followed it with a brief drum roll before he set down his sticks.

"I'm so proud of you boys," Leslie said, still a little teary. Jayson had to admit he found his mother's tender emotions rather endearing.

"You know," Will said to Leslie, "what Jayson does with the piano is amazing as well. I've enjoyed listening to him play while I work in the kitchen."

Leslie smiled at Jayson. "Has he played my favorite?"

"Would that be 'Funeral for a Friend?'" Will asked.

"It would," Leslie said proudly.

"He certainly has. I request it frequently."

"Well, you should hear it with the drums," Leslie said.

Will looked at Drew in astonishment. "You've cheated me out of hearing it with the drums?"

Drew shrugged and chuckled. "I didn't figure you'd really want a drum set in your front room."

"Well, not permanently, no," Will said, "but one evening wouldn't hurt. I want to hear it with the drums."

"Oh, yeah," Derek said with a delighted laugh. "We gotta hear it with the drums. I'll help you move 'em, Drew, my man. Let's do it."

Drew made a dubious noise. "I don't know if it's—"

"Oh, come on," Will said. "If you want me to keep feeding you, you're going to have to earn your keep."

"Oh, I would love to hear you do it," Leslie said. "It's been so long." She turned to Will and added, "I love it best when Jayson sings the second half and . . ."

She stopped when Will scowled at Jayson, saying, "Sings? So *you've* been cheating me as well?"

Jayson just shrugged. Drew said, "I guess we'll be moving the microphone upstairs for the evening, as well."

"Okay, but . . . put a sheet or something on the floor," Jayson said. "I don't think Mrs. Greer would appreciate what your drums could do to her white carpet."

Leslie helped Will in the kitchen while the boys moved drums and equipment up the stairs and efficiently set them up in the living room with the piano. Jayson occasionally peeked in on his mother, pleased to see that she appeared to be comfortable and having a good time. He wondered what Mrs. Greer would think to come home and find her husband cooking dinner with another woman—a lowly waitress, no less. But then, he'd often wondered what Mrs. Greer would think of the music going on in her basement. He hoped she didn't come home while the drums were set up in the front room. That would be a treat, he thought. After all this time to actually meet her when they were overtaking the most beautiful room in the house. He prayed that didn't happen. He'd barely thought it when he heard the door from the garage open. He straightened his back from adjusting the amp and held his breath.

"What *are* you doing?" Elizabeth asked.

Jayson gave her a quick glance and said nothing. Derek was her brother. He could answer the question.

"Well?" Elizabeth pressed.

Derek finally said, "After we eat, Drew and Jayse are gonna play this way cool song that they put together for their mom's birthday before they moved here. You just gotta hear it."

Elizabeth made a dubious noise, and Jayson decided he was uncomfortable with this situation, so he slipped into the kitchen to see how his mother was doing. Thirty seconds later, Elizabeth appeared there as well. He discreetly nudged his mother with an elbow.

"There are drums in the front room," Elizabeth said to her father as if he might have no idea.

"Maybe we should leave them there for a while," Will said brightly.

While they were talking, Leslie whispered to Jayson, "Is that her?"

"Yep," Jayson replied quietly, folding his arms over his chest.

"She's beautiful," Leslie whispered.

"Yes, indeed," Jayson said.

"Did you say something?" Will asked, turning toward them.

"No," Jayson said. "Can I help?" he added, hoping to lessen the strain in the room.

"No, thank you," Will said. "Elizabeth, this is Drew and Jayson's mother, Leslie Wolfe. Leslie, this is my daughter, Elizabeth."

"It's so nice to meet you," Leslie said, stepping forward with her hand outstretched. "I've heard so much about you."

Elizabeth looked surprised, but she just smiled and said, "It's nice to meet you too, Mrs. Wolfe. I have some classes with Jayson."

"So I've heard," Leslie said, and Jayson prayed the conversation would stop there.

Will called everyone to dinner, and for the first time ever, Jayson found Elizabeth actually sitting to share a meal with them. He wondered if his mother's presence had made the difference. He was amazed to hear the two of them talking comfortably. Leslie asked about Elizabeth's interests as if she had no idea what they were, and Elizabeth told her all about orchestra, chorus, drama, and being in the junior class presidency. Elizabeth and Will both posed questions to Leslie about herself. She said she worked as a waitress and left it at that. She told them she'd divorced her husband many years ago and got away with the best of him in her sons. Jayson appreciated the way she could so gracefully steer the conversation away from points that were too difficult—or embarrassing—to discuss in such circumstances.

Elizabeth actually felt glad that she'd left practice early and come home. She'd worked hard over the months since she'd met Jayson Wolfe to create an indifference toward him. She'd convinced herself that some silly fascination did not make him worthy of her attention. But she couldn't help noticing how perfectly polite and dignified he was at the dinner table. And his mother was a pleasant surprise. She wasn't certain what she'd imagined his parents to be like, but it wasn't this. Leslie Wolfe, wearing jeans and a sweatshirt, was adorable, pleasant, and even funny. She showed a genuine interest in Elizabeth and her family. She was everything that Elizabeth's own mother was not, and she found herself envious of Jayson in that regard. How might it be to have such an amazing mother? Jayson's interaction with his mother made it evident that they were close and comfortable. Of course, his father was out of the picture, and Elizabeth had to assume the guy was a jerk. Elizabeth was grateful for having a wonderful father, so she figured that balanced out.

Finding herself freshly intrigued with Jayson Wolfe, she couldn't resist sticking around for this performance that was apparently to take place after dinner. When the meal was finished, she offered to help with the dishes and ignored her father's teasing that such things rarely happened. Leslie helped as well while the boys went to the front room to finish setting up their equipment. While the two women were standing side-by-side at the sink and visiting, Elizabeth glanced up and noticed a scar on Leslie's cheekbone—very similar to the one on Jayson's face in nearly the exact same place. Discreetly looking more closely, she realized there were two other similar scars in the same area that were older and more faded. She wondered for a long moment what in the world could have caused them, but she honestly couldn't figure. Her assumptions regarding Jayson's scar didn't fit with this tender woman.

"Okay, they're ready," Derek announced.

"We're almost done," Will said. "Just give us a minute."

Elizabeth quickly finished loading the dishwasher and turned it on while Will exchanged some conversation with Leslie. She heard a quick sequence from the drums and a test on the microphone and said, "Wow, that's loud."

"That's the way we like it," Will said with a smile. "The neighbors are too far away to care."

Elizabeth wondered what kind of performance they were in for. Derek had been bragging about the Wolfe brothers and their abilities, but she'd never been terribly impressed with Derek's taste in music. She expected some mediocre, amateur song that these boys had done for their mother's birthday—something only a mother would love and their best friend would humor. And her father would wholeheartedly support anything that his children were excited about. Still, she was curious and eagerly took a seat between Leslie and her father on the couch in the front room.

Jayson made himself comfortable on the bench and told himself to not even think about the fact that Elizabeth Greer was sitting in the room. He couldn't decide whether he should feel terrified or elated. For what felt like endless weeks, he had longed for an opportunity to prove to this girl that he was not what he suspected she assumed him to be. The opportunity was before him, but if he blew it—or if she simply wasn't impressed—that would be it. There was no more to him than this.

With a perfect view of Jayson's profile where he sat at the piano, Elizabeth focused on him, almost grateful for an opportunity to view him from a different angle than the one directly behind him in English. Taking note of the way he wore his hair, she was suddenly reminded of some hero from a historical movie that took place during a time when *all* men wore their hair in ponytails. Or like Mozart, perhaps. It had a kind of haphazard look that she had to admit was thoroughly masculine, even rugged. Looking at it that way, it suddenly didn't seem so *rebellious*. More eccentric, perhaps. She tried to look at the earring in the same light and had to admit that it was tasteful, even if she didn't particularly like earrings on guys. She also noted a fine, silver chain around his neck that hung beneath his shirt. She was wondering what might be on the end of the chain when Jayson nodded toward his brother. Drew tapped his sticks together and began a slow, steady drum beat to accompany an even, poignant melody on the piano. *Not bad,* Elizabeth thought. Jayson was comfortable and composed with the piano. And he didn't have any music in front of him. The tempo picked up, and the piece he was playing became more intricate. *Okay, I'm impressed,* she admitted to herself. He's not just some third-rate kid on the piano. Then with no warning, the piece went wild with a controlled intensity that took Elizabeth's breath away. She watched in absolute amazement as the keyboard came completely to life beneath his hands. He played a strong succession of chords with such perfection and speed that she couldn't quite believe it was real. She had *never* seen *anyone* play the piano like that. Chills went down her back and up again while she looked at Jayson Wolfe as if she'd never seen him before. The song went on and on. Just when she thought it would end and he'd show exhaustion, he'd go into another twist, while the drums kept up with a perfect synchronization. It was as if the Wolfe brothers were breathing the same rhythm, alive with the same beating heart. And Elizabeth was transfixed.

At the moment when she thought she could bear no more, Jayson put his mouth to the microphone and belted out the lyrics with clarity and brilliance. The song went on while Elizabeth felt as if she were in a dream. She marveled once again at how he could fluidly continue playing and sing without missing a beat. Now she understood her fascination with Jayson Wolfe, or at least she thought she did. Had something in her spirit sensed the gift in him and felt drawn to him in spite of appearances and her gross misinterpretations of his character? This guy was not unfocused and flaky. He was a genius who was so thoroughly focused on music that all else surely felt superfluous. He was not an irresponsible rebel, kicking against the system. He was like an eagle attempting to exist in a world of sparrows.

When the song came to a sudden end, her father and Leslie applauded loudly, while Derek made a fool of himself by cheering and jumping up and down as if his favorite team had just made a touchdown. Elizabeth felt too stunned to move. She saw Jayson turn to take in her response, and in a split second she was struck with a mixture of emotion and understanding. In the same moment that it occurred to her that he actually cared what she thought, she realized that her lack of response had been misinterpreted—and that he was disappointed.

"Oh," Leslie said, drawing Jayson's attention to his mother, "it was even more incredible this time."

"Well, I hate to disillusion you, Mother," Drew said lightly, "but this piano is a whole lot better than Grandma's old upright."

"The acoustics in here are better, too," Jayson said, glancing around.

"Oh, do the other ones from that album," Leslie pleaded.

"Oh, Mom," Jayson said, "I haven't practiced those for . . . I don't know . . . too long."

"Oh, you can do it," Leslie pleaded. "It doesn't have to be perfect."

"What album?" Elizabeth asked Leslie.

"Elton John," she said. *"Goodbye Yellow Brick Road.* It's my favorite; or at least, some of the songs are. The boys grew up listening to them."

Elizabeth nodded. She'd never heard of it. She only knew that Elton John had a reputation for being a fabulous pianist, and obviously Jayson Wolfe had learned much from him.

"Do 'Grey Seal,'" Leslie pleaded like a child, making her children laugh.

"Okay, we'll give it a try," Jayson said. "But no critics here." He looked at Drew and asked, "Can you remember it?"

"I think so. If you can play it, I can follow you."

"Okay, go," Jayson said, and Drew hit a one-two-three-four that went directly into an amazing piano sequence that fell apart thirty seconds later with Jayson and Drew both laughing. "Oh, well," Jayson said.

"Oh, do that last chorus thing," Leslie said, "where the drums are so great. I love that part."

Jayson looked confused until Drew did a little drum sequence that seemed to jog his memory. "Okay," Jayson said, "the chorus." He nodded at Drew. "I'll follow. Go."

They played for only a couple of minutes while Elizabeth was struck with how equally fantastic Drew was on those drums. The overall experience was absolutely incredible.

"That was great," Leslie said, and the boys laughed as if she were crazy.

"You're our mother," Drew said. "You have to say that."

"Well, I think it was great," Will said eagerly.

"I think it was great too," Elizabeth said. Jayson looked toward her, surprised. Then he exchanged a look with his mother that seemed to have some silent meaning.

Leslie broke the awkwardness when she said, "Okay, just one more. Play 'Harmony.' It's a simple song. I know you both remember it, because it's like breathing to you. Do it for your mother."

"Okay, Mom," Jayson said. "'Harmony,' just for you. And then I think we should leave these people in peace."

"Oh no," Will said. "This is the most fun I've had in months."

Jayson said to Will, "This is the song that our mother made us both learn to play on the piano before she would let us get guitars and drums."

"Play *and* sing, mind you," Drew added. "And I don't sing nearly like my brother does. It was pathetic."

"You do backing vocals beautifully," Leslie said.

"So," Jayson said, "this song is something of a long-standing family tradition."

"How old were you when you got the guitars?" Elizabeth asked, and Jayson wanted to pinch himself. She was interested. She was genuine. That condescending air was completely absent.

"Eleven," he said, and Elizabeth was stunned. At eleven he was playing and singing Elton John, even if it was one of his "simple" songs.

Jayson turned on the bench to face the piano. He looked at Drew, and they seemed to read each other's minds as they both hit the beginning note at exactly the same time. It was a slow song with a soothing melody. And

Jayson's voice rang clearly, giving Elizabeth a fresh surge of goose bumps. Between bars he adjusted his seating on the bench and moved closer to the microphone without missing a note. This song showed off Jayson's vocal abilities more clearly, and Elizabeth was so in awe she could hardly breathe. When it was done, she did manage to applaud with the others this time, but Jayson didn't look at her. While Drew and Derek started talking and her father began chatting with Leslie, Elizabeth took a chance and moved to the piano bench where she sat next to Jayson.

Jayson turned to find Elizabeth sitting next to him, and he felt sure she could hear his heart pounding. *She was so beautiful.* And she was looking at him as if he had just spun straw into gold right before her eyes. He'd longed to see her look at him that way from the first time he'd met her. But now that she was, he felt almost angry. Still, he couldn't help but enjoy the moment.

"That was incredible," she said. "I had no idea."

"No, you wouldn't, would you."

"Well . . . you never said anything, so—"

"And what should I have said?" he interrupted. "Oh, by the way, Miss Greer, I'm not the rebellious derelict you think I am. In truth, I have a passion for music that makes me freakishly different from everyone else sitting in any given classroom."

Elizabeth was so taken aback that she felt momentarily stunned. His tone of voice had been perfectly kind and appropriate, but his words triggered something defensive in her. "What makes you believe I thought you were a rebellious derelict?"

Jayson chuckled and looked away. He realized he couldn't answer that without saying something that would likely create a rift between them. Not a smart move, he concluded, when he'd just barely begun to build a bridge. He was relieved to hear Derek say, "Hey, sis," and distract her attention from him. Jayson remained relieved until Derek added, "You haven't heard *me* play with these guys."

"Oh yes, Elizabeth," Will said. "You must hear the songs these boys have put together."

Drew said with mock chagrin, "I guess that means we're moving the drums back down the stairs."

"We'd have to do that anyway," Jayson pointed out and stood up to begin disassembling the microphone.

Everyone—including Elizabeth—pitched in to help move the equipment back down to the basement. Again Jayson didn't know whether to be pleased or aggravated to realize she was going to stick around and expect to hear the songs they'd done earlier for their parents. When she handed him the microphone stand that she'd carried into the music room, he smirked at her and said, "Now you get to hear the screaming guitars."

"How exciting," she said with subtle sarcasm.

Elizabeth sat on a chair in the basement, wondering when this show was going to start. She watched the boys efficiently preparing their instruments and equipment, her focus mostly on Jayson, although she attempted to be discreet. She couldn't help noticing how well her father was getting along with Leslie Wolfe. She wished her mother would be around even a little bit and share such simple conversation with her family members.

"Okay, I think we're ready," Jayson said, lifting an electric guitar over his head and settling the strap onto his shoulder. "Hit it," he said, and the song began with an impact that jumped into Elizabeth's every nerve. She quickly found herself caught up in a completely different kind of exhilaration than the kind she'd felt a short while ago in the front room. It was immediately evident that Jayson could handle a guitar much the same way he'd handled the piano. And her brother was a lot better on that bass than she'd ever given him credit for. He even did fairly well with the backing vocals. In fact, what they were playing sounded so close to professional that she had to admit she was astonished.

Unable to keep her eyes off of Jayson Wolfe for long, she had to wonder, *Who was this guy, and where had he come from? And why had she felt so thoroughly drawn to him, long before she'd realized he was a young man of rare talent?*

Elizabeth felt disappointed when the song ended, until she realized they were going to do another one. This one was more mellow, but still very catchy. She became so enthralled with watching Jayson sing that she was startled to find him looking right at her as he cooed into the microphone, *"Love is such sweet pain to me, 'Cause I can't touch but I can see."*

Jayson saw Elizabeth look away abruptly and wished he had the remotest idea what was going on in her head. He wanted desperately to just be able to talk to her, but he felt as if an invisible wall existed between them. He wasn't sure if he had helped put it there. He only knew his insides felt like a tangled mass of confusion, frustration, longing, and even some anger. And he didn't know what to do about it. He leaned into the mike and crooned the final chorus, *"Why can't I . . . say hello? When I try . . . my lips don't go. I get tongue-tied."*

When the song ended, Jayson flipped off the amps amidst the applause, then announced, "That's it."

Derek was bowing repeatedly and acting like a clown, provoking laughter from their audience of three. Jayson said, "Derek will now do a solo. We call it 'Weird.'"

Drew did a melodramatic drum roll and Derek imitated opera as he sang, "Me and my friends are so weird."

"You'd better believe it," Drew said and did another drum roll, provoking more laughter.

Will and Leslie dished out a number of compliments and encouragement, and in the midst of them, Elizabeth slipped from the room. Twenty minutes later Will and Elizabeth were in the kitchen pulling ice cream out of the freezer, while Derek and Drew gathered the makings for banana splits. Jayson didn't feel in the mood for ice cream and went to the piano where he toyed with it as quietly as possible, not wanting to draw any more attention to himself. He'd had more than enough of that for one day. He was startled to hear Elizabeth say, "The ice cream is in the kitchen."

He stopped playing and looked up to see that they were alone. "I'm not in the mood, thank you." When she just stood there, he added, "Did you like the screaming guitars?"

"They didn't sound screaming to me; it actually sounded like music."

"Imagine that," Jayson said.

"May I ask whose music you were playing? Not Elton John, I assume."

"No," he smirked, dearly loving this moment, "not Elton John."

"I've never heard either of those songs before, but they were very good."

"I didn't take you for a listening-to-rock-on-the-radio kind of girl."

"What kind of girl *did* you take me for?"

"Well," he chuckled, "I'd say you're more the kind of girl who would have tea and crumpets with your friends while listening to a string quartet."

She delicately snorted a laugh that he found endearing. "Well, I guess you don't know as much about me as you thought you did," she said with the subtlest bite to her words.

Jayson chuckled and had to say, "Touché." He figured she caught his intended humor when she smiled.

"So," she said, motioning toward the piano, "do you only play by ear, or do you actually read music?"

Jayson felt unexplainably angry. What she really meant was, *Do you have any brains or are you just an accidental artist?*

While he was struggling to come up with an answer that didn't sound as rude as he felt like being, she opened a drawer and pulled out a piece of sheet music. She didn't even glance at it; she just took out whatever happened to be on the top. She set it in front of him and sat on the bench beside him. "Can you play this?" she asked, looking into his eyes with a silent dare. But he had a feeling it had nothing to do with the music. He just didn't know exactly what she was daring him to do.

Without glancing at it he said, "If I can't, will you teach me?"

"Maybe," she said.

"In that case, I can't," he said, liking the idea of piano lessons with Elizabeth Greer—in spite of feeling angry.

She let out a disgusted sigh and pointed at the sheet music. "Can you play it or not?"

"Why do you want to know?" he asked, and Elizabeth felt certain he couldn't read music, that he was attempting to distract her attention from it.

"Just . . . curious."

"Well, curiosity killed the cat, Miss Greer."

"Can you answer a simple question, Mr. Wolfe, or am I to assume you're just trying to distract me from the question?"

Jayson turned to look at the music in front of him. "Mozart," he said.

"That's right," she said, having to glance at it to be sure. Then the connection struck her. She looked at him and said in an enlightened tone, "Mozart!"

"What about him?" Jayson asked.

"In English . . . Mozart."

"He's one of my heroes," Jayson said. He motioned to the music and said, "I have to memorize a piece before I can play it with any . . . meaning. I have to be able to . . . feel it."

Elizabeth was ready to declare him incapable of reading music and demand to know why he couldn't just admit it. And then he put his fingers on the keys and started to play. He went slowly, pausing occasionally to stumble over a difficult segment, but he certainly *was* playing it. He played about halfway down the first page, then stopped abruptly and said, "Satisfied?" She didn't answer, and he added, "Or maybe you're disappointed that you won't be able to give me piano lessons."

"Maybe you should give *me* piano lessons," she said, and he realized she'd just given him a compliment.

"Oh, no," he chuckled. "Your abilities are excellent in their own right."

Elizabeth was startled by the genuine nature of his praise, but she had to ask, "When did you hear me play?"

"Choral concert," he said. "You did beautifully."

"Thank you," she said and glanced down. "But I have to work very hard and practice a great deal to get something right—especially if it's complicated."

Jayson was struck with the reality of being closer to her than he ever had been. He could almost feel a tangible warmth permeating from her, and she exuded a subtle flowery aroma that made him heady. But still he felt angry without fully understanding why.

"So," she said in what felt like a feeble attempt to break the silence, "are you going to tell me whose music you were playing downstairs?"

Jayson couldn't hold back a chuckle. "Why, so you can go buy the records and see if our rendition is anywhere near the original?"

"Maybe," she said, looking away.

"Well, you're out of luck, baby. They're not for sale . . . yet."

"I don't understand."

"You just heard the original," he said and took great delight in her astonished expression.

"Are you saying that . . ." Elizabeth struggled to come up with the words to ask. She felt certain he was teasing her, but she didn't know him well enough to be able to read him.

While she was still wondering what to say, Derek came into the room and put his arm around her with a comical hug, saying, "How's it going, sis?"

"Just great," she said with mild sarcasm. "And you?"

"I'm fantastic. Did you hear how amazing we sounded?"

"I heard that," she said. "And where exactly did you come up with such amazing music?"

"Jayson wrote it," he said matter-of-factly. "He's a genius."

"So it would seem," she said and met Jayson's smirking eyes.

"Derek's pretty talented himself," Jayson said with a genuine humility that surprised her. "I've never been able to put it together quite right before now. Derek was the missing ingredient."

Derek comically shrugged his shoulders. "Ah, shucks," he said, making Elizabeth laugh. "Hey, come and get some ice cream," he added and left the room again.

"Derek is a funny guy," Jayson said.

"Yeah," Elizabeth said, "he's real funny when you've been in a car with him for about twelve hours, or when you have to share every meal with him. Weird is more like it."

Jayson chuckled and recalled Derek singing in the basement. *Me and my friends are so weird.*

Elizabeth stood up from the bench and asked, "Are you still not in the mood for ice cream?" When he didn't answer, she turned to see that his eyes looked distant as if he were suddenly a million miles away. "Jayson?" she asked and startled him.

"What? Did you say something?"

"Ice cream?"

"Uh . . . no thanks." He rose to his feet as if he'd just remembered that he urgently needed to do something. "I . . . uh . . . do you have a piece of paper? A pencil? Pen? Anything?"

"Uh . . . yeah," she said and led the way to a little study across the hall from the front room.

"Thank you," he said absently when she handed him a yellow legal pad and a pen. He leaned over the desk and frantically wrote something in longhand.

"May I ask what—"

"A song," he said as if he were annoyed with her talking. "It just . . . came to me."

"I see," she said, and then she just watched him, wishing she could see inside of his mind. He seemed completely oblivious to her presence. He wrote; he paused; he closed his eyes and hummed a few notes.

He wrote again, then he tore the top sheet off the notebook and rushed from the room, saying absently, "Thank you." She followed him to the kitchen where he said, "Drew, I need you." Then he hurried down the stairs.

"Oh, man," Drew said with a lilt of excitement in his voice, "he's doing it again." He shoveled the last two bites of his ice cream into his mouth and motioned for Derek to follow him. Elizabeth was left standing in the kitchen with her father and Jayson's mother, wondering why she felt so alone.

Chapter Five

Jayson was not easily lured away from the basement when his mother insisted it was time they went home. Driving home, the urgency of writing a song dissipated, and his mind went to the evening's encounters with Elizabeth Greer. He was gratefully distracted when his mother said, "Oh, that was so incredible. I'm just so proud of you both."

"Thanks, Mom," Drew said from the backseat.

"You okay, honey?" she asked Jayson.

"Just tired," he said, and Leslie talked about how much she liked Derek and his father, and how gracious they had been.

"And Elizabeth seems like a sweet girl," she added.

Jayson gave her a cautious glare; he didn't want anything said about his feelings in front of Drew, or he would never hear the end of it.

"Elizabeth is *hot!*" Drew said, and Jayson saw his mother trying to suppress a smile.

"She's too tall for you, Bro," Jayson said casually.

"I don't want to go out with her," Drew said. "I just think she's hot."

"Oh, that's right," Jayson said facetiously. "You'd rather keep company with science fiction."

"It's much less complicated," Drew said.

"Yeah, well you can't neck with a book," Jayson said lightly.

Drew laughed. "Yeah, well a book doesn't get PMS and bite your head off."

Leslie laughed as well. "Okay, that's enough female insults for one night. And you are both too young to be necking with anybody."

"He's eighteen, Mom," Jayson pointed out. "But he prefers books over girls, so I don't think you have anything to worry about."

"Not about him," Leslie said with a little chuckle.

"Not about me, either," Jayson said. "I've never even kissed a girl, and I don't see any obvious prospects at the moment."

Drew made a scoffing noise. "You kissed Belinda in sixth grade!"

"Does that count?" Jayson asked while his mother laughed. "A kiss that doesn't last a tenth of a second doesn't count, does it, Mom?"

"No, I don't think so," she said. "When you do kiss a girl, I want to be the first to know about it. Just remember what I've taught you. Be a gentleman and make certain it has some meaning."

"Elizabeth's not too tall for *you*," Drew said, as if it were a great epiphany.

"No," Jayson drawled with forced innocence, "but I don't think she's my type, or I'm not her type, or something like that. She's too highbrow for me."

"You never know," Drew said. "I think she was pretty impressed with you tonight."

"I think she was impressed with *us*," he said, hearing anger in his own voice. Apparently his mother caught it when she looked abruptly toward him. "The music," he clarified, his voice more cool. "She liked the music."

"But maybe she didn't like *only* the music," Drew said, and Jayson wanted to turn around and belt him.

Knowing that would just alert him to feelings he didn't want his brother to know about, he simply said, "Yeah, right."

Half an hour later, Jayson was sitting on his bed with his acoustic guitar, picking out the song that had come to him earlier. His mother knocked lightly at the door, then peered in after he'd called to her.

"How are you?" she asked, closing the door behind her so they could be alone in the room he shared with Drew, who was in the front room reading.

"I'm okay. How are you?"

"I'm great, actually," she said. "What I saw my sons do tonight is one of the highlights of my life."

Jayson chuckled. "You need to get out more, Mom. Maybe you should go on a date or something." He smirked and added, "You're not too young to neck."

"Now you're being silly," she said. "I'm too *old* to neck."

"Oh, if you're too old for that before you reach forty, then the world is doomed."

She laughed softly, then said, "Elizabeth really does seem like a nice girl."

Jayson sighed loudly and put the guitar aside. "Yes, I believe she is."

"But?" she pressed as if she'd read his mind.

"But . . . I . . . oh, I don't know."

"I think she was pretty impressed with you tonight; she was certainly watching you." He said nothing, and she added, "I would think you'd be pleased. Unless your feelings for her have changed."

"No, they haven't changed," he admitted. "She's . . . the most amazing girl on the planet." He smiled. "Next to you, of course."

Leslie returned his smile. "So, what's wrong then? You've wanted to get to know her better for a long time; now she's certainly seen what you're all about."

"I suppose she has," he said, "but I'm not sure I want her to be impressed with me because of the music. It might be what I'm all about, but it's not who I am. I'm not sure I want her to be taking notice of me just *because* of the music. Is it so bad to want her to just see me for me?"

"No, of course not," Leslie said. "And with time, perhaps the two of you can get to know each other better, now that your paths have crossed. Is it so bad that you've gotten her attention with something that might give her some incentive to get to know you better?"

Jayson absorbed what she was saying and had to admit that it made sense. "No, I guess that's not so bad."

"But?" she said again.

"But . . . I don't know if I could ever tell her how I feel. I get . . ."

"Tongue-tied?" she guessed with a smile.

"Exactly."

"I thought so," she said, and he knew what she meant. She'd figured out who he'd written that song about. She knew him too well. "Give that some time as well," she said. "You're young; you mustn't be so impatient. I have a feeling that Derek and his family are going to be a big part of your life."

"Yeah, I get that feeling too," he said, but he didn't necessarily know if that meant Elizabeth. He'd like to think so, but it just seemed too good to be possible.

* * * * *

Elizabeth found it impossible to sleep as thoughts of Jayson consumed her. The mystique surrounding him from the start now made so much sense. But how could she have known? The way she'd been instinctively drawn to him fascinated her almost as much as Jayson himself. She felt disconcerted, however, at the apparent evidence that Jayson Wolfe did not feel the same way about her. She'd caught him looking at her enough that she had to believe he felt some attraction to her, but it seemed more in the spirit of mocking. She felt much like a mouse being taunted by a very big cat. He likely saw her as some snobbish debutante, and he simply had no interest in a girl like her beyond putting her in her place. Wondering what she could possibly do about it, she decided that she simply had to try to convince him that she was not the kind of person he apparently assumed her to be.

The following day she saw Jayson in class as usual. She wanted to talk to him, but he barely said hi before he sat down, and she couldn't help but feel disappointed that he apparently didn't want to talk to *her*. She didn't get home until nearly seven and found her father in the kitchen.

"How're you doing?" he asked as she sat on the barstool and helped him put together a green salad.

"I'm okay," she said. They talked throughout dinner while she told him everything that was going on in her life—everything except for this obsession she had with Jayson Wolfe. They were clearing the table when she felt a subtle rhythm in the floor and said, "Derek's here?" She felt confused, knowing that if her brother was at home, he typically would have eaten with them.

"He's on a date, actually. That's Jayson. I told him he was welcome any time. I offered supper, but he said he'd eaten. Maybe you should go down and see if he wants some ice cream."

"Okay," she said nonchalantly, while inwardly she couldn't help being pleased with such an opportunity. She went down the stairs and opened the door to the music room. When she was assaulted with the blasting sound of whatever he was doing with Derek's bass guitar, she was surprised at how well the soundproofing worked. She closed the door loudly, and his head shot up as the music stopped.

"Hi," she said.

"Hi," he answered, not seeming displeased. But then, she couldn't tell if he was pleased, either.

"Dad said to ask you if you'd like some ice cream."

"Tell him thank you, but . . ."

"You're not in the mood?"

Jayson chuckled. "My mother has a passion for ice cream. I'm more a warm cookie kind of guy."

She smiled. "We don't get those around here very often. Dad's a great cook, but he doesn't bake. And Mom's never home."

"Well, my mother likes to bake, but she doesn't get the chance very often. She works long hours too."

Jayson looked down at the guitar and placed his fingers on the frets. It's now or never, she thought. "Mind if I sit down?" she asked.

"It's your house," he said.

"I don't want to . . . interrupt if you're in the midst of some great musical creation."

Jayson looked at her and wondered if he sensed a trace of sarcasm. Or was it his imagination?

"None of that at the moment," he said, and she sat down on the carpet, leaning back on her hands and stretching out her long, jean-clad legs.

"So," she said, "where is it that you came from, Jayson Wolfe?"

"Why do you want to know?" he asked skeptically.

"Just . . . curious."

"I didn't think you'd have any interest in a guy like me."

"A guy like you?"

"From the wrong side of the tracks."

"What tracks?" she asked, genuinely baffled.

He chuckled. "Just a figure of speech."

Jayson looked into her eyes and saw genuine interest there. Perhaps his mother had been right. Maybe now they could get to know each other better.

"Montana," he said.

"What was it like there?"

"Cold," he said.

"You like it here in Oregon?"

"Yes."

"So, what do you think of Oregon?"

"It's wet."

"Are you always such a great conversationalist?" she asked with sarcasm.

Jayson wanted to tell her he never had trouble talking to anyone but her. Instead he chuckled and said, "Sorry. I like the rain, actually. I like the way it sounds. I like the beach; we've managed to get there a few times."

"And you like Derek."

"Yes, I do. I've never had a friend like Derek. He's amazing."

"He thinks you're amazing."

"That works out nicely then," Jayson said, glancing down.

A tense silence fell over the room. Jayson didn't want to start playing again, fearing she'd take that as an indication that he didn't want to talk to her. She finally cleared her throat and said, "I really like your mother. She seems great."

"Yeah, she is," he said eagerly. "Your dad's great too. They're a lot alike, I think."

"Tell me about her," Elizabeth said.

Jayson was surprised. "You want to know about my mother?"

"Yeah, I do," she said. Elizabeth was genuinely curious about Leslie Wolfe, but she couldn't help recalling how her father had once said that you could tell a great deal about a guy by the way he feels about and treats his mother.

"Well . . . she's the most incredible woman on the planet," he said as if he truly believed it.

"Why?"

"Where do I begin?" he said. "She's risen above a lot of struggles, and she works hard. But what I really love about her is the way she believes in me and Drew—no matter what."

"My dad's like that."

"Yeah, I think he is. And my mom is easy to talk to. I hear other kids say they can't talk to their parents, and I can't even imagine how that would be. I don't know what I'd do without my mom."

"My mom is one of those you can't talk to."

"I haven't met her."

"Well, you wouldn't when she's rarely here except to sleep. And sometimes she even sleeps at the office."

"What does she do?"

"She's an attorney."

"Oh, I think Derek told me that once."

"I'm just glad I have my dad to talk to. He's pretty great. I don't think I've ever fought with my dad. I mean . . . sometimes we have our differences, but we get through them pretty easily, 'cause he really listens. You know what I mean?"

"Exactly," he said, wanting to pinch himself. He was having a civil, pleasant conversation with Elizabeth Greer. "I know that if I do what my mom expects of me, she won't give me any grief."

"Does Drew get along with your mom too?"

"He does," Jayson said. "But I don't think they have as much to talk about as we do."

Elizabeth smiled. "That's how it is here too. Derek and Dad get along great, but it's my dad and I that like to talk and do things together." She sighed and added, "So she really likes Elton John, I take it. I don't know if I've ever really paid much attention to his stuff."

"Oh, she *loves* Elton John; the old classic stuff he did, mostly. She listens to it as loudly as she can get away with when she's doing housework. Living in an apartment, that's not very loud. I got her some headphones with a long cord for Christmas." Elizabeth chuckled, and he added, "She likes all kinds of music, and she's always using music to try to teach us one thing or another."

"Like what?"

"Well . . . she says that a lot of her records have many good songs, but there are often some bad ones. She says that we need to learn to weed out the bad from the good, appreciate the good we get in life and make the most of it." He chuckled again and said, "She tells us how wonderful it will be when we're making records in LA, because they won't have those bad songs." He glanced down, feeling a little embarrassed, wondering if that sounded boastful. "She says things like that all the time, as if she just assumes we'll be great and famous musicians."

"That's not so difficult to imagine," she said, and again he felt a little embarrassed. "Is that what you want to do then?"

"Oh, yeah," he said with conviction. "I mean . . . I don't know that the fame appeals to me, but . . . the idea of having lots of people just . . . listening to my music is . . . the ultimate. I want people to feel better and find . . . hope and encouragement from my songs. Or just to have some fun. My mother talks about how certain songs gave her strength and hope to get through the tough times, and how songs remind her of good times in her life. I want my songs to do that for people."

"Wow," she said with enthusiasm. "That's a worthy goal."

"I don't know about that," he said, "but it's what I want to do, what I feel like . . . I'm supposed to do."

"And I'm sure you will," she said, feeling a little sad for some reason. Visions of her own future were so much different than that; she wanted a normal family life, with stability and security. She wanted to be a mother and raise a family and be there for them. She knew in her heart she could never marry someone who would either be starving and struggling to make it in a vicious industry, or traveling the world with fame and glamour. She told herself it was ridiculous to even consider that any kind of long-term relationship would occur between the two of them anyway. But at the moment she felt thoroughly entranced by him, and the obviously separate paths of their future saddened her.

Again silence descended, and Elizabeth struggled for something to say that might fill it. Thinking again of his mother, she couldn't help being curious over a certain matter. She hoped he wouldn't be put off by her asking. "May I pose a nosy question?"

"Sure."

"If you don't want to answer, just say so."

"Okay."

"I just . . . couldn't help noticing, and wondering . . . well, where did your mother get the scars on her face?" Jayson turned more toward her, startled. She added quietly, "They're the same as your scar. I assumed you'd gotten yours from some kind of fight, but . . . your mother is . . ."

"Not the kind of person who would be running with gangs in the streets?"

"No, of course not."

"But I am?" Jayson asked.

"Are you?" she asked, determined not to take offense from his defensive tone. She'd been judgmental, and she knew it. Perhaps he had good cause to be defensive.

"No, I'm not. But I'm not sure I want to tell you where the scars came from."

"Why not?"

"You might think less of me; of us." He sighed. "Still, it's part of our lives. There's no point in hiding it."

"Does Derek know?"

"Derek knows everything about me, but I doubt he'd tell you. I don't think he's the gossipy type."

"You don't have to tell me if—"

"No, it's okay," he said. "Truthfully, I'd rather you know everything about me, and then I don't have to worry about your finding out. If you hear all there is to know and don't want anything to do with me, I'll know now."

She laughed softly. "Just tell me. I promise I won't 'not want anything to do with you.'"

"Okay, well . . . it's really not something I enjoy talking about."

"Just tell me about the scars."

"I'm working on it. On the night of my mother's birthday, my father broke into the house. He was drunk." Elizabeth's heart quickened, and her stomach knotted tightly. She didn't know what she'd expected to hear, but it wasn't this. "I woke up and found him hitting her," he went on. "I think I surprised him, since the last time he'd seen me I'd been much shorter. I hit him. He hit me. I got the better of him, and Drew called the police. He's very good at getting a fist in just the right spot to split the skin over the cheekbone. It's the third time he'd done it to my mother." He sighed again. "That's when she decided we were moving."

"Will he find you?" she asked, sounding afraid on his behalf.

"No. He doesn't have the money or the gumption to do much of anything. We're not concerned about that. I think the biggest reason he'd show up was to try to get money out of her, and when she wouldn't give it to him, he'd get angry. It would cost him more to find us than he could ever hope to gain. We do keep an unlisted number."

"So . . . you've had a pretty tough life."

Jayson shrugged. "Tough is relative," he said. "I haven't had it so bad."

She smiled, and again there was silence. "Well," she said with a tense laugh, "I should let you get back to whatever you were doing and—"

"I can do that any time," he said, and she could almost believe that he was enjoying this conversation as much as she was.

She was just wondering what else she might say when Derek burst into the room. "Good, you're still here," he said, then turned to see Elizabeth. "Oh, hi, sis."

"Hi, Derek," she said, her tone bored.

"Mom's home. She wants to talk to you."

"Oh, great," Elizabeth said with sarcasm. She stood and moved toward the door.

"Hey, Elizabeth," Jayson said, "can I ask you a question?"

"Sure."

"Well . . . Derek calls you 'sis.' I guess I should call you Elizabeth, but . . . Elizabeth sounds so formal. Don't you go by Beth or Liz? How about Lizzie? Or maybe Eliza?"

Elizabeth scowled at him, realizing he behaved differently—if only a little—in Derek's presence. She said firmly, "My name is Elizabeth."

"Oh," Jayson said, pretending to sound embarrassed. "Forgive me . . . Elizabeth. However, I don't know if I can get such a mouthful out every time I speak to you. How about if I just call you 'Baby'? Then when I sing, 'Oh, Baby,' you'll know I'm talking to you." He paused, then sang a phrase from one of the songs he'd done at the piano the previous evening, "Hello, baby, hello."

Elizabeth smiled, and he was relieved to see that she could sense the humor he'd intended. "My name is Elizabeth," she said more lightly, "and I am not a baby."

Jayson smirked and looked her up and down. "Well, that's true. How about if I call you 'Lady'?"

"Like the dog in the Disney movie?" Derek said, then he pointed at Jayson and added, "*Lady and the Tramp.* You're kind of a tramp."

"Funny," Jayson said in a tone that indicated he didn't think it was. He turned to look at Elizabeth with serious eyes. "No, I would think Elizabeth is a lady in the truest sense." He said it firmly, as if he truly meant it, and she found herself staring at him while her heart quickened. Not knowing what else to say, she hurried from the room, hoping that time would give her the opportunity to get to know him better—without Derek around.

Once the door was closed, Derek raised his voice to mimic his sister, saying with mock arrogance, "My name is Elizabeth."

Jayson couldn't help but laugh, but he doubted Derek's sister would find it amusing.

"So, what are you working on?" Derek asked, sitting next to him. Jayson forced his thoughts from Elizabeth and showed him the bass-line he'd come up with for the new song. Derek picked it up quickly, and Jayson worked the electric guitar into it with little trouble. It was a simple equation, but it was working well. Then the door came open, and he knew the woman standing there had to be Derek's mother. He looked just like her. Except that Derek's bright countenance bore no resemblance; this woman looked angry and miserable, and it only took a split second for Jayson to dislike her. She wore a dark pantsuit and high heels; her blonde hair was pulled back tightly, and she was wearing too much makeup. Her nails were garishly long and painted a dark burgundy. She wore excessive jewelry. Jayson couldn't even fathom this being the mother of Derek and Elizabeth.

"Hi, Mom," Derek said without enthusiasm.

Mrs. Greer eyed Jayson while she said, "Your father told me I needed to come down and meet this new friend of yours. You must be Jayson."

"That's right," he said, moving toward her with an outstretched hand. She shook it firmly but didn't smile. "It's a pleasure to finally meet you, Mrs. Greer."

She made a dubious noise and glanced around. "Well, I guess it's good to get some use out of this room, if nothing else. You boys stay out of trouble now."

"Of course," Derek said, and his mother left the room, closing the door behind her.

"That was pleasant," Derek said with thick sarcasm.

"Now I see where you get your sense of humor," Jayson said, and Derek laughed loudly.

"And you're my *new* friend?" Derek said. "How long has it been?"

"I don't know; months."

Derek made a disgusted noise and started picking at the guitar.

* * * * *

Later that evening, Elizabeth was sitting in the kitchen with her father when Derek came in and said, "Hey, Dad, come down and hear what Jayson and I came up with. It's brand new, so it's kind of rough, but it's way cool."

"I'm coming," Will said eagerly, and Elizabeth impulsively followed him.

Jayson felt a little disconcerted to look up and see Elizabeth follow Will into the room. He'd become comfortable enough with Will that he could expose music to him before it was perfect. But Elizabeth?

When the door was closed, Derek said to Jayson, "Tell Dad what you told me."

"Okay." Jayson tried not to feel embarrassed. "Well . . . you know when Derek broke into song last night . . ." He motioned to Derek as if to cue him.

In mock opera he repeated, "Me and my friends are so weird."

"Okay," Will said with a laugh.

"Well, it stuck in my head," Jayson said. "So . . . we've been working on it. This is rough, but here goes . . ."

Derek started out with a simple melody on the bass, while Jayson sang, "Me and my friends are so weird."

And Derek *spoke* into the microphone, "Yes we are."

The guitar came in, and Jayson sang, "We just do things that are weird."

And Derek said, "You know it, baby"

"Have you ever known someone weird?"

"You're looking at him."

"Can you appreciate that we're weird?" Jayson sang, and then it shifted into a chorus. "Have to be weird to survive. Have to be weird to do what's right. This could be a very weird night. Let's just stay weird, you, and I, I, I." They stopped, and Jayson said, "That's as far as we've gotten."

"I really like it," Will said with a little laugh, and Elizabeth silently agreed. She couldn't help thinking that everything original she'd heard so far was unique. Their songs didn't all sound the same.

"Oh, but we have to do the best part," Derek said.

"This is Derek's idea for the ending," Jayson said, and the two of them did a simple thing back and forth with the guitars while they shared a mock conversation about weird things.

Derek finished the sequence by saying, "I want to thank my dog and my cat and my dad and my grandma and my best friend and my veterinarian and my dentist and everybody else I know because I really . . ."

While Jayson said at the same time, "Dude, dude, it's over . . . it's over. That's the end. Okay, that's the end. Man, you are weird. It's over. You're weird."

Will laughed boisterously, and Elizabeth couldn't keep from snickering. It really was funny. And it really was good. "That is great," Will said.

"Give us more than twenty-four hours," Jayson said, "and it might be a big hit." He laughed at himself, as the idea of actually hearing something like that on the radio seemed so unbelievable.

"What do you think, sis?" Derek asked Elizabeth as she came to her feet.

"I think it's weird," she said with a little smirk, and they all laughed. "It's great," she added, seeming to mean it, then she left the room.

The next day at school, Jayson was pleased to see that Elizabeth was more friendly than usual, but there was hardly time to really say anything to each other. He saw her nowhere but at school, and then the school year ended. Drew graduated, and Derek attended the ceremony with Jayson and his mother. Leslie cried when Drew received his diploma. Jayson teased her about her high water table and turned her tears to laughter.

Jayson quickly came to enjoy summer in Oregon, mostly because it gave him and Derek and Drew vast amounts of time to work on their music. They all managed to schedule their work time so they got lots of hours in the music room every week, and they were able to put together one project after another. They talked about record deals and big plans of going to LA once they were all out of school. Jayson began to feel that it wasn't just some faraway wish. The three of them together were a magic combination, and he felt sure that with time they would realize their goals. He often felt that something was missing, but he figured that eventually the missing piece would come together, the same way he'd been led to Derek in the first place. There were times when they simply needed another musician to achieve a certain sound. Jayson could play the keyboard and the guitar, but not at the same time. He felt frustrated occasionally, but reminded himself to be patient and enjoy these dreamy summer days that seemed almost like heaven. At least once a week the three of them drove less than an hour to the beach, taking Jayson's acoustic guitar along. They would gather driftwood and build a fire, cook hot dogs, and talk and laugh while Jayson picked at the guitar, certain that life couldn't get much better than this.

The only thing that made the summer imperfect was the fact that he almost never saw Elizabeth. Derek had told him that she was working with a local community theater on a play that would be running in August. She also got a summer job at a sewing factory. He wished she could work at a pizza place or something. At least he could go eat there and see her once in a while. As it was, he crossed her path about as often as he did her mother's. And he'd only seen Mrs. Greer a total of three times.

Jayson felt a secret thrill when the play *Joseph and the Amazing Technicolor Dreamcoat* finally opened in a tiny little theater where every seat had a perfect view. Elizabeth was the narrator, and she played the part with energy and finesse and a great deal of class. He went the first time to see it with Will and Derek, and then he went by himself twice more, leading Derek and Drew to believe that he was just busy elsewhere. She was amazing, and all these months had not dispelled his feelings for her in the slightest—just the opposite, in fact. However, he was getting tired of this loving her from a distance. *I can't touch, but I can see.*

When his third viewing of *Joseph* had ended, he went to Derek's house to see what he was up to. Will answered the door, looking pleased to see him as usual. "I'm glad you're here," he said. "There's something I want to show you."

"Okay. Where's Derek?"

"Bowling or something," he said. "Come into the study." Will sat down and tossed part of a newspaper onto the desktop, pointing at a small ad. "Read it," Will said.

Jayson bent over the desk to look more closely, and something inside of him came to life. It was an advertisement for a band to do regular weekly performances at some kind of dance hall.

"Where is this?" Jayson asked.

"Portland; forty-minute drive. I called and asked a few questions."

"And?" Jayson drawled.

"This place has been around for years. I used to go there when I was in college. It mostly appeals to college-aged people, although some older and younger folks go there, I believe. It's clean; it's got some class. Some nights they do records, but they have a longtime reputation of using live bands, and the manager told me they're in need of a good one. It would be every Saturday night for as long as it works. And it would pay enough that the three of you could quit your other jobs and still be better off."

"Are you serious?" Jayson asked.

"So, I took the liberty of scheduling an audition. If you don't want to do it, or the time doesn't work, just say so. I'll call him back."

"I'm game if the others are," Jayson said eagerly. "When?"

"Tomorrow, at seven. The place is closed Sunday through Tuesday. And tomorrow is Tuesday. He wants you to come and set up your stuff and play enough for him to know if you've got what it takes. And I know you've got what it takes."

"Wow," Jayson said.

"I haven't told you the best part."

"What?" Jayson asked, wondering what else there could possibly be.

"They have a grand piano, and you can use it on stage if you get the job."

Jayson let out a one-syllable laugh. Then another. "It's too good to be true."

"Well, we'll see," Will said.

"Uh . . . how do we get our stuff there? Drew's car isn't—"

"You can use my Suburban," Will offered easily. "You can put down all of the seats except the front and have plenty of room."

"Wow," Jayson said again.

Derek and Drew came in a few minutes later and were as excited as Jayson about the prospect. They went to the basement to go over some of their best numbers to make certain they were perfect. After they'd been down there for about an hour, Jayson went upstairs for a glass of water. He was standing in the kitchen with the glass in his hand when he heard Elizabeth's voice coming from the study—loud and clear.

"But tomorrow is the last night with any tickets available; everything else is sold out," Elizabeth said. "And you promised."

"I know, honey," Mrs. Greer replied, sounding subtly harsh, "but I just can't. It doesn't mean I don't love you. I just—"

"Love your job more, I know," Elizabeth countered.

"That's not fair. I have to be there. I—"

"Not every waking hour, you don't. Of course, I should know better. You promised you'd see *West Side Story*, and you never made it. And everything in between. What was I thinking? That my mother might actually come through this time? Forget it, Mom. It's not that important."

Jayson hurried into the shadows in the dining room before Elizabeth moved down the hall and up the stairs. He slithered quietly back to the basement, feeling a distinct heartache on her behalf. And he felt profoundly grateful for the mother he had. When he got home late that night, his mother was asleep. But he took a few minutes the next morning to thank her for all she did.

"What brought this on?" she asked suspiciously.

"Nothing. I'm just . . . grateful that you're interested in the things I do, and you're always there to support me, even though you have to work long hours."

"Okay. That's nice to hear, but . . . is there a reason you're so . . ."

"I overheard Elizabeth arguing with her mother last night." He briefly explained the situation, then finished by saying, "I just wanted you to know that I appreciate all you do for me. It's nice to know that you care about us more than anything else on the planet."

"Well, I certainly do," she said and gave him a loud smooch that made him laugh.

Jayson wished that he could be at the play this evening, although he'd already seen it three times. Elizabeth didn't know that, but he wondered if she might appreciate knowing that someone in the audience was there to see *her.* Knowing he couldn't be there, he said a little prayer on her behalf and focused on the evening's audition.

Chapter Six

Throughout a busy day, Elizabeth tried not to think about the previous evening's encounter with her mother. Of course, that was how she would describe her relationship with her mother—a series of brief and unpleasant encounters. She tried to tell herself that it didn't matter, that it wasn't such a big deal. But she'd put heart and soul into this project—just as she'd done with so many other similar projects in the past. And she simply wanted to know that her mother cared. Knowing that would never happen, Elizabeth resolved deep inside herself that she would be everything her mother was not. She would give her own children a home life with stability and structure. She would bake for them, be there when they came home from school, and give them everything—emotional especially—that any child deserved from a mother.

As the lights went up and the play began, Elizabeth focused on her performance, grateful that she really couldn't see the faces in the audience. Still, she felt an unmistakable heartache knowing that her mother was not among them.

* * * * *

Jayson felt distinctly nervous when they arrived at the destination of their audition. With Derek and Drew he went to a back door according to instructions the manager had given to Will.

"Hello, boys," a toneless voice said as they came into a little office that merged into a long, dark hallway. The man behind the desk was heavy and balding, and he didn't necessarily look happy about seeing them.

"Hello," they all said in haphazard unison.

"Are we in the right place?" Jayson asked.

"If you've come to audition for the Saturday night slot, you're in the right place." He stood and approached them, holding out a hand to Jayson first, since he was standing closest. "I'm Joe Wallace."

"Jayson Wolfe," he replied. "This is my brother Drew, and Derek Greer."

"Hello, boys," Joe said, shaking their hands as well. He moved a few steps and turned on a light switch that lit up the hallway. "You can take your equipment through that door and set up. Let me know when you're ready."

They went up the stage stairs, and Jayson caught his breath. *A stage.* He'd never performed on a stage in his entire life. In fact, he'd never *performed* except for neighbors and friends—and his mother. The stage was simple with a wood floor and black curtains. Rows of colored lights lined the ceiling. The stage curtain was closed, so he couldn't see the room beyond it, but a beautiful grand piano sat in one corner—on wheels, he noticed.

Jayson kept thinking as they hauled equipment from the Suburban that the weekly setup and takedown of this job could be a real pain, but it would certainly be worth it. He prayed that they would do well and that Joe Wallace would be impressed.

When they were set up and had everything tuned, Jayson went to Joe's office and quietly announced, "I think we're ready."

"Great," Joe said in a tone that indicated he didn't think it was great at all. Walking at Jayson's side to the stage door, he added, "You open the curtain. I'm going to the other end of the dance floor."

"How much did you want to hear?" Jayson asked.

Joe glanced at his watch. "You've got half an hour to flabbergast me. If I'm not flabbergasted by then, you'll have to try somewhere else."

Jayson went up the backstage stairs as Joe went farther up the hall. "Here goes," he said to Drew and Derek as he pulled on the cord to open the curtains. And again he was momentarily breathless. The place was huge, and just as Will had said, it had class. He could see Joe sitting on a chair some distance back, too far away for Jason to even remotely see his facial expressions. With the curtains open, Jayson picked up his guitar and put the strap over his head. He turned his back to the microphone, met Derek's eyes, and then Drew's. He nodded, and Drew hit the opening beat. It only took thirty seconds for Jayson to stop feeling nervous. It was just him and the music, and he was playing on a stage. He didn't care that it was to an audience of one. He was making progress. They went from one song to another, taking only a few seconds in between to make equipment adjustments. He played the piano on two of the numbers, even though he felt like the song was a little hollow without the guitar. Still, he wanted this guy to know he had a broad range of ability. After the fifth song, he heard Joe holler, "Okay, that's good."

Jayson set aside his guitar, watching Joe come toward them across the dance floor. He leaned his chest against the front of the stage and said in the same bored tone, "You guys are the best thing I've heard on this stage in a long time." Jayson let out a relieved chuckle and heard the others do the same. "I assume this stuff is original, 'cause I've never heard it before."

"That's right," Jayson said.

"Do you play anything by anybody else? Can you cover other people's songs?"

"Yeah," Jayson said, not certain he liked where this was going. "We can do it. We know a little Elton John. But it's not something you would have heard on the radio."

"Something people could dance to?"

Jayson exchanged a brief glance with Drew. They both knew that "Funeral for a Friend" was not dance music. But "Harmony" might work. There was nothing else they knew well enough to do with any confidence. "A slow dance," Jayson said. "We haven't gone over it for a while, but we could give it a try."

"Let's hear it," Joe said and walked back to his chair.

Jayson said to Derek, "Do you remember 'Harmony?' It's been a while."

"It's basic. I can do it."

"I need some oohs and aahs. If you don't remember, fake it."

"You got it," Derek said as if it was no big deal. He was a natural, and Jayson was grateful.

Jayson looked at Drew and said, "This is for Mom."

Drew smirked, and Jayson sat at the piano, adjusting the microphone. He nodded at Drew, and they hit the first beat with perfect synchronization. He felt completely comfortable with this song, and he knew Drew did as well. And the bass was perfect. He got chills when Derek hit those oohs and aahs with brilliance. Hitting the final notes, he knew they'd done about as good as they ever had—and without having practiced this number in weeks. Jayson smiled at the others and remained on the piano bench as Joe approached.

"I like that," Joe said, but Jayson wondered if he had a deformity that prevented him from having any inflection in his voice. He leaned his forearms on the stage and said, "Okay, here's the deal." He slid a piece of paper across the floor, and Jayson moved to pick it up. On it was a list of popular songs. "People come here to dance. The average age is between twenty and thirty; sometimes they're younger or older, but we need a variety of music from different eras. They like to dance to music they're familiar with. If you can learn to play those songs, you've got a job. I know your next question, and the answer is that you can put three or four of your own songs in between here and there, as long as it's good dance music. The job plays out like this. You play every Saturday—and I mean *every* Saturday. You're entitled to one emergency night off for illness or tragedy every six months. More than that, you're out of a job. You have your equipment set up and ready to go by seven-thirty—no later. The place opens at eight. We start out with recorded music for half an hour. You start playing at eight-thirty. You play for an hour. You get half an hour break. You play from ten to eleven. That's a total of two hours of music, and you can't repeat any numbers. Every week I'd like you to take one out and add a new one, and play them in different order so the regulars don't get bored. You have to wait until after midnight to take down your equipment; that's when the place closes. The amount of money you get is the same no matter how many musicians you got on stage. You do well for two months, you get a ten percent raise. Any questions?"

"Do we have the job?" Jayson asked.

"You come back two weeks from today; same time. You play me any five songs on that list and do them well, and you've got a job. If that's the case, you'll start the following Saturday. Will I see you in two weeks, or should I keep advertising?"

"We'll be here," Jayson said. "Thank you."

Joe grunted and walked away. Derck grabbed the list from Jayson who muttered under his breath, "We've got a lot of work to do in two weeks."

* * * *

Elizabeth felt exhausted after the performance, but it had gone well, and she felt gratified—as long as she didn't think about her mother. In the dressing room she shared with all the other girls in the cast, she hurried to change out of her costume and get rid of her stage makeup. Stepping into the hall, she was surprised to see Leslie Wolfe, apparently waiting for her.

"Oh, hello," Elizabeth said when their eyes met. "What brings you here? Aren't the boys doing their audition tonight?"

"Yes, that's right," Leslie said. "I came alone. I'd heard Jayson say what a wonderful play it was and what a great job you did, and I just had to see it. You *did* do beautifully. I just had to wait and tell you myself."

Elizabeth fought back a rise of emotion. She wasn't one to cry easily, but she could never tell this sweet woman what it meant to see her here—tonight. "Thank you," she managed to say. "It's nice to know my efforts are appreciated."

"Oh, yes!" Leslie said with enthusiasm. "It was wonderful. Anyway, I don't want to keep you. I'm sure you have plans and—"

"No, actually," she said, and Leslie smiled.

"Are you hungry?" Leslie asked. "Would you like to go get a hamburger or something?"

"Uh . . . I'm not really hungry, but . . . how about some ice cream or something?"

"Terrific," Leslie said. "I have a weakness for ice cream. Or," she drawled, "I don't bake very often, but I have a pretty fair peach cobbler at home, with ice cream in the freezer to go with it. What do you think?"

Elizabeth laughed softly. "That sounds great. Since I have my car, should I just . . . follow you or—"

"Perfect," Leslie said, and they walked to the parking lot together.

Alone in the car, Elizabeth *did* cry. She felt extremely envious of Jayson Wolfe for having such an incredible mother. She reminded herself that Jayson's father was a horrible person, and there was no father greater than her own. Still, at the moment, she felt motherless, and Leslie Wolfe's kindness was just what she'd needed.

Following the little car that Leslie drove, Elizabeth became suddenly curious about what their home might be like. She was surprised to drive into a lower-class neighborhood and then to pull up in front of an old apartment building. But stepping through the front door with Leslie, she wasn't surprised by the warmth of their little home. The furnishings were minimal and old, but the atmosphere was tidy and inviting.

"Make yourself comfortable," Leslie said, "while I heat this up a little; it tastes better that way." She noticed Leslie putting on a record and turning the volume low. A shelf filled with records and tapes reminded her of how Jayson had said his mother loved music—all kinds of music. She then realized that the decor in the little front room consisted only of several framed photographs—all of Leslie's sons. She laughed softly when she saw a matched set, one of Jayson and one of Drew in identical frames. They had obviously been taken with the help of a trampoline since they were each in midair, their bare feet tucked up beneath them. Jayson was holding an electric guitar, and Drew was holding drumsticks above his head.

"These could be worth something someday," she said.

"What's that?" Leslie asked from the other end of the room where the kitchen was located.

"These pictures. When Jayson and Drew are world-famous musicians, they could be worth something."

Leslie laughed with obvious pleasure. "Yes, I suppose they will be," she said as if she simply took for granted that they *would* be world-famous musicians.

Elizabeth then noticed that the music she was hearing sounded familiar—but not really. It took her a minute to realize what it was. "Oh," she said, "this is the song that Jayson and Drew played. Elton John, isn't it?"

"That's right," she said. "It's called 'Funeral for a Friend.' I don't know why I love this song so much, but I do."

"It's a pretty amazing song," Elizabeth said. "But I think I like the way Jayson plays it." She hurried to add, "And Drew."

"Yes, I do too," she said. "They play it with love."

"Can I call my dad and let him know where I am?" Elizabeth asked.

"Of course," Leslie said and motioned toward the phone.

Elizabeth made the call, then Leslie invited her to sit at the little table where they shared warm cobbler smothered with vanilla ice cream. They visited so comfortably that Elizabeth found it difficult to believe this woman was old enough to be her mother. She marveled that a woman of Leslie's generation could be so down-to-earth, so attentive, so understanding of Elizabeth's views and feelings. Of course, her father was that way. But he was a man, and it felt nice to have some female feedback that had some wisdom behind it.

"So, what will you be taking in school this year?" Leslie asked.

Elizabeth told her how she would be taking several classes that would help toward her college credit, and she would be in the orchestra, playing the flute. But she had decided against doing chorus this year, and she hadn't run for studentbody officer as she had the last three years. "I don't know that I'll do the plays this year like I have in the past, either," she said.

"Why not?" Leslie asked, in a curious way. The question was non-threatening, with none of the consternation her mother would express when she figured out the drastic change of pace.

"Well, I think I'm just tired of being so busy. My dad tells me I need to slow down and enjoy this time of my life—do something different."

"I think I agree with him."

"It's nice to know I've got you on my side. My mother won't be happy about it."

"Why is that?"

Elizabeth sighed. "She thinks I should do everything, the way she does everything. But then she never comes to see what I do, anyway. So I figure I'll do this year the way I want to do it."

"That sounds very wise," Leslie said. "But you will let me know when there's an orchestra concert, won't you? I'd love to come."

"I'll do that," Elizabeth said. "And if you . . ." She hesitated when they heard someone at the door. Her heart quickened as she turned around to see Drew and Jayson walk into the room. She'd hardly seen

Jayson all summer, but he still had an effect on her. She noticed that he had a guitar pick in his teeth.

Jayson was so stunned to see Elizabeth sitting there that he felt briefly frozen. He was trying to figure how this might have come about when his mother said, "Oh, hi. I went to see the play Elizabeth was in. It was even more incredible than you said it was, and we've been having some peach cobbler. Would you like some?"

"No thanks," Drew said and went down the hall.

"Jayson?" Leslie said.

"Uh . . . no thanks."

"Hello, Jayson," Elizabeth said with a little smirk.

"Hello, Lady," he said, returning the smirk.

"How did the audition go?" Leslie asked eagerly.

Jayson really didn't want to talk about it with Elizabeth sitting there, but he had to answer the question. "It went great, actually."

"So, you got the job?" Elizabeth asked, actually sounding excited.

"Well . . ." he drawled, "there are some stipulations. We go back for another audition in two weeks. So, I guess we'll see."

Jayson was wondering if he should sit down or leave when Elizabeth rose to her feet. "I really should get home. It's been a long day, and I'm exhausted."

"Don't run off because of me," Jayson said. "I can go away and leave the two of you to—"

"Oh, it's not that," Elizabeth said. "I just am really tired, and . . ." She turned to Leslie. "Thank you so much . . . for everything. The cobbler was wonderful and . . . you're so sweet."

"It was my pleasure, dear," Leslie said. "Call me if you ever need some female company."

"Thanks, I'll do that," Elizabeth said and hurried away.

When she was gone, Jayson sighed and said, "You didn't have to do that."

"Do what?"

"Go to the play just so—"

"I wanted to go," she insisted. "Elizabeth is a very sweet girl—talented too."

"Yes, she is," Jayson agreed, wishing it hadn't sounded so dreamy. "And you're very sweet too. She could use a good mother."

"And I suppose I could use a daughter. There's a little too much testosterone around here, if you ask me."

Jayson laughed and sat down where Elizabeth had been sitting.

"I'm sure, however," Leslie said, "that Mrs. Greer does the best that she can. We mustn't jump to conclusions."

Jayson appreciated his mother's effort to not speak badly of others, but he knew that Mrs. Greer was a workaholic who made no effort whatsoever on her family's behalf.

"So, tell me about the audition," she said. "What are the stipulations?"

Jayson told her everything, and then she asked, "Do you think you can do it?"

"I know we can do it," he said. "It's just going to take every waking minute. And I think he knows that. He's testing us to see if we can learn the songs quickly—if we're willing to put the time into it. The problem is that we all have jobs, and if we don't know for certain we'll be getting this job, we can't very well quit. Even if we could quit, we'd have to give notice."

"But if you know you can do it, then you know you've got the job. You should each at least talk to your bosses and see what you can do."

Jayson sighed. "Yeah. Well, first of all, I need to find recordings of these songs." He pulled the list out of his pocket and unfolded it.

"Five of them?"

"All of them," he said. "He wants to hear five, but he wants us to play for two hours, adding a new one each week. We're going to need to learn the whole list and then some."

"And sheet music?" she asked.

"Nah. The recordings will be easier to get hold of, and I can do it from that."

Leslie smiled. "You're amazing."

"I have an amazing mother," he said, lifting his brows comically.

"I think I have a few of these," she said, moving to the front room.

They sat together on the floor, sifting through records, and they found a handful of what they needed. The following morning Jayson called his boss to say he wouldn't be able to make it in the next couple of days. He didn't give an explanation. Leslie went to a music store with Jayson where they bought sixteen record albums, and she put the amount on a credit card that she saved for emergencies. Jayson gave her some cash to cover part of it and promised to pay the rest back as quickly as possible. They also bought a lot of blank cassette tapes. Jayson spent the afternoon copying the songs they needed to four sets of cassette tapes.

"Why four?" Leslie asked just before she left for work.

"A backup in case we lose or break one," he explained.

He felt good about where they'd come so far, since he now had an audio of every song on the list but one, and that was on an old Chicago album that he hadn't been able to locate. He gave copies of the tapes to Derek and Drew to listen to every possible minute. And that evening they listened to all the songs together, analyzing them and picking them apart. During the next several days, they each worked the absolute minimum they could get away with and managed to coordinate their work time for the most part so they could rehearse every possible minute. They worked on more than a dozen numbers enough to learn them, and they chose five that they all agreed would best represent their abilities. Four days before the two-week deadline, Jayson was actually feeling pretty good about four of the five songs. He was considering using a different one for the audition when Derek said, "You know the problem with this song."

"I'm sure you're going to tell me."

"It has a female vocalist, for one thing. You don't sound like Joan Jett. And there are some of these songs that need keyboards *and* guitar, and you can't do both."

"And the solution would be?" Jayson asked skeptically.

"We need another band member; somebody with a great voice and some real musical talent."

Jayson gave a scoffing laugh. "Did you have somebody in mind?"

"Yes, actually. And it's a *female* great voice."

"Who?" Jayson asked and then wondered why he hadn't seen it coming when Derek said, "My sister."

Once Jayson recovered from the shock of the very idea, he laughed more loudly. "You can't be serious."

"Do I look serious?" Derek asked with an unusually sober voice. "She could do it, Jayson. She's the missing ingredient."

"Oh, yeah," Jayson said with sarcasm, while he attempted to examine his feelings. He'd never even considered *performing* with

Elizabeth. It felt so foreign to his brain that he couldn't decide if he liked the idea or not. It would certainly give them more time together, but he wasn't certain she'd like the intensity with which he handled the music. Drew was used to him; Derek understood him. But the bottom line was that he could not even fathom her being able to do what Derek was suggesting.

"Yeah what?" Derek asked when he said nothing more.

"Are you trying to tell me that Miss Highbrow can do Joan Jett? I don't think so."

"Sure, why not? She loves this song."

"She does?"

"She can do it," Derek insisted.

Jayson felt intrigued with the idea, if only for the opportunity to see what she was capable of in that regard, but he wasn't sure she would *want* to do it. From things Derek had told him, he knew she had a bit of a stubborn streak. An idea came to him, and he hurried to retort, "You say she can; I say she can't—and even if she could, she wouldn't lower herself to do rock music on stage with people like me."

Derek shrugged. "Maybe you're right. It was just an idea."

Jayson felt a little disappointed. Now that he'd considered the idea, he couldn't help being intrigued with it, but he didn't want to talk Derek into asking her. The subject was dropped, and they continued the rehearsal as soon as Drew returned from the bathroom. But Jayson couldn't stop thinking about *the missing ingredient.*

* * * * *

Elizabeth was sprawled on her bed with a battered copy of *Pride and Prejudice* when Derek knocked at her door. She knew it was Derek, since her parents were both at work.

"Yeah?" she called.

"Hey, sis," he said after he'd opened the door. "Now that the play's over, I guess you're pretty bored, eh?"

"A little, why?" she asked skeptically.

"Well, we're working on this song that needs a female vocal. What do you say? We've got to put some stuff together quick for this audition. Please tell me you're interested."

Elizabeth felt momentarily stunned. Her feelings for Jayson tempted her to consider it, but then she didn't know if she could handle actually *working* with him. Jayson aside, she *knew* she didn't want to work with Derek. She loved him, but he was so annoying. She put her book in front of her face and insisted, "Not interested, sorry."

"It could be a paying job, you know," he said, and she lowered her book.

"Are you actually suggesting that I become a part of your little band?" She knew they were extraordinary, but she didn't want to admit that to her brother. Truthfully, she doubted that she could be talented enough to even consider being part of such a thing.

"That's what I'm saying. Sometimes we need another instrument, too."

"Was this your idea or—"

"Yep," he said proudly.

"And what does Jayson think of your little idea?"

"He doesn't think you can do it."

"Well, maybe I can't," she said, pretending to look at her book.

"Sure you can," he said. "You're a great actress and you have a great voice. Just . . . pretend you're doing the part of a rock star." He told her more details about what they needed and why, while Elizabeth's confidence waned. She felt sure it would be safer to just decline, as opposed to making any kind of fool of herself.

"Thanks, but no thanks," she said and returned to her book.

Derek sighed. "Just as well," he said. "Jayson thinks you're too highbrow for this sort of thing."

Elizabeth gasped. "He *said* that?"

"He did," Derek said proudly.

Elizabeth tossed the book on the bed. "What do I have to do?"

Derek laughed and sat on the floor to explain the details of his plan. Jayson had to work until six, but he and Drew were both off all day, so she could go over the piece with them enough to learn it. Then when Jayson showed up she would already know it. She appreciated Derek's insight on looking at this as a part in a play, and she liked the idea of getting comfortable with this in the absence of Jayson Wolfe. Still, as she followed Derek down to the music room, she wondered what she was getting herself into.

* * * * *

Jayson felt terribly impatient to get off work, and he couldn't help thinking that he'd prefer being a professional musician as opposed to changing oil. In fact, he decided that if he got this job, he would never work again doing anything *but* music. He arrived at the music room feeling a little down. He knew that Derek had been right about *the missing ingredient,* but he felt sure that Elizabeth would never consider the idea, even if Derek agreed to ask her. Either way, they only had a few days to be ready for the audition. He wondered if picking another song would be better; but he *did* like the song and how it felt to play it.

"Okay, let's do it," he said.

"Which one first?" Derek asked.

"The Joan Jett number," Jayson said.

Drew said, "You know, we really ought to have a girl sing this song."

"Well, we don't have a girl," Jayson said tersely. "So just . . ."

The door came open, and Jayson sighed. They had too much to do to deal with interruptions. He sucked in his breath when Elizabeth walked into the room. He had never seen her look like *that* before, and he wondered where on earth she might be going. The blouse she wore was pretty funky looking, and her curly hair was moussed out to double its usual volume. She wore slim jeans and red shoes with *very* high heels. In fact, with those shoes on, she met him eye to eye. He felt all over again like he had when he'd seen her in *West Side Story.* He couldn't help thinking, *Mercy, now I'm* really *in love.*

"Hot date, sis?" Derek asked with a smirk.

"Not really," she said, closing the door. Looking right at Jayson she added, "I heard you guys needed a girl to give this act some class." She continued with a defiance in her eyes that sent his heart racing, "Or maybe you'd prefer that somebody as highbrow as myself put my efforts elsewhere."

Jayson felt too stunned to speak. He glared at Derek, who had obviously repeated what he'd said, and he didn't know whether to feel angry or embarrassed. Derek just smirked, not seeming concerned in the least. He looked back at Elizabeth and realized that his fascination with her overrode every other emotion.

"Oh, no," Derek said, "come in. Let's see what you can do."

"Those are pretty amazing shoes, Lady," Jayson said.

"Until you get me a microphone of my own," she said almost snidely, "I'm going to have to be tall enough to share yours."

Jayson resisted the urge to just reach over and kiss her. Instead he chuckled and said with a trace of sarcasm that hid his true enthusiasm, "How pleasant."

"Okay, let's try it," Derek said. To Jayson he added, "You cover the backing vocals; and yes, you'll have to share the mic until we get another one."

Jayson just smirked and put the guitar strap over his head, adjusting it against his shoulder. He made some adjustments on the amp and then tapped a floor switch with his toe. He looked at Elizabeth and said, "Hit it, Lady."

Drew hit the introductory drum beats, and the guitars came in with well-practiced unison. Elizabeth leaned into the microphone and belted out the first phrase of vocals, giving Jayson a rush of goose bumps. He was so enthralled that he missed a couple of chords and the first cue for backing vocals. But halfway through the song, he had it down to a science. When he leaned into the microphone to back her on the chorus, their faces were nearly touching, and he could almost feel the heat of her energy. Together they sang the chorus as if they'd *always* sung together.

Following the last note, Drew let out of loud whoop and tossed his drumsticks in the air. Derek laughed and bellowed, "Yes! That was perfect!"

"Not perfect," Jayson said, "but it's getting closer." He met Elizabeth's eyes and added, "Welcome to the band, Lady. It would seem you're the missing ingredient."

Elizabeth tossed him a smirk, then said, "What else have you got?"

Jayson handed Elizabeth the extra cassette tape he'd recorded with all of the songs they needed to do. "Listen to this," he said. "Listen to it a lot."

Over the next few days, the four of them were able to put in several hours together, and Jayson felt magic evolving. Elizabeth was able to cover some keyboards on a number of songs that just added more depth and definitely made them sound better. While they would use the electric keyboard for some of the numbers, the piano would work better for others. They used the keyboard for practice for all of them since the piano was upstairs, but Elizabeth and Jayson spent some time at the piano just to be certain they had it right.

Leslie was thrilled when Jayson told her Elizabeth had joined the band. And Jayson couldn't deny that he was thoroughly enjoying her involvement. Their voices blended well. Her talent truly had added an ingredient that he'd not wanted to admit was missing. As of yet they'd had no interaction beyond actually practicing and sharing some meals in between with Drew and Derek. But he loved just having her around.

The day prior to the two-week mark, they had five songs in performance condition, and they had run through the others enough to be familiar with them. They each knew their parts—but they needed a great deal of work to be ready for the weekend. Derek started out practice by asking, "So, have we got every song on that list?"

"All but one," Jayson said. "I couldn't find the record and then, quite honestly, it slipped my mind, but we can put it in later."

"What is it?" Elizabeth asked.

"'Color My World,'" Jayson said.

Elizabeth chuckled. "I've got that record."

"Really?" Jayson laughed.

"I also have the sheet music," she said, and Jayson laughed again.

The four of them went upstairs to the stereo, and within minutes Elizabeth appeared with the album in her hand. The moment the song started, Jayson said, "I've heard this song; I just didn't know the name of it." They listened for a minute and all chuckled with relief. "Oh, man, this one's a cinch."

When the flute came in, Jayson said to Elizabeth, "You can do the flute on the keyboard. We have a flute sound on that thing, don't we?"

"We do," Elizabeth said, "but I'm not going to do it."

Jayson looked at her, startled. Until now she'd been relatively agreeable, and he wondered what her problem was with this. She added firmly, "I will play the flute part on the flute. I actually played this with a friend at a wedding."

Jayson let out a delighted laugh. "I forgot you could play the flute. Well then, let's go play it."

Chapter Seven

On Tuesday evening they arrived for the audition to find Joe every bit as bored and unenthusiastic as he'd been the last time. He showed the first spark of anything beyond bland when Elizabeth walked through the door with the microphones and asked, "Where do you want these?"

"You brought a girl," Joe said. "Is she in the band?"

"She is now," Jayson said as Derek walked past them toward the stage door, carrying an amp.

"That's great. Nothing like a pretty girl to liven up a show."

"Amen," Jayson said and comically lifted his brows toward Elizabeth, who just scowled and walked in the direction where Derek had gone.

As they set up the stage, he couldn't help feeling impressed with Elizabeth. He had expected her to do the prima donna thing and make herself comfortable while the men did all the work. But she kept going back and forth, carrying things in, and asking what she could do. Jayson showed her how to set up the mic stands and indicated which plugs went into which holes in the amps. Since he'd coded them with colored tape, it wasn't terribly complicated.

"Oh, I can do that," she said, leaning over the amp close to him. He glanced at her face, and for the thousandth time since he'd met her, he wanted to kiss her. He wondered if it would ever actually come to that or if they would forever be just friends. But then, he wasn't sure he could even officially categorize their relationship as friends. They were working together; they were friendly. Being friends was still a step or two away. But they were getting there.

When everything was set up, Jayson informed Joe that the show was about to start, and he took his usual seat at the other end of the dance floor. They began with the Joan Jett number. Jayson loved watching Elizabeth do it. He never would have imagined her being so comfortable with this kind of music. And he especially loved the way she moved to the music. She wasn't trying to be sexy or provocative. It was as if she simply felt the music, and it gave her a stage presence that he knew the audience would love. *He* certainly loved it. And he loved sharing center stage with her, and even sharing the microphone. He loved it when they would lean into the mic at the same time and their faces would nearly touch.

When the song ended, Joe actually applauded.

"He likes you," Jayson said to Elizabeth away from the microphone. "We couldn't get a sound out of him before."

Elizabeth just smiled and moved to the piano for the next number. They went through the audition smoothly, ending with "Color My World" and a standing ovation from Joe. He leaned his forearms on the stage, just as he'd done two weeks earlier, and said, "You kids have got yourselves a job. Pack your stuff up and meet me in my office."

Once Joe had left the room, they all exchanged high-fives and laughter, then they hurried to break down and load everything into the Suburban. When that was done, they all sat around Joe's desk. He cleared his throat and asked, "Are any of you eighteen?"

"I am," Drew said.

"Okay, I need you to sign this." He handed a paper to Drew. He handed one to each of the others. "The rest of you will need your parents to sign them. Don't come back Saturday without them. You don't have the release signed, you don't play. Nothing to be concerned about—just standard stuff. Read it over with your folks."

He gave them another paper that basically stated everything he'd told them previously about what was expected of them. He pointed out where it was written that they would do no smoking or drinking on the premises, and they would perform sober or not at all.

"That's not a problem," Jayson insisted while one of his mother's speeches came to mind.

"So, what do you call yourselves?" Joe asked. No one answered, and he added, "Does the band have a name?"

"A Pack of Wolves," Derek said, and Jayson glared at him.

"I like that," Joe said, writing it down. "Now, there's one more thing I need you to do." He handed Jayson a business card. "Some time in the next twenty-four hours, I want you to meet with this guy. He's going to take some pictures. He knows what I need; just do what he tells you."

"Pictures?" Jayson asked. "What for?"

"Advertising, son," Joe said. "Any questions?"

They didn't have any and were soon on their way home, all four of them squished into the front seat, since all the other space was filled with equipment. Elizabeth ended up between Drew and Derek, just as she'd been on the trip out. Jayson wondered if she was purposely avoiding being too close to him, or if it was just happenstance.

Once they were on the road, the first thing Jayson said was, "The name was a joke, Derek."

"What are you talking about?"

"A Pack of Wolves. It was a joke."

"It's a great name," Derek insisted. "Joe liked it."

"What does he know?"

"Joe likes us," Derek pointed out with dramatic humor. "Besides, what were *you* going to call us?"

"I don't know. I hadn't thought about it."

"Well, I like it," Derek said.

"I like it too," Drew added.

"I think it sounds kind of . . . savage," Elizabeth commented.

"I know. That's why I like it," Derek said.

"Okay, it's done," Jayson said, "but when we get a *real* job, playing our own music, we will not be A Pack of Wolves."

"Fine," Derek said, pretending to sound offended, then he laughed.

The four of them talked and laughed and speculated over where all of this would lead them. The boys talked of going to LA eventually, of record deals and world tours. Elizabeth broke in, saying, "I hope you guys have a good time. This is great fun, but I'm not following you guys to LA *or* around the world."

Jayson hated the uneasy prickle he felt when she said that. He forced a light voice and asked, "You're already sick of us?"

"No," she said. "My goals are just different, that's all."

"She likes goals," Derek said. "When she was five, she was setting goals."

Jayson asked, "So what lofty goals will you be achieving in life, Lady, while we're out making millions with music?"

"I'm going to school in Boston. And after I get a degree, I'm going to settle down in a cute little house and raise a family. I'm going to bake cookies for my children and always be there when they come home from school."

Derek chuckled, as if to imply that it was the stupidest thing he'd ever heard, but then, he was her brother. Jayson, however, felt a deep admiration. He wondered how many girls her age had the foresight to think of the importance of raising good kids in this world. Still, he couldn't help thinking he'd like to have her raising *his* kids. His version would be having her involved in his music as far as it was possible, and she could still get a degree and raise a family, and they would live happily ever after. He hoped with time that their goals might mesh, then he scolded himself inwardly for planning his life with a girl he hardly knew. And he reminded himself of what his mother would remind him of. They were still very young, and they had plenty of time.

Back at the Greer home, Will was thrilled to hear that they'd gotten the job, and he was obviously pleased with Elizabeth's involvement. He helped them unload the Suburban, then they all sat around the kitchen table eating Oreos after Jayson had called his mother to let her know where they were and to tell her the good news.

Mrs. Greer came home, and the laughter quieted immediately when she entered the room.

"Isn't this fun?" she said with obvious sarcasm, and he wondered what made this woman so miserable.

"It is actually," Will said. "Why don't you join us?"

Jayson noticed that there was no kind of greeting between them as husband and wife; no kiss, no hello, nothing.

"No, thank you, I'm tired," she said. "I'd appreciate it if you'd keep the noise down."

"Meredith," Will said as she started to leave the room, and Jayson realized he'd never known her first name. "Remember that dance hall in Portland we used to go to occasionally? The one that's been there for years?"

"Yes," she said, her tone bored.

"Our children just got a job there, playing live every Saturday night."

"You're kidding," she said with such astonishment that it was evident she'd never imagined they were actually doing anything productive in the basement.

"They're amazing," Will said. "You've got to hear them play."

"One of these days," she said, and Jayson heard Elizabeth sigh loudly. He felt sure her mother would never make the effort to hear them play.

Meredith Greer stood there for a long moment in silence as if she were trying to digest what she'd just learned. Then she said in a voice of astonishment, "Wait a minute. Did you say *children?*" She turned to Elizabeth, looking at her as if she'd broken out in polka dots. "You too?" she asked, her tone and expression implying that Elizabeth had just taken a job as a cocktail waitress. Jayson also felt she was implying that she expected Derek to do something stupid, but not Elizabeth. Jayson wondered how Derek must feel to know that his mother saw him as an inferior underachiever next to his sister.

"Me too," Elizabeth said with pride.

"School will be starting soon. How can you possibly do something like this and keep up with everything else you'll be doing?"

"It really won't take that much time," Elizabeth said. "But the only thing I have to work around is orchestra. That's like a few concerts through the whole school year. It's not a big deal."

"What about chorus?" Meredith demanded, apparently oblivious to the fact that others were present. "What about student government?"

"The officers were elected in the spring, Mom. I'm not in student government any more."

"You didn't run for office?" Meredith countered hotly.

"I would have thought you'd have noticed that months ago," Elizabeth said, her voice rising. "No, I didn't run for office, and I didn't try out for chorus, and I'm not doing any plays this year. I am, however, taking AP classes and getting college credits, and I will do my best to keep pulling straight As, the way I always have. Not that you would notice. Maybe you would notice if I got crappy grades and did *nothing*."

"Nope, that doesn't work," Derek said.

Meredith looked at her son as if she would like to slap him, good and hard. Before she got another word out, Will said with firm resolve, "Meredith, I don't think this is a good time to get into it. Derek's grades were improving on the last report card, and I've encouraged Elizabeth to back off a little and not exhaust herself so much."

Meredith's angry glare turned to her husband. "Well, you would do that, wouldn't you. If you were—"

"Meredith," he interrupted, still completely calm, "this is not a good time." He glanced discreetly at Jayson and Drew.

Meredith made a disgusted noise and hurried from the room. All was silent until they heard a door slam from somewhere upstairs. "Guess I'll be sleeping in the guest room tonight," Will said in a voice that attempted to sound light.

"More peaceful that way, I'd bet," Derek said, and Will made no comment.

"Sorry about that," he finally said, glancing again at Drew and Jayson.

"Not a problem," Jayson said. "It was much worse when our dad showed up." Drew made a noise of agreement. "But maybe next time we should just . . . discreetly leave and—"

"Oh, no," Derek said. "Your being here kept it from getting ugly. I think you should be here all the time." To his father he added, "Why do you put up with it? She's been like this ever since she got her degree and started working."

"No," Elizabeth corrected, "she keeps getting worse."

Will said, "I put up with it because I married her for better or worse, and marriage isn't something I take lightly. I have every hope that one day the woman I married will emerge again. She's just got some issues she needs to work through. We need to be patient with her."

"Yeah, well," Derek said, "I'm not going to hold my breath until she comes around."

The conversation lightened up again when Will started talking about how proud he would be when they got their first record deal.

The following day Jayson arrived at the Greer home midmorning. He rang the bell, and no one answered. He knew Derek was home, so he waited and rang again, hoping he hadn't already gone downstairs and couldn't hear a blasted thing. He doubted anyone would care if he just went in, but not actually having been invited to do so, he hesitated. He was about to go find a phone booth and *call* Derek when the door came open. It was Elizabeth, wearing jeans and a sweatshirt, looking like she'd just gotten out of bed. She looked mildly irritated.

"Sorry," he said, "I thought Derek was here."

"I think he's in the shower. Come on in."

"Thanks."

"Go ahead and go downstairs. I'll tell him you're here."

"Thanks," he said again and headed for the basement.

Elizabeth watched him go down the stairs and debated whether to go back to bed until they began practice when Drew showed up, or whether to follow him and confront him with the thoughts that had been keeping her awake at night. The more she got to know Jayson Wolfe, the more she liked him. But she often sensed that he was irritated, perhaps even angry with her, and she wondered why. Now that they were going to be working together, she didn't want this ongoing tension between them. But she wasn't sure what to do about it. If she confronted him, would he just scoff at her and become more angry? Or would it solve the problem? Deciding she had to at least try, she took a deep breath and hurried down the stairs.

Elizabeth peeked into the music room and found Jayson there alone, tuning his electric guitar. He glanced up and looked surprised as she stepped into the room and closed the door.

"Hi," he said, setting the guitar aside.

"Hi," she said back, and Jayson wondered what this might be about. He couldn't recall being alone with her since the day they'd talked in this room, and that was months ago. Her body language and the way she'd closed the door suggested that she'd come here with a purpose.

Searching for some avenue of conversation, he decided to ask her about her summer job. "So, how is the sewing . . . going?"

Elizabeth laughed softly. "Is that a question or a new song?"

He laughed as well. "Both, actually."

"It's fine," she said, and silence fell again.

"Is there something I can do for you?" he asked and silently added, *Like kiss you, for instance.*

"I just . . . have a question. It's been bugging me for . . . well, a long time. So, I decided I should just . . . ask."

"Okay," he said, wondering if he should be nervous.

She started wringing her hands as she leaned against the wall, and he realized *she* was nervous. Without looking at him, she said, "I just . . . wondered if there was a reason you seem . . . angry with me."

Jayson's heart quickened. While he was searching for an appropriate answer, she lifted her eyes to meet his. Something warm and vulnerable in them lured him to move closer to her.

"Is there something I've done to make you think I'm angry?" he asked.

"Nothing . . . obvious. It's just a . . . feeling."

"Well, I'm not angry," he said. She looked at him hard, silently asking for clarification. "Frustrated, perhaps."

"Why?" she asked, her brow furrowing.

"Are you sure you want to know?" he asked. "I mean . . . do you think we can handle brutal honesty?"

"If we're going to be working together, maybe we need brutal honesty."

"Maybe. But I should clarify what the others already know."

"What's that?" she asked.

"Rule number one is that we don't let personal matters interfere with the music. Drew and I can punch each other's lights out at home, but once we pick up the instruments, it's not personal. The same applies for Derek. The same applies for you."

"Do you and Drew really punch each other's—"

"No," he chuckled, "we actually get along rather well. I was just making a point."

"Point taken," she said.

"So, you want brutal honesty?"

"Give it a shot," she said, but her eyes showed an apprehension that contradicted her firm words.

"Okay, well . . ." Jayson cleared his throat and put his hands behind his back, if only to give him another moment to gather his words. "I just . . . got the impression early on that I wasn't the type of person you would ever be more than diplomatically polite to. I'm different from you, Elizabeth."

"But you're not," she protested, and it took him a moment to accept that Elizabeth Greer was trying to convince *him* that they had something in common.

"On the surface we *are* different," he said. "In every logical respect, we are different. I'm guessing that you took one look at me and assumed I was an irresponsible loser." She turned away quickly, but not before he saw a glimmer of guilt in her eyes. He hurried to add, "I confess that I was hoping for an opportunity to get to know you better, to let you know who and what I really am. But when that opportunity came, it didn't give me the satisfaction I'd been hoping for."

"Why not?" she asked, looking at him again.

"Well, I think you changed your opinion of me, but I had to wonder if your only interest in me was due to my musical abilities. And I suppose that's your answer. I get frustrated when people pay more attention to what I can do than who I am."

"I can understand that," she said. "And I'm sorry if that's the way it seemed. I admit that my first impressions of you were not accurate, but then . . . I think we're both guilty of that."

Jayson smiled. "Touché."

Elizabeth met his eyes and felt compelled to ask another question that had clung to her mind. She'd gotten through the first one all right; she hoped she wouldn't regret forging ahead.

"Can I ask you another question?"

"Sure," he said.

"Well . . . I was wondering why you're always . . . staring at me."

Jayson looked away abruptly as if that might convince her that such a concept was only her imagination. His heart began to pound. How could he possibly answer such a question without letting on to the truth of his feelings? But then, maybe it was time to do just that— tell her the truth of his feelings. Attempting a cautious approach, he looked at her and countered her question by saying, "I was wondering why *you* are always staring at *me.*"

"The same reason you're staring at me," she said quickly, and Jayson smiled.

"Well, that's good news for me," he said, and she looked suddenly nervous.

"Why *are* you always staring at me?" she asked.

He stepped closer and put a hand on the wall near her head. "Apparently you already know, or you wouldn't know that we're doing it for the same reason." She looked embarrassed, and he added, "Jumping to conclusions again, are we?"

"Just answer the question, Jayson, okay?"

"Okay," he said and forced a measure of humor into his voice, if only to buffer the intensity of his feelings as they came into the open. "It's because I'm madly in love with you, Elizabeth."

Elizabeth was so stunned she didn't know how to respond. While she wanted with everything inside of her to think he was serious, she just couldn't believe that he was.

Jayson felt a thick tension fall between them while he waited for her to respond. When he felt as if he might scream or burst into tears, he chuckled tensely instead and glanced down.

Elizabeth felt both relieved and disappointed at the evidence of humor in his manner. "Oh that's very funny, Jayson," she said with sarcasm and eased around him to put some distance between them.

"Is it?" he asked, feeling his heart plummet as he realized his nervousness had been misinterpreted. He was searching for a way to clarify himself when the door came open and Derek entered the room.

"What are you guys up to?"

Perhaps hoping to give Elizabeth another chance to hear his message, Jayson forced a firm, steady voice that didn't begin to express the heaviness of his heart, "I was just telling your sister that I'm madly in love with her."

Derek looked astonished. His eyes widened, and he gasped a little laugh. "You're madly in love with my sister?" he echoed.

"It's a joke, Derek," Elizabeth said. "Don't get yourself in a tizzy."

Derek let out a relieved chuckle and picked up his guitar, saying absently, "I was not in a tizzy. I just didn't think Jayson would be that stupid."

Elizabeth rolled her eyes and left the room. Jayson resisted the urge to call Derek a jerk—or worse, belt him in the jaw. If he drew attention to the truth of his mood, then his feelings would be all over the place—and obviously nobody was ready for that.

Later that day they went to Portland to meet with the photographer. He was an eccentric guy named Louis, who treated their photo session as if he were shooting professional models in Paris. A couple of times when they were trying a variety of poses, Derek said, "Jayson needs to stand next to Elizabeth because he's madly in love with her."

At one point the photographer asked, "Okay, who is doing the main vocals here?"

"Jayson," Derek said, pointing comically at him. "Except for when Elizabeth does them."

"Perfect," Louis said and told Jayson and Elizabeth to stand close together. "Now face each other; stand as close as you can get without touching. I want the back lighting to shine between the two of you just a tad." They did as they were told, and Jayson thought she was going to feel his heart pounding. Since she was wearing those red shoes, they met eye-to-eye, but he was more distracted by her lips. Such thoughts, however, always came with his mother's silent voice telling him to mind his hormones.

"Okay," Louis said, "now each of you put your hands behind your backs; clasp them—and look at me." They did so, and Louis said, "Perfect. Don't move. Don't smile. Now I want the drummer on the stool, right here." He put it directly in front of Elizabeth and Jayson, and Drew sat there. "And I want the bass player," he motioned for Derek, "on the floor, but . . . take your shoes off. Bare feet are good."

He took several shots of that pose and talked them through a dozen other poses, including a couple where Elizabeth sat on Jayson's lap. When the photo session was done, they hurried back to the music room to rehearse. Jayson was grateful for the soundproof room that allowed them to rehearse well into the night without causing anybody problems.

Throughout the next few days, Jayson kept reminding himself of his adage not to mix his personal feelings with the music. They had a lot of work to do to be ready to perform for two solid hours. Embarrassed over the outcome of his confession to Elizabeth, he opted to go with the "joke" theory, and at least once a day he reminded Elizabeth that he was madly in love with her.

It came out easiest in the midst of ordinary events. When he paid for her lunch, he said, "I only did it because I'm madly in love with you."

"Are you madly in love with me, too?" Derek asked with his mouth full of French fries. "You paid for my lunch too."

"No, you're a jerk," Jayson said, and they both laughed. Elizabeth just shook her head with disgust. Apparently, she didn't appreciate their humor. Obviously, she had trouble knowing when Jayson was serious and when he wasn't. He smiled and pointed at her saying in a simpering voice, "Next time, you can buy *my* lunch."

Later, when he was dishing up ice cream in the Greer kitchen, he gave Elizabeth hers first and said, "Only because I love you, Lady."

"You need to get out more, Jayson," she said.

On Friday afternoon, Will called from work while they were all taking a break in the kitchen, eating sandwiches. Elizabeth answered the phone, then hung up and grabbed her car keys.

"Where're you going?" Derek asked.

"Dad said we need to get some copies of the Portland paper."

"What for?"

"Because we're in it," she said. They hurried to put the food in the fridge and went with her, taking their sandwiches along. The boys waited in the car while she got out and left the door open and bought a paper. She got back in and turned to the page number her father had told her to look at.

"Holy asterisk!" Drew said as he saw it first, looking over her shoulder from the backseat.

Elizabeth laughed and moved the paper so Jayson and Derek could see the full-page ad. "That is way awesome," Derek said. Jayson just chuckled and tried to absorb the reality. Across the top of the page it read, *A Pack of Wolves.* A picture of the four of them took up nearly half the page, and below it was an ad for the hall where they would be playing the following evening. *Hot New Local Band,* it said in huge, bold type. *Don't miss their debut performance,* it said below that.

"Wow," Jayson said, then they all got out and bought six more papers.

Before going back to the Greer home, they stopped at the diner where Leslie worked. The hostess met them just inside the door, and Jayson said, "Could you please seat us in Leslie's section?"

"Sure. Come right this way," she said.

They were only seated in the booth for a minute before Leslie appeared, letting out a delighted laugh to see them. "What are you doing here?" she asked, hugging each of her sons, and then she insisted on a hug from Derek and Elizabeth as well. Derek acted like Bashful of the Seven Dwarfs as he sat back down.

"We want pie," Drew said. "I'm buying."

"Okay," Leslie said.

"And we have a present for you," Jayson added. "But first we want pie."

She took their order and was back shortly with four pieces of pie—all different flavors—and four glasses of water. "I'll be back," she said. "As soon as I take care of something, I can take a break."

Jayson took a couple of bites of his pie then slid it toward Derek and slid Drew's pie toward himself. Elizabeth watched them comically tasting each other's pie and sliding dishes back and forth, then she took the piece Jayson had in front of him and traded it with hers. Taking a bite she said, "Oh, I like yours much better." A minute later Jayson said, as if they were about to start a song, "Give me a one-two-three." Drew hit the table with his fork, and they all rotated their pieces of pie, took a bite, then did it again as they all fell into laughter.

"Sounds like you're having a good time," Leslie said, scooting onto the bench next to Drew.

"What kind do you like, Mom?" Jayson asked, and they all slid their plates toward her.

She took a bit of each one and said, "I like ice cream." They all laughed, and she added, "What's this present you have for me?"

"It's better than a tip," Jayson said.

"Which is good," Drew added, "because everybody spent their tip money buying it."

"Okay, I'm waiting," Leslie said, and Jayson pulled the newspaper from the bench to the table. He unfolded it to the correct page and handed it to his mother, watching her eyes closely. He wasn't disappointed by the way they widened, then filled with tears.

"Oh, it's incredible," she said, then she laughed, wiping at her tears with a napkin. "I knew you could do it." Her tears increased, and she added, "I have to work. I won't be able to be there."

"It's okay, Mom," Jayson said. "We'll be playing every Saturday night. Maybe you can make it next week."

She nodded and fought for composure. Jayson noticed that Derek and Elizabeth seemed concerned by Leslie's emotion. "Don't worry about it," he said to them. "She has a high water table. This is normal. She cries over everything."

"I'm afraid I do," Leslie said with a little laugh.

"Yeah, and Jayson inherited it," Drew said.

"Oh, thank you very much," Jayson said with sarcasm. "I really want everybody to know *that*."

"What, that you cry easily too?" Elizabeth asked, more intrigued than mocking.

Jayson looked at her and said, "If you see me crying, you'll know it's because I'm madly in love with you."

Leslie looked astonished, and Jayson hurried to say, "It's a joke, Mother."

"Oh, I see," she said, looking concerned. Knowing her, he could bet that she could see right through him. And that was fine, as long as nobody else could.

When Saturday came, Jayson felt decidedly nervous, but he did his best not to act that way, since he knew the others were nervous and they would look to him as an example. He would do well to be cool and calm.

When they were getting into the Suburban to leave, Jayson opened the door for Elizabeth and answered her questioning gaze by saying, "My mother taught me to open car doors for any girl I might be madly in love with."

She let out a disgusted sigh, but he saw her eyes smile just before she got in. And he couldn't help being pleased to note that he ended up sitting next to her. Deciding to press the joke a little, if only to distract him from his nerves, he put his arm up on the seat behind her and asked her softly, "How come you're sitting next to me? Are you madly in love with me?"

She turned slowly to look at him, saying coolly, "I told you my reasons for staring were the same as yours." She hesitated, then added, "But the truth is that I was just trying to figure out if that hole in your ear has any connection to the hole in your head that makes you want to hang around with my brother."

Jayson chuckled. "Derek's the one with a hole in his head."

"And in his ear," she mentioned with chagrin. "I'd wondered what provoked him to do something so silly as pierce his ear. Now I realize he was hanging around with you. You're a bad influence on him."

"And you," he said. "You've got holes in both ears."

She chuckled and shook her head. A minute later he asked, "You didn't answer my question. Are you letting me sit next to you because you're madly in love with me?"

Without looking at him she said, "I didn't want to sit next to Derek. He's so annoying sometimes."

"Yes, but you love him anyway."

Elizabeth admitted, "Yes, I suppose I do. It's a good thing he's funny; his sense of humor has saved his life many times."

"How is that?"

"It kept me from killing him," she said, and he laughed again.

Chapter Eight

After the stage was all set up, Joe showed them to the backstage lounge. It had a couple of couches, a vanity with a mirror, and some vending machines. Off the lounge were two restrooms where they took turns changing into the clothes they would wear to perform. Joe had told them he didn't care what they wore, as long as they didn't look sloppy. Leslie had insisted that they needed some way of being color-coordinated. A long discussion that almost turned into an argument had finally brought them to the conclusion that they would all wear black—except for Elizabeth, who would wear her red shoes and a shiny red belt with her black jeans and a black silk blouse. And flashy red earrings. Once the decision had been made, Leslie had gone out and bought matching black button-up shirts for her sons. They were lightweight with a texture almost like suede. Jayson wore his tucked into black jeans, with a black suit vest left unbuttoned over the shirt. Drew wore his shirt open like a jacket, with a black T-shirt underneath. Drew wore a black, long-sleeved T-shirt.

The boys were all sitting in the lounge, trying not to be nervous while Elizabeth took forever in the ladies room. In the distance they could hear loud music playing, and they knew the place was open and people were coming in.

"We look like we're going to a funeral," Derek said. "Are you sure this all-black thing is good?"

"It's a little late now," Jayson said, glancing at his watch. "We go on in less than twenty minutes."

"Oh, boy," Drew said and wiped his hands down the front of his jeans.

"Don't get sweaty palms!" Jayson ordered.

"I can't help it!"

"Well, whatever you do, hold onto those sticks."

"Once I get out there, I'll be fine."

"I hope so," Jayson said.

Derek went back to the clothing issue. "We're going to blend in with those back curtains."

"We will be in the spotlight," Jayson said. He glanced at his watch again. "What is taking her so long?"

"She's a girl," Derek said, as if Jayson might not have guessed. "She always takes forever in the bathroom."

Ten minutes later Jayson knocked on the bathroom door and hollered, "Are you dead in there, or what?"

"I'll be out in a minute."

"That's about how long we've got," Jayson called back.

Half a minute later, she emerged, and Jayson was dumbstruck. She looked gorgeous.

"What are you staring at?" she demanded lightly.

"I told you," he said. "I'm madly in love with you."

"She does look good," Drew said with admiration.

"I suppose," Derek muttered.

"You're my brother," Elizabeth said. "What would you know?"

Jayson was struck with a thought and hoped his friends wouldn't think him strange. "Hey," he said, "this might be weird, but . . . whenever we've had something big to face, our mom always had us hold hands and pray."

"You read my mind," Drew said, and Jayson felt a little better.

"Are you okay with that?" Jayson asked the others.

"Sure, why not?" Derek said. "As long as you know how to do it."

"Well, sort of," Jayson said. They stood in a circle and held hands while Jayson said a brief but sincere prayer that God would bless their performance for good and that all would go well. Following the "amen," he admitted, "Okay, I feel better. I'm ready now."

A loud knock at the door startled them, and Joe hollered, "Curtain's up in three minutes. Get yourselves out there."

"We're coming," Derek called. He gave Drew and Jayson a high-five, then kissed his sister on the cheek. "I really do like you," he said.

She smiled and said, "I like you too. But don't tell anybody I said that."

"Jayson, on the other hand," Derek added, "is madly in love with you."

"Oh, shut up and get out there," Drew said and led the way.

When they stepped onto the stage, they found it lit up in a variety of colors from the lights running in rows across the ceiling. They got into position behind the closed curtain and waited for only half a minute before a voice boomed, "Ladies and gentlemen, welcome the hottest new sound to hit Portland: A Pack of Wolves."

They exchanged quick smiles upon hearing applause. The curtain started to open, and the music began, prompting a new, more enthusiastic round of applause. The first hour of their performance went smoothly, their biggest surprises being how much they were sweating and how many people could get packed onto that dance floor.

"We'll be back," Jayson said into the microphone at the end of the first set. The crowd cheered, and the curtain closed.

In the lounge they collapsed onto the couches, exhausted but all in agreement that this was the coolest job in the world. The crowds loved them, and now that they had the pressure behind them of learning the bulk of the music, the hourly rate was excellent—especially for kids their age.

Joe came to the lounge and showed some measure of enthusiasm in telling them they were doing great. He then said, "There's a couple of people out there who claim to be related to you. I can't let them back here unless you tell me they are."

Jayson went with Joe to the door that led onto the dance floor. Just outside of it were Will and his mother. "Mom, what are you doing here?" he asked as she slipped into the hallway with Will right behind her.

"Oh, I just couldn't miss it," she said. "I prayed and prayed and found someone who would trade shifts with me. I'll have to work tomorrow, but it was worth it. Oh, Jayson, you're so amazing up there." She started to cry, and he hugged her tightly.

Will complimented him as well, and Jayson found out they'd not come together, but they'd soon found each other when they were among the few not dancing. Jayson took them back to the lounge where Leslie started to cry again as she hugged Drew and repeated her compliments.

The second half of the show went every bit as well as the first, then Will took them all out for a nice dinner, which the kids were grateful for since they'd all been too nervous to eat much before they'd come. They went back to the hall, arriving just a few minutes after it had closed, and they were able to load their equipment into the Suburban. While Derek drove home, Jayson sat with his arm on the seat behind Elizabeth, and he soon found her asleep with her head on his shoulder. *Oh please, God,* he prayed silently, *let my life be this way forever.* The moment felt like heaven to him.

The following day was equally pleasant as they took a picnic to the beach to celebrate. Jayson and Drew usually went to church on Sundays with their mother, but she was working, and they opted to make an exception. Derek and Elizabeth took them to a great section of beach where they were guaranteed they could almost always have it to themselves. They played in the water even though it was cold, then they gathered driftwood and built a fire where they roasted hot dogs and marshmallows. The four of them sat around the flames for hours, just talking and laughing and speculating about the places their music might take them. Elizabeth insisted, as she had in the past, that this was temporary for her—an idea that Jayson didn't want to think about. She assured them firmly, "I'm certain you can find someone to replace me, and you'll do just fine."

"I'm afraid you're irreplaceable," Jayson said, but she just laughed and told him he was silly.

* * * * *

The following day Elizabeth entered the music room tentatively. She'd been told to be there for rehearsal, but she wasn't really sure what to expect now that they'd gotten past the stress of getting the job and surviving their first performance. Since Derek and Jayson were evidently involved in some serious conversation over their guitars, she just sat down and waited. Drew was sitting on his drum stool, reading from a science fiction novel.

"Okay," Jayson said to Derek, "try it again."

Derek began a catchy bass-line on his guitar, and Jayson joined him with some pretty impressive picking on the electric. They did that for a few minutes while Elizabeth wondered if she should have brought a book to read, as well.

"Yeah!" Jayson said, and they both laughed as they apparently had it figured out. "Now," Jayson added, picking up a piece of paper from the floor, "I want you to *speak* these words, and I do the 'yeah, yeah, yeah,' echo."

"Speak?"

"Well, kind of a speaky-singy sort of thing."

Derek chuckled. "When I figure out what that means, maybe I can do it."

Jayson demonstrated in a speaky-singy kind of tone. *"Was it you or was it me?"*

"Okay," Derek said. "I can do that. *Was it you or was it me?"*

And Jayson followed with a very singy, *"Yeah, yeah, yeah, yeah."* Jayson added, "So you do these lines, and I echo each line."

"Okay, but I have a question," Derek said, pretending to be intently serious. "Why does it have to have an echo thing?"

"It just does," Jayson insisted, pretending to be defensive.

"Okay, why?" Derek asked, mocking anger.

"Because I can hear it in my head, and it has an echo thing," Jayson said, and Derek laughed.

"I love to hear you admit to it," Derek said.

"Admit to what?"

"That you can hear it in your head." He took on a dramatic voice. "We must honor the voice in his head."

"Just play the song," Jayson said with a chuckle.

Elizabeth pretended to be bored, even though she felt certain they were all oblivious to her presence. In truth, she was fascinated to observe Jayson's creative process and how he and Derek could almost read each other's minds. A short while after she'd entered the room, Jayson said, "Okay, let's walk through it without the drums."

"And what do you call this?" Elizabeth asked, if only to draw attention to the fact that she was in the room.

"'Photo Finish,'" Jayson said.

"It doesn't say that anywhere in the song," Derek pointed out.

"I know," Jayson said. "But it's the point of the song. It's the title. Just do it."

Derek laughed as if he thoroughly enjoyed provoking Jayson in such lighthearted banter—even if they were both only pretending to be angry.

"Was it you or was it me?" Derek said into the microphone.

And Jayson added, *"Yeah, yeah, yeah, yeah."*

"I couldn't tell 'cause I couldn't see."

"Yeah, yeah, oh yeah."

Derek continued with Jayson echoing each line, sometimes with the "yeah, yeah, yeahs," and sometimes with the lyrics. *"Neck to neck, we approach the line. Flying so fast I'm gonna lose my mind . . . Was it you or was it me? It looks like a tie to me."*

They both laughed with pleasure at having gotten the basic premise down, then Jayson said to Drew, "Okay, put the book down, Bro. We need you. Move a minute."

Elizabeth was surprised to see Jayson sit on the drum stool and take the sticks. He managed to play a simple rhythm, if only to show Drew what he wanted, what he could hear in his head.

"You play the drums, too?" Elizabeth said to him.

"No!" he insisted with a little laugh. "Drew *plays* the drums. I only hit them a little."

He stood up and gave the sticks back to Drew, who immediately imitated the rhythm Jayson had shown him, but with great finesse.

They went through a rough version of the song, then put down their instruments. She then watched in amazement as Jayson and Derek embarked on what seemed to be a well-versed ritual of messing up each other's hair and slapping each other playfully on the face. Then Derek started dancing like a boxer, laughing and egging Jayson on until Jayson put his arm around Derek's neck and gave him a noogie while Derek screamed and protested with exaggerated anguish.

"Good thing the room is soundproof," Drew commented and turned a page in the book he'd picked up the moment the song was finished.

Elizabeth couldn't help laughing at their antics, and she couldn't help thinking that she'd never seen Derek so happy in his entire life. Jayson Wolfe had obviously brought out the best in him, and the bond they shared was amazing. She could clearly imagine them taking the world by storm with the musical synergy they shared.

"This is all very entertaining," she said, pretending to be bored, "but if you guys don't need me, I'm sure I can find something better to do with my time."

"Oh, no. We need you," Jayson said, letting go of Derek, who fell to the floor and did a fairly impressive death scene while Jayson picked up his guitar and added, "Let's go through all the usuals."

Elizabeth took her place at the mic and said with a touch of drama, "I'm reminded of a quote."

"Oh, she's going to give us a quote," Derek said as if he were terrified.

Into the microphone she said, "'We are the music makers, and we are the dreamers of dreams.'"

Jayson stood still for a long moment, just to absorb the way the words flooded into him. "Wow," he said. "Who said that?"

"Who do you think said it?" Elizabeth asked.

"Mozart? Beethoven? Bon Jovi?"

"Wrong!" Elizabeth said and made a noise like a game show buzzer. Then with mock arrogance she said, "Willy Wonka." And they all laughed.

They quickly began a regular schedule of less intense rehearsals, working in a little more of Elizabeth's flute, and even some violin. Jayson was so in awe of her that he almost couldn't believe she was real. But he felt a deep frustration over the wall between them. He wondered if they would ever go beyond the musical relationship they shared.

More than once Elizabeth arrived at practice with warm cookies, and he couldn't help wondering if she was trying to impress him. Whether or not that was the case, it was working. He had, after all, told her he liked warm cookies. And she could bake them well. He concluded that her goal to make cookies for her children was definitely realistic.

The Saturday night gig quickly became an easy routine that they all thoroughly enjoyed. It took about twelve hours altogether from the time they started loading equipment from the basement, until they got home in the middle of the night and got it put away. But it was Jayson's favorite twelve hours of the week.

When school started, Jayson couldn't help feeling dismayed. He just didn't like it. He was naturally astonished when Elizabeth announced one afternoon, "I understand you guys didn't get very good grades last year."

"Or ever," Drew said.

"Sorry," Jayson said. "I hate to disappoint you, my love, but I'm not the straight-A kind of guy. It's hard to focus on schoolwork when you have music rolling through your head."

"Well, that's certainly understandable," Elizabeth said. "But I think you guys could probably manage to be the B-average kind of guys. In fact, I'm so certain of it that I'm willing to bet my job on it."

"What are you saying?" Derek asked, sounding angry.

"I'm saying that if you guys don't pull a B average, I'm quitting."

"You can't do that!" Jayson nearly shouted. "We need you. You're part of us now and—"

"I can and I will," she said. "You guys sit around and do nothing *but* music, thinking that you're totally stupid otherwise. Well, it's not true. You could do a lot better if you put a little effort into it. Three-point-O. That's not so much to ask. If I don't see at least that on your report cards at the term, I'm quitting."

"Why you . . ." Jayson began, then curbed his tongue. Instead, he pointed out a fact she was obviously overlooking. "I'm not so good at some of those subjects, little Miss Smarty-pants. Maybe it's just not possible for me to pull a B average. Is this just some excuse to get out of what you've committed to doing or what?"

"Of course not!" she insisted. "I love doing this." She smiled widely and added, "I will give free tutoring as much as you need. Since you guys don't have to work other jobs any more and our rehearsals are minimal, I'm certain you can find the time to keep up with your homework."

For about two weeks, Jayson felt so angry with Elizabeth he wanted to strangle her. Even while she was graciously helping him with his math, he wanted to hurt her. But he put all of his angry energy into doing school-work—even though he hated it. He felt relatively certain that she would indeed follow through on her threat. And then something astounding happened. He realized that he was completely caught up with every class in school, he had turned in every assignment, and he had actually gotten some decent test scores. And it felt good. She'd been right, blast her! He had come to believe that he didn't have any brain capacity beyond music, but he'd been wrong. He wasn't straight-A material, just as he'd told her. But he could do a B-average, and he could feel good about it.

One afternoon while Elizabeth was helping Jayson with his math at her kitchen table, she noticed a binder on the table that she realized he always carried with him, but she'd never seen him open it to do homework. When he went into the bathroom, she couldn't resist looking inside. She was intrigued to find pages and pages of lyrics and many pages of hand-written music with the notes created neatly on paper specifically printed for writing music. There were also many written descriptions of musical strategy, as if he'd been afraid he might forget it if he didn't get it on paper. She paused to read one in particular. *The bass-line breaks a steady one-two rhythm. Interject a three-two-one beneath the descant of the vocals, with lead guitar doing the major, and a synth harmony line.* It made absolutely no sense to her, but she felt sure he could read it and know exactly how it should sound. She became so enthralled that she forgot she was being sneaky and looked up to see him watching her.

"What are you doing?" he asked, sounding genuinely offended.

"Sorry," she said, closing the book. "I was just . . . curious. Your creativity . . . fascinates me."

Jayson made a dubious noise and took the book from her. He wished that something besides his creativity might fascinate her. For the moment he focused on her being his math tutor so he could keep up the decent grades.

A few days later, when midterm report cards came, Leslie was so impressed that she cried. Knowing Elizabeth was behind it, she made a point of taking her to lunch, and they had a glorious time. Jayson and Derek brainstormed about finding a way to show their appreciation to Elizabeth without making a big deal of it. They pitched in and bought her a new microphone, which they set up on stage with a big red bow tied to it. When they came onto the stage to perform, Jayson said to the audience, "Elizabeth has a new microphone."

"That's pretty cool," Elizabeth said into the mic.

"The bow matches your shoes," Derek said into his mic, and the audience laughed.

"She's pretty cute though," Jayson said to the crowd. "I think I'd still prefer sharing the mic with her. What do you think?"

A cheer went up, and Jayson started the song. From that time on, he occasionally still shared the mic with her, and she smiled at him when he did. Apparently she liked that too.

Their performances quickly became comfortable. Most of their money went into the bank with the intent of using it to get to LA to start a real career, although Jayson did buy himself a reasonable car. And they all used some of their earnings to acquire better equipment and a variety of performing clothes that were simple and tasteful. Only occasionally did they wear black. But Elizabeth always wore her red shoes. No matter what Derek wore, however, he always wore a hat. Every week Jayson waited to see what kind of hat he'd show up in. At first it was just a baseball cap worn backwards, then he wore a knit hat with long tassels, then a jester hat with bells that were thankfully drowned out by the music when he'd jump up and down. But the best was a colored beanie with a propeller on the top. Jayson could easily imagine him one day performing on the Grammy awards wearing that beanie.

Autumn settled in Oregon, and Jayson realized he had lived there a year. And what an amazing year it had been. The band was getting a good reputation, and they had started getting an occasional Friday-night gig doing high-school dances. The promo photos that had been taken showed up in ads and on posters preceding some of their events. And occasionally, one of the band members would be recognized and even asked for an autograph. Their success, however, remained in the Portland area, and people in their own high school were as oblivious to Jayson as they had ever been. And that was fine. At least he was getting decent grades, and he was enjoying life—except for this ongoing desire he had to actually share a romantic relationship with Elizabeth. His mother suggested that he just ask her out on a date and start from there, but he just couldn't bring himself to do it and he wondered why. It occurred to him that his feelings for her were so powerful that perhaps he preferred keeping them safe as opposed to exposing them to possible rejection. As long as she didn't know how he felt, he could admire her from a distance and keep his feelings secure in his heart. Still, the flaw in that plan was an aching for her that grew steadily with time. He tried to tell himself that he was too young to be feeling something so intense for a woman, but his heart disagreed. His heart knew she was the woman of his dreams, the love of his life. And time could never dispel such feelings.

While they continued to learn new songs and rotate them through their performances, Jayson kept writing songs of his own. He felt frustrated with not being able to play more of his own music, but his mother often reminded him to be patient and allow destiny to take its course.

On a particularly rainy afternoon at the usual practice, Jayson said, "Okay, I'm working on a new one, and I'd like Elizabeth to do the backing vocals; I want them kind of light and airy."

"I can do light and airy."

He said to Drew, "Give me a slow, light beat. This is a love song."

He started picking out a melody on the acoustic guitar, and he closed his eyes as he sang, *"You stand tall while I stand in awe, yearning from a distance. My awakened senses yearn to sense you . . . close to me. Our two hearts are only one divided by time and air and space. In another time and place . . . our two hearts were one . . . and they will be again."*

Elizabeth felt chilled by the lyrics and warmed by the way he sang them. She found herself wishing that he'd written them for her, but she knew the very idea was ludicrous. She kept wishing that he would just ask her on a date so they could have some time, just the two of them, to get to know each other better. Occasionally, she went out with someone else, but never more than once. Then she was asked out by a guy named Mark and actually had a good time. Still, she felt almost angry with the way her thoughts strayed to Jayson. Mark asked her out a second time and a third, and she accepted, certain it was better than sitting home waiting for Jayson to take notice of her.

The rainy afternoon following that third date, she went to rehearsal and found Jayson in more of a foul mood than she'd ever seen him. They started working on a new song that Joe had suggested they learn, and they did it over and over while Jayson had nothing good to say about what they were doing. With the way he kept tossing subtle glares in her direction, she wondered if the problem was with her.

Elizabeth felt thoroughly exhausted by the time they'd gone through the song for what seemed the hundredth time. The moment it was done, Jayson said, "Okay, we're doing it again."

Elizabeth was grateful that Drew, being Jayson's brother, would say what he felt more easily than she or Derek. "Oh, come on, Jayson. The song is fine. It's—"

"It's *not* fine!" Jayson snapped in a tone of voice she'd never heard before. "It's mediocre; and mediocre isn't good enough!"

"We're exhausted, Jayse," Drew said firmly but without anger. "We can't perform when we're exhausted."

Jayson looked at Drew hard, then Derek, then Elizabeth. "Fine," he snarled and lifted the guitar strap over his head. "We'll meet back here in two hours, and we'll do it until it's perfect." He set the guitar down with a gentleness that defied his sour mood and hurried from the room.

Elizabeth moved to follow him and Drew said, "You might be better off to let him cool down. He's very intense about his music."

"So I've noticed," Elizabeth said. "But I think I can handle him."

She found Jayson in the backyard, beneath the awning, looking out into the continuing rain. He tossed her an angry glare when he heard the door.

"I thought you needed a nap or something," he said.

"A break should be sufficient," she said. "They have child labor laws in this country, you know."

"Oh, very funny," he said with sarcasm. "Especially since you're older than I am."

"By a few months," she pointed out. "What's eating at you, Jayson? I know you're upset with me, and I want to know why. Am I not singing well enough for you? Is there something I've been doing to ruin your music?"

"You do just fine," he said.

"Then what's the problem?"

Jayson looked at her hard, then looked away again. He paused a long moment to just listen to the sound of the rain. No matter its tempo or intensity, he felt that rain always had a musical quality to it. Its distraction helped him straighten out his thoughts. Answering her honestly would open a can of worms, and he knew it, but since Derek had mentioned to him something about Elizabeth's recent activities, the question he wanted to ask her had rattled around so much in his brain that he couldn't force himself to hold it back. "Who is this . . . idiot you've been dating?"

Elizabeth let out a surprised chuckle. "He is not an idiot. And what does my personal life have to do with making the song perfect?" He tossed her a guilty glance, and she growled, "You hypocrite! Aren't you the one who told me in no uncertain terms that we don't mix our personal lives with the music? And you're angry with me? For what? For going out on a few dates?"

"Yes I am, actually."

"What right do you have to be angry over my love life?"

"Love life? Is that what it is? You're in love with this guy? And what is he? Straight-As, no doubt. Or a jock perhaps. Is he—"

"Just answer the question, Jayson," she said, feeling her own anger rise as she considered that Jayson Wolfe was so thoroughly intense over his music—and her part in it—that he felt he had the right to control every aspect of her life. "What gives you the right to be angry over this?"

"Maybe I don't have any *rights,* but when you are well aware of how I feel about you, I don't know how you could just turn around and—"

"*Feel* about me?" she interrupted. "Is that what you said? Jayson, just because you're constantly joking about being madly in love with me, does not mean that—"

"It's not a joke, Elizabeth," he said with an intensity that was a close match for the passion he felt toward his music. "It was *never* a joke! Not to me. You're the one who brushed it away and laughed it off."

Elizabeth felt suddenly breathless. Was *she* the cause for this intensity in him that was in such close running to his music? Could it be possible? Had he been feeling all along the way she had wanted him to feel? She couldn't believe it!

Jayson watched the enlightenment fill her expression, and he felt suddenly terrified. He'd done it. He'd lost control of his senses and said what he'd been resisting for months. If she rejected him now, he wondered if he could ever cope. Could he keep his personal feelings out of the music? Not likely. How could he sing and play by her side and be utterly disconnected from her emotionally? But how could he go on in this ridiculous limbo, frustrated and aching inside?

Without warning, the ache rushed from his chest up to his head, burning into his eyes. He turned away and cursed under his breath. He *had* inherited his mother's high water table, and he *hated* it. When tears leaked out, he didn't want to lift a hand to wipe them away or she'd be onto him. So he hurried into the rain and lifted his face skyward to allow it to bathe his tears away. He was grateful to find the rain warm for this time of year, and the overall effect was soothing to his emotions. Focused on the sensation of water running over his face, he was surprised to find Elizabeth facing him. He looked into her eyes and swallowed carefully. If only to end the silence he said, "Give me the verdict, Lady. Get it over with."

"What verdict?" she asked.

"You know how I feel about you. Tell me whether or not I'm a fool."

Elizabeth lifted her chin slightly, and he became preoccupied with the way the rain slithered over her face. "If I told you that you're a fool, would you write a song about it?"

"Maybe," he said, his voice cracking.

"I can only guess how you feel about me, Jayson. Honestly . . . I believed you were joking. If that's my misinterpretation, then . . . I'm sorry, but . . . I need you to tell me; tell me again. Tell me so that I could never believe it's a joke."

"And then what? Should I pour my heart out to you just so you can tell me I'm a fool?"

Elizabeth understood the vulnerable look in his eyes and realized he needed some measure of trust, something to reach toward. And she was willing to give it. "Jayson," she said, "you have to understand that . . . all this time I thought that *I* was a fool. I admit that at first I didn't see you for who and what you really are. But the more I got to know you, the more I realized that you are . . . the most . . . amazing person I have ever known. The first time I saw you walk into school, it was like . . . my soul just reached for yours, and . . ."

Her voice broke, and she hesitated while Jayson felt his breathing become shallow. Had she just said what he thought she'd said? Had she just described what had happened to *him* the first time he'd seen *her*? He couldn't believe it!

"I didn't understand those feelings; I fought them, thinking you and I could never be compatible. But every day I realize more and more that we are of the same mind, the same spirit. You and I are so much alike, Jayson, that it scares me. And the way I feel about you scares me." A little sob erupted from her mouth. "And all this time, I thought . . . that you thought . . . I was just a spoiled . . . debutante or something, and you would never see in me what I wanted you to see. I was just so . . . in awe of you . . . your gifts . . . and the way I feel, but . . . I thought you were teasing me—mocking me. I kept hoping you'd just . . . give me a chance."

For what felt like minutes of silence, Jayson just watched her, countering her unwavering gaze, listening to the sound of the rain while he attempted to accept the reality of what she'd just told him. Her sincerity was readily evident, which was perhaps the most amazing thing of all. It was easy for him to say, "When I first came to Oregon, I paid attention to no one, nothing. I kept my eyes down. I didn't see you in class; I didn't see anybody. Then I went to see *West Side Story.* You were . . . incredible. Sitting in that auditorium, it was like . . . well, I told my mother that it was like . . . I had known you in another life; like my soul was supposed to be linked with yours." Elizabeth gasped and felt her heart quicken. "I started looking for you, but I was looking for someone with dark hair." She smiled, and he went on. "I had no idea you'd been sitting behind me in English all that time until you stood up to give your book report on *Pride and Prejudice.*" He chuckled as he said it, then added, "That pretty well describes us, doesn't it?"

"Yes, it does, actually." She took in a deep, slow breath. "Forgive me, Jayson."

"For what?"

"For being proud and prejudiced."

"If you'll forgive me as well, we can start over."

"Done," she said. He smiled, and she held out her hand. He took a step forward and took hold of it, and then he didn't move. She found herself just gazing into his eyes, while he gazed into hers. The moment was so incredible that she felt compelled to say, "This is pretty amazing, Jayson. Maybe you should write a song about it."

"Not about being a fool?"

"No, not about that. Write a song about . . . the way we feel about each other."

"I already did," he said, then his voice broke the sound of the falling rain as he sang softly, *"You stand tall while I stand in awe, yearning from a distance. My awakened senses yearn to sense you . . . close to me. Our two hearts are only one, divided by time and air and space. In another time and place . . . our two hearts were one . . . and they will be again."*

"You wrote that about us?"

"I did," he said.

"I was wishing you had the first time I heard it. If only I had known how you feel."

"How do *you* feel, Elizabeth?" he asked, taking a step toward her.

She looked up into his eyes and murmured, "I love you, Jayson Wolfe."

He laughed softly and lifted his free hand to touch her face. "Oh, how I have dreamt of hearing you say that to me."

"And what did you dream would come next?"

"First I would say, 'I love you too, Elizabeth Greer.' And then . . ." He took her chin into his fingers and closed his eyes as he bent to kiss her. Elizabeth gasped when she realized his intention, then she closed her eyes as well and lifted her face to his, taking hold of his upper arms to keep herself standing.

Jayson had imagined so many times what it might be like to kiss her that the reality felt completely surreal, impossible, *a miracle*. Something magical happened as their lips met. The feelings that had drawn him to her initially, feelings he had fought and struggled with for more than a year, came back to him with such intensity, such clarity, that he knew beyond any doubt she was destined to be a part of his life. He drew back and looked into her eyes, seeing his own awe reflected there. He was grateful to still be standing in the rain when he felt his emotion over-flowing from his eyes. Then he saw a glisten of moisture gathering in *her* eyes, and he wondered if she could tell that he was crying. Rather than worry about it, he closed his eyes and kissed her again, feeling as if he might drown in this, the most perfect moment of his life.

"Oh, Jayson," she murmured as their lips parted reluctantly. She nuzzled her face against his throat and felt his arms come around her, "this can't be happening to me. It's too wonderful to be real."

He chuckled and pressed a kiss into her wet hair. "That's what I was going to say."

Jayson's mind went back to where this conversation had begun, and he felt that one point needed to be clarified. He drew back to look at her and said, "So, what are you going to do about this idiot you've been dating?"

Elizabeth smiled. "Oh, I won't be needing him any more." She laughed softly and added, "He is a jock, you know. And he does get straight A's." Jayson's brow furrowed, and she laughed again. "However . . ." Her voice sobered, and her expression became sincere, "He's really very nice, but he's musically illiterate, and he's dull. I prefer a B-average, musically gifted, passionate-about-life kind of guy."

Jayson smiled. "Does this mean you won't be going out with him any more?"

"I didn't really think I would anyway, but you've certainly clinched it for me. I must confess there was a little part of me that couldn't help hoping he might make you jealous enough to get your attention." She grinned. "I guess it worked."

"I guess it did," he said and kissed her again.

A few minutes later, they decided they'd both better get out of the rain. They were soaked to the skin. Elizabeth laughed when Jayson picked her up and carried her beneath the awning to the door. Before going inside they took off their wet shoes and stockings and did their best to wring the excess water out of their clothes.

"Okay," she said, stepping into the house, "you go in the bathroom there." She pointed to the door close by. "I'll go change and find some of Derek's clothes for you to wear. It wouldn't be the first time you guys traded clothes."

Elizabeth hurried upstairs, grabbed some clothes and changed in the bathroom off of her bedroom, leaving her wet clothes in the bathtub. She got some of Derek's clothes and took them to Jayson, along with a plastic grocery sack for his wet things. She then retraced her steps, wiping water up off the vinyl floors, and sponging it out of the carpet with a towel. She was nearly finished when Jayson found her at the foot of the stairs. She stood to face him and realized he'd taken the elastic out of his hair and had combed it through. She'd never seen him without his hair in a ponytail, and she couldn't resist touching it. He touched her hair as well, saying, "It's more curly when it's wet. Were you born with this much curl?"

"I was," she said, "and sometimes I hate it."

"I love it," he said earnestly.

They sat together on the bottom step and talked while they held hands. Jayson kept looking at her and at her hand in his, in awe of the bridge they had crossed. He'd never dreamed he could feel so happy, so thoroughly content. They were both surprised to hear Drew and Derek coming up the stairs from the basement, laughing about something as they did.

"There you are," Derek said. "You guys hungry?"

"Maybe," they both said at the same time, then laughed.

"Hey," Derek said to Jayson while Drew went into the kitchen and opened the fridge as if he lived there, "you're wearing my clothes—and your hair's wet."

"Very observant," Jayson said. "We were out in the rain and got pretty wet. I didn't think you'd mind."

Derek noticed their clasped hands, and his brow furrowed. "What were you doing in the rain?" he asked.

"Talking," Jayson said at the same time as Elizabeth said, "Kissing."

Jayson and Derek both looked at her in surprise. Jayson chuckled. Derek just stood there with his mouth open. "Which?" Derek asked.

"Both," they answered at the same time, then laughed again.

"You're joking, right?" Derek said.

"Well, that depends," Jayson said. "If you're going to hit me for kissing your sister, then I'd say we were definitely talking."

"Yeah, we were talking," Elizabeth said with a snigger.

"You were kissing my sister?" Derek asked, seeming astonished, maybe even angry.

"Yes, actually, I was," Jayson said seriously. "Is there a problem with that?"

Derek chuckled, and it became evident he'd been teasing. "No. I just can't imagine why you'd want to."

Drew came out of the kitchen, eating a banana. "So, are we gonna work on the song some more or what?"

"No, it's fine," Jayson said. "We'll work on it tomorrow."

Derek bent over and looked at Jayson with mock amazement. He checked his brow for fever, then lifted his wrist as if to check for a pulse. "The boy is apparently ill," he said to Drew. "First the song is not fine, then it's fine. He's completely mentally sick; I'm certain of it."

Jayson laughed, and Elizabeth kicked her brother in the shin. "Ow. See what I mean," he said to Jayson. "Why would you want to kiss somebody like that?"

"She doesn't do things like that to me, because I'm nicer to her than you are."

"Did you say *kiss?*" Drew asked.

"She's mine!" Jayson said, pretending to be afraid Drew might steal her away.

"You told me a long time ago," Drew said, "that she was too tall for me."

"Yeah, that's true," Jayson said. "And you said she was hot."

"Now you guys are embarrassing me," Elizabeth said. "Maybe we should go get some pie."

"Maybe we should get some real food before we eat pie," Drew suggested.

"Maybe we should get both," Derek said.

"Okay." Elizabeth stood up. "It's on me. Let's go."

"Cool," Derek said and followed Elizabeth and Jayson to the garage.

Elizabeth drove to the diner where Leslie worked, and they were seated in her section. They ordered lunch and four different flavors of pie. When the pie was brought to the table, Drew did a little beat on the table, and they each picked up their forks in unison, took a bite, then passed their plates clockwise to the next person. They laughed and did it again, and life was perfect.

Late that evening when Jayson came home, his mother said, "You seem awfully happy."

"I am, actually."

"Quite a contrast."

"Is it?" he asked, wondering if his struggles with his feelings had been that obvious. Of course, he should have known that his mother could see right through him.

"Yes," she drawled. "What happened today to put you in such a fine mood?"

"Well," he chuckled, grateful that Drew had gone to bed, "it finally happened."

"It?" she questioned.

He leaned toward his mother and whispered loudly for effect. "Elizabeth Greer loves me."

"Really?" Leslie said and laughed softly. "I mean . . . I suspected that she did for quite some time, but . . ."

"You did?"

"Oh, yes."

"And you didn't say anything?"

"It's none of my business," she said and laughed again. "So, tell me what happened."

Jayson repeated the experience while Leslie beamed. She asked in a hushed voice, "Did you kiss her?"

He smirked and felt his face go warm. "Yes, actually."

"And?" Leslie asked with a grin.

"It was incredible," he said.

"Good," she said. "As any first kiss should be." She put a hand over his. "Just be careful. Don't let those hormones take over and get into trouble."

"I'll be careful," he said, well aware of what she meant. She'd always been very frank in teaching her sons about how powerful passion could become, and how careful a person had to be to remain in control. Jayson was determined that he would never do anything to hurt or compromise Elizabeth. He cared for her far too much for that.

They talked a while longer about Elizabeth and her fine qualities, and Jayson had to ask, "Mom, do you think every guy feels this way when he first falls in love or . . ."

"Or what?"

"Well . . . it's just that . . . it's been more than a year since I first fell for her, and my feelings have only grown since then. It's like . . . she's a part of me somehow. I hear people talk about high-school romances as if they're no big deal. They say that once you grow up, you realize it was just silly. It doesn't feel silly to me."

"I'm sure that some high-school romances *are* silly," she said. "You can't really measure your feelings against someone else's. You're the only one who knows your heart."

Jayson sighed. "Sometimes . . . what I feel . . . almost scares me."

"Why?" she asked gently.

"It's just so . . . overpowering."

"As long as you don't let your heart rule your head, as long as you can make your decisions wisely and keep your relationship appropriate, with time you will come to know and understand the purpose of your feelings. You're both young. Enjoy your time together and don't worry about such things."

Jayson looked at his mother and wondered if there was a better mom in the whole world. He hugged her and told her he loved her before he finally went to bed, but it was still a long while before he slept. He couldn't believe it. Elizabeth Greer loved him.

Chapter Nine

The following evening Jayson took Elizabeth on their first official date. He was glad to have a decent income and money in the bank so that he could take her out for a really nice dinner. They went to a place called Mo's that Elizabeth had declared was one of her favorites. They were famous for their clam chowder, seafood, and Marionberry cobbler. And since Jayson could easily include those items among his favorites, he was all for it. The food was incredible, and the company incomparable. They had a glorious time, and Jayson liked the way she made a point of clarifying where their relationship stood. Dating exclusively suited him fine, since he'd not been on a date with anyone else in more than a year anyway. They both agreed that their relationship would not interfere with their work, but they enjoyed working together so thoroughly that Jayson doubted it would ever be a problem.

After dinner they walked barefoot on the beach, even though the evening was a little cool and they kept their jackets on. He loved the feel of her arm around his waist as much as he loved keeping his arm around her. She often set her head on his shoulder as they ambled slowly through the sand, talking as comfortably as if they'd known each other forever.

Back in the car they faced each other and held hands, still talking. Elizabeth marveled at how closely related their views were on so much of life and love and everything in between. And when he put a hand into her hair and kissed her, she felt as if life could begin and end with such a moment.

"Oh, Jayson," she murmured, reaching up a hand to touch his face, "tell me I'm not dreaming."

"You *are* dreaming," he muttered, and she laughed softly. "And I pray you never wake up." He pressed his lips to her brow, and she let her hand slide to his throat. When her fingers found the chain hanging around his neck, she drew back, wanting to satisfy her curiosity. She lifted it from beneath his shirt, wondering if he might stop her. But he didn't. She didn't know what she'd expected, but she was surprised to see a little silver cross.

"Don't look so surprised," he said. "You know I go to church."

"Yes, but I didn't realize it was so . . . personal for you. You've worn this for as long as I've known you."

"That's right," he said.

"So . . . you're a Christian," she said.

"Yes," he drawled. "Aren't you? I mean . . . you don't have to go to church to believe that Christ is real and that what He did was real."

"I guess that's true," she said. "And if you put it that way, then . . . yes, I suppose I am. I've never actually been to church, but . . . well, I believe all that Christmas and Easter stuff is true. It just feels right."

"Yeah, it does," he said.

"So . . .what church do you belong to exactly?"

"I don't really belong to any church," he said. "I go to church with my mother, and she's gone to a few different ones. I don't think she cares what denomination it is as long as she can just go to church. Personally, I don't believe it matters which church you go to or belong to. What matters is the personal relationship you have with God. I don't have to go to church for that. I go because my mother wants me to be there."

"Did your dad go to church?"

"No," he scoffed. "He was always drunk on Sundays. Well," he chuckled, "he was drunk every day. But I know he came from a Mormon family."

"Ooh," she said as if he'd said his father had belonged to a satanic cult. "That's a little scary. I mean . . . I haven't heard much, but from what I've heard they're . . . weird. They're not even Christians."

"Yeah, well . . . I've heard some pretty strange things myself. I only know that anything remotely connected to my father is something I intend to steer clear of."

"So . . . do you think when you're a father that you'll take your children to church?"

"I don't know about that, but I will teach them—the way my mother taught me—that God is real and that prayer is important. As a father I could make good use of the Bible, I think."

Elizabeth smiled. "Yes, I bet you could." Holding the little cross in her fingers, she asked, "So, do you have extended family? I've never heard you talk about any."

"I don't actually," he said. "According to my mother, there was no family on my father's side worth knowing about. My mother pretty much disowned her family when she was very young, because there was so much abuse and garbage going on. She kept in touch with her mother, but she died when we were pretty little. So, it's just us. But I'm okay with that. How about you?"

"Oh, we've got relatives here and there on both sides, but no one we're really close to. All of my grandparents are dead, and the families just aren't close. So, I guess it's just us, as well."

"Well," he smiled, "our two families seem to get along pretty well. Maybe we should eventually connect them officially."

Elizabeth knew what he was implying, and she couldn't deny the fascination she felt with the idea of becoming his wife—eventually. Still, she knew their goals differed greatly, and they had to be practical. But eventually was a long ways off, and for the moment she was going to enjoy this place in her life. She just smiled back and said, "Maybe."

* * * * *

Jayson had never enjoyed school quite so much. Walking the halls with Elizabeth's hand in his was incredible. It quickly became evident that their peers, for the most part, were surprised by the match. Some thought it was great; others seemed appalled. It was also evident that no one at school was aware of the fact that Jayson and Elizabeth worked together—onstage. Their performances went on as usual, except that Jayson would always take Elizabeth's hand when they took their bows before leaving the stage. And occasionally they'd go out on the floor during their break and share a slow dance. As they moved among the crowds they always received many compliments on their performances, although the average age of the audience was much older than their seventeen years. Jayson figured that was likely the biggest reason why their band had remained unknown at their school in a different city. And he actually preferred it that way.

A few weeks after her first official date with Jayson, Elizabeth was approached by a member of the senior class presidency while opening her locker. She'd never been fond of LaRee, since she was one of those girls who was highly focused on her own good looks, and her personality was just a little too perky.

"Hi, Elizabeth," she said as if they were best friends.

"Hello," Elizabeth said and focused on putting on some lip gloss with the use of a little mirror hanging inside her locker door.

"I heard a rumor that your boyfriend is actually a brilliant musician."

Elizabeth swung her locker door closed enough to see LaRee's face. "Where did you hear that?" she asked, hoping she wouldn't regret it. LaRee had a way of talking with the impetus of a freight train once she got started. She kept picking up speed as the words got moving.

"Well, Melissa Wilkins told me that Stacey Lewis said her big brother went to this dance place in Portland where college kids go . . . and older people, too. And they have live bands part of the time, and one of the bands was really great, and he said that he heard a rumor that a couple of guys in the band went to this school. He said the band was called . . . something about wolves, and that's because of Jayson Wolfe and his brother. He said they're actually in this band and they were amazing. I told Melissa I just didn't know if it could be true. He just doesn't seem like he could be that amazing, but obviously you see something in him, so I just have to know if it's true. So is it true?"

"Now what makes you think that a guy like Jayson Wolfe couldn't be amazing?"

"I didn't mean that—"

"The thing is," Elizabeth interrupted before the train got going again, "Jayson is the most amazing guy at this school, and that has nothing to do with the fact that he is likely one of the greatest musicians of his time."

LaRee's eyes widened. "It's true then?"

Looking beyond LaRee's shoulder, Elizabeth saw Jayson approaching. "Why don't you ask him yourself?"

"Ask me what?" Jayson said behind LaRee, startling her.

"Oh, hi," she said to him, seeming flustered and nervous.

"This is LaRee," Elizabeth said, her tone bored.

"Hi, LaRee," Jayson said, taking Elizabeth's hand.

When LaRee seemed hesitant to talk, Elizabeth said, "LaRee heard a rumor that you were in a band that played at some dance place in Portland and that you were pretty amazing. I told her you *were* amazing, but it didn't have anything to do with your being a brilliant musician."

Jayson chuckled. "Did you now?" He looked at LaRee and said, "It's just a vicious rumor. The truth is that *Elizabeth* is in a band that plays at some dance place in Portland. And she wears these cool red shoes. Sometimes she wears black jeans. Sometimes blue ones. She's got all kinds of different funky shirts she wears. I mean, she performs every Saturday night; a girl can't wear the same thing every week. Although, the black is my favorite, but whatever she wears, she always wears these red shoes. And boy can she sing! She's a genius, especially with the oohs and aahs. You really should go see her sometime."

LaRee looked as if she didn't know whether to believe him or not. Elizabeth said, "Maybe you could have Melissa ask Stacey to ask her brother where this place is, and then you'll see that the real genius on stage is not me." She laughed and added, "I'm just there to make him look good."

"That's true," he said, looking into her eyes as if LaRee were not present.

"So, are you guys just pulling my leg or what? Just tell me what the real deal is."

"Why do you want to know?" Jayson asked in a gruff voice that seemed to frighten her.

"Because I'm in charge of getting a band for Girls' Preference and for Prom. And the last three bands we've had have been pathetic, and I just hate it when the band is pathetic. I'd rather have records than a pathetic band, but the committee insists that we should have a band, so when I heard that there was somebody at our school in a band and it was a good band, I just thought that I needed to find out if it was true, and if you're really as good as Stacey's brother says, then we could have you play at the dances, and they wouldn't be pathetic." While LaRee talked Elizabeth watched Jayson's eyes grow steadily wider with amazement, which made her chuckle. "So, I wish you'd stop teasing and just tell me whether or not it's true."

"I'm not playing at Prom," Jayson said firmly. "I have a date. And I can't dance and perform at the same time."

"It's true then!" LaRee said.

"Whether or not we're pathetic is for you to decide," Jayson said. "But yes, Elizabeth wears red shoes when she's on stage."

LaRee made a disgusted noise and walked away. Jayson just laughed. "You have a date for Prom?" Elizabeth asked, pretending to sound insulted. "Who is she? I'll beat her up."

"Will you go to Prom with me?" he asked.

"It's still months away."

"I know. Will you go to Prom with me?"

"Will you like . . . wear a tuxedo and buy me a corsage?"

"You'd better believe it."

"In that case, yes. It's a date."

"Good," he said. "And with any luck LaRue will—"

"LaRee will think we're pathetic and you can take me to Preference."

That afternoon Jayson got a call from Joe Wallace. He and Jayson talked for about ten minutes, then Jayson went to the Greer home and found the others all in the music room waiting for him in order to begin rehearsal.

"Hi," he said when he walked into the room, and Elizabeth's heart quickened just to see him.

"Hello," she said back. Drew and Derek just nodded in his direction, then Drew went back to his book and Derek to picking something out on the bass.

"Hey, Drew," Jayson said brightly, and his brother looked up. "I just talked to Joe."

"And?"

"Guess what song Joe wants us to do?"

"What?" Drew asked with anticipation, judging by Jayson's attitude that it must be good.

"Are you ready for this?" He paused for emphasis. "'Saturday Night's Alright . . .'"

"By Elton John!" they both said together, then laughed and did a high-five.

"Okay," Jayson said and passed out cassette tapes. "I recorded it as soon as we got off the phone. I'll be doing the guitar." He pointed at Elizabeth. "You're on the piano, Baby."

"I've told you before, I'm not a—"

"Oh, my mistake," Jayson said with sarcastic self-recrimination. "You're on the piano, *Lady.*"

"I can't do Elton John on the piano."

"This one you can," he said as if it was no big deal. "This song is heavy on the guitars. You can hardly hear the piano at all on the recording—except in the places when you *really* hear the piano, and that's the part you need to work on until it's perfect. You *have* to do the piano, because Derek and I need to be on guitars."

Elizabeth sighed. "Okay, so . . . have you got sheet music for this? I can't play by ear the way you can."

"I'll teach it to you," he said.

She followed him upstairs to the piano, and they sat side by side on the bench.

"Okay," he said, "this is it." He pressed his right hand from the low end to the high end of the keyboard in a split-second run. Then he grinned.

"That's it?"

"That's it," he said proudly.

"I can do that."

"Yes, I know you can. The timing is crucial, but you'll get the feel for it. Between the runs we just need . . . well, basically this in the verse." He tapped out a simple five-chord sequence, then did the same one octave higher.

"I can do that," she said again.

He responded, "Yes, I know you can. And on the chorus line, you're going to do this." He did a three-chord set in three different places while he sang softly.

"Okay," she said and moved a little closer to him on the bench, looking at him instead of the piano. "Show me that part again."

"You're not even looking," he chuckled.

"Yes, I am." She smiled. "I'm just not looking at the piano."

She put a hand to his face and touched her lips to his just in time to hear a loud, "Ahem."

They both turned to see Will standing in the doorway, his hands on his hips. With astonishment he said, "You're kissing my daughter?"

Jayson wondered how he was supposed to respond. Will knew they'd been dating, and he'd seemed happy about it. Jayson didn't see any reason to pretend that things weren't as they appeared. He tried to keep it light by saying, "Actually . . . she was kissing me."

Will smirked, and Jayson realized he'd been teasing. "At least she's got good taste," Will said. "Just mind your manners, now," and Jayson chuckled.

"Of course," he said.

Will left the room, and Elizabeth said, "Sorry."

They both laughed, then went back to the music room and sat together to listen to the Elton John version of the song. Before Jayson turned on the tape, he smirked at Elizabeth and said, "This is a rebel song, Lady. In fact, I would call this song Elizabeth's first impression of Jayson Wolfe."

"Some of it could be true," Drew said.

"Just play the song," Elizabeth said, and he did.

Elizabeth found him smirking at her again as they listened to Elton John singing about getting drunk and fighting, about switchblades and motorbikes, about rebelling against discipline. And that certainly wasn't the Jayson she'd come to know. But there were a few lines that stood out to her as actually suiting him rather well—in a positive kind of way. He was just a *little* bit of a rebel. And that's the way she liked him.

When the song was over, she repeated what Drew had said, "Some of it could be true."

He just smiled at her and played the song again.

The following day, Elizabeth went down to the music room, knowing Jayson was there by himself. She entered the room to find him playing the guitar for the *Saturday* number. He was wearing headphones with an extremely long cord, and his eyes were closed while he played the guitar with energy and a studied power. She sat and watched him and realized he was listening to the original in the headphones. He stopped in the middle to rewind the tape a little, but with his back turned, he didn't see her before he started again, and this time he sang the song with a tough demeanor and a rugged edge to his voice that suited the song so well. She could easily imagine how much fun this would be to play onstage with him.

Completely oblivious to her presence, Jayson kept his eyes closed, singing, dancing, jumping, playing his soul out on that guitar. Then the song ended, and he turned around to shut off the tape. And that's when he noticed her sitting there, leaning back in a chair, her arms folded.

"How long have you been there?" he asked, pulling off the headphones.

"Long enough to know that I'm in love with you," she said, and he laughed.

A moment later Derek and Drew showed up. They went over the song several times before Jayson said, "You know guys, this song is perfect for the Mannheim Steamroller effect."

"So it is," Drew said, seeming pleased. "We can have the audience so pumped they won't know what hit them."

"Mannheim Steamroller?" Elizabeth said. "You mean like 'Fresh Aire'?"

"No," Jayson drawled, "as I understand it, the people who do 'Fresh Aire' named themselves after the Mannheim Steamroller effect. It's basically when the music continues to build momentum. And that's what we're going to do with this song."

"Cool," Elizabeth said and sat at the keyboard. "Let's do it."

By the time Saturday rolled around, the new song was ready for a debut, and Elizabeth had never had so much fun with a number as she had with this one. They used it as an opener for the second hour of their show, and the room was bursting with positive energy by the time the song ended. Never had she heard such applause. They'd had some newspaper guy in the lounge during their break to talk with them, and she hoped that he'd stuck around long enough to hear that number. She felt so completely proud of these boys she was playing with that she had trouble resisting giving them each a big hug right there on stage. They were amazing—all of them. But especially Jayson. She wondered if he had any idea how talented and full of musical energy he really was.

Two days later they were all sitting on the floor of the TV room at the Greer home when Will appeared and set a newspaper in the middle of them. "You got a review," he said with a grin.

"Holy asterisk!" Derek said as their heads all bent toward two different pictures of them onstage, with an impressively large headline that read, *Saturday Night's Alright for A Pack of Wolves.*

"Here, I'll read it," Elizabeth said, picking up the paper. She cleared her throat dramatically and began to read aloud. "'I've been reviewing hometown bands for years, you know. I'm certain many of you reading this have been following the trends right along with me. I know how these local dance halls work. If you get there at opening, it's practically empty, and the crowds fill in slowly. So naturally, I wondered what might be going on when I arrived five minutes before the band was set to play and the place was packed. It soon became evident the regulars knew something I didn't know. The show was going to be good, and they didn't want to miss a minute. The curtain went up to a deafening roar, but when these four teenagers appeared onstage, I wondered what all the fuss was about. Then, as casually as breathing, they jumped into an impressive rendition of some of rock's hottest songs. And the crowds were psyched. The place cooled down a little with recorded music while the band took a half-hour break, and we had a little chat in the lounge. I felt sufficiently impressed and ready to be on my way when, working my way through the crowd to the door, I was struck by a hot current in the air and couldn't resist holding out for just one more number. Pretty boy Jayson Wolfe stepped up to the—'"

"What did he call me?" Jayson interrupted, clearly insulted.

"Oh, be quiet and listen," Elizabeth scolded, then read on. "'. . . Stepped up to the microphone and greeted his fans with the announcement that it was Saturday. The fans' response alone threatened to bring the house down, then the mercury jumped to the top of the thermometer with a near-perfect clone of Elton John's classic, *Saturday Night's Alright for Fighting.* By then I was so caught up in the feeding frenzy that I had to sit out the rest of the show.'"

Elizabeth lifted her eyes and smirked at Jayson before she continued to read. "'Lead singer, guitarist, pianist Jayson Wolfe is everything a front man should be. He seems to have taken a quantum leap from some unknown platinum musical cosmos where rare musicians are bred. It can be the only explanation to the questions on every tongue on the dance floor. Where did he come from, and where did he learn to woo these instruments with such finesse at such a tender age? One simply wouldn't guess that he's pulling a B-average—'"

"How did they know *that?*" Jayson asked.

"Obviously, they called the school," Will said.

"Good thing you got your grades up," Elizabeth said. "Who'd have dreamed they'd advertise them in the papers?"

"Get on with it," Derek said impatiently.

"'. . . a B-average at a local high school? Were these Wolfe boys weaned from Gerber to guitars? Jayson is kept on beat by his brother, Drew, who obviously eats and sleeps with perfect rhythm. Derek Greer, who expertly monopolizes the bass-line, is clearly as much at home with his instrument as the rest of his mates. Elizabeth Greer, the only female member of Wolves, improves the scenery on stage, although—'"

Derek started to laugh, and she glared at him.

"Well, it's true," Jayson said, nudging him with an elbow.

"Keep reading," Drew said.

"'. . . Although, it's not difficult to imagine these good-looking lads gracing the covers of teen rock magazines. Beyond adding some feminine grace to the stage, Miss Greer adds texture to an already-rich sound with a variety of unique additions to rock and roll. Appearing onstage with a flute or violin, one might expect something classical to roll off, but she blends the sound into a well-performed montage of rock classics as well as a few originals that bring the house down. The blended voice of Wolves is the icing on a cake that any rock fan should take a big, hearty bite of. Sit up, Portland, and pay attention. Better yet, get on the floor and dance. The opportunity isn't likely to last forever. I smell a record deal in the wind.'"

"Wow," Derek said. Jayson just let out a little laugh. He could smell it too.

* * * * *

The following day LaRee practically assaulted Elizabeth and Jayson when they walked into the cafeteria together for lunch. She'd obviously attended their Saturday-night performance but had missed school the previous day and was so excited now that she'd caught up with them. She talked like a freight train for a good ten minutes about how incredible it had been, while Jayson and Elizabeth ate their lunch and nodded occasionally. They were officially invited to play at Preference, and Jayson reluctantly agreed. When LaRee finally left them in peace, Elizabeth said, "You don't seem very happy about that."

"I'm not sure I want to play for . . ." he looked around at the crowded lunchroom, "these people."

"These people ought to know how incredible you are."

"*We* are, you mean," he insisted.

"It's *your* brainchild," she said. "You're the genius, you know." She lowered her voice to mimic the newspaper reporter, "'everything a front man should be.'"

He made a dubious noise and finished his lunch.

That evening the band was in the basement rehearsing another new number that Joe had suggested, even though Drew was on a date. They figured they could put the drums in later. They were interrupted when Will came into the room looking more somber than Jayson had ever seen him. His stomach actually tightened when Will said, "Derek, Elizabeth. Your mother and I need to talk with you. It could take a while." He glanced toward Jayson and said, "You're welcome to stay and practice if you'd like."

Jayson saw Elizabeth and Derek each toss him a concerned glance before they left the room with their father, who closed the door.

Twenty minutes later Jayson decided that maybe it would be better if he just left. He crept quietly up the stairs and found it impossible not to overhear the conversation coming from the dining room. And what he heard guided him to the firm conclusion that maybe he'd better stay. He had a feeling Derek and Elizabeth were going to need a friend. So he went quietly back down the stairs to wait until the fireworks died down.

* * * * *

"What's up?" Derek asked when they entered the dining room to see their mother sitting at one end of the table.

"Have a seat," Will said, and Elizabeth had a sudden attack of nerves. She couldn't remember the last time she'd seen her mother actually sitting at the table, and it had been even longer since the four of them had gathered to talk. In fact, the four of them hadn't done *anything* together for years.

When they were all seated, Meredith looked at her husband and said with a bitter edge, "Well, are you going to tell them, or do you want me to do it?"

"You're the one who wants this, Meredith. This isn't my doing. Why don't *you* tell them."

Elizabeth exchanged a concerned glance with Derek. She'd *never* heard her father speak that way in all her life. The bitterness in his voice consumed her with uneasy chills.

"Fine," Meredith said. "It's time the two of you were made aware of the situation. Your father and I are getting a divorce."

"What?" Elizabeth practically shrieked. She looked at the despair in her father's countenance and couldn't imagine how any woman could be crazy enough to leave a man like William Greer. "How can you be so stupid?" she shouted at her mother. "Don't you know how he loves you?"

"You have no idea what you're talking about," Meredith said. "Now be quiet for a few minutes and listen to what I have to say."

For nearly half an hour, they sat in silence while Meredith harped about the hardships of her life, the insensitivity of her husband that her children could never understand, and the pressures of a career that they were all oblivious to. She rambled vague references about needing to find herself and how she couldn't be expected to be a wife and mother when she was under such strain. To Elizabeth it sounded as if she were not only announcing divorce, she was declaring the official abandonment of her children. She noticed Derek sitting quietly, his arms folded, his expression hard. Occasionally, his chin quivered, and she knew he was fighting back tears. She cried silently, unable to hold back her emotion. She noticed her father doing the same while her mother went on and on. When it seemed she was finally finished, Elizabeth stood from the table, saying hotly, "It's not a surprise, really. You haven't wanted anything to do with any of us for years. At least now we won't have to dread your coming home and making us all miserable."

"Why, you ungrateful little—"

Will interrupted Meredith with a firm voice. "I think you've said enough, Mrs. Greer. Why don't you just pack your things and go."

Elizabeth rushed from the room and down to the basement, praying that Jayson hadn't left. She heard Derek right behind her and knew they had two strong common bonds at the moment. They were both losing their mother, and they both needed the support and understanding that they knew Jayson could give them. She opened the door to the music room, and their eyes met. The compassion in Jayson's expression melted what little resolve she had left. She moved abruptly into his arms, clinging to him tightly as the tears rushed out. Attempting to offer an explanation, she muttered, "My mother . . ."

She had trouble finishing due to her emotion, but he said gently, "I know. I heard. I went up, wondering if I should just leave. I heard what she was saying and decided I'd better stay."

"Oh!" She clung to him more tightly as if to express her gratitude for his staying, then she turned her attention to Derek as he sat down and pressed his head into his hands, obviously crying.

Jayson took hold of Elizabeth's hand and moved to sit beside Derek, with Elizabeth sitting on the other side of Jayson, her head on his shoulder. "Hey there, bud," Jayson said. "You gonna be okay?"

Derek just shook his head and kept crying. Jayson cursed his own high water table when tears quickly surfaced on behalf of his friends. He kept a hand on Derek's back and put his other arm around Elizabeth while she cried on his shoulder. He caught movement in the room and looked up to see Will standing in front of them. Derek and Elizabeth were oblivious to his presence until he said to Jayson, "Have you got room for me to cry on your shoulder as well?"

Will's children looked up at him, both wiping at their tears. He looked at each of them, then looked down and shook his head. "I'm so sorry," he said.

"It's not your fault," Derek said vehemently.

"It's hard to say what went wrong," Will said, "or when. I wonder what I could have done differently. I suppose that's irrelevant now, but . . . I'm sorry you had to be hit with it so suddenly." Emotion was evident in his voice. "I . . . don't suppose it will change the way we live much, but . . . I guess I just kept holding onto the hope that . . . she would come around. Now that hope is gone." His voice broke, and he sat down on a chair that was facing them, lowering his head into his hands the same way Derek had.

"How long have you known," Jayson asked, "that . . . it had come to this?"

"A couple of hours," Will said and wiped tears from his face.

"I'm truly sorry," Jayson said.

Elizabeth sniffled and stated the obvious, "Your parents are divorced."

"Yeah," he chuckled without humor, "but my situation is much different."

"How is that?"

"Divorce was the best thing that ever happened to us. I'm not saying divorce is a good thing; I'm saying that when it's better than living a lie—or living in hell—then it's a positive option." He sighed and added, "At least your mother is leaving quietly."

"I take it your father didn't," Will said.

"No, he certainly didn't," Jayson said.

"Tell me about it," Will urged, and Jayson wondered if he wanted some distraction for his children—or perhaps even himself. There had been a time when he'd felt hesitant to have people know about his history, fearing it might diminish his standing in their eyes. But he'd long ago learned that these people would care for him no matter what.

"Well," Jayson said, "my earliest memory is waking up in my bed to hear my father yelling . . . drunk . . . and my mother screaming . . . because he was beating her."

Will gasped. Derek and Elizabeth had both heard pieces of this story before.

"It happened regularly. I mean . . . not *all* the time, but far too often. When I was seven I got angry and tried to protect her. I was in the hospital for nearly a week. That's when my mother got the divorce. She told me that it was one thing to have him hurt *her*, but when he'd hurt one of her children, she'd reached her limit. I remember her talking to a police officer and a social worker in my hospital room. They thought I was asleep. She was gutsy. She told them she would be having the locks changed, she wanted a restraining order immediately, and she wanted two officers to be present when my father came home from work to be told that he was no longer welcome. I was still in the hospital when that happened, but Drew said there were some pretty nasty fireworks. Mom put his stuff in the carport and told him he had twenty minutes to put it in his truck and leave. I think if the police hadn't been there, he'd have killed her."

"I had no idea that your mother had endured so much," Will said.

"She's quite a woman," Jayson said with overt admiration. "Her father and brothers treated her at least as bad, but . . . I guess that's not my place to talk about."

"So, have you seen your father since then?" Will asked.

"I'm sorry to say that I have," Jayson said. "He'd show up once in a while, usually when he wanted money. Of course, she'd never give it to him, but he'd keep trying. Sometimes it was weeks; sometimes years. The last time he showed up was in the middle of the night after . . ."

"What?" Will asked when Jayson hesitated.

Jayson sighed loudly. "It was my mother's birthday—the day we'd given her that song."

"'Funeral for a Friend,'" Derek said.

"We'd had a great evening, and then I woke up to hear her screaming, and it all came back to me. I surprised him, though. He hadn't seen me for a few years, and I was big enough to let him have it."

"That's how Jayson got this scar," Elizabeth said proudly while she touched his cheekbone.

"And that's when Mom decided we were moving—and here we are."

"Well, I for one am grateful," Will said, "that you came here. My children have never had a finer friend, Jayson. We're glad to have you as part of the family."

Jayson felt choked up. "I'm the grateful one," he said. Wanting to divert the attention from his own emotion, he cleared his throat and said, "You know one of the things I hate most about my father?"

"What?" Elizabeth asked.

"The fact that I was named after him," Jayson said with chagrin. "His name is Jay."

"Oh," Derek said, "so that's why your name is spelled that way. Jay-son." He chuckled. "I get it."

"You're quick," Jayson said with light sarcasm.

"Well, Jayson is a fine name," Will said. "And so far, you're making great use of it. I want you to know that I think it's admirable to see the way you and Drew have chosen not to follow in your father's footsteps."

"Who would want to?" Jayson asked. "But I think our mother deserves the credit for that."

"Well, some of it, I'm sure," Will said, "but don't sell yourself short. You've made choices on how to live and behave in spite of some great challenges."

Jayson felt embarrassed and was relieved when the topic turned to the new turn of events for the Greer family. They talked for nearly two hours about how they felt and how they were going to handle the situation. As Will had said, life wouldn't actually change much. It was more the loss of hope they were grieving over. Jayson knew that Derek and Elizabeth had always longed to feel some validation and evidence of love from their mother, and now she had delivered the final blow in turning her back on them completely and officially. Will believed they would likely see her very little, that she had found a life for herself elsewhere, a life that she preferred. He felt certain the divorce would be quick. She was taking little beyond her personal belongings and her own income.

Over the next few days, Jayson saw the shock of the divorce settle into his friends and then wear off. It seemed that once they'd become accustomed to the idea, their biggest concern was how it would affect their father. He was accustomed to living without his wife around much, but Will loved Meredith, and it seemed his heart was broken. Jayson looked up to Will as a father and hoped and prayed that he would find happiness in the future.

Chapter Ten

Weeks passed, and Jayson settled more comfortably into his place among the Greer family. For him, Meredith's absence made him feel more at home. He'd rarely seen her, but he'd always feared she might come in and find him in her home and get angry. Now it was Will's home, and he treated Jayson like one of his own children. Drew spent a great deal of time in their home as well, but he had his own friends and was rarely around beyond rehearsal times. Leslie often came by to hear them practice and see how they were doing, declaring that she would rarely see her sons if she didn't see them at the Greer home. She and Will got along well, and Jayson couldn't help thinking that it was nice the two of them shared some level of friendship. After Will's divorce was final, he and Leslie occasionally rode together to Portland to hear their children play, and went out to dinner as well. The kids speculated on whether or not their parents might ever develop a romantic interest. They all agreed that it would be a little weird, but not necessarily a bad thing. Still, they felt that it wasn't ever likely to really happen. Leslie hadn't dated *at all* since her divorce, and Will was still pretty brokenhearted.

During the month of December, the band put a few jazzed-up Christmas songs into their repertoire and had everybody dancing to "Jingle Bells," "Winter Wonderland," and "Rockin' Around the Christmas Tree." The holidays were the best Jayson had ever known. While he shared the heart of the Christmas celebrations at home with his mother and Drew, they all spent time with the Greers, and he found joy in the season like he never had. They all went caroling a couple of times, and several times they gathered in the Greers' front room to sing carols while Jayson and Elizabeth took turns playing the piano.

For Christmas Jayson gave Elizabeth a beautiful, rather large, wooden jewelry box with four little drawers in it. When the bottom drawer opened, a music box was activated. Elizabeth listened for half a minute, then smiled when she recognized the song as "Somewhere," the love theme from *West Side Story*. "That's when I first fell in love with you," he said. Even though the character she'd played had not actually sung this song, he felt it was appropriate. While the music tinkled, Elizabeth sang the lyrics in a soft voice.

In one of the other little drawers, she found a gold necklace with a tiny treble clef hanging on it. She squealed with delight and let Jayson fasten it around her neck before she kissed him.

Elizabeth gave Jayson a very classy brocade vest and a beautiful, long black leather coat. It was designed like a classic raincoat, but made of fine, soft leather. She told him she'd seen it months earlier and had felt drawn to it, thinking it went so well with his personality and the unique way that he dressed. He truly loved it and wore it practically everywhere.

For Jayson, the year began with great hope on the horizon. Life felt perfect to him, and he could see good things ahead as graduation came closer. When the time came, Preference was a huge success. Performing at their own school was something that they all agreed felt a little strange, but it went well, and the response was more zealous than normal. Literally overnight, Jayson and Derek became more popular at school than the jocks. Jayson took it in stride beyond an occasional comment to Elizabeth about how flaky people could be. Derek thoroughly enjoyed it, making it a personal challenge to see how many different girls he could go out with before graduation. Jayson was just glad to have Elizabeth at his side and really didn't care about anything else. The only thing in life that bothered him at all was a subtly growing restlessness he felt concerning his music. More and more it became a topic of discussion among the band. They enjoyed their job, but it was getting a little monotonous, and the boys all agreed that this was not what they intended to spend the rest of their lives doing. They speculated over a future of making it big, of hearing their own music on the radio, of touring the world and going platinum with record sales.

When they talked like that, Elizabeth had trouble admitting—even to herself—how uneasy it made her feel. She knew they were capable of doing it. She was also realistic enough to know that it was a dog-eat-dog world and that getting that kind of success—and keeping it—could be a difficult life. She also knew that the music industry world was famous for a lifestyle she wanted no part of. When she privately shared her feelings with Jayson, he asked, "What are you saying? That I shouldn't do this? I can't keep playing other people's music, Lady. I can't."

"I'm not saying that at all," she said. "You *have* to do it. It's who you are. It's in your blood. Your music is amazing. I'm saying that *I* can't do it. That's not what I want for *my* life, Jayson. I love being onstage with you, but I don't want to spend my life on the stage. It's just not for me."

"Okay, but . . . we don't have to be onstage together to be together. We're supposed to be together, Elizabeth," he insisted. "I know it with everything inside of me."

"I feel that way too, Jayson," she said, "but . . . I just don't know how it could ever work. I want to get a degree. I want to raise a family in a stable home environment, with a father that comes home every day. I want a life that's . . . calm and predictable."

"So you're saying that we can't raise a good family in a stable environment if I'm making records and going on tour?"

"Well, what do you think, Jayson? I know you're not naive about what that kind of life can be like. We would either be starving because nobody has the sense to see how amazing you are, or we'd never be together because I'd have to share you with the world. I see the potential in you, Jayson. I see it more than anybody. You're capable of doing it, and I know you will. But it's going to be a tough life, and I just don't know if I can live it with you." When he said nothing, she went on, "I can't be raising children alone while you're out dazzling the world—or starving because you can't find anybody with the right connections to believe in you."

"So . . . what? I'm doomed to be a horrible husband and father because I have music in my heart?"

"That's not what I mean."

"Then what do you mean? There must be a way to make some compromise."

"Maybe," she said, "but . . . LA is a long way from Boston."

"Boston?" he echoed as if he'd never heard of it.

She drew courage and just said what she needed to say. "I've got a scholarship. I'm going to Boston to go to school."

He looked at her as if she'd told him she was becoming a nun. "When did this happen?"

She looked down. "Last week."

"And you didn't tell me? You were applying at schools in Boston and you didn't tell me?"

"I was afraid you'd be angry."

"You bet I'm angry. You tell me I'm supposed to be a great musician and I need to go to LA to make that happen. You tell me we're supposed to be together. And you tell me you're going to Boston. How does this add up, Lady? Explain it to me."

She drew the courage to look at him. "Maybe it just doesn't add up. Maybe it never will."

Jayson gave a scoffing chuckle. "How can you and I not add up? I feel as strongly about you as I have ever felt about my music. How can I be forced to choose?"

"Maybe we just need some time," she said.

"Maybe we do," he agreed, certain that with time she would come to understand what he knew with every molecule of his being. They were destined to be together. He just knew it. He was grateful to drop the subject and to resume their relationship as usual. As long as they ignored that one point, everything was fine. He just didn't want to think about Elizabeth going away to Boston. So he didn't.

With the coming of spring, Jayson found himself anticipating Prom and the opportunity to take Elizabeth. He'd never been to a formal dance before, and when he finally arrived at her door, wearing a tux, a corsage in hand, he actually felt nervous. When Will answered the door, Jayson was surprised to find his mother there. She'd told him she had somewhere to go; he'd not realized that her intent was to be present when Jayson picked up his date. Jayson teased her while she straightened his tie and brushed her hands over the shoulders of his jacket. But he became oblivious to everything but Elizabeth when he looked up to see her coming down the stairs in a shimmery blue gown, her hair pinned into an array of curls on top of her head. He felt Will nudge him with an elbow, and Jayson said quietly, "You have a beautiful daughter, Will."

"Yes, I do," he said with pride.

"Wow," Elizabeth said at the foot of the stairs, "you clean up well."

Jayson chuckled. "You look incredible," he said, reaching out a hand toward her.

He was grateful for his mother's help in pinning on the corsage, and she helped with the boutonniere as well, even though her water table was obviously a problem. Will insisted on taking several pictures, then they each shared careful embraces with their parents and left.

For Jayson, the evening was like heaven. Dinner was wonderful, Elizabeth was beautiful, and at the dance he only had eyes for her. He was even relatively oblivious to the mediocre band that was covering the music. The only problem was that the evening came to an end.

Elizabeth watched Jayson closely as he drove toward her home. With her hand in his, she felt somehow close to heaven. He was such an incredible person that she was continually amazed at how much he loved her. She wondered what she would ever do without him, and it occurred to her that maybe they *could* compromise and come up with a future together. She had a very clear image in her mind of what her future would be like, and it was easy to imagine Jayson a part of it. The problem was that her visions were not the same as his, and she wasn't sure how to make that work. But for the moment she just enjoyed basking in his presence, wishing they could be young and in love forever.

At the door of her home, she asked, "You want to come in?"

He smiled. "No . . . thank you. I want this evening to end right here. Not laughing in the kitchen over Derek's bad jokes."

She smiled back. "Good point."

"But I'll see you tomorrow . . . of course."

"Of course," she said. "Tomorrow's Saturday. We have to work."

"How miserable," he said with light sarcasm and a little smirk. He bent to kiss her, and Elizabeth closed her eyes, savoring the feel of his lips over hers. His kiss had become familiar to her over the months they'd been dating, but it had never lost its ability to make her tingle. There were moments when she sensed his passion and moments when she felt the stirrings of passion within herself. But never had she felt threatened by his affection or concerned that it might get out of hand. Now, just as the first time he'd kissed her in the rain, his kiss was sweet, meek, unassuming. There was something so perfectly giving and gentlemanly in his affection. Still, she marveled at how he could continually surprise her. As his mouth softened over hers, she felt something newly electric surge through her, making her want for this moment to never end. He eased back and looked into her eyes as if he could find the answer there to the meaning of life.

"Thank you, Lady, for a perfect evening."

"Thank *you,*" she said and laughed softly. "It *was* perfect, wasn't it?"

"It think it was the highlight of my high-school career."

Elizabeth smiled. "Mine too."

Jayson smiled in return. Considering her popularity and all she had accomplished and participated in, he had to take that as a huge compliment. He kissed her once more and resisted the urge to kiss her still again, not wanting to dilute the experience.

"I love you, Elizabeth," he said, touching her face.

"I love you too, Jayson," she replied, returning the gesture. He kissed her once more quickly, then walked away. Elizabeth watched him go, certain that life could be no better than this.

The following day Jayson felt so thoroughly enchanted from the previous evening that when he saw Elizabeth he felt as if he were falling for her all over again. He marveled at the intensity of his feelings and knew he was destined to share his life with her. Following typical greetings, while her eyes sparkled toward him, they embarked on the usual routine of loading their equipment and driving to Portland. While Elizabeth was in the ladies' room changing, and Drew was reading, Derek sat beside Jayson on the couch in the lounge and spoke in an unusually somber tone. "So, are you going to marry my sister?" he asked.

"I'd sure like to," Jayson admitted, taking note of a rare serious moment between them. "I really do love her, Derek. I hope you're okay with that."

"Well, that just gives us one more thing in common. I love her too." He chuckled. "But don't tell her." More seriously he added, "I know you'll take good care of her."

"I'll certainly do my best—if she'll let me." He nudged him with an elbow and added, "So you think you could handle being my *official* brother."

"Oh, yeah," Derek said. "But I don't need you to marry my sister to consider you my brother." Their eyes met, and Jayson wondered what had brought on this tender moment from a guy who was always so full of fun and laughter.

Rather than analyzing it too deeply, Jayson just smiled. "Amen," he said and playfully slapped Derek's face.

Two weeks before graduation, Jayson, Derek, and Elizabeth were speculating over how they might celebrate the big event. While Jayson felt some concern over the uncertainty of what might happen beyond that, he couldn't help but anticipate achieving this milestone and being able to press forward with his dreams. He had difficulty with the idea that he and Elizabeth might temporarily be separated while she went to Boston and he went to LA, but he felt certain that eventually they would be married and be able to make their every dream come true. They had talked about continuing to work through the summer, if only to keep adding to the savings accounts that would help them through the coming months.

The school asked if the band would play at the graduation dance, but Jayson firmly declined. It would be a night for celebration, and he didn't want to spend it working. While he certainly enjoyed his time on stage, he was still playing other people's songs for the most part, and the work of setting up and taking down the equipment was tedious.

Eleven days before graduation, Jayson and his mother went to the Greer home right after church and had Sunday dinner with them while Drew spent the day with friends. They all pitched in to make the meal and had a glorious time visiting over the table and then cleaning it up together. In the middle of the afternoon, Derek excused himself to go and visit a girl at her home. Jayson teased him, since this was the only girl he'd ever taken out more than once. Derek took it in stride, then made a comical display of hugging everyone in the room good-bye, as if he would be leaving for a year.

"Don't worry about me, Jayse," he said with mock emotion, his hands planted on Jayson's shoulders. "I'll be all right. Wherever it is they send me, I promise to never forget you." He pretended to sob and hugged Jayson once more. "You're the best friend a guy could ever have."

Jayson laughed and surprised Derek by putting him in a headlock and giving him a noogie. "The feeling is mutual, buddy," Jayson said.

When he let go, Derek fell on the floor, pretending to have a seizure until his father laughed and said, "Where do you get your talent, son?"

"That's what I'd like to know," Elizabeth muttered with mock disgust.

Derek jumped to his feet and startled Elizabeth by hugging her tightly. "Oh, Elizabeth," he said with exaggerated drama, "did I ever tell you that you're my favorite sister?"

"Not recently," she said with a chuckle. "But since you mentioned it, I must admit that you're my favorite brother."

"Oh, I knew it. I knew it."

Derek did a little dance around the kitchen, and Leslie said, "Where does he get all of his energy?"

"It's hard to say," Will said, and Derek finally headed toward the door.

An hour later, Jayson and Leslie went home, since Sunday evening was traditionally a time when Leslie liked to visit quietly with Jayson and catch up on life. Elizabeth knew that Jayson was spending some quality time with his mother, so she did the same with her father. While they sat at the kitchen table, she appreciated the way they could talk about anything, and she hoped that they would always be close. She thought how much she would miss him when she went away to school, and how lonely he would be with both her and Derek living in different cities. It occurred to her that Leslie would be in the same boat. She couldn't help hoping that they might enjoy each other's company. For her, the idea of a romance developing between them was appealing. Leslie was everything Elizabeth had ever wanted in a mother, and in spite of her relationship with Jayson, she felt sure that her father and Leslie could enrich each other's lives even more than they already had.

Elizabeth heard the doorbell and remained at the table while her father went to answer it. She heard an official-sounding voice ask, "Is this the Greer home?"

"Yes," Will said with obvious concern in his voice, and Elizabeth hurried to the door, wondering who on earth it could be. Her stomach knotted up when she came into the front hall to see two police officers at the door.

"Are you the father of Derek Greer?" one of the officers asked in a voice that was unusually compassionate. His tone didn't imply that Derek was in trouble—as if he would be.

"Yes," Will said again, his tone expressing a subdued panic.

Elizabeth put a hand over her mouth as the implication began to sink in. A montage of memories swirled in her mind, as if her brain had absorbed an hour's worth of thought in a single moment. And somehow she knew. Somehow in the deepest part of her soul she knew what had happened even before the officer said, "There's been an accident."

What Elizabeth heard through the next few minutes felt cloudy and obscure, while it pierced her to the very core. She couldn't think. She couldn't breathe. She couldn't accept what she'd just heard as reality until she watched her father crumble, and his pain seemed to connect with her own. It was true. Derek was dead.

When she and her father were left alone, they clung to each other and sobbed. The horror was coated with disbelief, but not enough to buffer an anguish unlike anything she'd ever experienced. When they had both calmed down, holding hands in stunned silence, Elizabeth could only think of one thing. "I need to tell Jayson."

Will squeezed his eyes closed as if he couldn't bear the thought. But he said with a hoarse voice, "We should go together."

Elizabeth nodded. She didn't want to go alone, and she didn't want to face Jayson on her own, but still she said, "I need to be the one to tell him."

"I understand," Will said.

Until the car pulled out of the garage, Elizabeth hadn't realized it was raining—good and hard. As they drove, they both went through bouts of tears, taking turns muttering, "I can't believe it. I just can't believe it."

Elizabeth looked out the window as familiar scenery passed by. She marveled that life was going on and people were behaving normally. The world should have stopped. For her it had. And she knew that in a matter of minutes, the world would stop for Jayson as well. The very thought pressed her into helpless sobbing. She wrapped her arms around her middle and curled around them, amazed at the literal pain inside. Her tears continued while the wipers scraped frantically over the windshield of the car, futilely trying to keep up with the continuing downpour. She tried to calm down as her father parked the car; then they ran to the apartment door, where she pounded with her fist, praying he would be there, that he'd be awake. She didn't even know what time it was. Her relief when he opened the door was so intense that she practically collapsed into his arms, crying without control.

Jayson took in Elizabeth's emotion the same moment he realized that Will was standing in the doorway. His expression provoked Jayson's quickened heart into a painful thudding. As Will stepped inside and closed the door, Jayson wanted to ask him what might be wrong, but Will gave a little nod that seemed to say he needed to ask Elizabeth.

"Good heavens, Elizabeth. What is it?" Jayson asked. "What's happened?" She just cried harder and held to him more tightly until he took her shoulders into his hands and shook her gently. "Talk to me! What's happened?"

Elizabeth swallowed hard and coughed in an effort to find her voice. "He . . . Somebody . . . ran a red light and . . . he . . . he . . ."

Jayson's pounding heart threatened to jump out of his throat. He couldn't recall ever feeling so afraid in his life. "Who? *Who?*"

"Derek," she said, and his thudding heart came to a dead stop, dropping to the pit of his stomach. "He . . . he was hit . . . broadside. He . . . he was gone . . . before they . . . even got to him."

Jayson sucked in a hard breath, as if a shock of wind had rushed into his lungs then refused to be let out. His chest began to burn for want of air. He teetered and dropped to his knees, still holding to Elizabeth's arms. "I can't breathe," he muttered. "I can't breathe." He pulled in more air, but he couldn't let it out. His surroundings began to blacken. "Oh, please help me. I can't breathe."

Elizabeth was startled by her father urging her aside. He knelt to face Jayson, taking his face into his hands. "Breathe, Jayson," he said, looking into his eyes. "Come on, breathe with me." Will took a deep breath and let it out slowly. "Breathe with me," he said again, and Jayson forced out a long breath, and with it came a whisper of a sob. "Breathe with me," Will said once more.

Jayson let out another breath and felt his surroundings become more solid. As the fear of losing consciousness subsided, the reality washed over him. A tangible weight settled onto his shoulders, tightening around every muscle in his body, like a lead blanket that wrapped around him and held fast. He looked into Will's eyes and saw the reflection of his own shock and disbelief. "No," he heard himself say. He shook his head as if he could make what he'd heard not be true. "No, no, no!" he sputtered. "It's not . . . it can't . . . he wouldn't . . ."

"I'm afraid it's true," Will said, and Jayson groaned and doubled over, collapsing against Will, whose arms came around him.

"No!" Jayson howled, holding to Will as if he might die himself otherwise.

Elizabeth felt her own emotion recede into shock as she stood, dazed and afraid, watching the reality sink into Jayson. The intensity of his reaction was somehow frightening. She loved Derek, and the loss was deep; she couldn't imagine life ever being the same for her. But her love for Jayson made the loss doubly difficult. She knew Jayson, heart and soul. She knew the depth of his bond with Derek. Elizabeth had lost her brother. Jayson had lost a friend who had become a brother, and he had lost an integrated part of his music. In that moment she felt so afraid on his behalf that she began to tremble all over again.

While Jayson sobbed helplessly in Will's arms, Elizabeth saw Leslie come into the room, her expression full of panic. Her eyes took in the scene, then turned to Elizabeth. "What's happened?" she demanded quietly, apparently knowing she'd never get an answer out of Jayson in his present state.

With a croaking voice she managed to say, "Derek . . . an accident . . . he's dead."

Leslie put a hand over her mouth and another to her heart. Tears came fast and hard. She took a step toward Elizabeth and wrapped her in a warm, firm embrace. Elizabeth held to her tightly, longing for a mother of her own to share this grief. Leslie then turned her attention to her son, and Elizabeth sank onto the floor beside her father. Leslie knelt beside Jayson and pressed a hand to the back of his head. He turned to look at her and shifted himself into her arms, sobbing freshly against her shoulder while she whispered soothing words and cried silent tears, holding her to him as if he were fifteen years younger.

Will opened his arms to Elizabeth, and finding herself in the comfort of her father's embrace, her own tears began again. They held to each other and cried with no sense of time. Gradually the four of them settled into stunned silence. Will leaned back against the couch with Elizabeth's head on his shoulder. Jayson kept his head in his mother's lap, holding to her as if he might face destruction otherwise. The silence was finally broken when Jayson said, "I can't believe it. It can't be real."

"That's what I keep thinking," Elizabeth said.

Silence fell again until Drew came through the door. They all looked toward him at the same time, just as he tossed the door closed then stood, looking stunned as he took in the scene before him.

"What's wrong?" he asked.

Jayson waited for someone else to say it. He wasn't sure he could get the words to come out of his mouth. When no one answered, he found Drew looking at *him*. He cleared his throat, which caused the others to relax slightly as it became evident he intended to speak. "Uh . . ." Jayson croaked, "Derek . . ." Just saying his name pressed fresh tears into his eyes. He squeezed them closed, and the tears fell down his face.

"What?" Drew demanded.

Jayson forced it out. "He's dead."

Drew sank unsteadily into the nearest chair while Jayson heard the words echo over and over in his head. It was unusual to see Drew cry, and seeing his emotion now induced Jayson back into a state of sobbing helplessly. The tears had a contagious effect, and soon they were all crying.

Jayson had no idea what time it was when Will and Elizabeth finally went home to try to get some sleep. And it seemed hours beyond that when he finally drifted into a fitful sleep himself, filled with horrid images in his dreams. He was startled awake by his mother nudging him. He attempted to focus on her face as she said, "Will's on the phone, honey. He wants to talk to you."

Jayson pulled on his jeans and staggered to the phone. "Hi," he said, his voice hoarse.

"We have an appointment with the mortuary," Will said, "to make . . . arrangements." His voice cracked with emotion as he said, "I would really like you to be there. You knew him better than anyone. Please tell me you'll come."

Jayson cleared his throat and wondered how he could ever cope with this. But how could he refuse such a request? He already knew he wouldn't be going to school; he'd never be able to get through the day. "Uh . . . sure," he said. "If . . . you want me there, I'll be there."

"Good. Thank you," Will said, sounding extremely relieved. "We'll pick you up in an hour, if that's okay."

"Uh . . . yeah. I'll be ready. Do I need to . . . dress up?"

"Not for this, no," Will said and ended the call.

An hour later Jayson was pacing by the door, resisting the urge to go back to bed and never get up again. Drew had gone to a friend's house, and his mother had gone to work. A tap on the horn startled him, and he hurried outside, locking the door behind him. He was relieved to see that they'd come in the Suburban, and Will was driving. It was the only vehicle in either family that had a bench seat in the front. He opened the passenger door and slid in next to Elizabeth.

"Hi," she said and gave him a quick kiss while she touched his face. Then she looked into his eyes, creating a silent connection between them that insulated the grief. How grateful he was for her!

"Hi," he replied and pulled the door closed.

"Thanks for coming, son," Will said.

Jayson flinched inwardly at the use of that word, *son*. Will had always called him that, but it took on a whole new irony—and poignancy—with this turn of events. "Thanks for including me," he said, and had to admit inwardly that as difficult as it was to be facing this task, he felt privileged to be in on the plans, rather than excluded from them.

When Jayson said that this didn't feel real, Will assured them that it was. He'd gone to the mortuary already and had seen Derek's body. Following this statement, there were only grueling minutes of silence.

As they entered the mortuary, Jayson was grateful to feel Elizabeth's hand in his. He couldn't tell which one of them was trembling, then he concluded that they both were. He knew Derek's body was somewhere in the building, probably on some cold slab, waiting to be embalmed. He resisted the temptation to ask to see the body himself. While a part of him couldn't accept that Derek was really gone until he saw him, he preferred to wait until the body was prepared to be seen, and preferred to take Will's word for it.

They all managed to remain relatively emotionless throughout the process of making each decision for the funeral, and they left with forms to fill out and bring back later for the program and the obituary. With that much done, they went directly to order a headstone, since Will insisted that he wanted it done, and he wanted Jayson's input. While Will was writing out the pertinent information on a form, Jayson whispered to Elizabeth, "I really hate this."

"Yeah, me too," she whispered back. "I still can't believe it's real. It's like some kind of . . . warped dream."

"Nightmare, more like," he muttered.

"Yeah," she agreed and leaned her head against his shoulder, pushing her arms around him. He returned her embrace and pressed a kiss into her hair, reminding himself to be grateful that at least he still had Elizabeth.

Will turned and said to Elizabeth, "Check this for me, will you?"

Elizabeth and Jayson both moved to look at the form. Jayson felt something knot up inside of him to read, *Derek William Greer, Beloved Son, Brother, and Friend.* And there below his birth date was the date of death—yesterday. It just didn't seem possible. That word "friend" lingered in his mind. He felt a little in awe of the fact that Will was putting that on the headstone, carved in granite forever. Jayson knew he was the only real friend Derek had ever had. The implication felt hugely complimentary—and comforting, somehow.

"It's perfect," Elizabeth said, tightening her arm around Jayson's waist.

"Yes, it's perfect," Jayson added.

The man helping them then asked if they wanted any artwork on the headstone. He showed them pictures of trees and flowers and leaves and a variety of other designs. They all looked at each picture in silence, then Will asked with hopeful expectancy, "Do you have any guitars?"

Jayson felt sure he wouldn't and was surprised to hear him say, "We do, actually."

He then produced a few possibilities. Will turned to Jayson, who easily pointed to the one that looked closest to what Derek had played. "That one," he said firmly, and a design was created with a beach effect across the bottom, a simple border moving out of it and over the top to the guitar that would be carved just above his name.

Will took Jayson and Elizabeth out for a late lunch, but none of them ate much or had much to say. It just didn't seem possible that yesterday at this time Derek had been alive and breathing and full of laughter. And now he was gone. Jayson couldn't begin to fathom how he would ever come to accept this. And just the thought of ever playing music without Derek made him sick to his stomach. His thoughts were on that very thing when he heard Will say, "Jayson, I have a very big favor to ask you."

"What?" Jayson asked. He looked up from where he had been playing with his food rather than eating it.

"I want you to play . . . at the funeral."

Jayson felt his eyes widen as Elizabeth's hand reached for his beneath the table. He knew she understood how difficult the very idea was to him. Unable to think of ever playing anything at all, ever again, he could only say, "I can't. I just . . . can't."

"You can," Will said firmly. "You have to. It came to me last night when I was alone." Will got tears in his eyes. "It came to my mind as clearly as if Derek had been standing there telling me. You *have* to play at the funeral. Nothing meant more to him than your friendship and the music you shared."

Jayson couldn't argue with that, and he couldn't deny sharing Will's conviction on that count. He had to ask, however, "What would I possibly play? Everything we played, we played together."

Will leaned back and sighed. "It's obvious, isn't it?"

Jayson wondered if his mind was too clouded with grief to think clearly. He had to admit, "No, it's not obvious. I'm afraid you've lost me."

Will sighed again and said with a broken voice, "'Funeral for a Friend.'"

Jayson felt as if a dagger had gone straight through his heart the same instant that his brain absorbed the words. "No!" he whispered a shout and rushed from the restaurant.

Elizabeth followed him out and found him at the back of the building where there was an enclosed parking lot and nothing else. They were completely alone. He had both hands pressed against the bricks, his head hanging between his arms, gasping for breath. She could understand his hesitance, his grief, his fear. But she had to admit that she couldn't fully understand his pain, any more than she could understand the gift inside of him. He'd spent his life hearing music in his head. He'd told her more than once that the song he loved to play on the piano most was the one that represented his conquering of the piano, the one he'd learned to play as a gift to his mother, the one that Derek had loved to hear him play and had often begged him for. Derek had understood and connected to Jayson's gift more than anyone ever had. Jayson had told her that even as close as he was to his brother, and the way they understood each other's talent and the drive behind it, Derek had been able to draw out aspects of Jayson's music that no one or nothing else had ever been able to do. She could well understand the irony of what her father was asking him to do and how difficult it would be. On the other hand, Elizabeth knew her father was right. Derek would want this song at his funeral. And deep inside she knew what she believed her father knew—if Jayson wasn't forced to play music now, she could see the possibility of him falling into a trap of never being able to play again at all. He'd allowed Derek to become such an integral part of his music that he needed to find the ability within himself to play without Derek. And this was the song to do it. This was the song that Derek had never played with him; he'd only listened—over and over with an expression on his face that Elizabeth could recall clearly—awe and admiration. The irony of the title of this song left Elizabeth with a formless belief that destiny was somehow at work in their lives, in a much broader and deeper sense than they could ever imagine. She didn't know how she could ever find the words to express all she was thinking and feeling, especially when she doubted she could say much of anything without falling apart. She set her hands on his back, then pushed them around to his chest, hugging him tightly from behind. "I understand," she said.

"I know you do," he muttered.

"I think he's right, Jayson. I think you need to do this."

"I . . . don't know if I can ever play again," he admitted tearfully. "I feel like my right hand has been cut off."

Elizabeth sighed as his confession validated her suspicions. "And that's exactly why you need to play," she said. "This gift was in you long before you met Derek. It will be in you forever. Derek would want you to honor your gift, Jayson. It would break his heart to see you let go of your gift . . . after all that the two of you accomplished together. He can't live the dream with you, Jayson, so you're going to have to live it for both of you."

Jayson could never explain what her words did to his heart. He only knew that he felt the tiniest glimmer of hope that he could get beyond this, the tiniest speck of light against an otherwise black sky. He turned to look at her, wiping his face with his sleeve. When their eyes met, she said softly, "You have to play this song, Jayson. You have to play it for him—and for me and Dad. There is nothing that could have more meaning for Derek than this."

"I don't know if I can do it," he admitted.

Elizabeth just held out her hand, saying, "Let's go talk about it."

He took her hand and followed her back inside where they found Will sitting with his chin resting on his clasped fingers. He glanced expectantly at each of them as they were seated. "Forgive me," Will said. "It was not my intention to upset you, Jayson. I'm not going to make you do it, and I'm not going to make you feel guilty if you choose not to. I just . . . really think it's . . . right. Your playing this song is a tribute to the friendship you shared."

Jayson cleared his throat and muttered in a hoarse voice, "In spite of the title, I'm certain it's not typical funeral music. People won't understand. They'll think it's . . . strange."

"And I don't care what people think," Will said with fervor. "The three of us sitting here are those who loved him—and knew him— the most. *We* will understand, and that's all that matters."

"I cry too easily," Jayson argued. "How can I get through it without crying all over the place?"

"So, what if you do?" Will asked. "This is not a performance, Jayson. It's a tribute." He sighed and added, "Besides . . . they'll get it if you explain it before you play." Jayson bristled visibly at the suggestion. "Just a few words," Will said, "then you play the song. Whether or not you want Drew to play with you is up to you; or maybe it's up to Drew. I noticed that the funeral home doesn't have a very good piano; I'll rent one and have it brought in. I need you to play the song. That's all I ask. Do it for Derek. Do it for *me*." His voice broke as he added, "I need to hear you play that song, Jayson."

Jayson sighed and hung his head. "Drew won't do it," he said, knowing it would be easier to not have to do it alone. But in his heart, he knew Drew would protest. But then, Drew hadn't loved Derek the way Jayson loved him. It was different.

"That's okay," Will said. "The drums might be a bit much for a funeral anyway."

"This *song* is a bit much for a funeral," Jayson said. Then he looked up at Will. "But if you want me to do it, I'll do it."

Will sighed, and his shoulders slumped with visible relief. "Okay," he said. "Thank you. Anything else is just . . . superfluous in my opinion."

They discussed plans for the remainder of the program. Elizabeth reluctantly agreed to sing "Amazing Grace," but only if Jayson accompanied her. He told her he would. For him, playing something less personal was not an issue—and the focus would be on Elizabeth. If she could get through singing *that* song at her brother's funeral, he could certainly play it.

Will dropped Jayson off at his apartment in the early evening. He got out of the Suburban to hug Jayson tightly, then he took his shoulders into his hands and said with emotion, "Promise me you will always be a part of our family, Jayson. Promise me."

"I promise," Jayson said, and Will hugged him again.

Chapter Eleven

Will nodded and got back into the Suburban, waiting while Jayson hugged Elizabeth tightly and gave her a quick kiss. "I'll see you in the morning," he said. They'd made the decision to skip school until the funeral was over. Their parents had readily agreed to excuse the absences. Graduation was just around the corner, and there was no problem with either of them graduating. Attending classes just didn't seem important at the moment. Instead, Jayson intended to spend the day practicing for the funeral.

Elizabeth nodded. "Call me later," she said, and he nodded in return.

Jayson was relieved to go in and have his mother there. Had he been gone so long that she'd completed an eight-hour shift? He glanced at the clock and realized that he had.

"How are you?" she asked, reaching a hand toward him from where she sat on the couch.

Jayson sat beside her and muttered, "I don't think I can answer that without falling apart. And I'm tired of falling apart."

"Tell me what you've been doing," she said, and he did. He told her every detail of their day, often wiping tears as he spoke. She offered perfect compassion, perfect understanding, and complete acceptance. The last thing he told her was the hardest. "Will wants me to play at the funeral," he said with hesitance. "He wants me to play . . . 'Funeral for a Friend.'"

He wasn't surprised to see her eyes fill with new tears at the irony. He *was* surprised by her conviction when she said, "And so you should."

They kept talking until Drew came in, and it was evident that he was grieving Derek's loss greatly—he was just more reluctant to talk about it. Jayson told him, "Will's asked that 'Funeral for a Friend' be played . . . at the funeral."

Drew sounded angry as he insisted, "Well, I'm not playing it! You can do the piano. I'm not playing it. To me, he was a member of the band, and I'm going to miss him immensely." His voice cracked. "But he was your best friend. You should play it. That's the way it should be."

Jayson didn't argue. He slept better that night, only because his mother gave him half of an over-the-counter sleeping pill when he'd admitted to needing a good night's sleep. His mother had gone to work when he got up. He tried to orient himself to the reality that his best friend was dead, then he ate a piece of toast and went to Elizabeth's house. Just seeing her face reinforced the reality of what had happened, and then he walked into the house, feeling a defined emptiness. Without a word uttered, Elizabeth pushed her arms around him, clinging to him as tightly as he clung to her.

"I love you, Jayson," she muttered. "I don't know what I'd do without you."

"You will never have to do without me," he said.

She drew back and looked at him as if she didn't believe him, then she led the way to the front room and pointed at the piano. "There's the sheet music for 'Amazing Grace.' Why don't you run through it while I grab something to eat, or . . . are you hungry? Did you eat?"

"I'm fine," he said, sitting at the piano.

He was glad to have Elizabeth out of the room when he found it extremely difficult to just put his hands onto the keys. A clear image came to his memory of the first time he'd played this piano while Derek had looked on. He kept Derek's expression foremost in his mind and muttered, "This is for you, Derek," before he put his hands to the keys with a tentative reluctance. Going through the song in front of him, he was grateful that it wasn't something familiar. It was a beautiful song, and he'd grown up hearing it in church; he knew the lyrics well. But he'd never played it. When Elizabeth returned, she sat beside him and said, "That sounds pretty good."

"I have to memorize it," he said. "I can't play it with feeling if I don't memorize it."

"Is that a problem?"

"Not if you and your father don't mind me spending every waking minute at the piano. I have to practice . . . the other one. I'm only doing the first half; I'm not going into the second part with the lyrics, so I have to figure out a suitable ending, and . . . I just need to do it . . . a lot so I can . . ."

"So you can what?" she pressed when he hesitated.

"So I can hopefully get the emotion out of my system."

"Okay," she said. "Well, that's exactly why I need to sing this song a lot."

"Let's get to it then," he said.

They went through it once, and Elizabeth thought it didn't sound too bad, but she could see what he meant by needing to memorize it. He managed to play it, but it lacked the passion that usually came through when he played. Together they did the number several times, stopping twice for a good cry. She mentioned more than once, "You need to put some great embellishment in there to hide the way my voice will be cracking."

"You're going to do just fine," he insisted over and over.

Jayson determined that they needed to practice with a microphone, because she would be singing with one at the funeral. He went to the music room to get it and barely had the door open before he froze with his hand on the knob. He'd not been in here since the accident. There sat Derek's guitar, leaning in its stand as if he might appear and pick it up any second. There was a jacket of Derek's and a pair of shoes. And one of those stupid hats.

He forced himself to get what he needed, then he closed the door, wanting to never go in there again. He barely had the microphone and amp set up in the front room when he heard the phone ring, and Elizabeth went to answer it.

"Hello," Elizabeth said, praying it wouldn't be another concerned relative wanting to offer comfort or ask details of the event. On the chance that it might be her father, she knew she had to answer it.

"Elizabeth?" her mother's voice said, and she wanted to throw the phone at the wall.

Instead, she said, "Uh . . . yeah . . . hold on a second. I'll be right back."

Elizabeth set the phone down and went to the front room. She took hold of Jayson's hand, saying, "My mother's on the phone. I need you to hold me up."

"Oh, boy," Jayson said, going back to the kitchen with her.

"Does she know?"

"No. My dad's been trying to call her, but . . . I know he didn't want to be the one to tell her. I don't want to do it, but I'd rather do it than have him subjected to the dirty deed." She blew out a long breath. "Okay, here goes." Into the phone she said, "I'm back."

"Well, actually I need to talk to your father." Meredith's voice had a typical irritated tone. "Apparently, he's been trying to get hold of me. I tried his office, which is where I would assume he'd be on a weekday, but they said he's not in. Now, I can't help wondering why you're not in school. Are you sick?"

"No, I'm not sick," she said.

"So, what's the problem? My assistant said your dad's called several times. He should know how busy I am. I can't imagine what in the world would be so important."

"Well, if you'll stop whining for a minute, I'll tell you," Elizabeth said, unable to avoid mimicking her mother's irritated tone. Jayson put his arms around her, and she wished she could tell him how grateful she was just to have him with her.

"I was not whining," Meredith said. "I don't know where you get such a belligerent attitude these days. If I—"

"Mom!" Elizabeth interrupted. "Just be quiet a minute and listen to me." She heard no response, so she forged ahead and just forced herself to say it. "There was an accident, Mom." Elizabeth heard no anger in her own voice; there was only perfect sorrow as she added, "Derek's been killed." When she heard no sound at all for half a minute, she finally said, "Are you there?"

"I'm here," Meredith said in a tone of voice that Elizabeth hadn't heard in years; it almost sounded human. "I can't believe it."

"Well, that would actually give us something in common," Elizabeth said. "Everything's been arranged. The viewing is tomorrow night. The funeral is the day after tomorrow. The obituary will be in this evening's paper." She paused but got no response, no sign of emotion, nothing. "That's all really. Dad will be home in a couple of hours if you want to talk to him. He's doing something with the life insurance. I've gotta go. I'm singing at the funeral, and somebody's here to practice with me."

Elizabeth ended the call and hung up the phone before she clutched onto Jayson, muttering softly, "Oh, just hold me." The composure she'd fought for on the phone faltered completely, and she held on to him and cried.

After a few minutes, he lifted her chin with his fingers and wiped her tears away with his other hand. "Hey," he said, "we're going to get through this . . . together. We can get through *anything* together. Understand?"

She nodded and wiped at his tears as well. "Have I ever told you," she said, "that I love the way you cry so easily?"

Jayson made a scoffing noise. "It's ridiculous; it's *embarrassing.*"

"It shows how tenderhearted you are," she said, "and that's one of the things I love about you." Their eyes met with a familiar intensity, and she added, "I love you, Jayson."

Jayson inhaled deeply. He never grew tired of hearing her say it. Her love for him was like a miracle, in his opinion. And never had he been more grateful for it than now. "I love you too," he said and couldn't resist kissing her.

He was surprised at how the grief and sorrow he'd been feeling seemed to pour into his kiss, sparking something between them that he'd never felt before. It was as if the intensity of their present emotion intensified the sensation. He drew back to look at her, surprised to see evidence that she had felt it, too. They shared a lengthy gaze before she murmured, "Oh, Jayson," and lifted her mouth to his. In the span of a heartbeat he found himself engaged in a kiss unlike anything he'd ever experienced. He'd always made a point of keeping their affection within certain limitations. Through months of dating, every kiss they had shared was not unlike their first. His mother had taught him to be very conscious of such things, and beyond that he knew that his feelings for Elizabeth had been so overpowering that he almost feared what might happen if he allowed them to fully surface. In a way, he was so in awe of her that he instinctively felt compelled to treat her with the delicacy of fine porcelain. But now *she* was initiating a kiss that passed all boundaries he'd kept carefully established in the past. As their kiss went on and on, he felt a tingling erupt deep inside and found himself pulling her completely into his arms. Never had he experienced anything so thoroughly pleasant, so completely intoxicating. He could only compare it to the thrill of feeling a new song pour into his mind or the elation of performing onstage and having the audience eating out of his hands. But this was better, so much better! When his own heart quickened and he felt her become breathless, he began to get a glimmer of understanding concerning the lessons his mother had taught him. *Passion is like a slippery slide,* she'd said a dozen times. *When you're sitting at the top, you're completely in control, but once you start to slide, it becomes increasingly difficult to stop.* As her words trickled into his mind, he could feel himself sliding into a sensation that he ached to explore. His desire was only enhanced when he withdrew his lips from hers and looked into her eyes. What he saw there clearly told him that he had more power over her with his kiss than he'd ever had with an audience hanging on his music. But her obvious vulnerability and abject trust were the very reasons that he forced distance between them. He wanted to tell her that they needed to practice the song, but the moment felt so perfect that he felt hesitant to shatter it with the reminder that Derek was gone and they had to find a way to cope. Impulsively he sang to her, easing her effortlessly into the rhythm of a slow dance, while he crooned the lyrics. He added a dramatic, slightly comical tone to his voice and saw her smile. He turned her in a wide circle around the kitchen while he made noises to imitate the piano notes that led into the next string of lyrics.

"You're pretty amazing," she said while he eased her through a smooth series of dance steps to imaginary music. "You can dance and do a pretty fair Elton John imitation at the same time."

"Oh, I can't dance," he said. "This is just . . . feeling the music."

"Is that what it is?" she asked and smiled again. It was good to see her smile. "Whatever it is, it works." Jayson just smiled back and sang the second verse.

Elizabeth watched him as he serenaded her a capella, not missing a beat. She felt so in awe of him, his gift, his love for her. She marveled over the moment as he closed his eyes and lifted his face to belt out the chorus, hitting the notes with brilliant clarity.

When the song was finished, Jayson stepped away from her, resisting the urge to kiss her again. He wondered how to break the spell of the moment without bringing the harsh reality crashing down around them. Then Will came in through the garage door, looking strained and completely sad. It was evident he'd been crying as he drove.

"How's the song coming?" he asked.

"Maybe you should be the judge of that," Jayson said, and they moved to the front room.

They went through the song a couple of times while Will discreetly cried, then he declared he was going to cook something. Eventually Elizabeth went to the kitchen to help her father, declaring she needed a break. Jayson stared at the piano for several minutes, trying to talk himself into playing the song he needed to play.

From the kitchen Elizabeth heard the beginning of "Funeral for a Friend," and she had to just stop and listen. She saw her father doing the same, and then they were both crying. While the song itself spurred memories and emotion, she could feel the hesitancy in Jayson's playing, and the lack of passion that she knew he usually put into it. And then she heard it fall apart. Then silence. She perked her ears to listen, sensing that her father was doing the same thing. They both started in the same moment when a fist obviously came down on the piano keys, followed by the slamming of the key cover and then a loud thud. Will ran toward the front room, and Elizabeth followed him, arriving just in time to see Jayson kick the piano bench that he had obviously just kicked over. Oblivious to their presence, he kicked it again and cursed aloud before he clenched his fists and shouted heavenward, "How could you do this to me? How could you leave me like this?"

"Jayson," Elizabeth said, moving toward him with her hand outstretched.

"*Don't* touch me!" he snapped, and she stepped back, unable to hold back a little sob. She'd never seen him so angry, and it scared her.

Jayson heard Elizabeth crying and attempted to subdue this consuming anger long enough to absorb the concern on her face—and Will's. He wanted to tell them he was fine. But he didn't feel fine. What he really wanted was to have a sledgehammer in his hand and to smash the piano into a thousand pieces. He reminded himself that it wasn't his piano, and he could never pay for it, especially when he no longer had a job. Without Derek he was unemployed, useless, incapacitated. The music had no meaning any more. And he felt so angry. So blindly angry. Feeling as if he might explode from the inside out, he rushed from the room, needing something, anything to take this rage out on. His mind focused on an object that belonged to him, and at the moment it seemed the only means to fully express what he was feeling.

Elizabeth watched him rush past her, and a split second later she heard him open the basement door, and she knew where he was going. "Oh, no," she said, barely meeting her father's eyes before she ran after Jayson. She entered the music room just in time to see him pick up his acoustic guitar by the neck, holding it like a baseball bat. "Jayson, no!" she said, and their eyes met while he froze for just a moment.

Will appeared beside her, saying gently, "Please don't, Jayson."

"It's my guitar," he growled, "and I'll do with it whatever I please." Without a second's hesitation he swung it with force against the carpeted wall.

Elizabeth screamed at the sound of it breaking and tried to move toward him, but Will put his arms around her to stop her, whispering close to her ear, "It's already broken. Just let him get it out of his system." She cried helplessly in her father's arms while Jayson cursed and raged and smashed the guitar into the wall over and over, until there was nothing left to smash.

Elizabeth screamed again when he threw it down and turned around, setting his eye firmly on his electric guitar. She was relieved when her father rushed toward him and grabbed both of Jayson's wrists just as Jayson grabbed the guitar. "That's enough destruction," Will said firmly, as if Jayson were his own son.

Jayson looked toward him, his eyes blazing as he snarled, "It's mine and I'll—"

"And you'll regret it tomorrow," Will said, and Elizabeth could tell he'd tightened his grip on Jayson's wrists by the way Jayson groaned and let go of the guitar. He lifted his arms in an attempt to be free of Will's grip, but her father held tight, and they ended up facing each other, their hands at their sides. Jayson's expression was defiant and filled with rage. He struggled again to free his arms, but Will shook him gently. "I know you're hurting, and I know you're angry," Will said, close to Jayson's face, "but this isn't going to make it go away. He's dead, Jayson. He's gone, and nothing is going to bring him back. We have to live with that."

"Well, I *can't* live with that!" Jayson shouted. "How can I ever play music without him?"

"Because it's who you are," Will said through clenched teeth. "You're a musician. And a true musician finds a way to follow the music wherever it leads him no matter the cost, no matter the heartache, no matter the obstacles that are put into his path. You were his hero, Jayson. You made him happier than he had *ever* been. He died happy because of you. Do you hear what I'm saying? And if you turn your back on the music now, you might as well be spitting on his grave."

Elizabeth saw Jayson wince at the metaphor, but it seemed to startle him back to himself. He hung his head and groaned, but Will still didn't let go of his wrists. "I can't do it," Jayson said, then he sobbed.

"You can," Will said. "You have to."

Jayson sobbed again, and his arms dropped abruptly, as if he had no strength left to hold them up. Will let go and put his arms around Jayson. He practically collapsed into Will's embrace and sobbed like he had when he'd first learned of Derek's death. It was another hour before they left the music room. On his way to the door, Jayson stared long and hard at the pieces of his guitar scattered on the floor, but he left them as they were. The three of them worked together to finish preparing the meal that Will had barely started. What had been intended as a late lunch ended up being supper right on time. In the middle of the meal, the phone rang, and Will rose to answer it. Elizabeth heard him sigh loudly, then say, "Hello, Meredith." Following some silence, he said, "You should know your children better than that. One assumption is as ludicrous as the other. I have to go now, Meredith. I assume we'll see you at the viewing."

Will hung up the phone and moved back to the table. "What did she say?" Elizabeth asked.

"It's not important," Will insisted.

"How is it that she should know her children better?" Elizabeth pressed. "What ludicrous assumptions did she make?"

Will sighed and leaned his chin on his clasped fingers. "Fine," he said. "She said she'd been hoping that you had just been playing some kind of sick joke on her."

"What?" Elizabeth practically shrieked. "She thinks I would actually tell her that—"

"Obviously, she knows now that it's true."

"Why is that?" Jayson asked.

"She's seen the obituary."

They all sighed, but none of them seemed to want to go get the paper off the porch and look for themselves. "What else did she assume?" Elizabeth asked.

Will sighed again. "She implied that perhaps Derek had been drinking or doing drugs."

Jayson cursed and slammed his napkin on the table. "That's the stupidest thing I've ever heard," he growled.

"Yes, it is," Will said, but he said it calmly. "We all know it isn't true, and getting angry over it will not bring about anything good."

"Well, you're a better man than I am," Jayson snapped and left the table. For a moment Elizabeth was worried that he'd go back to the basement and resume the destruction of musical instruments. But a few seconds later, she heard the piano. He was playing "Funeral for a Friend," but he'd begun in the middle of song, right where the music was fast and hard—and it sounded angry. But at least he was playing it. And it *did* have the passion he was capable of. He finished and started over at the beginning of the song. He played it over and over while Elizabeth and her father finished eating and cleaned up the kitchen together. While the music was resounding through the house, Will went to the porch and got the paper. Without a word spoken between them, he laid it on the table and turned the pages until the obituaries appeared. And there, at the top of the page, was a printed copy of Derek's senior picture. It was true, Elizabeth thought as she stared at it. It was actually in the newspaper. Her brother was dead.

Jayson played the song until his arms and back couldn't take sitting at the piano another minute. Then he read the obituary and went home, where he cried himself to sleep. The next morning he got up late and found his mother waiting for him at the kitchen table.

"How are you?" she asked, putting some breakfast in front of him.

"How am I supposed to be?" he countered.

"I didn't ask how you're supposed to be. I asked how you *are.*"

"I'm angry," he admitted, perhaps expecting her to tell him that he had no cause to be angry.

Leslie put a hand over his and said softly, "I would be disappointed if you weren't."

"Why?"

"Because you can't lose someone so suddenly who means that much to you without being angry. You have a right to be angry. With time you'll come to terms with the anger. It's one of the stages of grief."

"It is?" he asked, wondering if that meant he wasn't crazy.

"Oh, yes," she said. "I don't know all the psychological babble, but I know there's shock and anger and . . . I don't know—some other stuff. And eventually there's acceptance, and then I think there comes a determination to keep going in spite of whatever it is you may have lost."

"And who did you lose to death that gave you all this wisdom and experience?" he asked.

"Oh, I didn't learn that through death. I learned that through divorce."

Jayson was a little taken aback, but as he let that settle in, he knew she was right. He had to ask, "Did you ever do anything you regretted when you were angry?"

"Oh, yes," she said, "but I don't know that I should admit to my son what I did; maybe someday." She tightened her eyes on him and asked, "Did *you* do something you regret, Jayson?"

"Yes," he admitted and couldn't hold back tears.

"What?" she asked, wiping them from his face.

"I smashed my guitar," he said and wasn't surprised to hear her gasp.

"Which one?" she asked.

"The acoustic."

"That was a beautiful guitar," she said. "You worked and saved a long time to buy it."

"Yes, I did. And now it's in a few hundred pieces on the floor of the music room."

"Why did you do that?" she asked.

Jayson took a deep breath. "I just . . . felt so angry."

"Okay, but . . . there are a lot of things you could have taken your anger out on. Why the guitar?"

He swallowed hard. "Because I don't know if I can ever play it again."

"Do you think that's what Derek would want?"

"No," he admitted, and his emotion deepened. "Will told me that . . . if I turned my back on the music, I might as well be spitting on Derek's grave."

"That must have hurt," Leslie said gently.

"Yeah," he said and wiped his tears on his sleeve.

"Was Will there when you—"

"Oh, yeah. And Elizabeth was there, too. And they still love me, or so they said."

"They understand."

"Yes, I think they do. And so do you. Sometimes I think I'm the only one who doesn't understand."

"Understand what?" she asked.

"What I'm doing . . . and why."

"May I offer some advice?"

"Sure," he said.

"Just worry about getting through the funeral, and don't be too concerned about life's great questions at the moment. Give it time; get some perspective."

Jayson appreciated his mother's advice, and he fought to keep it foremost in his mind as he went to the Greer home and practiced the song over and over while his thoughts wandered. He worked on "Amazing Grace" until he had it comfortably memorized, then he went over it with Elizabeth a few times before she left him so he could work on the other number. Again he played it over and over until he decided that he could do it no more. He started it over once more, reasoning that this would be the last time until he did it at the funeral the next day. As the music surged through him, he realized that he was finally coming to understand it. He'd played this song more times than he could count, but only now did he realize what it meant. The music went through every stage of grief that he'd experienced in the few short days since

Derek had been killed. Shock, anger, sorrow, acceptance, and a determination to keep going—just as his mother had so wisely explained. And yes, he had to keep going. For Derek, he could keep going. With Elizabeth at his side, he could keep going.

Will came in late in the afternoon; he'd gone into work for part of the day to put out the biggest fires and came in just as Jayson and Elizabeth were doing a final run-through of the song they would do together. "It's beautiful," Will said when they were finished, but neither of them commented.

"Hey," Will added, "I haven't wanted to bring this up, but . . . have you called Joe? He needs to know you won't be playing this Saturday."

Jayson blew out a long breath and hung his head. "No, I haven't called him. I couldn't bring myself to do it, but . . . I guess I should."

"Do it now and get it over with," Elizabeth said. "I'll hold your hand."

Together they went to the phone, and Jayson dialed the number. "Hi," she heard Jayson say. "Uh . . . I need to let you know that you're going to have to get somebody else to cover Saturday nights." He was silent for a long moment, obviously listening. "I don't have a bass player," Jayson said, his voice cracking slightly. "No, you don't understand. I am permanently without a bass player. No, I can't find another bass player." His voice became agitated as he said, "He was smashed in a car, Joe. He's dead. He was my best friend, and I'm not doing the gig any more without him. That's it." Elizabeth heard him calm down as he said, "Well . . . okay. Thank you. I'm truly sorry. It was great while it lasted." Tears spilled down his face, and Elizabeth wiped them away.

He ended the call and cried on her shoulder until Will came into the room. "Sounds like that went well," he said with sarcasm.

"Oh, yeah. As long as Joe can fill the dance floor, little else matters."

Will went on to say, "The two of you had better get cleaned up."

Jayson felt startled and glanced at the clock. "What for?"

"The viewing. We need to get there early so we can have some time alone . . . to adjust . . . before people start coming."

Jayson felt sick to his stomach as he realized what Will was saying. But he didn't have time to stew about it. He had to hurry home and take a shower and put on his best clothes. Will and Elizabeth came by to get him, and not one of them uttered a word during the drive to the funeral home. And going inside felt tantamount to being led to the guillotine. He was only distracted for a moment with the realization that Elizabeth was dressed entirely in black, wearing a dress he'd never seen before and black high-heeled shoes over black stockings. "You look beautiful," he whispered to her. She gave him a wan smile and put her hand into his.

Jayson was grateful to be alone with Elizabeth and Will when the shock of seeing Derek in a casket was even harder than he'd expected. Together they cried and attempted to come to terms, just as they'd done several times already. The good thing about actually seeing him was the absence of disbelief. He could no longer attempt to believe that it wasn't real. Derek was cold and lifeless, and the evidence could not be denied.

Jayson was touched to see Derek's bass guitar near the casket, leaning in its stand. There were also many framed pictures of Derek set out where they could be seen by guests as they arrived. Jayson found himself in a few of those pictures.

Meredith arrived about ten minutes before the viewing was actually scheduled to begin. She became hysterical when she saw Derek in the casket, and Will was there to hold her and help calm her down. Jayson couldn't help thinking it was likely the most contact they'd had in years. When Meredith was finally composed, she approached Elizabeth, who was standing next to Jayson. Taking Elizabeth's face into her hands, she asked gently, "And how are you?"

"I'm fine, Mother," she said, barely civil, and Jayson was reminded of how he would likely greet his own father if they ever came face-to-face again. He was grateful to know that it would never happen.

Meredith tossed a cursory glance toward Jayson but said nothing to him before she took her place by the casket, next to Will. Jayson had never been to one of these things in his life, and it took him a few minutes to realize the procedure. The family stood close to the casket while those who came to pay their respects waited in line to speak to the family and offer condolences. While there were many people here whom he didn't know, he was surprised to see a great number of people he recognized from school—faculty as well as students. He suspected that some of them had not known Derek all that well, but they had still come to pay their respects.

Watching the line quickly lengthen, Jayson felt disoriented by a sudden distance between himself and Will and Elizabeth. But he felt compelled to remain near the casket, as if doing so might somehow help him feel closer to Derek. About ten minutes into the ritual, he was surprised to see Elizabeth at his side, and even more surprised when she said, "Dad wants you to come and stand by him."

Jayson wasn't sure if he liked that idea. "I don't know any of these people," he insisted quietly.

"You don't have to say anything. Just . . . come and stand by him."

Jayson sighed and followed her to where Will was standing. She stood between her parents, and he stood on the other side of Will. While he'd expected to just blend into the background and offer some silent support, he heard Will tell nearly every person who went through the line, "This is Derek's dear friend, Jayson. He's like a part of the family." People would shake his hand and say they were glad to meet him. Jayson could do little beyond force a smile and nod. Occasionally, Will put an arm around his shoulders. And more than once Will impulsively hugged him, saying softly, "I'm grateful for you."

Jayson was grateful for Will, too. But he was way too emotional to even speak, so he just returned the embrace, hoping he understood, praying that eventually he would become an official and permanent member of the family. Being a father to Will's grandchildren was something that felt amazingly right.

The following morning Jayson stood in front of his closet for ten minutes before he put on the black shoes and slacks he usually wore to church. But instead of the white shirt and black jacket he'd worn the previous evening, he put on the black shirt his mother had bought for him the first time he'd performed live. And over it the black suit vest, left unbuttoned. He was ready just a couple of minutes before Will knocked at the door. He was startled to step outside and see a black limo. They got inside, where Elizabeth was sitting with her black-clad legs crossed at the knees, wearing the same dress she'd worn the previous evening. Jayson gave her a quick kiss and sat beside her. When she put her hand on his knee, he put a hand on hers.

"You look nice," Elizabeth said to him.

"So do you," he replied, "as always." Then nobody said anything.

If only to break a miserable silence, Jayson said almost lightly, "I've had big dreams of riding in one of these, but this isn't exactly what I had in mind."

"What did you have in mind?" Will asked, almost smiling. "Pulling up in front of a concert hall with thousands of screaming teenage girls wanting your autograph?"

"Something like that," Jayson said.

"It'll happen," Will said matter-of-factly. "But I think you'll probably go in the back way and avoid the crowds."

"Probably," Jayson said, and the silence fell again.

At the funeral home, they found no one there except for Meredith. Her first comment to her ex-husband was in a tone of disbelief. "I understand you spent some ridiculous amount of money to rent a piano."

"It was a perfectly reasonable amount of money," Will said, "and what I do with my money is certainly none of your concern."

Jayson and Elizabeth exchanged an incredulous glance, but could do nothing beyond stand there and listen.

"Don't these people already have a piano?"

"A very lousy, out-of-tune piano," Will stated. "And that's not good enough for Derek."

Will motioned Jayson and Elizabeth to walk past him, then he followed them into the large chapel where the service would actually take place. Jayson caught his breath when he saw the piano. It was black, not too unlike the one in the Greer home. But it was shinier, and obviously brand new. *It was beautiful.* One day he would have a piano just like it in his own home, he thought. Derek would want it that way. Will said, "I thought the two of you might want to get a feel for the piano and the mic before anyone else gets here."

"Good idea," Elizabeth said, and they went to the front. With Will and Meredith sitting on the same row but several feet away from each other, Elizabeth took her place at the microphone and put her hands on either side of the pulpit. Jayson warmed up a little before they went through "Amazing Grace." Elizabeth was relieved to get through it with no emotion, and she prayed that ability would hold out for the actual performance.

As they were coming down from the platform, holding hands, Meredith said, "That was lovely, Elizabeth. You really have done well with your voice."

"Thank you," Elizabeth said and walked on. Meredith said nothing at all to Jayson.

The formalities preceding the funeral felt like purgatory to Jayson, especially the closing of the casket. He was grateful to have Elizabeth on one side of him and his mother and Drew on the other. Still, he felt as if his insides were going to burst from the anguish, and he could only pray that he could get through the funeral without making a fool of himself. He noticed on the printed program that "Amazing Grace" was slated early on. The title of the song was stated, followed by Elizabeth's name and then, *Accompanied by Jayson Wolfe*. Further down on the program, after a few other things, it stated simply, *Special Musical Number, Jayson Wolfe*. Just reading it made him nervous.

When it came time for the first number, Jayson sat at the piano and waited for Elizabeth to get situated at the pulpit before he began. He felt immeasurably proud of her as her voice rang clear and strong. She got through the next few verses with strength and brilliance, then he heard her voice break. When the final verse was supposed to begin, he realized he was playing—but she wasn't singing. He did a little embellishment as if it were meant to be that way, and an obvious introductory bar, but still she didn't sing. He played what sounded like a well-planned conclusion, then he quickly moved to her side, singing the lyrics into the microphone. Elizabeth met his eyes while he sang, and he was glad to see that he'd done the right thing. He saw her gain composure as he sang the last phrase, and together they finished with a harmony that sounded as if they'd practiced it a dozen times. He was surprised when she closed her eyes and lifted her face and began to sing that last verse again, this time an octave higher. He joined in at a point that felt natural, and they finished together on a high, clear note. A quick glance at the audience made it evident that there was hardly a tearless eye in the room. With an arm around Elizabeth's waist, he escorted her back to their seats, where she leaned her head on his shoulder and whispered, "Thank you."

"It was my pleasure," he said and pressed a kiss into her hair. He saw Will tightly squeeze Elizabeth's hand, then he reached across her to take Jayson's hand, and did the same.

Chapter Twelve

Jayson became so caught up in the speakers and the wonderful things being said about Derek that he was startled to realize it was time for his tribute. Elizabeth nudged him, and he moved to the microphone to do as Will had suggested and give some explanation for what he was about to do.

He cleared his throat and tried not to sound nervous. "Uh . . . Derek's dad asked me to play this song. It's not typical funeral music, but it's something that Derek loved and . . ." His voice broke with emotion. "Derek is my best friend, and the most important thing we shared was a love of music. Even if most of you here don't understand what this song means, Derek does, and I have to believe that he can hear me." It occurred to him that he didn't want any kind of applause to detract from the spirit of the funeral. He impulsively said, "At the end of the song, I would ask for a minute of silence." He paused and added, "Ironically, this song is called, 'Funeral for a Friend.'"

Jayson wiped the tears from his face as he moved to the piano. He wiped the moisture from his hands by pressing them over his pant legs as he sat down. He clenched his hands into fists, then stretched his fingers and prayed that their trembling would cease as he put them down to play the first notes. "This is for you, Derek," he said quietly as those first, sad, poignant bars filled the room with music. Once he began, it was just the keyboard and him, and thoughts of Derek. The people in the room and what they might be thinking all became irrelevant. He felt tears falling down his face, but he ignored them and played the song as if doing so might bring Derek back to him. Never had he done it with such intensity. Never had he felt the music moving through him so completely.

When the song was done, Jayson hung his head and remained as he was for more than a minute, while the room was so still he could hear the beating of his own heart. He returned to his seat, pressing a hand over the casket as he passed by it. He was grateful to be sitting between his mother and Elizabeth when a fresh surge of emotion overtook him. They each handed him a tissue, then put an arm around him. "It was perfect," Elizabeth whispered and kissed his cheek.

When the service was over, Jayson and Drew were among the pall-bearers that carried the casket to the hearse. Drew and his mother rode to the cemetery in the limo with Jayson and Elizabeth and Will. The brief service that took place around the grave was over far too quickly. While others slowly filtered away, Jayson stood with his family—and Derek's—not wanting to leave, not knowing what to say. He felt as if he might explode into violent sobbing, but for the moment his emotion was barricaded behind a dam of shock. The finality of Derek's open grave felt too stark, too close, too real.

Jayson was surprised to hear Will whisper in his ear, "Would you please sing that song again? You and Elizabeth?" Elizabeth apparently heard him as she looked at her father, obviously not wanting to. "Please," he added.

Jayson didn't wait for Elizabeth to make a decision; he just started to sing. He'd discovered something about singing today. With his voice he could release his emotion in a way that seemed to echo a formless comfort back to him. After the first verse of "Amazing Grace," Elizabeth joined him, and he marveled at how well they could harmonize without even trying. He felt there was symbolism in that. It was simply a new experience to make music together with only their voices, music that came solely from the heart.

When the song was finished, Jayson opened his eyes to realize that everyone was in tears. His own composure failed, and he cried until he could hardly breathe. Will finally urged them all away and back into the limo; not a word was said, but the crying continued. By the time they got to the Greer home, where many people were gathered and food was being served, Jayson felt numb with shock once again. He didn't feel hungry, and he didn't want to talk to anybody, but

Elizabeth seemed to understand. They sat together on the piano bench with their backs to the piano, holding hands. He was surprised to look up and see Elizabeth's mother standing in front of them. He expected her to speak to Elizabeth and ignore him completely as she'd done before, but she spoke directly to him in a voice more positive and animated than he'd ever heard from her.

"Your performance was astounding, Jayson," she said. "All that time you were practically living under our roof and I had no idea you were capable of such incredible music."

Jayson rose to his feet, mostly so he could look down at her. He counted to ten, willing his anger down to a place that was moderately reasonable. Still, he couldn't help the curt tone when he said, "Mrs. Greer, I'm absolutely certain there was a great deal going on under your roof that you had no idea of. First and foremost, there was incredible music in your home long before I came around. And what I played today was not a performance; it was a tribute. If you will excuse me, your daughter and I have something we need to be doing. Maybe I'll see you at the wedding."

He walked away, pulling Elizabeth along by holding to her arm. They walked out the back door and stood beneath the awning before she asked, "What wedding?"

"Ours," he said. In response to her concerned gaze, he added, "No matter when you and I get married, I suspect it will be the only other time I will ever see her. At least I can hope."

"And what makes you so sure that you and I are going to get married?"

Jayson looked into her eyes and wondered how she could possibly believe that any other course could be right. He countered almost hotly, "What makes you so sure we *won't* get married?"

"I didn't say we wouldn't; I just wanted to know what makes you so sure. You're taking a lot for granted."

Jayson turned more toward her and asked, "Will you marry me?"

"Someday . . . maybe." She sighed and looked away. "They say you shouldn't make crucial decisions in your life when you're in the middle of a crisis."

"Who is 'they'?"

"I don't know."

"Then why should I care what they say?"

"It's just common sense, Jayson."

"I'll tell you some common sense," he said. "I've wanted to marry you since I first laid eyes on you. That's hardly making a decision in the middle of crisis."

Elizabeth shrugged. "Still, we're very young."

"Must you be so blasted practical?" he asked.

"Must you be so starry-eyed?" He looked at her hard, and she added more gently, "Yes, I suppose you must. Great musicians don't become great without being starry-eyed. And that's your destiny; I'm certain of it."

"I'm not so certain any more," he said.

"Why, because Derek's gone?"

"Exactly."

"I thought we'd had this conversation before. You can't give up on the music, Jayson. You can't."

"No, I can't," he admitted, sounding less terse. "But . . . that doesn't mean I have to perform onstage and make records. I could . . . play at funerals, for instance."

Elizabeth attempted to lighten the mood as she looked him up and down and said, "You do look good in black."

He looked her over as well and countered, "So do you. But you should have worn your red shoes."

She sighed. "I doubt I'll ever wear them again."

Jayson could understand that, but he had to say, "Don't ever get rid of them."

"I promise." Their eyes met, and she added, "I would never be able to get through this without you."

"No, you got that wrong," he insisted lightly. "*I* would never be able to get through this without *you*."

"Then we're even," she said.

"No, we'll never be even. I could never repay what you give to me, Elizabeth. Not in a lifetime; not in eternity. Never."

She looked away, almost feeling embarrassed. To ease the tension she said, "You're talking like a songwriter, Jayson Wolfe."

"How ridiculous," he said tonelessly.

"By the way," she said. "You told my mother there was something we needed to be doing."

"I did tell her that, didn't I," he said and glanced around to be assured they were alone before he pressed his mouth to hers, gratified with the way she melted in his arms. He was longing for it to go on and on when they heard the door open and both turned to see Meredith staring at them as if they'd turned green.

"Oh, great," Elizabeth muttered under her breath as she tried to ease away, but Jayson kept his arm firmly around her to prevent her from moving.

Meredith closed the door behind her and said, "I had no idea the two of you were . . . romantically involved."

"We've been dating for several months, Mother—since last fall."

"I see," Meredith said and glanced down. She looked up again and said, "I would really like to hear your band play. When will your next performance be?"

"There won't be any more performances, Mother," Elizabeth said, unable to keep from sounding terse.

"Why not?" she asked, sounding astonished.

"Our bass player is dead," Jayson said with blatant anger.

"But surely you can—"

"One plus three does not add up to four," Jayson interjected.

"As usual, Mother, you're a little late to catch the performance."

Elizabeth felt sure her mother would erupt with anger, but before she had a chance, the back door came open, and her father called, "Hey, Jayson. Could you come here a minute? There's someone I want you to meet."

Jayson cast a cautious glance toward Elizabeth, not wanting to leave her alone, but she nodded subtly. "Excuse me," he said and went into the house.

"So," Meredith said with no apparent sign of anger, "how old is your boyfriend?"

Attempting to be civil, Elizabeth answered, "He's eighteen—the same as me."

Meredith's surprise was evident. "Really? He looks and acts much older, but then you do as well, I suppose."

"Mom, he's Derek's best friend. How much older did you think he would be? Actually, Jayson is between us in age."

"I see," Meredith said. "And did I hear him say the two of you are getting married?"

"It was a joke, Mother," she said, glad Jayson wasn't here. He likely wouldn't agree.

"Well, I'm glad to hear that. He seems like a very nice young man, but you're much too young to be getting married."

"You think I don't know that? I'm going to Boston. I have a scholarship."

"Really?" Meredith sounded extremely impressed, but Elizabeth had to resist the temptation to point out how ridiculous her ignorance was in relation to her children's lives. "Well, I hope you have the good sense to follow through and get a degree. Don't be doing anything to blow your chances for some real success."

"I have no intention of messing up my life, Mother, but I'm certain our definitions of success are entirely different. My goals would likely not impress you."

"What *are* your goals?" she asked in a tone that implied she would like to hear them if only to discredit them.

"It really doesn't matter; I don't want to talk about it."

"And what of Jayson?" she asked as if she were cross-examining a witness in the courtroom. "Is he going to college?"

"No, actually. Jayson is one of those rare individuals who has the potential to make millions with very little education. And I'm certain he will."

"What do you mean?"

"You heard him play . . . and sing. He's brilliant. And you haven't heard the half of it. He's going to LA, and he's going to be world renowned."

"LA is a long way from Boston."

"Yes, it is. But that's just temporary."

"You're in love with him," she stated, as if it were a criminal action.

"Would I be dating him this long if I weren't?"

Meredith folded her arms and looked at her daughter hard. "Are you using birth control?"

It took Elizabeth several seconds to convince herself that she'd not misunderstood the question, and then the fury she felt erupted out of her mouth with a sharp, "What?"

"You heard me. You're old enough to talk frankly with your mother. I know how kids are these days."

"You know *nothing!* Absolutely nothing inappropriate has ever happened between us, not that it's any of your business. He is a gentleman in the truest sense."

"Men are all alike, Elizabeth. Just give him half a chance, and he'll have you pregnant, and your life will be shot. Trust your mother on this."

"Why should I trust you on anything? You've never given me one lousy reason to trust you. And obviously you don't trust me."

Meredith sighed as if she were exercising great patience. "I truly did leave you far too much in your father's care. If he—"

"My father is the most amazing man in the world, and you have no idea what you're talking about. If you—"

Elizabeth's words were interrupted by her own scream when her mother slapped her hard across the face. She was amazed at how badly it hurt, and she couldn't even think how to respond. She was relieved beyond words when the door came open and Jayson demanded, "Are you okay?" With her hand pressed over her face, she could only stare at him. She saw his eyes go to her mother as he closed the door and said firmly, "I heard you scream. Are you okay?"

Elizabeth wondered if that meant everyone else in the house had heard her as well, or if Jayson's ears were simply more tuned in to her. "No," she admitted with a shaky voice, "I don't think I am."

As he moved toward her, Meredith said, "This is between me and my daughter, and you'd do well to—"

"What?" Jayson interrupted, standing directly in front of Meredith. "Tell me what you'll do *Ms.* Greer. Will you hit me, too? I've got scars to prove I can survive much worse than you. I know how people like you work. You're just like my father. But at least he had an excuse. At least he was drunk when he started hitting the people he was supposed to love."

"This is none of your business," she growled. "And you'd do well to—"

"Elizabeth is a lot more my business than yours. You have no business calling yourself a mother. All they ever wanted was your approval, but you couldn't give even that. Now Derek's dead, and you have the nerve to actually hit your own daughter."

"With that kind of belligerence, *any* parent would have done the same," she countered as if she were in a courtroom.

"Belligerence?" Jayson gave a scoffing laugh. "We're not talking about the same person. She is wonderful and brilliant and kind and good—clearly nothing like you. You're nothing but an overgrown bully in a skirt. And if you ever—*ever*—hurt her again, I will have you slapped with domestic violence charges so fast you won't know what hit you. I might be just a kid to you, but I have a lot of experience with that. I wonder how that would reflect on your brilliant legal reputation. And don't think I wouldn't do it."

Meredith's expression softened slightly, as if she knew he had her. In a terse voice, she said to Elizabeth, "Your boyfriend is charming. It's no wonder the two of you get along so well. But don't be thinking that—"

The door opened, and Will demanded, "What's going on?"

Jayson waited for one of the women to speak. When they didn't, he took great pleasure in tattling. "Your ex-wife just hit your daughter."

Will closed the door with a studied fury showing in his face. In a voice that was barely calm, he said to Meredith, "I don't want to know why; I don't want any excuses or rationalizations. There is no justifiable cause for hitting a child."

"She's no child," Meredith snapped. "She's a woman, full grown."

"You bet she is," Will said. "And a fine one, at that—in spite of growing up with a lousy mother. Now get out. You are no longer welcome here—ever."

"Will you cause a scene at our son's funeral?" she snapped.

"You bet I will," he said firmly. "So you can graciously walk out and get in your car and drive away, or I will escort you out by any means necessary."

Meredith looked hard at Will, then at Jayson, who looked as if he'd like to tear her to pieces. "Fine," she said. "I'm leaving. Now I don't have to wonder why I left this wretched place to begin with."

Meredith gave Elizabeth a harsh glare, then went through the house to leave. Will followed her to make certain she did. The moment her mother was gone, Elizabeth allowed her composure to falter. She was grateful to feel Jayson's arms come around her, giving her perfect love and acceptance, as well as a firm shoulder to cry on.

"Let me see," he said, taking hold of her chin and tilting her face to his view. He made a noise of disgust. "It's pretty red," he muttered, "but I don't think it will bruise. Does it hurt?"

"Not really; not any more," she admitted. "I just . . . can't believe she'd do that."

"I can't either," he said. "What did she say to get you so upset?"

"How do you know I was upset?"

"Well, I don't *know*. But the last time I heard you argue with your mother—months ago—I heard her say some deplorable things to you, and you got pretty upset. And that's when she looked like she was going to tear you to pieces until your father intervened. I'm just assuming it was something similar."

"That about covers it."

"What did she say?"

Elizabeth said nothing. She just held more tightly to Jayson, and he wondered why she would be hesitant to tell him. "It was about me, wasn't it," he said with disgust. "That's why you don't want to tell me."

"It was indirectly about you."

"Indirectly? Would that be something about your taste in men?"

"No, I think she was rather impressed with you, now that she's witnessed your talent."

"Oh," he said lightly, "you *do* have something in common with your mother."

"That is not funny!" she insisted.

He let out a brief chuckle, then said intensely, "Sorry."

"Well," she added, "she was impressed until you threatened her brilliant attorney reputation." She actually laughed. "You really said that to my mother."

"I really did," he said, wondering if he should regret it. But he didn't. Still he had to say, "I'm sorry if I did something—"

"Don't be sorry," she said. "You were brilliant. My knight in shining armor." She smiled up at him.

Jayson looked into her eyes and asked, "What did she say that was indirectly about me that got you so upset?"

"It's not important."

"Oh, no you don't. Obviously, it was important enough to create a heated argument. You and I have never kept secrets from each other. As close as we are, I think I have a right to know what she said."

"You probably do," she said. "But it's . . . embarrassing."

"You're not going to embarrass me."

"I might embarrass myself."

"Just say it, Lady."

Elizabeth sighed and put her head to his shoulder, if only so she wouldn't have to look at him. "She asked me if I was using birth control."

She felt him take a sharp breath. Then he took her shoulders into his hands and looked at her hard. "She *said* that?"

"She did."

"And what did *you* say? I hope you told her that . . ." He didn't know how to put it without making a difficult conversation more difficult.

"I told her you were a gentleman, that nothing inappropriate had happened between us."

"And . . ." he drawled, knowing that's not where it ended.

Elizabeth looked up at him, and huge tears appeared in her eyes. "She said that . . . men were all alike and . . . you would get me pregnant . . . and my life would be shot."

Jayson felt an unfathomable anger rise inside of him. His desire to run after Meredith and bust her in the jaw was close to the motivation he'd felt to smash his guitar. But he felt sick now at the thought of what he'd done in anger, and he knew that anger would not help him—or Elizabeth. Instead, he counted to ten and touched her face as he spoke in a soft voice. "I hope you know I would never do that."

"I *do* know," she said. "So let's just . . . drop it. I'm glad she's gone. We just need to . . . forget about it." She said it firmly, but Jayson noted the look in her eyes and felt certain that for Elizabeth, forgetting about it would be easier said than done.

* * * * *

With the funeral over, adjusting to Derek's death became a study in dreariness. Jayson felt as if he'd go insane, simply from the absence of noise and laughter that had been left in Derek's place. He'd been so full of life and humor and energy. And now that he was gone, the whole world just looked a whole lot darker. What was bad became worse when Jayson woke up Saturday morning and realized that for several months now, every single Saturday had been spent focused on performing live with Derek at his side. Now he had no job, nowhere to go, nothing to do. And his heart felt like it would burst from the continual aching. He wanted to be with Elizabeth, but he couldn't find the motivation to even get out of bed and call her. She shared his grief more than anyone, except perhaps Will, but Elizabeth was his peer. She knew him, heart and soul, and he knew her. Thoughts of her finally prompted him to at least get on his feet. He went into the bathroom before he headed for the phone, but his mother intercepted his trek.

"What are your plans today?" she asked in a bright voice that he found annoying.

"Absolutely nothing," he said, "except for calling Elizabeth. But I can't do that because you're standing between me and the phone."

"Oh, I'll let you call her," she said. "But when you do, I want you to tell her you'll pick her up in an hour and you're going to have a picnic on the beach."

"We are?" he asked, wondering if he was still too asleep to recall something he was supposed to recall.

"You are," she said. "By the time you get a shower and have a piece of toast, I will have everything you need packed and ready to go." While he was trying to think of something to say, she added gently, "You need to get out and do something—something normal. Just . . . be with Elizabeth. Talk about how you're feeling. Just . . . relax. Next week you can both get through graduation, and then you can make some decisions on what to do beyond that."

Jayson felt suddenly grateful that his mother had the insight and brain capacity that he was obviously lacking. He couldn't come up with any words beyond, "Thank you." Then he hugged her, and she handed him the phone.

Elizabeth answered, sounding as unenthusiastic about life as he felt. But she seemed pleased with his mother's idea and said she'd be ready when he came to get her.

Elizabeth hung up the phone and glanced at the clock. She'd been up early and was already showered and dressed well enough to go to the beach. She'd been unable to sleep due to the echoes of her argument with her mother the day of the funeral. There was one point that continued to haunt her, and sometime around dawn she'd finally come to the conclusion that she just needed to talk to her father about it. Knowing that Jayson was coming in an hour, she knew she would have an eventual out if the conversation became difficult. She didn't want to upset her father, but there was something she had to know. She found him in the front room, sitting alone, looking dazed, staring at the piano.

"Can I talk to you?" she asked, startling him.

"Sure," he said, patting the couch beside him. Elizabeth sat down, and he added, "What can I do for you?"

"This is . . . hard for me, but . . . there's something Mom said that's been eating at me, and I . . . just have to know if there's a reason she would feel that way."

"Okay," he said with a hesitancy that increased her nervousness.

Elizabeth looked at the floor as she said, "She told me that men were all alike; and she said that if I gave Jayson half a chance, he'd get me pregnant and my life would be shot." She turned to look at her father, startled to see his eyes squeezed shut, his expression a painful grimace. Her heart plummeted as she felt this was one more piece of evidence to substantiate her suspicions. When he said nothing, she felt compelled to say, "That's it, isn't it? That's the reason she's so unhappy." She heard anger in her own voice but couldn't help it. "She married you because she was pregnant, and she's resented it ever since." Will turned to look at her with tears in his eyes, and she added firmly, "And she was pregnant with *me*."

"You're partly right," he said, "but I think you need to calm down and listen to the *whole* story. Yes, your mother was pregnant when I married her, but it was *not* my baby, and it was *not* you." She opened her mouth to respond, but no sound came out. He went on to say, "She'd become involved with some jock she went to college with. He was a jerk. He left her high and dry. I'd had a crush on your mother for months. When she suddenly didn't have a boyfriend, I made a point of putting myself into the picture. When I asked her to marry me, she admitted that she was pregnant. I told her I was willing to live with that. And truthfully, I think that's the biggest reason she married me. I think I always loved her a lot more than she loved me.

She miscarried that baby about a month after we got married. Things were actually pretty good between us for a few years. We had some good times, but it was never what it should have been."

"Do you wish you hadn't married her?"

He smiled and shook his head. "Oh, no," he said, pressing a hand to her face. "You and Derek are the best things that ever came into my life. If for no other reason, I would choose no differently if I had it to do over. Even with Derek gone, I wouldn't trade away a day of his life for anything in the world. The joy he brought to me is priceless, and I feel no less love for you, my sweet Elizabeth. You are such a light in my life."

He hugged her tightly, and before he let go, she realized he was crying. They sat together on the couch, crying all over again for the losses they had shared. In that moment, Elizabeth realized for the first time the common bond they shared, not only in losing Derek, but in losing Meredith—a long, long time ago.

They were still sitting there when Jayson came. Elizabeth answered the door with her father standing just behind her, and she knew it was clearly evident they'd both been crying. Jayson took a good, long look at them and said, "Another party, eh?"

"Oh, yeah," Will said. "You'd think the river would have run dry by now."

"You'd think," Jayson said, reaching for Elizabeth's hand.

"You kids have a good time," he said, forcing a smile.

"We're going to try," Jayson said. Elizabeth kissed her father on the cheek and walked out to the car with Jayson.

As he drove a familiar highway toward the coast, practically nothing was said between them. "Come on," he finally spoke, "we must have something to talk about. How about this weather?" he added in an attempt to lighten the mood, but she didn't even smile.

"Fine," she said, "here's some fodder for conversation. My mother was pregnant when she got married."

Jayson stared at her in amazement for as long as he could keep his eyes off the road. "Well, that's quite a jump from the weather. When did you find this out?"

"This morning. I asked my dad about what she'd said."

"She was pregnant?"

"Yes."

Knowing Elizabeth was older than Derek, he had to assume, "With you?"

"No. Actually, she miscarried that baby, but it was *not* my father's baby."

"Wow, that certainly puts a whole new light on their marriage, doesn't it."

"Yes, it certainly does. As I see it, she married him because he was a way out. He told me he knew that he loved her more than she ever loved him."

They talked a while longer about this revelation and how they felt about it, then silence descended again. Jayson was relieved to finally arrive at the beach. They parked in the usual place, and he carried his mother's picnic basket while Elizabeth carried the blanket he'd brought. After walking less then ten minutes, they came to a secluded section of beach where they'd come together many times—usually with Drew and Derek. More often just with Derek. And the three of them had always had so much to talk about, so much to laugh over.

"You hungry yet?" Jayson asked, spreading out the blanket in their usual spot.

"Not really; let's wait . . . unless you're—"

"I'm fine," Jayson said, and they both sat down. He watched her tuck her feet up beneath the blue and white flowered skirt she was wearing, then he moved his gaze to her face. She was so beautiful. But her sorrow was evident, and the reasons for it broke his heart as surely as he knew her heart was broken.

"Mom sent sunscreen," he said, reaching into the basket. "She said if I love you I'll make sure your beautiful skin is well protected." Elizabeth smiled, then let him rub sunscreen on her face and arms, and she did the same for him.

When minutes of silence passed, he stretched out on his side, leaning his head into his hand. "Talk to me, Lady," he said.

"There's nothing to talk about except Derek, and that's too . . . hard."

"Maybe we *need* to talk about him. Why don't you just tell me what's on your mind."

Elizabeth sighed and rested her arms on her knees. "I've never been to church, you know."

"I know."

"Do you think if I'd gone to church I would be able to cope with this better?"

Jayson made a dubious noise. "I've gone to church a great deal, and I don't think I'm coping with it any better than you are."

"Does that mean with all the time you've spent in church, you've never heard anything that explains death enough to give you any peace?"

"Not that I recall. I mean . . . I've heard sermons on death, but . . . the overall impression I've gotten has just been some vague mumbo jumbo that really doesn't answer anything at all. It's almost like the preacher pretends he has the answers to keep the congregation in awe of him, but I'd bet if I got in his face and asked some hard questions, he wouldn't know diddly-squat."

"So, do you think anybody has the answers? Or is the world just full of bogus religions that are . . . what? Making money off of God, or something?"

"Oh, I'm sure there are good people out there who have some of the truth, but personally, I don't think anybody has all of the truth. You know what I think?"

"What?" she asked, turning toward him.

"I think that when Jesus was on the earth, he taught the truth— and all of it. But I think that after He died it all fell apart with time. And I think most of the scriptures are distorted because they've been translated so many times, and we don't know *who* translated them."

Elizabeth sighed. "So, that pretty much leaves us in the dark, doesn't it."

"Yes, I suppose it does."

"But there must be a lot of good in the Bible. It can't all be wrong."

"No, I don't think it's wrong as much as it's . . . not complete. That's just my personal feeling, anyway."

"It makes sense, I suppose. So what does the Bible say about where people go after they die?"

"I don't know. I've never read it."

"A lot of good you are," she said, and he actually chuckled. A minute later she asked, "So what's your opinion? Where do you think Derek is now? Do you think this is it for him? Is he just . . . gone?"

"I don't know, Lady," he said intently. "I'd like to believe that his spirit lives on somewhere, but he sure feels gone to me."

"Yeah, me too," she said. "It would be nice to think that there is such a thing as forever, but I just don't see how it's possible."

"Okay," Jayson said, sitting up abruptly, "that's about as depressing as a conversation can get. Could we change the subject?"

"I don't know what else to talk about," she said, and Jayson just sighed. He didn't either.

Chapter Thirteen

Jayson was finally able to generate some pleasant conversation about Derek. They reminisced about the good times they'd shared, and Elizabeth told Jayson stories from their childhood he'd never heard before. But eventually they both ended up crying. Jayson just couldn't believe the body was capable of producing that many tears, any more than he could believe that Derek was actually gone.

They didn't eat their picnic until the middle of the afternoon, then Jayson stretched out on the blanket and fell asleep. He woke up to find the sun sinking toward the horizon over the sea and Elizabeth sitting beside him. Without a word he took her hand, and they walked the beach in bare feet. He rolled up his jeans and stepped into the water, bringing her along. Its coldness was initially startling as usual, but they soon became accustomed to the temperature. With the waves rushing over their lower legs, he pulled her into his arms to kiss her. It was such a pleasant distraction from his grief that he kissed her again, not surprised when she apparently shared his enthusiasm. When his feet began to go numb, he took her hand, and they walked back to where they'd left their things. Impulsively, he sat down in the sand, a short distance from the blanket, mostly because his feet were wet. She sat close beside him and put her head on his shoulder. In silence they watched the sun go down, then Jayson laid back on the sand and let out a heavy sigh. She stretched out beside him and looked into his face. "What are you thinking?" she asked gently.

"A week ago right now we were on stage with Derek. It had all become so . . . comfortable, so normal. And now it seems like a dream."

"Yeah, I know what you mean."

"How can he have been here a week ago, and now his funeral's over and he's in the ground?"

"I don't know," she said, putting her head on his shoulder. A moment later she lifted her head to look at him. She pressed a hand over his face then touched her lips to his. "I love you, Jayson. I would be lost without you."

"It's the other way around," he said and pressed his hand through her hair, urging her to kiss him again, as if her affection could somehow save him from the pain burning in his chest.

Elizabeth quickly became caught up in a kiss unlike anything she'd ever experienced before. She clung to him as if his kiss alone could give her everything she needed to live and breathe. She felt herself drawn completely under his power to a place where she couldn't feel the bite of death or the heartache of life. She became intoxicated with the ethereal effect of being drawn so fully away from the pain that had so quickly become a familiar part of her existence. Jayson loved her. And she loved him. Nothing else mattered. Instinctively, she believed that this tangible evidence of his love for her could somehow compensate for the lack of love and acceptance she'd had from her mother. While he kissed her on and on, Elizabeth found her mind wandering, wondering what these sensations inside of her might lead to. A flicker of logic in the back of her head told her she needed to use some common sense and stop now. But logic was quickly squelched by a voice more powerful, a voice telling her that crossing this line with Jayson would eliminate the confusion going on inside of her, this battle between her heart and her head that seemed to have no defined answer. If she made the choice now to give herself to him completely, then it would be done, and she could stop feeling torn between the life she'd convinced herself she was supposed to live and the life that she could share with Jayson. And while she knew at some level that she was being rash and foolish, a string of thoughts paraded through her mind, telling her that life was too short to care about being noble and moral and that there was no such thing as forever. And resounding through it all was the voice of her mother, bellowing expectations that Elizabeth suddenly felt determined to fulfill.

While Jayson marveled at the experience of holding Elizabeth close with a kiss that he believed could never end, he told himself he needed to enforce some reason between them, along with some distance. He could feel himself slipping toward that edge he'd been warned about, and he was astonished by how alluring the cliff could be. Caught up in an unearthly release from the pain he'd been holding so close, the impact of her affection was all the more intoxicating. Forcing some measure of sensibility, he detached his lips from hers and eased back enough to look into her eyes. Through the little remaining light of dusk, he absorbed the blatant desire on her face and became preoccupied with how thoroughly beautiful she was—and how he loved her. A moment later, he was completely unprepared to find her urging him toward boundaries that were clearly marked "No Trespassing Before Marriage."

"Elizabeth," he muttered, "we mustn't—"

"I don't care," she said as if she were someone else. Three times he found the strength to stop and retreat. And three times she urged him back toward the edge of some beckoning cliff. Dusk filtered into darkness while Jayson tried to tell himself he couldn't let this happen. He tried to tell himself he was stronger than this. But how could he not want what she seemed so eager to give? He was human, and nothing was more consuming to him than Elizabeth. Oh, how he loved her!

In one last desperate measure, he prayed silently. *Please God, give me the strength to stop this.* Immediately he recalled his mother telling him more than once, *If you truly love a girl, you will wait until you marry her.* And following his own mother's words, he heard Meredith Greer snidely saying in his mind, *I knew you were just like all the rest; I knew you'd get her pregnant and her life would be shot.*

"I can't do this!" Jayson muttered and moved abruptly away from her. Elizabeth felt a tangible shock from the sudden separation.

Jayson dug his fingers into the sand, so consumed with frustration he wanted to scream. He wanted to cry like a baby for reasons that had nothing to do with Derek's death. Instead, he jumped to his feet, needing to catch his breath and clear his head. "I'll be back in a few minutes," he muttered and hurried away.

Elizabeth felt suddenly cold and starkly alone. Her mind felt hazy as if she'd just emerged from a deep sleep filled with heavenly dreams, and now she was disoriented with the reality of being plucked from such an ecstatic state and drop-kicked back into the cold, cruel world. While she knew Jayson had only been gone a couple of minutes, his absence felt harsh, and she was suddenly afraid, uncertain, overwhelmed.

"Jayson!" she called and waited for a response, but it didn't come. "Jayson!" she heard herself scream with an urgency that made her realize how emotionally fragile she'd become.

Jayson heard her scream, and he quickly splashed ocean water on his face and shook it from his hands. He wiped his hands on his jeans as he ran in bare feet across the sand toward her. He found her curled up on her side, breathing sharply. He sank to his knees beside her and touched her face. "I'm here, Elizabeth. I'm here." She moaned and clutched onto him, and he realized she was shaking. "Are you cold?" he asked, and she nodded. He grabbed the blanket they'd been sitting on earlier and shook the sand out of it before he put it over her.

"Hold me," she murmured. "I need you to hold me."

"I'm here," he said, but kept his embrace discreet and impersonal. He pressed a kiss to her brow, wishing he knew what to say. Hovering somewhere between the brief moments of bliss they had just shared and a sick, smoldering regret, he wanted this moment to never end. In the deepest part of him, he knew that the further they moved from this experience, the deeper the regret would become. He wanted to just be here this way for as long as the world kept turning, and never have to face the cold, hard reality of the trust that had been broken between them.

"Jayson," she whispered and put her fingers to his face, and then her lips to his. "I love you, Jayson."

"I love you too, Elizabeth," he said with fervor. "I love you more than I could ever tell you . . . ever show you in a thousand years."

She let out a stilted laugh. "You're talking like a songwriter again."

"I could never write a song to express how I feel about you. Never."

"There you go again," she said.

Following several minutes of silence beyond the distant lapping of the ocean against the shore, she whispered close to his ear, "What happened, Jayson?"

"I don't know," he admitted, still trying to figure it out in his own mind.

More minutes passed with a quiet that Jayson knew was likely the calm before an inevitable storm. He'd been taught plainly that the universe was ruled by cause and effect. If you jump off a tall building, you will hit the ground. If you play with sharp objects you will get cut and bleed. If you play with fire, you will get burned. He knew it was true. And he knew that the boundaries of marriage and intimacy were in place for reasons of security and happiness. He knew that some might say it was an old-fashioned precept put into place by people attempting to control their children with the threat of God's punishment. But Jayson believed in his heart that God's dictates were more a matter of guidance and safety. *Don't play with fire or sharp objects. Don't mess around with sex. You'll get hurt.* And already he could feel that hurt settling in. He'd disappointed her. He'd disappointed himself. And he'd disappointed his mother—even if she didn't know it yet.

"I should take you home," he said, pressing his fingers through her sand-filled hair. She clutched tightly to him as if she couldn't bear the thought. "I don't want to go home either," he said, "but we have to."

In the car Jayson held Elizabeth's hand while he drove, but they had little to say. She was wrapped in the blanket, curled up on the seat, turned toward him. He felt her hand on his face and glanced toward her while he pressed her hand to his lips. He put his eyes back to the road and felt her hand in his hair. "You didn't do it," she said.

"Do what?" he asked, glancing briefly toward her as if that might help him understand what she meant.

"You . . . stopped . . . before it went too far."

Jayson took a deep breath and focused on the road. "Too far is relative," he said. "It went *way* too far."

"But not all the way," she said, and he wondered if that was dismay he heard in her voice.

"I'm sorry if I disappointed you," he said, if only to determine where he stood with her. "But I just couldn't do it."

"Why not?" she asked, and he tossed her a sharp glance.

"Because you would have hated me in the morning," he said, unable to avoid sounding terse, if only slightly. "I would have hated myself. If that disappoints you then—"

"No," she said, "I'm glad you stopped. I mean . . . I was disappointed then, but now I'm . . ." her voice cracked, "grateful. You obviously have more discipline than I do."

Jayson sighed. He didn't know her reasons for allowing herself to get so caught up in that kind of situation, but he had to say, "I think it's more complicated than that."

"What do you mean?" she asked, sounding alarmed.

Not knowing how to explain without putting his foot in his mouth, he simply said, "I don't know what I mean, Lady." He was surprised to feel tears come into his eyes and crack his voice. "I'm eighteen years old. I know nothing about such things. Quite frankly, it scared me to death. Now that it's gone that far, what about next time? Can I even be alone with you and trust myself? Can I ever expect you to trust me again?" His breathing sharpened as he bared his soul. "Can I pretend that it didn't cross my mind that . . ."

"What?" she pressed gently, squeezing his hand more tightly.

"That . . . if you *did* get pregnant, I could marry you and take you to LA with me and I wouldn't have to let you go to Boston, and I would never have to be away from you. But I know that's not right. The last thing I want is to take away your choices. But it scares me." He turned to look at her, then forced his eyes back to the road as he admitted, "If I'm completely honest, I have to wonder . . . with the time that you and I spend together, how am I supposed to deal with this?" He sounded angry, especially when he added, "If Derek were here to be our chaperone, maybe we could cope with this." He heard her sniffling and knew she was upset. "Hey, I'm sorry. I just . . ."

"It's okay," she said. "I just feel so . . . overwhelmed . . . and confused. I don't understand what happened, or . . . why I did that . . . and I don't know how to deal with it." She sniffled loudly. "I wish I had a mother I could actually talk to about such things, and . . ." Her voice faded into tears, and Jayson put his arm around her. She eased as close as it was possible while sitting in bucket seats with an emergency brake between them.

"You could talk to *my* mother," he said, "if you want to. I've heard her tell you if you ever needed some female company, that she would be there for you."

Elizabeth felt strangely comforted with the idea. She could feel comfortable enough talking to Leslie, even about this. But one problem stood out. "You want me to talk about this with your mother?"

Jayson sighed loudly. "She'll figure it out even if I don't tell her. She can see right through me, and she won't let it drop when she knows something's wrong." He sighed again. "Besides, I'm not sure I could get through this without her."

A minute later Elizabeth said with a teary voice, "Okay, then . . . will you take me to your place? Will she be home?"

Jayson glanced at the clock on the dashboard. "Yeah, she'll be home by the time we get there."

"I love you, Jayson," she said tearfully. "I'm so sorry for—"

"Don't apologize to me, Elizabeth. You know what they say. It takes two to tango."

Her tears increased. "But I was the one who—"

"Stop," he insisted. "I could have stood up and walked away long before I did, but I didn't. Enough said."

When they arrived at his home, he opened the car door for her and put his arm around her as they walked toward the apartment. Just before he reached out to open the door, she took hold of him and sobbed against his chest. "It's okay," he muttered, pressed to tears himself. "Everything's going to be okay. I'm going to take care of you. No matter what happens, I will always be here for you—as long as you want me to be."

"I would die without you, Jayson," she said and held more tightly to him.

"Hey, you're shaking again. Let's go inside."

She nodded and attempted to compose herself while he wiped his face with his hand before opening the door. Leslie looked up from where she was sitting on the couch. "Hi," she said brightly, then her countenance faltered when she saw their faces. "What's wrong?"

"I told you she could see right through me," Jayson said to Elizabeth. Then to his mother, "Elizabeth needs to talk to you. I think she could use a mother right now." He met Elizabeth's eyes and added, *"We* need to talk to you."

Leslie came to her feet, setting aside the book she'd been reading. "What's happened?" she asked, putting her arms around Elizabeth, who was still wrapped in the blanket.

Elizabeth became emotional, only managing to say to Jayson, "Will you call my dad . . . and tell him where we are?"

"Sure," he said and left Elizabeth in his mother's care to go to the kitchen phone.

It only rang once before Will answered.

"Uh . . . hi, Will. It's Jayson."

"Is everything all right?"

"Relatively speaking," Jayson said. "We're at my place; my mom is here. Elizabeth's pretty upset, and she wanted to talk to my mother. We didn't want you to worry."

Will sighed loudly. "Does this have something to do with what she and I talked about this morning? I assume she told you."

"Yeah, she told me. But it's . . . not *only* that. She's talking to my mom. I'll bring her straight home when they're done, but I don't know when that will be."

"It's okay. Let her talk. Thanks for calling."

"Sure," Jayson said.

"Uh . . . Jayson?"

"Yeah?"

"Would you and your family come over for dinner tomorrow? I don't know that I can bear the quiet of a Sunday otherwise."

"I'll be there," he said. "I'll have to ask the others."

"Good enough," Will said. "Let me know."

Jayson ended the call and turned around to see his mother and Elizabeth sitting on the couch, Elizabeth crying silently in Leslie's arms. Jayson moved one of the kitchen chairs to face them, but he remained on his feet and stuffed his hands deep into the pockets of his jeans. Leslie looked up at him over the top of Elizabeth's head. "Do you want to tell me what's got her so upset?"

"No, but I'm going to anyway."

"I'm waiting," Leslie said as if she sensed she wasn't going to like it.

Jayson just forced himself to say it. Beating around the bush would get him nowhere with his mother. "We got carried away."

She tightened her eyes on him and furrowed her brow. "Are you talking about what I think you're talking about?"

"Probably."

"How carried away?"

"Very," he stated, his voice trembling.

He saw his mother's eyes go wide—with fury—and the regret settled into him more deeply. Little in life gave him more joy than making his mother proud. And disappointing her was creating an equivalent grief.

Her voice was calm with barely suppressed panic as she demanded, "Are you trying to tell me that this girl could be pregnant?"

"No!" he insisted, immeasurably grateful that his answer wasn't any different.

"What *are* you telling me?" she asked, holding Elizabeth more tightly as if she suddenly saw him as some ravenous beast from whom Elizabeth must be protected.

"It didn't go that far," Jayson said with quiet humility. "But close; too close. We need your help, Mother, so we can understand what happened and not let it happen again."

Leslie let out a visible sigh, and her eyes grew distant, as if she were trying to absorb the information she'd just been given. She then looked up at Jayson, sorrow mingling with anger in her eyes. "I really thought you knew better. I thought I had taught you the importance of maintaining appropriate boundaries."

"I *do* know better," he insisted.

"Then explain to me how this could happen."

"I . . . don't know," he admitted, his emotion threatening. "I . . . just . . . I don't know . . . what happened. It was just . . ."

"It was my fault," Elizabeth said, sitting up straight to look directly at Leslie.

Leslie gave her a hard stare. "Trying to be noble will get you nowhere with me, Elizabeth. I want to understand what happened and why, so I can help you. But I can't do that if you distort what happened for the sake of protecting him."

"It's true," she insisted. "I'm the one who initiated it. He kept trying to stop, but I . . ." Her words faltered.

Leslie looked hard at Jayson and said, "Well, he should have tried harder."

"Yes, I should have," Jayson said with anger, but Elizabeth couldn't tell exactly who he was angry with—her for encouraging all of this to happen, his mother for her recrimination, or himself for allowing it to go on. "But I didn't!" he went on. "I just was not strong enough to be everything you want me to be, Mother, and I apologize for that. Maybe if my best friend hadn't been smashed in a car six days ago, I could have been more superhuman. But I'm *not!* I blew it, and I'm asking for your help, Mother." He groaned and kicked the chair beside him, knocking it over. He saw Elizabeth wince and his mother's expression harden.

"Okay, that's enough anger," Leslie said. "That move was a little too much like your father, and I won't tolerate such behavior in my home."

The very idea made Jayson sick to his stomach, but something base and angry inside himself blurted the words, "Maybe I *am* like my father. Maybe deep inside I'm just selfish and irresponsible and destined to hurt the people I love."

"That's ludicrous, and you know it."

"Right now I don't know anything!" he shouted.

"Jayson!" Leslie shouted back. Then in a firm, quiet voice she added, "Sit down and calm down and tell me what you're afraid of."

Jayson met his mother's eyes, then Elizabeth's. He blew out a long, slow breath before he picked up the chair and put it upright. He sat down with a hard sigh and pressed his hands through his hair, finding it full of sand.

"What are you afraid of, Jayson?" she repeated.

Jayson sighed and admitted, "I'm afraid . . . it will happen again . . . and I won't be able to stop and . . . I'll ruin her life . . . and mine. I don't want her to marry me because she *has* to. I want her to marry me because she knows that I love her and respect her. I want her to trust me." The expected tears began to flow as he hit on the hard truth. "Now I wonder if she'll ever trust me again . . . if she'll ever believe I respect her."

"Of course I trust you," Elizabeth insisted, but Jayson felt too absorbed with confusion to know whether or not to believe her. "This changes nothing between us. The only thing I'm afraid of," she said more to Leslie, "is having it get out of control like that again. I don't know what happened to me." Her tears began again. "I never dreamed that . . . it could be that way. I mean . . . my dad told me that passion could overtake a person and make them lose control, but . . . I don't know. Maybe I didn't completely believe him. It was like . . . I wasn't even myself. It actually *scared* me. But it was so . . . incredible. How could I not want to feel that way again? But . . . I don't want to mess up my life, or Jayson's."

Leslie blew out a long breath. "Okay, well . . . I have to say . . . now that I'm adjusting to the shock, I'm glad you're willing to be so honest with me. It takes a lot of courage and maturity to admit you've made a mistake."

Jayson was grateful to hear Elizabeth express his own thoughts. "It's not so hard to be honest with somebody you know will love you anyway and not bite your head off."

"Well, I'll admit to some . . . shock," Leslie said and looked at her son. "But I do think Jayson still has his head attached. And yes, I love both of you no matter what." She took Elizabeth's hand. "So let's talk. What do you think went wrong?"

During the course of the conversation, Leslie got them to admit that the first problem was their sharing any affection at all when they were both struggling with grief and depression. Their emotions were too vulnerable to be kissing like that. She suggested that they needed to have enough self-discipline to recognize their own moods and not be alone together if either of them were struggling. Jayson was amazed to hear Leslie delicately draw out Elizabeth's concerns in attempting to understand what had happened to her physically. Jayson understood his own physical functions, but he learned by listening to his mother's frank but appropriate explanations that while a guy could get turned on more quickly and easily, a woman was capable of all the same sensations, but her experience could be far more intense. Leslie made it clear that what they had experienced together was meant to be shared within a marriage relationship for many valid reasons. It was her belief that within the bounds of a good marriage, such intimacy could be one of the greatest aspects of life.

Jayson felt compelled to ask, "Was there ever anything good between you and Dad?"

Leslie's expression became typical of when they talked about him—mildly disgusted. "When he was sober, we had some great moments. But that became less and less frequent as time went on. When he was drunk he just treated me the way my father did."

Jayson took a sharp breath. He knew her father had been guilty of some heinous abuse, which made the implication clear. To see the way she could talk about sexual issues so freely—and with such a healthy attitude—was a miracle in Jayson's opinion. He knew she'd suffered a great deal, and her emotional recovery had been difficult. He and Drew had watched her go through a breakdown after the divorce, and she had eventually told them why. It was one of many reasons that Jayson admired her so much. And looking at her now, hearing her talk about the treatment she'd endured from his father, he felt as amazed as he felt sick. She must have read his mind when she said, "Yes, it's difficult to hear, but you're an adult now. And you need to understand the power behind your choices. Your decision regarding marriage will have more impact on your lives than any other single choice. When you marry the right person, at the right time, in the right way—for the right reasons—you determine a great deal of the outcome of your life."

Jayson asked her firmly, "Do you regret marrying my father?"

"No," she said so quickly and firmly that it startled him. "You and your brother are the best things that ever happened to me. Believe it or not, there was good in your father. I married his potential, and he chose to drown that potential in alcohol. But the two of you got the best of his qualities, and you would not be who you are if not for him. I wouldn't want you or Drew to be any different. For that reason and none other I would do it all again."

"Funny," Elizabeth said, "that's what my dad told me just this morning."

"Your father's a good man," Leslie said to her, then she turned to Jayson, "which is one of many reasons that you need to go and talk to him."

"About what?" Jayson asked, feeling his heart pound.

"You need to come clean and tell him what you told me."

"He'll never respect me again," Jayson protested. "He's . . . like a father to me."

"Exactly," Leslie said. "Which is why you need to come clean with him." She leaned toward Jayson and said intently, "Listen to me, Jayse, you have crossed a line that will now be ten times more difficult not to cross again. And if you are any kind of man, if you love Elizabeth as much as you claim, you won't let it happen again. It's not a matter of knowing when to quit making out; it's a matter of not making out at all."

"So . . . what are you saying? That I should never kiss her again?"

"No," she said firmly, "starvation is only going to make you feel desperate. But you need to keep it to an appropriate minimum; not the kind of kissing that leads to lovemaking. I'm your mother, and I will be happy to spend time with the two of you any time I'm available. But I'm not always available. I'm going to trust you. I'm not going to nag you or wonder what you're doing, but I expect you to remain open and honest. And I will do the same and not be afraid to ask how you're doing or talk openly about this. Because I love you—both of you. If we can be honest and open, then you're less likely to have any further problems. You know you'll have to face me, and you know I'll be able to tell if you're keeping something from me. And for the same reason, you need to talk to Will. He loves you both, and he can help you get through this. His home will be another safe refuge where the two of you can be together when he's home, and you'll know somebody cares enough to keep track of what you're doing."

Jayson looked at Elizabeth and admitted, "I don't know if I can tell him."

"You have to, Jayson," Leslie said. "He needs to know what's going on. Elizabeth is all he has left." Jayson winced, and she went on. "He may be upset, but I know he's not a harsh or unfair man. He will respect you more if you talk to him. Don't think he won't notice the change in your behavior toward Elizabeth—and him. He's smarter than that. Most kids think they're so sly and clever, keeping things from their parents. But if you talk to any parent who is paying attention, they can tell when something changes. If he knows how much you care for Elizabeth, he can help you make sure it doesn't happen again, the same way I can. That way the two of you can be at either of your homes, with one of us around, and be comfortable and not have to pretend." She stood up as if to conclude the conversation and added firmly, "You would also do well to ask God to help you. And He will." She hugged them both and said, "I'm going to bed. You both know where to find me if you need anything—anytime."

After Leslie went into the bathroom, Jayson looked at Elizabeth and felt as if they were existing together in some kind of altered state, some kind of strange time warp, a dream that kept them hovering in some bizarre limbo.

"Come on," he said, coming to his feet with his hand extended, "I need to take you home."

The short drive passed in silence. At the front door Jayson hugged her tightly and kissed her quickly before he said with fervor, "I love you. I'll see you tomorrow. Your dad invited me to dinner; Mom will probably come with me, but . . . maybe I should come over before she does so . . . we can talk to him."

Elizabeth nodded and looked down. "I'll see you tomorrow, then."

The minute Jayson got back into the car, he started to cry. By the time he got home, he was crying so hard he could hardly breathe. He didn't know if he was crying over Derek's death, or what had happened between him and Elizabeth. Both, he reasoned. He forced himself to calm down before he went inside and took a shower. He hardly slept that night and got up early. Knowing it was a few hours before his mother would be wanting him to go to church with her, he phoned the Greers, knowing if they were still in bed they'd let the machine get the call and he'd not be disturbing them. Will answered after only two rings, sounding fully awake.

"Hi," Jayson said, "my mom and I will be there for dinner. Drew's got plans."

"I'll look forward to it," he said.

"Can we bring something?"

"No, just your company."

"Uh . . ." Jayson forced the words out, "I need to talk to you, Will. Is it too early to come over?"

"No, we're up. Elizabeth is cooking pancakes. Come over and have some, and we'll talk."

"Thanks," he said. "I'll be there in a few minutes."

"Was that Jayson?" Elizabeth asked when her father hung up the phone.

"He's coming over; he says he needs to talk to me." Elizabeth unconsciously stiffened, then realized her father had noticed. "Does this talk include you?"

"Yeah, I believe it does," she said and was relieved when he didn't press her.

Jayson arrived within minutes. He gave her a quick kiss in greeting, and the three of them sat to share a quiet breakfast. When they'd finished eating, Will leaned back in his chair and said, "So, what did you want to talk to me about?"

Jayson exchanged a concerned glance with Elizabeth. She opened her mouth to speak, but he put up a hand to stop her. "I need to do this," he said quietly to her, then he turned his attention to Will, taking Elizabeth's hand across the corner of the table.

Will became more attentive and visibly concerned as he apparently took in their terrified expressions. "What's up?" he asked with obvious trepidation.

"There's something we need to tell you," Jayson said, "and I know you're going to be angry with me, but . . . I've been praying that you would hear me out and that you would be willing to help us get through this."

Will took a sharp breath, looked at them both, and said, "Are you trying to tell me Elizabeth is pregnant?"

"No!" Jayson blurted, then chuckled tensely. "No, no, no. That's not possible."

Will sighed visibly and relaxed some. "Okay," he said. "Knowing that much, I think I can take just about anything."

"Does that mean if she *was* pregnant, you couldn't take it?" Jayson asked.

Again Will looked at each of them, but he spoke directly to Jayson. "If that were the case, I would certainly be disappointed and concerned, but we would work together to manage the situation in the best possible way. You should both know that I would love you—no matter what." His eyes deepened on Jayson. "Both of you."

Jayson took a deep breath, holding those words foremost in his mind as he admitted, "I'm glad to know that, because . . . we need your help . . . to make certain that . . . it doesn't come to that."

"What are you saying, Jayson?" Will asked. "Just . . . get to the point."

Jayson lifted his chin and squeezed Elizabeth's hand more tightly. His heart was pounding, and his palms felt clammy. He forced himself to just say it. "We got carried away, Will. I think we were both . . . taken by surprise at how . . . overpowering it could be. We just . . . lost control."

Will seemed to be absorbing this, then he asked, "But it didn't go all the way?"

"No," Jayson said, "but close. Too close. And once we got some distance from the moment, it scared us both . . . a lot."

"Well, that's some credit to both of you," he said, but his tone of voice indicated his displeasure at what he was hearing.

Elizabeth said tearfully, "We love each other. We don't want to mess up each other's lives."

"So," Jayson went on, "that's why we're here. I'm willing to take responsibility for what happened and make sure it never happens again, and—"

"Your attitude is admirable, Jayson, but Elizabeth is equally responsible, and she needs to be equally accountable in handling the problem."

Now that he'd crossed the line of getting the confession into the open, Jayson relaxed somewhat and held Elizabeth's hand in his while they talked with Will, much as they'd talked with his mother. Will looked Jayson in the eye and expressed his disappointment, then quickly added that his respect for both of them had deepened in seeing their willingness to be honest and open about the problem. He basically gave them all the same messages Leslie had given them, from a slightly different perspective. He added a powerful point when he said that people can sit and watch a half-hour sitcom on TV and see two people go to bed together, as if it were no big deal—even a source of humor. But they never show the consequences or results. Beyond the obvious concerns of sexually transmitted diseases and unwanted pregnancy, Will talked about studies he'd read of the adverse emotional impact of such things throughout people's lives. Those same studies had stated plainly that people who live together prior to marriage have a much higher rate of divorce. He mentioned that sharing physical intimacy with a person creates an emotional closeness; you instinctively feel more responsible for them, more connected. But when you're not in a position to continue that closeness or be a part of their lives, it creates confusion and puts a strain on your spirit.

Elizabeth mentioned that, feeling as she did about the experience, it was difficult to believe the casual talk of sex she'd been exposed to at school. She knew beyond any doubt, as did Jayson, that many of their peers were actively involved in casual sex and talked about it freely, as if it were no big deal, as if it were a natural part of the dating experience.

Will commended them for being able to recognize that such attitudes were distorted and unhealthy. But having been regularly exposed to such talk surely made remaining chaste more difficult. When the conversation was done, Will hugged each of them tightly and told them he loved them.

"You're the best father I've ever had," Jayson told Will with sincerity.

Will gave an emotional smile and hugged him again, saying close to Jayson's ear, "Promise me it will always be that way, Jayson. No matter what happens, promise me that you'll always be a son to me."

Jayson looked into his eyes. "I promise," he said firmly.

Chapter Fourteen

Elizabeth impulsively decided to go to church with Jayson, even though she never had before. She hurried to change her clothes, and they picked up Leslie and Drew before going to the little chapel at the edge of town. She enjoyed singing the hymns and liked the feeling there. The sermon was on the story of the good Samaritan. She'd never heard it before, but she really liked it. When the meeting ended, she whispered to Jayson, "Do you think we could ask the preacher some questions?"

Jayson looked at her in surprise, but it only took him a moment to know what she meant. "Sure. Why not?" he said, but he felt instinctively skeptical.

Jayson asked his mother if she would mind waiting. Drew overheard their purpose and said, "This I gotta hear."

They waited for the rest of the congregation to clear out, then the clergyman turned to Jayson and said, "What can I do for you, young man?"

"I just have a question," he said, and the man smiled. Jayson wished he could remember his name. "My best friend was killed a week ago and—"

"Oh, I'm so sorry," he said. "I didn't know."

"Thank you, but . . . I just can't help wondering where he is now. I would appreciate any insight you might have."

"You can rest assured that his spirit has gone to a far better place."

Jayson liked that answer, and he could tell that Elizabeth did as well when she squeezed his hand. He felt compelled to ask, "That is good to know, but . . . I have to wonder if we will ever see him again. Will we be with loved ones after this life is over?"

Jayson noticed Drew looking at him in surprise, then he turned abruptly to the preacher, as if to echo Jayson's question.

"You must understand," the minister said in a tone to indicate he had bad news, "that our existence there will be much different than it is here. Relationships will not have the meaning there that they do here. Your question, therefore, is irrelevant, young man."

Jayson was highly tempted to yell at this man and tell him exactly what he thought of *that,* but Leslie seemed to sense his mood and said quickly, "Thank you. We appreciate your time." She took hold of Jayson's arm, and they all moved outside.

"He's wrong, you know," Jayson said to his mother.

"How do you know that?" she countered.

"I just do. How can our relationships mean nothing in heaven? How can it be heaven without being with those we love? The very idea is ludicrous."

"Well, it may feel ludicrous," Leslie argued, "but maybe that's just the way it is. If you ever find proof otherwise, I'd sure like to hear about it."

They drove in silence back to the apartment to drop Drew off, and Leslie went in to get the cobbler she'd baked that morning. Jayson and Elizabeth waited in the car, and he took the opportunity to say, "I don't believe it, Elizabeth. My deepest gut instinct tells me there has to be more." He looked into her eyes. "We *will* see him again. We just have to."

Elizabeth sighed, feeling strangely comforted by his conviction. "I hope you're right," she said. "Otherwise, there doesn't seem to be much point in caring about anything."

"Well, I think we should keep caring, just in case I'm right."

Elizabeth kissed his cheek. "Good plan."

When they arrived at the Greer home, Will was ridiculously happy to see them. He made a fuss over Leslie's cobbler, and she offered to help him in the kitchen.

"Can I help, too?" Jayson asked.

"Yes," Will said, "you can give us some background music."

Jayson opened his mouth to protest, but Elizabeth nudged him with her elbow and said, "He'd love to." She took his arm and urged him into the front room, where she said quietly, "He's having a hard time, Jayson. He loves to hear you play. Do it for him."

Jayson sighed and thought of all that Will had done for him. He sat at the piano and decided he could handle playing some of the stuff he'd played before he ever came to Oregon—which mostly consisted of Elton John. He started out with "Harmony," singing the lyrics to Elizabeth with an edge of humor. When that was done, he moved right into the energetic, "Your Sister Can't Twist, But She Can Rock and Roll," making Elizabeth laugh with his exaggeration of certain words.

Elizabeth then got out some sheet music by Mozart, and she played a piece that sounded pretty good, even though she'd not done it in a while. By then dinner was ready, and the four of them gathered around the table to eat. They weren't far into the meal before Will admitted his disbelief that a week ago Derek had been sitting at the table with them. They talked about those final moments before he'd left, his humorous antics, and the color he'd brought into their lives. But they managed to talk about him without the intense emotion they'd been enduring previously.

Jayson expressed his biggest challenge when he admitted, "Everything's just gray without him. It's like the world used to be colored; now it's gray. I feel gray. Everywhere I look it's just . . . gray."

Elizabeth said to the others, "He's talking like a songwriter again."

"He does that," Leslie said proudly. "But I have to agree with him. Everything is just more . . . gray without Derek."

"Do you suppose it will get easier with time?" Will asked.

"I sure hope so," Jayson said. "If I had to feel this way for the rest of my life . . . well, I just couldn't do it."

"I don't think we'll ever stop missing him," Elizabeth said, "but surely we will adjust."

"I'm certain you're right," Will said. "It was that way with my parents' deaths. Time really did help, even though I've never stopped missing them."

Leslie agreed it had been that way with losing her mother. Then the conversation shifted when Will said, "So, it's graduation Thursday. This is a pretty big milestone for the two of you. Although, I must confess you both seem way too mature to just be at this point."

"I feel ten years older than I did last week," Jayson admitted.

"I think we all do," Will said, then brightened his voice. "I assume the two of you will be going to the graduation dance and the big party afterward at the school."

"I hadn't really thought about it," Jayson said.

"I suppose we will," Elizabeth added.

"Well," Will said, "I've already asked Leslie if she would go to the graduation exercises with me. It starts at noon, I believe. Would the two of you like to go out for an early dinner afterward, before the dance begins?"

"Sure," Jayson said after glancing at Elizabeth.

"I'd rather do that than anything else," she admitted.

It took a great joint effort to get through the remainder of the day without thinking too hard about the previous Sunday's events. They washed dishes, played board games, watched a movie, made sandwiches, and they all cried here and there. But they all had to agree on how grateful they felt to have each other.

When the evening was growing late, Jayson sat in the front room with Elizabeth, talking quietly, waiting for his mother to come and tell him they should be going. Elizabeth started playing the piano, and Jayson went to the kitchen for a drink of water. He stopped cold in the doorway when he found Will kissing his mother. For a long moment, he just stared, unable to believe his eyes. When their kiss went on and on, he realized this was far from the first time it had happened. He cleared his throat loudly, and they both turned toward him, startled.

"Am I supposed to pretend I didn't see that?" he asked, not certain why he felt angry.

"No, of course not," Leslie said.

"So . . . how long has this been going on?" Jayson asked, feeling disconcerted for reasons he didn't understand.

"How long has what been going on?" Elizabeth asked, appearing at his side.

Jayson didn't know how to answer, didn't know what to say, so he just turned and walked away, aware that Elizabeth was following him. He was surprised to find himself at the door of the music room. Habit had drawn him there. He felt hesitant at first to go in, but once he did he felt strangely comforted. In this room he felt some tangible evidence of Derek's existence. His guitar had been returned here following its display at the funeral, and he noticed there was no evidence of the destruction he'd created with his own guitar. He stood in the middle of the room with a thousand thoughts rolling through his mind, the most prominent being what he'd just discovered about Will and his mother. If nothing else, it was a distraction from the grief of Derek's absence.

"What's wrong?" Elizabeth asked, startling him to an awareness that he wasn't alone.

For a long moment their eyes met, and the memories of what they'd shared on the beach made his heart quicken and his stomach flutter. He forced his eyes elsewhere and swallowed hard. Sticking to the issue at hand, he asked, "Did you know our parents were romantically involved?"

"No!" she said, laughing.

"You think it's funny?"

"Obviously, you don't," she said and laughed again. He just glared at her, then looked away. "So . . . what happened?"

"I just walked in on them . . . kissing. And they looked like they'd had a fair amount of practice."

Elizabeth laughed again before she said, "Is that such a bad thing? They've both got to be pretty lonely, don't you think? They're very much alike in many ways. It's not such a surprise when you think about it."

"No, I suppose not," Jayson admitted.

"Then, what's wrong?"

"I don't know," he said. "It just . . . took me by surprise, I suppose."

"I can understand that, but . . ." She stopped when Will and Leslie appeared in the open doorway, holding hands.

Will looked directly at Jayson, saying, "You asked me a question and didn't give me a chance to answer it."

"Sorry," Jayson said.

"If you'll sit down, we can talk," Will said, and the four of them moved the chairs in the room to positions where they sat in some semblance of a circle, Jayson holding Elizabeth's hand, Leslie holding Will's.

"Okay," Will said. "You asked how long this has been going on. The answer is that we've been friends for a good, long time. When your mother left," he said looking at Elizabeth, "Leslie and I started talking a great deal on the phone, mostly late at night. Until last week we had never actually gone out together except to see your performances. Our first official date was last Saturday night, while you kids were working. We'd intended to talk about it when both of our families were together last Sunday, but then Drew didn't come for dinner, and we wanted you all to know at the same time." He hung his head and sighed, and they all knew what had happened only hours beyond that. He looked back up at Jayson and said with a breaking voice, "Your mother has helped me get through this last week, Jayson. There just wasn't a good time to tell the two of you that something had changed between us."

"Okay," Jayson said, but Will seemed dissatisfied with his response.

"Is there a reason you think I shouldn't be dating your mother, Jayson?" he asked.

"Obviously, you're both adults, and it's none of my business."

"Jayson," Will said gently, "we *are* both adults, and we don't need your permission. But it is *certainly* your business. You have a right to know what's going on."

"I guess that's the problem," Jayson said. "I didn't know *anything* was going on. It just took me off guard, that's all. At least when you caught me kissing your daughter, you knew we were dating."

"Yes, that's true," Will said. "And I'm truly sorry that we didn't talk about it sooner. It just didn't seem relevant with everything else that's happened."

"Okay," Jayson said. "Is there anything else we should know?"

"No," Will said. "If something changes, we'll be sure to let you know."

Elizabeth said, "So I guess this means that our going out to dinner Thursday is more like . . . a double date?"

"I suppose it is," Will said, smiling at Leslie.

The following morning when Jayson picked Elizabeth up for school, she said, "I get the feeling you're not very happy about our parents dating."

Jayson admitted honestly, "No, it's not that. Once I got used to it, I was okay. I can see it's a good thing." He smirked and kissed her hand. "Maybe we could have a double wedding."

"That would be ironic," she said, looking out the window.

"I was just . . . surprised, that's all. I mean . . . my mother hasn't dated *at all* since the divorce. And that's been a long time."

"How old were you when she left your dad?"

"Seven," he said.

"That is a long time," she said, then turned to look at him. "My dad's a good man, Jayson. He'll treat her well."

"I know he will," Jayson said. "I'm not worried about that. I'm just . . . overwhelmed, I guess. Far too much has changed in far too short a time."

"Yeah," she said, and silence fell until they arrived at school and went their separate ways for classes. At lunch they were just sitting down across from each other in the cafeteria when they were approached by the studentbody president. Jayson didn't know his name, but he knew the face.

"Hi," he said more to Jayson, then he nodded at Elizabeth. "I was told I could find you here. May I sit down?"

"Sure," Jayson said, "but I wouldn't recommend the rice stuff; the chicken is much better."

Their visitor laughed softly and sat at the end of the table. "You probably don't know who I am," he said more to Jayson. "Elizabeth does, but—"

"This is Alan," she said.

"Hi, Alan," Jayson said.

"I was at the funeral," Alan said. "I didn't know Derek, but he was a student here, and I felt I should be there. It was a beautiful service."

"Yes, it was," Jayson said, wondering if this was simply an attempt to offer condolences or if Alan had another purpose.

"You know," Alan said, "Derek should have walked at graduation this week." He looked more at Elizabeth and said, "His name will be read along with the other graduates." Elizabeth nodded, and Jayson saw moisture brim in her eyes. He reached across the table to take her hand. "But I feel we need something more," Alan said. "Something that will make it possible for every member of Derek's class to remember him well. Even for those who didn't know him, the loss of a fellow student can have a lasting impact. They're all mourning his loss in some way. The principal just got off the phone with Derek's father. They're putting together a slide show of pictures. And when that's over, we would like you to play that song you played at the funeral."

Elizabeth saw Jayson bristle. "The slide show's a great idea," he said. "But I don't really think that—"

"I can understand your reluctance," Alan said. "I know it must be difficult to play it, but—"

"I just don't want to perform at graduation—especially *that* song," Jayson said.

Elizabeth leaned toward Jayson and said gently, "I don't think they're asking for a performance, Jayson. I think what they want is a tribute."

"Exactly," Alan said. "Will you do it . . . for Derek?"

Jayson sighed and met Elizabeth's encouraging eyes. "Fine," he said hesitantly, "on one condition."

"Anything," Alan said.

"Make that two conditions; no, three," Jayson added, and Alan chuckled.

"I'm listening," he said.

"First of all, the piano needs to be professionally tuned."

"Done."

"You make the explanation before I play it; make it clear that it's not a performance, and it's not a musical number. It's a tribute to Derek."

"Done," Alan said again.

"And no applause. A minute of silence, and then we go on."

"You got it," Alan said firmly. "I'll make that very clear."

After Alan thanked him and left, Jayson said to Elizabeth, "And what are you going to be doing while I play this tribute?"

"Crying," she said.

"Yeah, well . . . I'll be doing that too, but everybody will be watching *me.*"

"It's good practice," she said. "Someday millions of people will be watching you when you perform on the Grammy Awards." Jayson made a scoffing noise. Such dreams felt very hollow without Derek. "Before that happens," she said, "you'll have to buy your mother a TV so she can watch it."

"I'll put that on my list of things to do," he said with a cynical edge to his voice, then he finished his lunch.

When graduation day arrived, Jayson hung his freshly pressed, navy blue graduation gown in the backseat of the car and drove with his mother to the Greer home. Drew would be attending the graduation, but he'd be going later with a friend. Elizabeth answered the door, already wearing her white gown. It was still unzipped, however, and he could see that she was wearing the black dress she'd worn to the funeral. She pointed at his own black attire and said, "Great minds think alike."

"It seemed appropriate," he said, and she nodded. She hugged Jayson, then insisted he put his gown on as well.

Jayson teased Elizabeth about the special collar and gold tassels she wore. "That's pretty impressive, Miss Highbrow. I'm not smart enough to get things like this."

Elizabeth smirked and kissed him quickly. "I'm not talented enough to be the great Jayson Wolfe."

Will and Leslie teased them a little while Will snapped several pictures of them, separately and together. "Now put the hats on," Leslie said.

"Who invented these?" Jayson asked with a scowl as Elizabeth put his on for him. "It's got to be the stupidest hat I've ever seen."

"But you look so smart," Leslie said.

"Derek would have loved it," Elizabeth said. "He loved stupid hats."

"Yeah, he would have loved it," Jayson said sadly, then he forced himself to lighten up as he scooped Elizabeth into his arms, making her laugh, and Will snapped a picture.

They drove together to where the event would take place. Jayson and Elizabeth went to join the other graduates, while Will and Leslie found a seat. As Elizabeth got into the line of students that were standing in alphabetical order, she found it difficult to remain composed. Derek should have been standing right in front of her. She could well imagine his possible antics and how she would pretend to be annoyed and embarrassed by his behavior. When "Pomp and Circumstance" began to play over the loudspeakers and the procession began, she had to quickly wipe a few tears before she walked out. She hated not being able to sit by Jayson, but the Greers were a long way from the Wolfes in the alphabet. When she'd mentioned this to him at rehearsal the previous day, he'd pointed out that if she'd married him, they could sit together. She didn't want to admit how tempting such an offer really was.

Early in the program an explanation was given of the recent tragic death of Derek Greer, one of their classmates. The slide show was announced, and Elizabeth was grateful to have tissues stashed in the little purse that hung on a long strap beneath her graduation gown. With a tender song playing as background music, a series of photographs representing Derek's life flashed across a huge screen. The pictures were incredible; the memories they stirred were difficult, but comforting somehow. While Elizabeth cried silently, the girl sitting next to her put an arm around her shoulders. And Elizabeth barely knew her. The last few pictures included her and Jayson, since they were taken at their performances. And the final shot was Derek's senior picture where he was wearing a tux—just like the one he'd been buried in.

Following the slide show, Alan stood at the pulpit and said with solemn dignity, "In a spirit of tribute, we have asked Derek's closest friend and fellow musician, Jayson Wolfe, to share with us the song that he played at the funeral. This song was one of Derek's favorites, and Jayson has agreed to play it now, as a tribute to our fellow friend and classmate. He has requested that to honor Derek we withhold our applause at the end and that instead we join together in a minute of silence. As Jayson mentioned at the funeral, this song is ironically called 'Funeral for a Friend.'"

Jayson left the hat on his chair and moved to the piano. He'd only gone through the song once the day before, and he attempted to focus on the piano and put his emotion elsewhere. In a way, this was more difficult than the funeral, he decided. Today he missed Derek beyond belief. They had talked about this day for so long, planned for it, reached toward it, mostly because it signified the beginning of a new season in life for them. And now Jayson would be embarking on that season without him.

He forced such thoughts away and focused on the keys. He took a deep breath and began. It only took a few seconds for him to become lost in the music, and it occurred to him that as long as he could play music, he might actually be able to get through whatever this life dished out to him.

When the song was done, he put his hands in his lap and bowed his head until more than a minute later when he heard a voice over the microphone say, "Thank you." Jayson returned to his seat.

When it came time for the names to be read, Jayson felt unbelievably nervous about hearing Derek's name. When the senior class president said into the microphone, "Derek William Greer," a huge roar of cheers and applause filled the room, and everyone who wasn't standing rose to their feet. Jayson took in the moment while tears rolled down his face. He was grateful for Alicia Woolley at his side, who gave him a clean tissue, even though he'd never known her before rehearsal yesterday.

When the applause finally died down, the next name was read. "Elizabeth Meredith Greer." Again there was a roar of applause, as if everyone in the room was expressing compassion for her grief. Jayson realized then that he'd never known her middle name was after her mother. It was an irony he understood, being named after his father. The ceremony went on, and it seemed forever before his name was read. He wondered if they would read his full name, but he was relieved when they said, "Jayson A. Wolfe." He was met with an unexpected surge of applause, which he figured was likely a delayed reaction to the song he'd played.

After all the names had been read and everyone had returned to their seats, Alan came again to the microphone and said, "We would like to ask Derek's father, William Greer, if he would accept the diploma on Derek's behalf."

Derek wondered if Will had been forewarned of this; he'd not mentioned it. Again Jayson was moved to tears as Will came forward and was presented a graduation hat, a tassel, and the diploma. He returned to his seat amidst more applause. The tassels were moved, the ceremony ended, and while every other member of their class broke into laughter as they dispersed, Jayson stood where he was, feeling somehow lost and alone. He closed his eyes and could easily imagine Derek's response to this moment. And his heart ached! He opened his eyes to see Elizabeth standing directly in front of him, mirroring his every emotion in her beautiful face. She wrapped her arms around him, and together they cried, oblivious to the celebrating going on around them. They were still standing there when Will wrapped his arms around them from one side, and Leslie from the other. They all shared a tearful moment, then Will urged them to be on their way.

In the car, Elizabeth searched for an outlet to lighten the mood. She found it when she said to Jayson, "I didn't know your middle initial was A."

"I didn't know your middle name was Meredith," he said like a snotty child, making her laugh.

"So, what's the A for?" she asked.

"Why don't you guess?"

"Alexander," she said, and he laughed. "Okay, Anthony. Antoine."

"No, no, no," Jayson said, and his mother chuckled.

"I know," Elizabeth said, "Alfred."

"Not even close," Leslie said.

"Albert? Adam?"

"You'll never guess," Jayson said.

"Okay, I give up."

"Well," Leslie said, "the name—"

"Don't tell her!" Jayson said.

"I was just going to give her a hint," Leslie insisted. "As I was saying, the name Wolfe always reminded me of the name Wolfgang, which as you know is the first name of—"

"Mozart!" Elizabeth said, then she laughed. "Amadeus? Your middle name is Amadeus?"

"That's right," Jayson chuckled. "I told you he was a hero of mine."

"The amazing thing," Leslie said, "is that I obviously had no idea when I named my infant son that he had such a musical gift in his blood."

"You must have been psychic or something," Will said.

"Or inspired," Leslie said, smiling at her son.

Dinner proved to be immensely pleasant, in spite of a few tears. The four returned to the Greer home where Will announced, "Now it's time for presents." He led the way to the front room where they all sat down. The cedar chest he had given to Elizabeth that morning was still sitting there with a big blue bow on it. Jayson knew he'd also given her a significant amount of money to help with her schooling.

"Presents?" Jayson said, pretending to sound surprised. He strategically retrieved the little wrapped gift he had for Elizabeth that he'd hid the previous day. "Oh, you mean like *this* present?" He set it into her hands, and she let out a surprised laugh. "I hope you like it," he said. "Mom helped me pick it out."

"Your mother has good taste," she said and unwrapped the little package. She opened the box and gasped at the beautiful gold watch, obviously very expensive. "Oh, it's beautiful," she said, then she laughed again as she threw her arms around Jayson's neck. "Thank you. It's perfect."

She then produced a gift for him and laughed when he opened it to reveal a beautiful gold watch. "I think our parents have been conspiring," he said.

"That's ridiculous," Will said facetiously, then he added, "Now you can synchronize your watches and keep track of each other better."

"That's a nice thought," Jayson said and quickly kissed Elizabeth. "Thank you," he said. "I love it. And I love you."

"I love you too," she said and hugged him again.

They each put on their watches and Will took pictures of them both holding their arms up, their left wrists side-by-side to model their his-and-hers watches that had obviously been made to complement each other.

"Now," Leslie said, handing a small wrapped box to Jayson.

He felt a little taken aback and said, "I don't need presents, Mom."

"I'm giving you the same thing I gave your brother," she said, and he gasped.

"I'd forgotten about that," he said and opened the little box to reveal a savings bond that she had purchased when he was born. It had now matured to a significant amount, and she said softly, "To help you get your career off the ground."

Jayson hugged his mother tightly. "Thank you, Mom. I'll use it wisely."

"I know you will," she said, getting teary. She then turned toward Elizabeth and said, "I have a little something for you, too."

"Oh, you didn't have to—" Elizabeth began, but Leslie interrupted, pulling a little wrapped box out of her purse.

"I want you to have this," she said firmly. "I didn't go out and buy it; it's something I've had for a long time, tucked away. And it just feels right that you should have it."

Elizabeth opened the box to reveal a fine gold chain with a delicate little angel hanging from it. "Oh, it's beautiful," Elizabeth said.

"It is real gold," Leslie said. "Other than my sons, it's one of the few things Jayson's father ever gave me that had any real value—sentimental and otherwise. We had some good moments, and this necklace represents one of the best. He gave it to me the day Jayson was born."

"I didn't know that," Jayson said while Elizabeth struggled for composure.

"Thank you so much," Elizabeth said, hugging Leslie tightly.

"You're welcome," Leslie said, "and I want you to remember that whatever happens in the future, whether you and Jayson end up permanently together or not, I want this to be a reminder that you have been an angel in our lives; you've been like the daughter I never had, and I want you to promise that it will always be that way."

"I promise," she said, and they hugged again.

"I guess that just leaves one more thing," Will said, coming to his feet. "I have a little something for you, Jayson."

"This is silly," Jayson said as Will left the room. "There is no need for you to . . ." He stopped and lost his breath when Will returned, holding in his hands a beautiful acoustic guitar, with a big blue bow tied around the neck. Will stood in front of him and held it toward Jayson. But he couldn't bring himself to take it. Their eyes met, and Jayson watched him become blurry behind the tears that clouded his own vision. "How can I . . . when . . ." Jayson couldn't get any more words out than that; he could only hope that Will understood the regret he felt over the incident that had left him without an acoustic guitar.

His tears fell, and his vision cleared as Will set the guitar on his lap. Jayson touched it with reverence, and it only took a moment to know this was no cheap guitar. It was of a far higher quality than the one he'd destroyed in a fit of rage. Will sat back down, and Jayson looked up at him, feeling bewildered and dumbstruck.

"This is not just a graduation gift, Jayson. This is a meager token of appreciation for the music you brought into our home and into our lives. And it's for all the happiness you gave to Derek—and consequently, me."

"And me," Elizabeth added.

"And Elizabeth," Will said with a smile. He tightened his gaze on Jayson and added, "I want you to take this, Jayson, with the knowledge that you will forever hold a large place in my heart; you will forever be a son to me. I anxiously look forward to the great things you will do with this guitar." He chuckled. "I thought of giving you a piano, but I thought you might have trouble getting it to LA." Jayson chuckled as well and wiped a fresh stream of tears, grateful that these people had become well-accustomed to his high water table.

"You have a remarkable gift, Jayson," Will went on earnestly. "I want you to honor Derek through your gift, and take it to the top, and I will always be cheering you on, and I will always be a phone call away if you need a father—*always!*"

Jayson took the guitar by the neck with one hand and stood up to embrace Will tightly. "Thank you," he said. "I won't let you down."

"I know you won't," Will said and pulled back. "But you're not leaving for that dance until you play something on it."

Jayson felt momentarily hesitant. He'd not played a guitar since they'd lost Derek, but he reasoned that he had to do it sooner or later. He sat down and took a few minutes to tune it.

"Okay," he said with a strum for emphasis. "I wrote this song for Elizabeth." He efficiently picked out an intricate strain, then closed his eyes and tenderly sang the first verse while Elizabeth marveled at his voice range, his intensity, the passion that emanated from him. He then moved into the chorus that she loved so well. *"You stand tall while I stand in awe, yearning from a distance. My awakened senses yearn to sense you . . . close to me. Our two hearts are only one, divided by time and air and space. In another time and place . . . our two hearts were one . . . and they will be again."*

Listening to him sing that way, seeing how he looked at her when he did, she could almost believe that what he sang was true. A part of her couldn't help hoping, while another part of her just couldn't see how it was possible. And she dreaded the day when the battle inside her could no longer be put off.

For now, however, she was determined to enjoy the moment. He loved her, and she loved him. They were as good as family, regardless of whether they ever married. With Jayson in her life, Elizabeth felt the tiniest measure of hope that she could overcome the grief of Derek's death and find happiness in her future.

Chapter Fifteen

On the Monday following graduation, Jayson realized that he either had to go to LA or get a job. If he wasn't going to be able to immediately pursue his musical career, he at least had to be making some money to help it along. He applied everywhere he could think of, but there weren't even any oil-changing positions available. Drew had already gotten steady work at the movie theater where he'd continued doing a few shifts all along. He said many times that he'd be ready to go to LA whenever Jayson was ready. He had no terribly strong ties in Oregon, but he wasn't necessarily in a hurry to leave. Drew, for all his passion about music, admitted readily that he was more passive about actually taking it somewhere. He shared Jayson's dream of success, but he'd said many times that without Jayson's passion and drive it would never happen. Drew was behind him all the way—as long as he could stay behind.

Elizabeth got her job back at the sewing plant, but rather than working part-time as she'd done in the past, she was working forty hours a week, and Jayson felt like a fish out of water. He spent time every day applying for jobs and following through at every place he'd applied, but work just seemed to mystically elude him. He dabbled some with his new guitar, but there was no new inspiration to keep him occupied, and playing the old stuff felt hollow without Derek. He expressed his concern to Elizabeth. "What if I'm all dried up? What if there's no more creativity in me? I feel dead inside in that respect since we lost Derek."

"You are *not* all dried up," she insisted. "Give it some time. However, even if you take the stuff you've already written and keep refining it, you could have enough to do more than two albums."

"That's true," he had to admit, but he had to go to LA to do anything about *that,* and the thought of being away from Elizabeth seemed more than he could bear. He knew that come August she was planning to move to Boston. High school was behind them, and some big choices lay ahead. He could no longer ignore the dilemma between them. For months he had pushed it to the back of his mind, telling himself that he didn't have to worry about that yet, certain that when the time came, everything would fall neatly into place. But that time was here, and he felt no more prepared to face this fork in the road than he had the first time Elizabeth had told him she had no intention of going to LA. He knew he needed to talk to her, but the very idea was terrifying. Addressing the problem would make it impossible to ignore. Their relationship was comfortable, and he didn't want to disrupt that. But the very idea of living without her threatened to break what little of his heart hadn't been broken with Derek's death.

Still, he kept putting it off, trying to enjoy each moment he had with her. But it reached a point where he couldn't bear the uncertainty and limbo any longer. On the last Friday in June they went to a movie that ended up being relatively stupid, then he took her back to her house where they sat together on the couch, just enjoying each other's company without talking. Jayson knew that Will was in the house, and that's the way he wanted it. Although, just the thought of having to face Will with a bad choice was probably chaperone enough. It had become a frequent battle to deal with the memories of his intimate moments with Elizabeth, but his motivation to keep control was equally powerful.

Jayson loved the way Elizabeth held his hand, threading her fingers between his, smiling at him as if he meant as much to her as she did to him. In his heart he knew that was true, but he also knew they had a huge dilemma before them, and it couldn't be denied any longer.

"Oh, Jayson, I love you," she said, breaking minutes of silence. And as if her thoughts were on the same track as his, she added, "I'm going to miss you so much."

Jayson looked into her eyes and took a deep breath, knowing he'd get no better opening than that. "Can I ask you a hypothetical question?"

"Sure," she said, putting her head on his shoulder.

"Well . . . life has certain . . . expectations, certain . . . rules, if you will. Rules that are there for the purpose of helping us be . . . successful . . . and happy. But do you think there are times when those rules can—and should—be bent to achieve a greater purpose when extenuating circumstances are present?"

Elizabeth lifted her head to look at him. "You're not talking like a songwriter; you're talking like a philosophy professor. What are you getting at? Tell me in English. Give me an example."

"Well . . . for instance, it's generally known that divorce is not a good thing, and it should be avoided. But in the case with my parents, having my father in the home was damaging to our spirits—and a physical danger. Therefore, due to extenuating circumstances, divorce was a good thing."

"Okay, I agree with that." She put her head back on his shoulder.

"And with your parents, your mother wasn't willing to make any effort to be a part of the family. Her presence in the home was damaging to your spirits. So, divorce was better than living a lie."

"I agree with that too. What are you getting at?"

"So, you agree that sometimes altering the general expectations of society can be the right thing . . . when there are extenuating circumstances?"

"I do," she said firmly.

"So . . ." he took a deep breath, "even though it's not necessarily considered smart for two people to get married right out of high school, there might be cases when it's the best thing."

Again she lifted her head to look at him, this time her eyes were wide. "What are you trying to say, Jayson?"

Jayson took her hand into his. "Will you marry me, Elizabeth? Now, right away? I'll go to Boston with you. I'll help you get through school. We can be together."

Elizabeth sat up straight, putting some distance between them, as if that might make her think more clearly. She looked at him hard and asked, "And what about LA? What about your music?"

"That will come with time. Who knows? Maybe there are opportunities for me in Boston that could help me along. I never dreamed I'd find such opportunities in Oregon, but I did. Eventually, we'll go to LA—together. You can bake cookies, and I'll make music—and we'll raise a family. As I see it, this is a matter of compromise. We love each other; we need to be willing to make some compromises."

Her eyes turned skeptical. "Does this have to do with what happened at the beach?" she demanded. "We can't expect getting married to suddenly make everything right just because we could go to bed together."

Jayson was momentarily stunned. "No! This has nothing to do with that. I mean . . . I'll admit it's been hard; it's difficult not to think about it . . . and sure, it would be nice to be married in that respect. But I do have some measure of self-discipline. Have I not been a perfect gentleman?"

"Yes, you have," she said, looking down.

"This is not about sex, Elizabeth. This is about you and me being together, working together to help each other achieve our goals. It's about both of us becoming successful, not in spite of each other, but because of each other. I've asked myself a thousand times if what we feel is really what it seems to be, and honestly, Lady, I believe with everything inside of me that you and I are supposed to be together."

Elizabeth looked away and said, "And what if I believe otherwise?"

Jayson made a noise of disbelief. "How can you even say such a thing? I know how you feel about me, Elizabeth. You just told me not three minutes ago that you love me."

"I *do* love you," she said and turned back to face him. "But maybe love isn't enough. My father loved my mother when he married her. Your mother loved your father when she married him."

Jayson leaned toward her and said in an angry whisper, *"This* love is enough! I am *not* my father, and you are *not* your mother. We're better than that."

"Maybe we are," she said, "but that doesn't mean marriage is going to magically solve our every problem."

"And I'm not naive enough to believe that it would. But if we're supposed to be together, we can't just sit back and expect life to spin some potion to make it happen. *We* have to make it happen. I need you, and I believe you need me, too. We might have some extra challenges by getting married sooner than later, but it would eliminate other challenges, and I believe it would be worth it. I believe that with the way we feel about each other, and with what we have already endured together, we can do anything if we are committed and have some mutual respect—which we do."

Elizabeth sighed and turned away, as if she had no retort. Then she said, "Do you really think our parents would want us to get married—now?"

"I don't know; maybe we should ask them."

"You go for it," she said, coming to her feet. "I'm tired. I'm going to bed."

She hurried from the room, leaving him alone. He cursed under his breath and drove a fist into the couch where he was sitting. He wondered if she had PMS, or if this was really as bad as it seemed. He was still sitting there trying to figure it out when Will appeared. "You okay?" he asked.

"Not really."

"Want to talk about it?" Will asked, taking a seat.

"Not really, but I probably should." He didn't want to bring this up with Will when he'd had absolutely no time to think about how he might approach it, but the opportunity was before him and he didn't want to pass it up. "Can I ask you a question?"

"Anything. Ask away."

"How would you feel about me marrying your daughter?"

Will's eyes widened. "What, now?"

Jayson sighed. "Maybe," he admitted. "I know we're young, but I also know we're supposed to be together."

Will leaned forward and looked at Jayson more closely. "I want Elizabeth to marry someone she loves and who loves her. I want her to spend her life deliriously happy. You're a fine young man, Jayson, and if the two of you feel that way about each other, then nothing could please me more than having you as part of my family. You're already practically that. However, I think timing is important. You *are* young. You both need some time and experience—some education. I think the two of you should live on your own for a while before you make such important decisions."

"I love her, Will."

"I know you do."

Jayson said again, "I really believe we're supposed to be together. And I think we can help each other more by being together now, rather than being apart."

"And how does she feel about that?"

"It's hard to say," Jayson admitted. "She gives me every reason to believe she feels the same way, but she's always telling me that because our goals are so different, she doesn't see how that's possible."

"And what do you think?" Will asked.

"I think if we love each other enough we can find a way to compromise and still achieve our goals."

"And how would you go about that? Is there more than one way to follow the path to musical stardom?" Jayson didn't answer, and he added, "Your goals are very defined, and for a good reason. Your gifts make those goals obvious. I think you're one of those rare people where a college education would be fairly irrelevant. And I don't say that lightly; I'm a strong advocate of education. But you have the ability to make a viable income with what you already know. That doesn't mean, however, that the road will be easy. Whether your success comes quickly or takes years, your life will be far from conventional."

"I know that," Jayson said, looking down. "But I can't make a choice between my music and Elizabeth. I need them both in my life."

Will leaned his forearms on his thighs and looked at Jayson intently. "I'm not sure exactly what it is you're seeking from this conversation, Jayson. If you want my permission to marry my daughter, I can only tell you this: you're both technically adults. You don't need my permission to do anything. If the two of you decide to get married soon, I will love you both, and I will do my best to help you in any way I can. I would prefer that you wait, but believe it or not, I understand where you're coming from. My opinion may not matter, but truthfully, I believe the two of you *are* supposed to be together. It just feels incredibly right, Jayson."

Jayson let out a long breath of relief. "However," Will added, lifting a finger, "whatever choice you make, if it involves the two of you equally, then you need to be in complete agreement. If she is the tiniest bit reluctant to marry you—or marry you now—it will plant seeds of doubt and trouble in your future. I've taught my daughter to use her brain and follow her heart. Whatever you do, you must respect that completely. Do you understand what I'm saying?"

"I do," Jayson said.

Will sighed and leaned back. "And Jayson."

"Yes?"

"It's important to understand that sometimes things just don't work out the way we want—or even expect—them to. I think we would all like to see you and Elizabeth together, but maybe it's just not meant to be."

"I can't believe that," Jayson said firmly.

"I know. And I understand. But you're only one-half of the decision, and you can't force or control the power of choice in another human being. I know it may be difficult to understand at this point of your life, but you need a wife who will support you one hundred percent in your career. And maybe Elizabeth's right. Maybe your goals *are* too different from hers. Maybe she is wise enough to see that she's simply not capable of giving you what you need in that regard. Perhaps the role she will play in your life is significant, but maybe it's not marriage."

Everything inside of Jayson wanted to scream in protest and tell him he was crazy. But he didn't want to behave like a child or make a fool of himself. He was relieved when Will broke the ongoing silence by adding, "Talk to her . . . honestly, and let her be honest with you. Give it some time, and you'll both know what's best."

Jayson nodded, but he felt near tears and certain that Will had to be sick to death of seeing him cry. He'd cried more than Will and Elizabeth combined since Derek's death—at least as far as he'd seen. Feeling a sudden need to be alone, he came to his feet, saying, "Thank you. I appreciate your time."

"It's not a problem," Will said, standing as well. "I'm here for you any time; I mean it."

"Thank you," Jayson said again, and they exchanged a familiar embrace.

Alone in the car, Jayson cried. He couldn't even fathom accepting that his life might be lived without Elizabeth in the center of it, but he had a feeling that deep inside, Elizabeth didn't agree with him.

When he arrived at home, his mother was sitting on the couch with a book, but he knew she was waiting for him. "How are you?" she asked.

"I've been better. How are you?"

"I'm okay," she said. "Did you want to talk to me?"

"Maybe," he said, wondering if she was psychic or if she'd been talking to Will. He didn't know whether it was an advantage or a disadvantage to have his mother dating his girlfriend's father. Right now, he was thinking he'd prefer a little more distance between the families.

"Elizabeth called me," she said.

"And what did Elizabeth want to talk to you about?" he asked, as if he didn't know.

"She said you asked her to marry you."

"Can't a guy keep a secret for an hour?" he asked, not entirely serious.

"No," she said in the same tone.

"So, now that you've talked to Elizabeth, maybe you can explain to me why she's so hot and cold. Is it PMS, or do I have a problem?"

"Both . . . maybe," Leslie said, and Jayson sat down beside her. "Do you want my opinion?"

"I'm waiting."

"Elizabeth is highly oriented by her logic and practicality."

"Boy, you're telling me."

"She's very accustomed to figuring something out according to logic and going with it. You, on the other hand, are more focused on your feelings. If you feel something is right, you go for it. Any human being needs to find the balance between their heart and their head. I've always taught you that, and I think when it comes right down to it, you do that for the most part. You follow your heart, but you do it sensibly."

"I think that's a compliment."

"It is," she said. "Elizabeth, however, is not that way. Now, this is just my opinion; I'm speculating here, and I don't want you confronting her with this. It will get you nowhere in that regard. But maybe it will help you understand her better. It's my opinion that she's closed off a portion of her heart and trained herself to be motivated by logic, because her mother's rejection has been so traumatic for her."

"Where did you learn to talk like that?" he asked with a little chuckle.

"I've endured thousands of hours of counseling, my son. Now be quiet and listen to me."

"I'm listening."

"It's really quite simple, Jayson. Elizabeth is used to following logic, but what she feels for you comes completely from the heart. She's hot and cold because she doesn't know how to mesh the two."

Jayson took that in for a minute. "Okay," he said, "that makes sense. But what am I supposed to do about it?"

"I'm not sure there is anything *you* can do about it, beyond what you're already doing. I told her she needs to come to a place where her heart and head can agree. When she can make a decision that is free of confusion, then she'll know she's doing what's best for her."

Jayson had mixed feelings on that. In truth, he had to admit he was terrified of Elizabeth deciding that she could live without him. Praying that wouldn't happen, he asked his mother, "Do you think we're too young to get married?"

"Yes," she said, "but that doesn't mean I wouldn't support you in that decision—as long as you come to that decision for the right reasons and you're prepared to take on every responsibility associated with marriage."

They talked for a while longer, and Jayson told her how much he appreciated her being there for him—and for Elizabeth. Then he went to bed, his heart heavy and his brain clouded. The sound of pouring rain outside meshed with a pounding rhythm in his head. But it had nothing to do with music.

During the following week, Jayson spent a great deal of time with Elizabeth, as usual. And he was pleased to see that there was no apparent strain between them. But he wondered where her head was— or rather, her heart. Or most accurately, he wondered if she had been able to come to a place where the two could agree. And he prayed they would agree that her life should be spent with him. He concluded that he *could* live with giving the matter some time, but he didn't want to.

Jayson had three job interviews that week, but every one of them fell through, and the jobs were given to somebody else. When he mentioned to his mother that the universe seemed set against his getting a job, she suggested that maybe the universe was telling him that he just needed to go to LA. *Not without Elizabeth,* his mind protested, but he said nothing aloud.

The Fourth of July proved to be a pleasant day. Jayson and his mother barbecued with Elizabeth and Will, and they found a great place to watch fireworks together. The following evening Jayson gave Drew a ride to work, since his car was in for some minor repairs, then he drove toward Elizabeth's house. He braked at a four-way stop, then moved into the intersection when there were no vehicles at any of the other three stop signs. When he heard screeching tires, he had a split-second awareness of another car flying past one of those other stop signs. He felt the jolt, heard the crash, then everything went black.

* * * * *

Elizabeth heard the phone ring and was glad her father went to answer it, since she was momentarily involved in a good book. She absently glanced at the clock and realized Jayson was late just before she heard her father say, "What is it? What's wrong?" His panicked tone sent her heart racing, and she tossed her book, moving toward him. "Calm down, Leslie, and tell me what's wrong." While he was obviously listening, Elizabeth saw him meet her eyes with an alarm that put her stomach in knots. "Okay," he finally said. "We're on our way. We'll meet you there. You be careful too."

Will hung up the phone and turned slowly to meet Elizabeth's eyes, as if he were drawing great courage. "What?" she demanded. He hesitated, and she nearly shouted, "It's Jayson, isn't it? Something's happened to Jayson."

Will took hold of her shoulders, and she realized he was shaking. "We have both got to stay calm and not jump to conclusions," he said.

"Just tell me!" she screamed.

"He's been taken to the hospital. They wouldn't give Leslie any information over the phone." He visibly drew courage again and added, "Yes, it was a car accident."

"No!" Elizabeth shrieked and clutched onto her father as the memories consumed her with a fear beyond her ability to bear.

"Now, calm down," Will murmured, even though she could tell he was shaking. His voice quavered. "We don't know how bad it is. Maybe he's fine."

"And maybe he's not!" she shouted. "If he . . . If he . . ." She couldn't get the thought out while she could hardly breathe.

"Come on," Will said, urging her to the garage. "Let's get down there and find out what's going on. I'm not going to assume anything but the best until I'm told otherwise."

In the car Elizabeth struggled to breathe while her chest and stomach became steadily more constricted. She knew she could never bear losing Derek *and* Jayson. She couldn't. She simply couldn't. She found herself praying silently, even though she'd never actually prayed in her entire life.

At the hospital they found Leslie pacing the emergency waiting area. She took one look at Will and flew into his arms, sobbing uncontrollably. Elizabeth felt something die inside of her as she observed this through a veil of shock, fearing the worst. She wanted to shake Leslie and demand that she calm down and give them the verdict. When Will took Leslie's shoulders into his hands, she knew he had the same thought. "What?" he demanded gently. "Tell us what."

"I'm sorry," she said. "He's going to be all right."

That was all Elizabeth needed to hear before she sank into a chair and sobbed, fully understanding why Leslie's emotions were so out of control. The relief was as intense as the fear had been a moment ago. She was just managing to get control of herself when a male nurse came out and said, "Mrs. Wolfe?"

"Yes," Leslie said.

"You can come back now."

She motioned toward Will and Elizabeth and asked, "Is it all right if—"

"Sure," the nurse said, "I think he's up to company." While they walked with the nurse through two sets of double doors and down a hallway, he explained, "He's pretty bruised up and needed a few stitches, but beyond that he appears to be fine. In a few minutes, they'll take him to radiology for a CT scan and an MRI, just to be certain there's nothing going on that we can't see, and they'll probably keep him overnight so they can keep an eye on him."

"Thank you," Leslie said. Just then they came to the door of a room, and the nurse pushed the door open.

"Your family is here," the nurse said, and Jayson looked up to see his mother, Will, and Elizabeth all come into the room.

"So they are," he said and couldn't hold back a rise of emotion when he observed their expressions. He could easily guess what they'd gone through in the last little while. If he'd been conscious he would have insisted that his mother not be called with such news. He would have preferred to call her himself. As it was, he could only be grateful that they were here now, and they could see that he was fine—relatively speaking. While he suspected his loved ones had just endured a repeat of the emotions they'd been met with at Derek's death, Jayson had become assaulted with the sounds and sensations that he felt sure Derek must have experienced in the last few seconds of his life.

Elizabeth felt frozen as her eyes took in Jayson, his bare legs showing from beneath a hospital gown and hanging over the edge of the bed where he was sitting. As he turned to look at them, she was stunned by the dark bruising on the left side of his face, and the stitches close to his hairline, just above the temple. She watched Leslie move abruptly toward him, then take him carefully into her arms. "Oh, you're alive," she muttered tearfully, then she gently took his face into her hands. "You look terrible," she said with a teary laugh. "What happened?"

"Uh . . . as far as I can figure . . . with what they told me . . . and what I remember . . . some guy ran a four-way stop and hit the back end of my car, sending it into a spin. I guess the side of my head hit the side window, and my right knee hit the steering column." He lifted his leg slightly, and Elizabeth gasped to see the horrible bruising there. "But I'm fine," he said. He glanced toward Will and Elizabeth, seeing something in her eyes that frightened him. "I'm sorry you had to—"

"It's all right," Will said gently. "We're just glad to have you still with us."

"Yeah, me too," Jayson said, but Elizabeth didn't say anything, didn't move. He met her eyes, wondering what to say to assure her that everything was all right, but before he could form the words, she rushed from the room.

Will and Leslie watched her go and exchanged a concerned glance. Will gave Jayson a careful hug, saying, "I'm sure glad you're all right, kid. You need to stay safe."

"I'll do my best," Jayson said.

Will said to Leslie, "I'm taking Elizabeth home; you call me if you need anything."

"Thank you," she said, and Will kissed her quickly before he left the room.

* * * * *

Jayson was relieved, as was his mother, to learn that there were no internal injuries, no concussions, no broken bones. His night in the hospital was long when he found it difficult to sleep. He kept recalling the moment of that accident while the memory meshed with thoughts of Derek's death. The resulting images in his mind were horrible. Forcing his mind from that, he had to admit that not knowing where he stood with Elizabeth was making him crazy. Nothing had been said for days about his proposal of marriage, but he knew she was weighing her future carefully, and his deepest fear was that she would weigh him out of it. Everything had felt all right between them—until she'd seen him at the hospital. Now, something was wrong, and he knew it.

He was relieved to finally leave the hospital. After waiting to be officially released, he had to wait until his mother got off work. The minute he knew Elizabeth would be home from work, he asked his mother if she'd drive him over there.

"I don't have a car," he reminded her, since he'd been told that it was considered totaled. "And I'd drive myself but that little label on the prescription bottle says I'm not supposed to."

"Sure," she said, "just let me finish what I'm doing."

In the car she asked, "What's bugging you?"

"I'm just wondering why Elizabeth didn't say a word to me last night, and I've not heard a word from her since. I know she had to work, but she has a lunch hour. She knew where to call me. Her father called me."

"Well, you just need to ask her."

"Which is what I intend to do . . . if she'll even talk to me."

"I don't think she's that immature," Leslie said.

When they arrived, Leslie followed Jayson to the front door, making the comment, "You've got a definite limp there, son."

"Yeah," he said with chagrin, telling himself he was grateful to know the pain was only from bruising and swelling.

Will answered the door and kissed Leslie in greeting before he said to Jayson, "Elizabeth's upstairs in her room. I was just cooking some stir-fry and hoping you'd show up."

"A true man," Leslie said and went to the kitchen to help him.

With his leg reluctant to bend at the knee, it took Jayson longer than usual to get up the stairs. He found Elizabeth's bedroom door closed and knocked on it lightly.

"Come in," she called, and he opened the door. She was wearing jeans and a sweatshirt, fluffing her wet hair with a towel. She'd obviously just taken a shower. He loved the way the natural curl in her hair was more intense when it was wet. When she turned toward him, she was obviously surprised, and he figured she was expecting her father.

"Hi," he said.

"Hi," Elizabeth replied and almost hated herself for the way her heart quickened just seeing him. She'd gone through a gamut of emotions since she'd last seen his face at the hospital last night, but she still felt as confused now as she had then. And he just had to show his face and make it worse. She resisted the urge to throw herself into his arms, and instead, she simply said, "Your face looks worse today."

"Oh, thank you very much," he said, lightly sarcastic. "It's nice to see you too."

"Does it hurt much?" she asked.

"No more than when my father busted me in the face. It's the leg that hurts, actually. But nothing's broken."

"That's good then," she said and looked away. He could feel the same mood she'd been in last night.

"Mind if I sit down?" he asked, moving to the chair beside her study desk. "It hurts to stand very long."

"Go for it," she said.

"And then why don't you sit down and tell me what's wrong," he said firmly. Elizabeth looked mildly astonished, and he added, "Don't even begin to think that I wouldn't be able to tell you're upset, and don't think that I wouldn't expect a reason." He scrutinized her countenance and concluded, "You seem angry." When she didn't protest, he said more conclusively, "You *are* angry. With me, I assume." Still she said nothing, and he added, "Okay, we're narrowing it down. You're angry with me. Apparently, I did something wrong. And since we had no interaction yesterday before I saw you at the hospital, I have to assume that your anger has something to do with that."

"You're practically psychic," she said, only subtly terse.

Jayson took in the implication. "Let me get this straight. You're angry with me because I was in an accident? I hate to point out the obvious, but it wasn't my fault."

"Yeah, well. The accident Derek was in wasn't his fault, either. But you were certainly angry with *him.*"

"Okay," Jayson said more gently, "but I'm fine. It's over. Except that you're angry with me."

"I'm not angry with you," she insisted in a contradictory tone. "I'm just angry. I'm angry because . . . because . . . you're so blasted . . . lovable."

"Oh, now that makes sense," he said with sarcasm. "Maybe you would prefer me to be a little more obnoxious."

"That would be good, actually. And then it wouldn't be so blasted hard to think of . . . living without you."

Jayson's heart quickened. "Who said you have to live without me?"

She started to cry. "I nearly lost you yesterday."

"No, you didn't. I was fine. You didn't know I was fine, but I was fine."

"I thought I had lost you, okay? And I can't live through that again."

"So . . . what? You don't want to be emotionally attached to me because you're afraid you'll lose me?" Her eyes silently admitted there was some truth to that, and he gave a humorless laugh before he added, "That's ludicrous. Isn't it already too late for that? Aren't you already emotionally involved?"

"There are all kinds of ways to lose someone, Jayson. Whether I lost you to death or to another woman or to the music industry, I would still be losing you."

Jayson made a noise of frustration and pushed his hand through his hair. "What are you saying, Elizabeth? What do you want me to do? I can promise you that you will always and forever be the only one. I can stay grounded in the right priorities no matter what my life's work might entail. But I can't promise I won't die. Nobody can. Even you can't do that. Am I not risking as much of my heart to love you as you are to love me? Have I not suffered equivalent losses in Derek's death? Don't try to tell me you loved him more than I did and that it hurt you more than it hurt me."

Elizabeth softened her voice. "I would never try to tell you that," she said. "I know how much you loved him."

"*Love,*" he corrected. "It is still in the present tense. His absence does not diminish the way I feel. I will always love him, and I will always love you." He reached a hand toward her. "I'm sorry, Elizabeth," he said gently. "I know what happened was hard on you. And I'm so sorry."

She tossed the towel she was holding over the foot of the bed and moved toward him, slipping her hand into his. He came to his feet and felt bathed with relief when she touched his face and looked into his eyes. "I love you, Jayson," she said and pressed her lips to his. "I'm so grateful you're all right."

"Yeah, me too," he said and kissed her again. She eased more fully into his arms, and their kiss quickly became warm. When Jayson began to enjoy it a little too much, he eased back and murmured, "I think we'd better go downstairs."

"I think you're right," she said, but she seemed reluctant to move out of his arms. He finally forced himself away and started down the hall.

"You might want to go ahead," he said to her at the top of the stairs. "It could take me a while."

"Does it hurt that bad?" she asked.

"No. It only hurts *bad* when I try to bend it, and that makes stairs a bit of a challenge."

"I'm not in any hurry," she said and took his hand, matching his pace until they arrived in the kitchen, where Jayson sat down and propped his leg up on another chair.

Will stopped what he was doing for a moment and looked right at Jayson. With a little chuckle, he said, "You really look terrible."

"Oh, well, thank you," Jayson said with sarcastic appreciation. "That makes my day."

Will laughed and added, "It's good to have you here."

"It's good to be here," Jayson said. Leslie smiled toward him. Elizabeth did as well, but he saw a hesitancy in her eyes that frightened him.

Chapter Sixteen

Again Jayson had trouble sleeping that night. He drifted in and out of a fitful rest, floating in and out of strange dreams. He finally got up a little after six and unlocked the front door to get the morning paper, then he sat at the kitchen table, drinking a cup of coffee that he hoped would counteract the effect of what the pain pills were doing to him. He heard the bathroom door open and figured his mother must have an early shift. He looked up expecting to see her; instead he saw William Greer. It only took a moment to assess the evidence. The front door had been locked, as it was only when everyone was gone—or at night. Will's expression made it clear he'd not expected to be seen before he left. Jayson's tone of voice clearly expressed the disgust and astonishment he felt as he stated the obvious. "You spent the night here!"

"Yes, I did," Will said coolly. Jayson felt immediately angry, but before he could even think how to respond, Will added, "Now don't go jumping to conclusions, son. I spent the night. I did not do anything inappropriate. Don't think that I would lecture you about keeping your hands off my daughter and then turn around and have my way with your mother. I'm not a hypocrite, Jayson. I care very much for your mother, but our relationship is not like that. She's struggling and discouraged. She needed a friend. We talked. I slept on the couch. Okay?"

Jayson glanced toward the folded blankets on the couch and swallowed his misjudgments, muttering quietly, "Okay. I'm sorry if I—"

"It's all right, Jayson. I'd be disappointed if you weren't concerned about her. If any other guy is here before breakfast, you have my permission to belt him in the jaw."

They both chuckled, but it felt tense, just as everything had become much of the time since Derek had left them, leaving only a dark cloud in his absence.

Jayson had to ask, "What's she struggling with?"

"Maybe you should ask her."

"I don't think she'll tell me," Jayson said. "She is very good at bearing her burdens quietly and with dignity. I learned a long time ago that no amount of coaxing or pleading will get her to tell me something if she thinks I would worry. Why don't you just give me a hint so I'll know whether or not I'm the cause of the problem."

Will sighed and said quietly, "It's nothing major, really. She's struggling with Derek's death, as we all are. That little accident of yours really shook her, as it did all of us. And she's concerned about you and Elizabeth—as we both are. She's also dreading the fact that her sons will soon be on their own, and she's questioning her purpose. There. That's it. It's just life, and we have to deal with it the best we can. There's nothing any of us can really do except try to be understanding and help her through." Will put a hand on his shoulder and added with sincerity, "She tells me often how sweet and sensitive you are, more so than your brother. You stay that way, okay? Wherever you end up going, don't ever stop looking out for your mother."

"Of course," Jayson said.

"I need to get to work." Will moved toward the door. "I'll see you later, I assume."

"I would assume," Jayson said, but when Elizabeth got off work, she called and told him she needed some time and space to think things through.

"What things?" he asked.

"You know very well what things," she said. "I need to go. I'll talk to you in a day or two."

Three days later, he'd had only one very brief phone conversation with Elizabeth. He felt as if he would lose his mind, wondering hour after hour what the outcome would be when he felt as if his very life was hanging in the balance. The fact that she had withdrawn from him and didn't want to talk was a bad sign, and he knew it. His mother tried to console him with such statements as, "If it's meant to work out, it will." Or, "Elizabeth's a smart girl with a good heart;

she'll do what's best." He felt no consolation in either respect. Deep inside he feared that Elizabeth would find a way to rationalize that it was *not* meant to be, and that what she might deem best for her would not necessarily be best for him. But all he could do was wait— and pray.

* * * * *

After days of stewing and nights of little sleep, Elizabeth finally came to the point that Leslie had advised her to find—a point where she had an answer that didn't cause any confusion. When she'd firmly made up her mind as to what she had to do, she found her father in his study.

"I've come to a decision," she said, well aware that he knew what was going on.

Will sighed loudly. "You don't look very happy. What decision would you have come to that would make you so unhappy?"

"There're only two possible answers to Jayson's question. If I was ready to get married, I'd be happy, don't you think?"

"There're three possible answers," Will said, and Elizabeth felt disoriented. "There's yes, no, or not yet but maybe someday."

Elizabeth shook her head slowly. "No, Dad, I'm afraid there're only two possible answers."

Will squeezed his eyes shut as if he could feel Jayson's pain. "As I already mentioned," he said, "you seem awfully unhappy. Can it be right if it makes you feel this way?"

"It's not pleasant, and I'm *not* happy about it, but I know it's what I have to do. I've considered every possibility carefully. I've weighed the options, both long term and short term. I can never be what he needs; he can never be what I need. It's just not in us to make each other happy for a lifetime."

Elizabeth wondered if her father was trying to change her mind when he added, "That sounds awfully logical. What does your heart tell you?"

"My heart tells me it would be better to let him go now rather than drag it out any longer. There's a part of me that can logically assess my love for him . . . if that makes any sense."

"Yes."

"And I know I should love him enough to make it work, but . . . all I can say for certain is that my deepest instincts are telling me this is the way it has to be."

Will sighed again and looked as if he might cry. "And I always taught you to trust your instincts," he said. "But . . . oh!" He shook his head. And then he did cry. "This is like another death in the family, Elizabeth. And it will be at least that bad for him."

"I know," Elizabeth said, wiping her own tears. "That's why I need you to spend some time with him. You told him you would always be a father to him; he's going to need a father very badly in a matter of hours." He lifted his eyes in question, and she said, "He's picking me up any minute. We're going to the beach to talk." Her voice broke as she added, "I love him, Dad. I love him too much to drag this out any longer. I love him too much to hold him back. He'll find happiness without me, probably a lot sooner than he realizes."

"I hope you're right," Will said, and the doorbell rang.

"That's him," she said and wiped at her tears. "Will you be home when we get back?"

"It's Saturday; I'm not going anywhere."

Elizabeth pulled open the front door and forced a smile. "Hi," she said, hating the way her heart always quickened just seeing him.

"Hi," he said brightly. "You look great; I've missed you."

"I've missed you too," she admitted honestly, and they walked out to the car.

The drive to the beach was strained with silence, but Elizabeth didn't want to get into it on the road. Once they arrived they held hands and walked to their usual spot while the late afternoon sun moved toward the west horizon. Elizabeth was a little taken aback by the memories associated with this place since the last time they'd come here. But she forced her mind to the moment. The expectation in his expression made it evident that this couldn't be put off any longer.

"So," Jayson said, attempting to quell the trembling in his stomach, "what did you want to talk to me about?" He sat beside her on the sand, hating some memories of this place and cherishing others. He turned his attention to Elizabeth, sitting beside him. Seeing her obvious nervousness, he wanted to scream. Whatever she needed to say, it wasn't going to be good. Still, he never would have dreamed . . .

"Get on with it," he said. "Just say it and get it over with."

Elizabeth looked up at him and just forced the words out of her mouth. "I can't go to LA with you, Jayson."

He considered this a moment and said, "Not yet, I know. You're going to school in Boston and—"

"I can't go to LA with you . . . ever. I can't marry you, Jayson."

Jayson chuckled tensely. He knew there had to be a "yet." He knew there was some explanation to come. The very idea of them not being together *ever* was too ludicrous to even consider. And then she lowered the final blow. "I don't love you . . . that way. I don't love you . . . enough . . . to do what you're asking. I could never love you the way you love me."

He looked into her eyes, longing to see any evidence that she didn't really mean it. But her expression was firm, her eyes sincere. And that's when it hit him. He was reminded of the time his father had struck him and knocked him to the floor. He felt like he'd been kicked in the stomach and busted in the jaw at the same time. He felt a burning pain in his chest, and everything started to spin. In one final effort to keep from being suffocated by the pain, he muttered, "You don't mean that. You can't possibly mean that. Not after what we've felt for each other. You can't."

"I do mean it, Jayson," she said.

He erupted to his feet, gasping for breath as if a whirlpool of despair was sucking him helplessly downward. His dizziness increased, and he bent over, pressing his hands over his thighs, staring at the sand beneath his feet. Her words kept spinning in his head, attempting to make sense, attempting to attach themselves to his brain. It was Derek's death all over again. He didn't want to accept it, couldn't accept it. It was too horrible to even consider. "No," he muttered, and then he howled it, grateful they were completely alone. "No! You can't do this to me. You can't!"

"I'm not *trying* to hurt you, Jayson," she protested, coming to her feet. "It's just the way it is."

"No, it's not! It can't be." He stood straight as anger catapulted him to his senses. "You and I are of one heart, one soul," he shouted.

"We are supposed to be together. I know it with everything inside of me."

"Well, I don't know it!" she shouted back. "You can't force me to feel something I don't feel. I know in my heart this is what I have to do, Jayson. I can't give up my dreams for yours. And I can't let you give up yours for me."

"I would," he said.

"No!" she insisted hotly. "It would be a crime for you to let go of those dreams, Jayson. You have to do it. You would shrivel up and die if you didn't."

He knew she was right, but he also knew something else. "And what makes you think I won't shrivel up and die without *you?*"

"Because you're stronger than that," she insisted.

"No, I am not!" he shouted. "I am nothing without you! Do you hear me? You cannot expect me to live without Derek *and* you. You can't!"

"Well, you're going to have to," she said, and Jayson felt the anger flood out from him, draining away his strength. He fell to his knees in the sand, ignoring the pain from his injuries, and wrapped his arms around his middle.

"I can't," he muttered over and over. "I can't. I just can't."

"You can, Jayson," she said, kneeling beside him. She put her arms around him. "You can, Jayson. You have to."

He clutched onto her and realized he was sobbing. "Don't leave me, Elizabeth. I beg you."

"It has to be this way, Jayson. I beg you to understand."

"I don't understand," he muttered. "I don't."

He pressed his head into her lap and cried himself into exhaustion, while Elizabeth attempted to offer comfort, crying silent tears of her own. When she realized he was asleep, she shifted carefully in order to see his face, wondering how she was ever going to live without him.

Jayson woke in the dark, feeling chilled. He heard the rushing of the waves and remembered being on the beach. Then he remembered what had taken place, and he groaned. He shifted and turned to see Elizabeth lying nearby.

"Are you all right?" he heard her whisper.

"Tell me it was a dream and I'll be all right," he whispered back.

"It was *all* a dream, Jayson. Every precious moment we spent together; it was all a beautiful, perfect dream. But dreams don't last. We have to wake up and live our lives."

"We can live them together, Elizabeth. I know we can."

"It's just not meant to be," she said gently.

"You will never convince me of that."

"Time will convince you," she said as if she knew it beyond any doubt, then she stood up. "We should get back."

Jayson numbly walked to the car with Elizabeth's arm around him. He felt every bit as stunned as he'd felt with Derek's death. It didn't feel real. The shock was indescribable. He was grateful to feel momentarily emptied of tears, but when they got to the car he felt the emotion rising again and said, "I think you'd better drive."

Throughout the ride nothing at all was said. Jayson did his best to keep his tears silent while Elizabeth held his hand. He was surprised when the car stopped, and he looked up to see that they were in front of her home. "There's something else I need to say," she muttered, turning off the ignition.

"Let me have it," he said with obvious cynicism.

"No, it's not like that," she insisted quietly. "I need to say that . . . we were friends long before our relationship became romantic, Jayson. I don't want this to be good-bye."

He turned to look at her and asked with the same cynical tone, "And you really think we can be friends after all we've shared?"

"Yes, I do," she said firmly. "Your mother has promised to always be a mother to me. My father has promised to always be a father to you. They care very much for each other. Whatever happens, there is no reason we can't still be close."

"As friends," he said. "Well, you know what? I fell in love with you the first time I saw you. I was never content with that, and you can't expect me to be content with it now."

Elizabeth sighed, realizing she needed to stop trying to reason with him. He was grieving, and he had a right to do so. "I'm truly sorry, Jayson. Maybe it would have been better if we had never—"

"Don't even go there!" he insisted.

"So, you're not wishing we'd never met?"

"Not yet," he said. "Give me a few minutes."

Elizabeth couldn't bring herself to get out of the car, and Jayson was obviously too upset to do much of anything. She felt compelled to say, "My dad wanted to talk to you when we got back."

He turned toward her abruptly. "Does he know?"

"Yes, he knows."

"And what's his take on your cutting me off at the knees?"

"You're being cruel, Jayson."

"What goes around comes around, Baby," he said bitterly. "Maybe you'll get lucky and I'll write a song about it." He got out and slammed the car door, moving as quickly as he could manage with his knee still giving him grief. He went in without knocking and left the door open for Elizabeth, even though she was barely getting out of the car. He heard Will in the study and stood in the door frame until he looked up, his expression immediately showing compassion. But Jayson felt too angry to absorb it. "So, what's your take on this, *Dad?* Was I too pushy? Too impatient? Too possessive? Was I too obsessed with music? Inattentive? Neglectful? Did I not love her enough?"

"None of the above," Will said gently.

Jayson kicked a chair over with his good leg and groaned. "Then why do I have to live without her?"

Will stood and moved around the desk, saying calmly, "You need to settle down before you hurt yourself, son."

"There's nothing left to hurt," Jayson snarled.

Will put his hands on Jayson's shoulders, and he hotly pushed his arms away, but Will immediately took hold of his wrists, holding them in a firm grip, just as he'd done after Jayson had smashed his guitar. In a voice that sounded way too gentle to Jayson, given the circumstances, Will said close to his face, "I'm not going to let you hurt yourself or anybody else. I'm not going to let you break anything that you love or do anything that you'll regret tomorrow. I'm going to stay with you every minute, if I have to, if that's what it takes to let you know that I meant what I said when I told you I would be a father to you." He looked into Jayson's eyes and added more softly, "I know it hurts, Jayson."

"I'm so sorry, Jayson," Elizabeth said, and he turned to see her standing in the doorway, tears streaming down her face. "I will always love you."

"Yes, I know," he said bitterly. "But not enough," He turned to Will and added, "Tell your daughter to leave me in peace. I've had enough rejection today to last me a lifetime." He was vaguely aware of Will nodding toward Elizabeth, who slowly left and closed the door.

Once Jayson was alone with Will, he felt the anger filtering into tears again and teetered slightly. He was grateful to feel Will's arms come around him, and again he was reminded of the night Derek had been killed. He lost all sense of time as he cried in Will's arms, not unaware of the irony that this was the father who would never be his father-in-law, as he had deeply hoped.

Jayson was finally able to calm down, and a numb shock blanketed his emotions. Will tried to get him to talk, but he couldn't think of anything to say. "I'd better just go home," he said, glancing at the watch on his arm that Elizabeth had given him. "I don't want my mom to be worried."

"I can call her if—"

"No, that's okay," Jayson said. "I need to go."

"Will you be all right? Do you want me to drive you home or—"

"No, really, I'm fine," Jayson said.

Will hugged him once more at the door, saying gently, "I'm here for you, Jayson, anytime. I mean that."

"I know; thank you."

"You remember you promised me that you would always be a son to me, no matter what."

Jayson looked into his eyes and tried to accept the ironies of this situation. "I remember," he said. "I promise."

When Jayson pulled the car up in front of the apartment, he couldn't even remember getting there. He sat for a long while just staring into the darkness before he found the motivation to go inside. He came through the front door, both relieved and disappointed to find no one home. His tears had gone dry, leaving in their wake an unbearable heartache and a debilitating shock—not unlike the aftermath of Derek's death. But this was worse, somehow, and he couldn't even fathom how he would ever go on living. He sank onto the couch and pressed his head into his hands, feeling as if his life's blood had been drained right out of him.

"Jayson?" he heard his mother say and looked up to see her standing close beside him, deep concern etched into her expression. He couldn't recall even hearing her come in. "Jayson, what's wrong?" she asked gently, sitting close beside him.

As he struggled to form the words to answer her question, hot tears burned past the barrier of shock into his eyes from a seemingly endless source. "Uh . . . I . . ." He sobbed and Leslie pushed her arms around him.

"What?" she asked gently.

"Elizabeth . . . she . . . she . . . left me."

"No!" Leslie murmured, her shock evident as his emotion broke fully past the dam holding it back.

"Oh, God help me!" he cried and pressed his head to her shoulder. She held him and let him cry, as if she had all the time in the world to just be with him. When his tears finally receded once again into shock, he just held to her like a lost child, feeling terrified and alone, abandoned and cast off.

"I can't believe it," Leslie said. "Tell me what happened."

"I don't know what happened," Jayson muttered, his voice hoarse and raw. "She just . . . said she couldn't marry me—not now, not ever."

"But . . . why?" Leslie asked, now crying herself.

"I don't know *why!*" Jayson said, feeling his grief become swallowed by a sudden return of his anger. "I just know she's gone, and I . . ."

The door opened, and Drew walked in. Jayson knew a friend must have dropped him off, since Jayson had been using his car. He took a long look at their faces and spoke in a panicked voice. "Don't tell me somebody else died."

"Might as well have," Jayson snapped. "Elizabeth dumped me."

"No!" Drew said with a stark astonishment that was somehow validating to the intensity of Jayson's grief. He sat down and reiterated their mother's reaction. "I can't believe it. You two were like . . . destiny."

"That's what I thought, too," Jayson said. Suddenly wanting to be alone, he stood up and added, "I'm exhausted. I'm going to bed."

A few minutes later, he crawled under the covers of his bed, wondering how he could ever find the will to get out of it again. He cried into his pillow until he heard Drew come in, then he fought to keep the tears silent. He tossed and turned far into the night and was surprised to hear Drew say, "So, when do you want to go to LA?"

Jayson glanced at the clock. 3:42. "I'm sorry if I kept you awake," he said.

"You didn't. I just . . . can't stop thinking about what happened. I'm so sorry, little brother. I wish there was something I could do."

Jayson thought about that for a minute. LA. It had been a distant beacon on the horizon for almost as long as he could remember, and now the opportunity was within his grasp. There was nothing holding him back now. With determination he said, "There *is* something you can do."

"What? Anything; just name it."

"You can get me to LA as quickly as possible. Get me out of here, Drew, so I can put it behind me."

"When do you want to leave?" Drew asked, and Jayson could barely make out his form in the dark as he leaned up on one elbow in his bed.

"When *can* you leave?"

"Say . . . three or four days."

"I'll be ready," Jayson said, and they talked for another hour, formulating a plan.

Jayson finally got out of bed at dawn with absolutely no sleep behind him. Just thinking of Elizabeth made his insides knot up, and the threat of tears was almost constantly right behind his eyes. And as if that weren't bad enough, he'd then think of Derek, and the sensation would intensify. He made up his mind that all he had left was his music. If only to honor Derek's memory, he would give everything he had to his music, and he would make it to the top.

When his mother got out of bed, he said without preamble, "Mom, we're leaving in a few days."

She sighed loudly, and he wasn't surprised by the tears evident in her eyes. "I suspected you might," she said.

"Mom, there's no reason for you to stay here. As soon as we get settled, we'll come back for you."

"You don't need to come back for me," she said. "If you take your beds and your equipment, there's nothing here that has any value that won't fit in my car. I assure you I'm capable of driving a car to LA. But I don't want to be an intrusive mother, and I don't want to be a bother. You're both adults now, and you need to live your own lives and—"

"You could never be intrusive or a bother if you tried," Jayson said, taking her hand. "We're family. We need you. And you need us."

Leslie smiled as if his attitude gave her great peace and comfort, then she hugged him tightly.

As soon as Leslie left for work to begin a mid-morning shift, Jayson called Will at his office.

"How you doing, kid?" he asked gently.

"I'm okay as long as I don't think about it," Jayson said. "Hey, Drew and I need to get the equipment out of your house."

Will hesitated, and when he spoke there was emotion in his voice. "Of course, but . . . you know the two of you can practice there any time you want. Truthfully, I hate to see it go, and . . ."

"I understand," Jayson said, well aware that Will was crying—and not just a little. He felt suddenly so sick to death of crying, especially when new tears appeared on his own face. "But . . . we're not practicing, Will. We're going to LA in a couple of days."

"I see," Will said. "Well . . . it's what you've always wanted. I'm sure you'll make it big in no time."

"I guess we'll see about that, but . . . I was wondering if . . . I know it's a lot to ask, but . . . do you think we could use the Suburban to take the drums and amps to the apartment? I won't have it long, but it would take four trips with the car and—"

"It's not a problem, Jayson. I'm glad to let you use it. You know the code to the garage door, and you know where the keys are. Just help yourself."

"Thank you," Jayson said. He had to ask, "Will Elizabeth be at work?"

"Uh . . . yes, as far as I know."

"Okay, thanks," Jayson said. "I'll talk to you again before I leave."

"I'll be counting on it," Will said, his emotion growing deeper.

They ended the call, and Jayson could well imagine him sobbing the moment the phone was hung up. Will had blatantly loved the music the band had played in his home, and today it would officially be leaving. Jayson suspected that for Will this was just one more repercussion of Derek's death. Jayson couldn't even think too hard about that or he would completely fall apart.

That afternoon Drew went with him to the Greer home. They went in through the garage and down to the basement. While they were loading the equipment into the Suburban, the routine felt so familiar that Jayson had to stop more than once and remind himself that Derek and Elizabeth were not going to cross his path on the stairs or in the garage. With everything loaded that belonged to Jayson and Drew, the room looked much as it had the first time Jayson had come here. He pondered the memories for a long moment, then forced them away when they became too painful. Since he knew where the vacuum was, he decided to spiff up the room a little and leave it looking half decent while Drew was adjusting the equipment in the Suburban for the safest traveling. While he was vacuuming, he was surprised to glance up and see Will leaning in the doorway. He turned off the vacuum and said, "You're supposed to be at work."

"I forgot to tell you something, and I knew you wouldn't answer our phone if it rang."

"Okay," Jayson said.

"I want you to take Derek's stuff." He motioned toward the guitars and amps.

"Oh, no." Jayson shook his head. "I can't do—"

"Jayson," Will said, putting a firm hand on his shoulder, "what else would I possibly do with this stuff? Look at it and miss him? I don't need to look at it to miss him. I have photographs. I have memories. And that's all I really need. I need you to take them, and I need you to play them and keep them alive. They were played with his hands. I want you to just do with them what you think best. Here they'll only collect dust."

Jayson reminded himself to be gracious and to recognize what this obviously meant to Will. "Thank you," Jayson said, embracing him. "At least this way something of Derek will be going to LA."

"That's what I was thinking," Will said. "And while we're at it . . . I know it's difficult, but . . . if there is anything else of Derek's— anything at all that you would like—I want you to take it. Is there anything especially sentimental to you? I know you were close to the same size. Take some of his clothes; take whatever you want."

"Uh . . ." Jayson wasn't sure what to say. "Let me think about that while I finish up here."

"No problem," Will said and picked up Derek's bass guitar, setting it reverently into its case. "In the meantime, let me help you."

"What is this?" Drew asked when Jayson came into the garage with one of Derek's amps.

Knowing Will was coming close behind him, he said quietly, "He's giving me all of Derek's stuff. Just smile and be gracious or you'll break his heart."

When all of the music equipment was loaded up, Jayson told Will he'd be back with the Suburban in less than an hour, which would give him plenty of leeway in missing Elizabeth before she got home from work. At the apartment, Jayson quickly helped Drew unload everything into the front room, then he left to return the Suburban, leaving Drew to put all the stuff in order.

Jayson parked the Suburban in the garage and returned the keys to where he'd found them earlier. He found Will in Derek's room, just sitting on the bed, twirling the little propeller on the top of Derek's favorite beanie hat.

"He looked like an idiot when he wore that on stage," Jayson said, and Will chuckled.

"Yes, I know. That's what everybody liked about him." He held it toward Jayson. "Do you want it?"

Jayson shook his head. "I don't need that to make a fool of myself on stage. I think you'd better keep it."

"Actually," Will set it aside and picked up the jester hat, "I think I'll keep this one. I think you need the one with the propeller. You can put it in a display case someday with your Grammy Awards."

Jayson reluctantly took it and twirled the propeller a few times, trying not to cry.

"Is there anything else you'd like?" Will asked. "I want to box up a few things that have value to me, and I just need to get rid of the rest. I refuse to let this room turn into some kind of holy shrine or something. It's just stuff, you know. It's all relatively meaningless in the big scheme of things." While Jayson was too choked up to speak, Will stood and opened the closet. "Surely you could use some of these clothes. You're going to be on a tight budget for a while, I bet. You could make good use of them." He looked over his shoulder, "Please . . . take them."

Jayson recognized the depth in Will's plea. He would rather see them taken by someone who loved Derek than to just see them go randomly to charity. But Jayson didn't want to take so many of Derek's things that the memories associated with them became diluted. He forced himself past his own internal trauma and picked out a few things from the closet. He took some guitar picks and a lapel pin with a guitar on it. Will found a box and helped put the items into it, then he put it into Jayson's hands with tears in his eyes.

"I'm going to miss you, son," he said.

"I'm going to miss you too," Jayson said and had to set the box aside to give him a firm embrace. While they held to each other with trembling arms, Jayson muttered, "I could never tell you how grateful I am . . . for everything you've given me. The first time I walked into your house, you treated me better than any man ever had. You opened your heart and your home to me, and I will never forget that."

"You brought life into our home, Jayson," Will said without relinquishing his embrace. "You filled our home with music, you brought out the best in Derek, and you brought my children closer together."

Jayson drew back enough to see Will's expression, silently questioning this. "Oh, yes," Will said. "They could hardly tolerate each other until you got them into the same band." Will shook his head. "I still marvel at the miracle you've been in our lives—especially mine."

Jayson hugged Will again, then forced himself to step back, fearing he'd have a complete meltdown otherwise. "Thank you for everything," Jayson said, picking up the box. "I will keep in touch, I promise. And I'll always let you know where I am."

"I'd appreciate that," Will said. "If you ever need anything, please call me. If I can't help you, I won't be afraid to let you know, but I don't want you going without. Do you understand?"

"Yes, thank you," Jayson said.

Will walked Jayson out to Drew's car. He put the box into the backseat, then hugged Will again. As Jayson walked around the car to get in, Will said, "You'll see Elizabeth before you go?"

Jayson was startled by the question, but it only took a moment to know the answer. "Yes, of course."

Will surprised Jayson when he said, "Just between you and me, I keep hoping she'll change her mind."

Jayson looked down and forced his emotion down where he couldn't feel it. "I can't hope for that, Will. I just don't have the strength. I have to find a way to let go."

"I understand." Will nodded. "I wish you every happiness; you deserve the best."

"So do you," Jayson said. "Tell her I'll see her before I go."

"I'll do that."

Jayson got into the car and drove away, marveling that he was actually holding himself together. Either he'd become accustomed to dealing with unfathomable heartache, or he was getting better at finding a place to put it where he couldn't feel it and didn't have to face it.

Chapter Seventeen

Three days later, Jayson and Drew were all but ready to leave. They'd rented a small U-Haul truck, and in it was the furniture from their bedroom, all of their music equipment, and their personal belongings. Drew's car was hooked behind it and ready to be towed. Leslie would follow through on the insurance settlement related to Jayson's accident and see that he got the money when it came so that he could replace his own car as quickly as possible.

Leslie had done little but cry most of the day, but she assured them repeatedly that she would be fine. "You can come with us now, if you want, Mom," Jayson said.

"No, it's okay," she said. "I need to keep my job until the two of you get some work. I know you have a lot of money in savings, but it will go quickly. Use it—"

"Wisely," Drew interrupted. "Yes, we know. And we will."

After Jayson had vacuumed their completely empty bedroom, Leslie stood in the doorway and said, "I think I'll make a sewing room out of it or something."

"You don't sew," Jayson pointed out.

"Well, maybe I should start. Elizabeth could teach me how."

Jayson gave his mother a sharp glance, then hurried to roll up the vacuum cord. She put a hand on his arm, and he said quietly, "Keep track of her, if you can. Make sure she's all right."

"I will," she said firmly.

"I need to go see her." He glanced at his watch. "She should be home soon." He sighed. "I need to tell her good-bye."

Leslie just gave him a hug and walked away.

Driving his mother's car to Elizabeth's home, Jayson thought of his behavior the last time they'd been together, and he felt mortified. His grief related to Derek's death had been shared by those around him, but his grief over losing Elizabeth was something that had hit him harder than anyone else. He'd made a fool of himself with her, and he knew it. Now he was determined to maintain some pride and dignity and handle this like a man.

Pulling up in front of the house, he prayed she would be there. He'd asked Will to let her know he would be stopping by this afternoon. If he didn't see her now, he might not get the chance. As he rang the doorbell, he feared his heart would pound right out of him. Only a few seconds later the door came open and there she stood. Why did she have to be so beautiful, so amazing?

"Hello," she said with a little smile. "It's good to see you."

"You too," he said, and she motioned him inside. As she closed the door, he added, "I can't stay long. We're all loaded up, ready to go. Drew's waiting for me."

Elizabeth looked astonished. "I see," she said. "Wouldn't it be better to leave . . . early in the morning, or . . ."

"We're going to take turns driving through the night. We'll be there tomorrow morning sometime, and hopefully we can find someplace cheap to stay before too long so we don't have to keep paying rent on the truck."

"I see," she said again. "Do you want to sit down?"

"Uh . . . no thanks. I just . . . came to say good-bye."

Elizabeth nodded and looked away; he saw her chin quiver slightly.

"Also," he added, "you must forgive me."

"For what?" She looked back up.

"For getting so upset, for making such a fool of myself, for making it so hard for you."

"I understand. And you didn't make a fool of yourself." She looked at him deeply. "You're not the only one who's hurting."

Jayson felt fresh anger overtake him, but he preferred it over any other emotion. Anger he could handle. "If I could make any sense of that whatsoever, I might be able to accept what you're doing."

"What do you mean?"

"How can your hurting and my hurting make this right?"

"It just is. Sometimes the right thing is the hardest thing. At least know you're not alone in your grief."

"Maybe not. But I will sure be alone."

"You'll find someone," she said, and he gave a scoffing laugh.

"Okay, Lady. Let's stop this conversation here before I either get really angry or start bawling and make a fool of myself all over again. I'm leaving now. I don't know when I'll see you again."

Elizabeth looked at him and couldn't hold back a stream of tears. "I'll always love you, Jayson," she said.

"Yes, I know," he said, unable to help the bitter tone, "but not enough. Well, I love you too, Elizabeth . . . and I love you *enough.* I love you enough to wonder how life could possibly go on for me. But as you have pointed out, it has to. So, I'm going to buck up and try to act like a man. And I am going to LA, and I am going to fight and claw my way through the muck and do whatever I have to do to make it work. I am going to sing the songs I wrote for you on stages all around the world. You will hear those songs on the radio, and you will see me on television, and you will know that I did it because I loved you enough. And some day when you have your cozy, stable life with your knight in shining armor and you're baking cookies for your children, I hope you remember what we shared and miss it as much as I'm going to miss it every day for the rest of my life."

"Maybe you won't," she said. "Maybe this will all just pass with time like most high-school romances. And we will both look back on what we felt and wonder what we were thinking."

He looked at her hard, almost cruelly. "If you can do that, I will give you my second million."

"Not your first?" she asked, attempting to lighten the mood.

"No, I'll be giving the first to some other woman who will futilely be trying to make me forget you."

"That's hardly fair to her."

"No, it's not. But I can only do the best I can do. Nobody can force me to feel something I don't feel." Jayson glanced at his watch. "I need to go. Drew is waiting for me."

Elizabeth felt an unexpected panic and reached for his hand. "You'll keep in touch."

"Of course," he said, but he wondered if such words were an empty promise.

"A kiss good-bye?" she asked and lifted her face to his.

He gave her a slow, savoring kiss, then stepped back. "Good-bye, Elizabeth. I will always love you."

"And I will always love you," she said, unable to hold back a fresh surge of tears.

Jayson forced himself to turn and move toward the door. He'd only taken two steps when a thought came into his mind with such urgency that he had no choice but to turn back around and take her by the shoulders. "Promise me that we *will* keep in touch, Elizabeth. Promise me."

"Of course," she said.

"No, not like some . . . empty promise that we say to be polite because it's difficult to say good-bye. Not like when you said, 'I'll keep in touch' to all the girls in the school orchestra when you know you'll never see them again—and never care to. I mean that we *will* keep in touch. I mean that I will always let you know my address and phone number, wherever I may go, and you will do the same. I mean that we will call or write and share every significant event of our lives with each other—no matter what. I believe Derek would want it that way. Our parents would want it that way. I believe that we can both help keep Derek's memory alive if we truly stay friends, Elizabeth. Promise me."

"I promise, Jayson," she said, looking into his eyes. Then she pressed her mouth to his with a kiss that didn't begin to express the desperation she felt in letting him go. He drew her fully into his arms and kissed her on and on. She realized she was crying the same moment she felt him sob in the midst of their kiss. She kissed him harder, drew closer still, and her tears increased.

He finally severed his lips from hers and looked into her eyes. "Elizabeth," he whispered, "why can't you see that this is all wrong? Can you not feel that we need to be together?"

She touched the tears on his face. "I know in my heart this is what's best, Jayson. It's necessary. I don't know why. I only know that it's what my heart tells me I must do." She sobbed quietly. "Letting you go is the hardest thing I've ever done, but . . . it has to be this way."

Jayson knew there was no convincing her otherwise. He also knew if he stayed another minute he'd be bawling like a baby. He kissed her quickly once more and turned and walked away. Once he was outside, he practically ran to the car and managed to hold the full extent of his emotion back until he'd driven a few blocks, then he had to pull over. He pressed his head to the steering wheel and cried as he had so many times over Derek's death. But Elizabeth was *choosing* to leave him, choosing to not be a part of his life. And he wondered how he could ever learn to live without either of them.

* * * * *

Jayson felt almost as if he'd been catapulted into some eery time warp as he stood and looked out over the ocean. It had been Drew's idea, before heading south, to stop first at the place where they'd come with their mother less than two years earlier. They talked briefly of all that had happened in their lives since they'd first stood in this spot. And Jayson couldn't deny that for all the grief and heartache he was taking with him, he was also taking a great deal of experience, insight, and personal growth. His musical abilities had grown through the experiences he'd found in Oregon, and his heart had been touched in ways that had changed him forever.

He closed his eyes and listened to the sound of the waves, the seabirds, and the laughter of children down the beach. And then it started to rain. It was a gentle, soothing rain, but the sound of it hitting the sand around him was comforting somehow. And that's when Jayson felt it. A sensation overcame him that was more abstract than literal, but undeniable nevertheless. A different kind of tears stung his eyes as a blanket of warmth seemed to wrap around him, easing the pain, soothing the grief, and offering a wealth of hope for the future so real he felt as if he could reach out and hold it in his hands. He could never put the experience into words, but in his deepest self, he found a sudden strength to go on and a certain belief that, somehow, everything would be all right—for him *and* for Elizabeth.

As they got back into the truck and Jayson drove it onto the highway, he made a firm resolve to hold the good memories close to him and to put the bad ones away where they couldn't be felt. A few miles later, he said to Drew, "I feel like we're moving into some altered state of existence."

"We are," Drew said. "It's called California."

They both laughed and shared a high-five. What would he ever do without his brother—and his music? Somehow, they would make it together.

Special Thanks

I would like to express a special thank you to the members of Reflect for allowing Jayson to borrow their music. The lyrics to "Predator" and "Weird" were written by Sam Pehrson. "Tongue-Tied" and "Photo Finish" were written by John Stansfield. All songs © 2001, Reflect, from the album *Broken Glass*. All other lyrics were written by Jayson Wolfe.

About the Author

Anita Stansfield, the LDS market's number-one best-selling romance novelist, is a prolific and imaginative writer who wants her readers to know that she is "real." She and her husband, Vince—whom she calls "her hero"—have three boys and two girls: John, Jake, Anna, Steven, and Alyssa. She loves butterscotch chip cookies, long walks, and romantic movies. She loves to go out to eat, especially for seafood and steaks. Her favorite color is black. She loves lemonade and French fries with fry sauce. She loves her husband. She loves her kids. She loves her sisters, her brothers, her dad, and her friends. She loves her house and her neighborhood. And she loves Alpine, the little town she lives in. And—oh, yes—she loves to write stories.